# La Bella LUNA

## NICOLE SHARP

## The Simply Trouble Series:

Big Trouble in Little Italy
Simply Protocol
Worth The Trouble
A Simple Avalanche

## Secrets of the Moon Trilogy

Tears of the Moon

## Standalone Books

The Italian Holiday
La Bella Luna
Surviving Thirty
Home for the Holidays

## Novellas

Let It Snow
The Museum Guide
Italian For Christmas

For all those facing ghosts and sifting through the old stories ...
You're never too old and it's never too late.

# La Bella LUNA

In My Defense,
the Moon Was Full
and I Was Left
Unsupervised.

-anonymous

# Chapter One

Luciano's restaurant did a good business on Thursday nights. They weren't as generic or economic as the Olive Garden, but they weren't as expensive as the four-star Italian restaurants across town with their hoity-toity, al dente, authentic homemade dishes that put on airs.

There were other options for Italian restaurants, but for those you had to drive forty-five minutes into the city and deal with traffic and parking and reimagined recipes that were often described as "East meets West" or "Italian inspired."

Luciano's didn't make everything from scratch and some of their wait staff had trouble with the law every now and then. There were a few after-hours poker games that had turned raucously quarrelsome; but there was a level of consistent quality and treatment that kept customers returning.

Owner Rita Campitelli, a third-generation Italian, told people she named the restaurant for her grandfather, the first of her family to come to America. The truth was that it was cheaper to keep the name of the previous restaurant; it came with the proper business licenses and she liked the existing sign, a rectangle with yellow backing and a maroon flourish of script reading Luciano's.

Years later it didn't even matter, as no one recalled that there'd been a different owner of the restaurant. After twenty years, Rita had a loyal customer base that were like family.

She worked the room Thursday through Sunday night; shaking hands, inquiring as to whether or not her customers were having a good meal, and plugging in a few familial details of those she knew: "How's your daughter? Ready to graduate high school soon, right?" "I saw your son and his fiancé in here the other night, you should be so proud to have raised such a well-mannered young man."

Rita also used her third-generation Italian-ness to her advantage. She put on a bit of an accent when she pronounced the names of dishes and sprinkled her customers with overused Italian phrases like 'mangia' (*eat*) and 'va bene' (*very good*). Her superpower was putting her guests at such ease they offered their own declaration of 'grazie' and grinned at their attempts of being 'Italian.'

Rita just finished a round of meet and greet and was headed back to the kitchen when she noticed one of her waiters peeking around the corner, staring intently at one of his tables.

"What are you doing?" she hissed in a whisper when she was close enough.

He pointed toward one of Luciano's loyal customers with his nose. "Mr. Anthony, he's gonna propose," he said, still in shock.

"Really?"

Ten years ago, 'Mr. Anthony' started coming to Luciano's twice a week. A year ago, he began coming in every Thursday night with Diana, a woman in her early fifties, maybe late forties; it was hard to tell. Rita felt Diana could be described with one adjective: average. Average height, maybe five six. Average face, drawn, showing signs of her age and indifference to makeup. Average body weight, maybe. She wore sensible, drab clothes that hung in straight shapes; clean and in place, but not flattering and without even the remotest hint of flare. And her dark auburn hair, always up in a tight, practical bun, showed more signs of age in the gray streaks throughout.

Diana was simply average. Which, in Rita's opinion, made Diana a good fit for the doughy, fidgety, Mr. Anthony. It was only a matter of time before the lifelong bachelor figured out marrying the woman might be a good idea. In fact, looking between the couple, marriage might do them both some good. They'd have stability and comfort. Not passion though. Rita shook her head sadly, it wasn't everyone who got passion.

"Do you think she'll say yes?" the waiter whispered, covering his mouth as if the words might jinx Mr. Anthony's chances.

"Probably." Rita shrugged.

"She'll probably start cooking for him. You think we'll see them anymore if she says yes?"

Bachelors. Lonely, older bachelors, were the backbone of Rita's business. Luciano's bread and butter, she liked to joke.

The waiter didn't wait for Rita to weigh in on his questions and continued his confused diatribe, "Why would a man get married so late in life?"

Rita thought about trying to explain human nature to her employee, but he was young and there wasn't enough time; and really, she didn't have the patience.

"Did he tell you he was going to propose?" she asked instead.

He gave a distracted nod. "He got my attention earlier when she was in the bathroom. He's gonna propose and when she says yes, he wants me to bring two glasses of champagne over."

"Not a whole bottle?" Rita raised an eyebrow.

"Mr. Anthony ..." the waiter glanced around as if he were trying to figure out how to explain it, "he's not flashy."

That was one way to put Mr. Anthony's frugality.

"No, he's not." Rita hid a smile as she watched the moment unfold across the room. After several seconds, she slapped the waiter on the back and continued to the kitchen. She had better things to do than worry about losing one bachelor customer.

Anthony nervously wiped his hands on his napkin then gently set it down on the table beside his plate. "Diana. Do you ..." He cleared his throat as the question lodged itself in his esophagus. He took a drink of water and started again, "What I mean is ... I mean ... I know it's Thursday, and I'm leaving tonight." Another clearing of his throat gave Diana time to patiently ask, "What is it Anthony?"

He stuttered for a moment and then choked out, "Happy Birthday."

"Thank you." Diana smiled and took a bite.

Anthony leaned forward. "I know it's two days late. I had that big project and then, with getting ready to go out of town ..." He held out his hands in an apology.

Diana gave an understanding wave of her fork. "I know. It's alright."

"The flowers were nice?" He asked after the large bouquet he'd sent her.

"They were lovely." She paused and tilted her head, watching as worry pulled his eyebrows up, unearthing his subtle charm; something others tended to miss about him. "It was such a big arrangement, it takes up the whole coffee table."

"I told the florist you loved wildflowers and she said she had an idea."

Diana reached out and patted his hand. "They're beautiful."

"Good." Anthony nodded and again cleared his throat then licked his lips nervously.

Diana turned her attention back to her food. Anthony quietly tried to clear his throat, but made a strange sound, began to cough and stood abruptly, pushing the chair back so fast it fell over with a thud.

Diana's eyes widened in alarm.

Continuing to cough and apologize with a nod to the people around him, he reorganized himself and the chair.

Concerned, Diana asked, "Are you okay?"

He took a shaky drink of his water and nodded. Gathered once more he assured her, "I'm okay."

She narrowed her gaze and waited a moment. "You sure?"

"Yes. I'm okay." He picked up his fork and twirled his pasta around with it.

Diana shook her head before turning her attention back to her food. So, it was out of the corner of her eye that she saw Anthony's slight movement.

He slipped out of his chair and onto his knees. Slowly. Quite ungraceful. The movement was awkward; like a small child trying to sneak out of a chair without anyone noticing. Only, he was fifty years old and slightly overweight, so the table wobbled when he pressed against it and moved onto the floor. When he was finished with the maneuver, he was kneeling next to the table.

Diana's frown increased as she watched the strange display. "What are you doing?"

He opened and closed his mouth but no words came, causing Diana to drop her fork and hold out her hands toward him. "Are you having a stroke?"

"What? No. No!" He took her hands in his. "Diana, I'm trying to ask if you ... if you ..." He took as deep a breath as he could muster before forcing words. "Diana, will you marry me?"

Diana raised an eyebrow in answer. She felt as if the rush of breath that held the question she'd not been expecting on a Thursday night, their usual date night, had flipped the tables and it was Dianna's turn to feel unsure. But instead of forcing her chair back in shock, she took her time to consider Anthony.

The passing moments became so painfully awkward Anthony let her hand drop and pulled the handkerchief out of his jacket pocket to dab at the gathering sweat on his brow.

"Is there a ring?" Diana whispered the question when he put the handkerchief away.

"A ring?" He looked confused.

Diana patted the side of his face and instructed him to sit back in his chair. He did, then leaned forward with rapt attention, anxiously awaiting her reply.

"Anthony," she began, "you know I was married before."

"He left you widowed and alone with no money." He recited her past with such a conciseness it shook Diana more than the proposal. Anthony quickly added, "I can take care of you. I *want* to take care of you and build a life with you."

She shook her head to realign herself with the moment. "We eloped then, but I always regretted not having a wedding."

Anthony nodded as if he understood, but the frown of confusion contradicted his agreement. Diana knew she wasn't making much sense, so her face softened as she explained, "Anthony, I'd like a wedding this time. And a ring." She winked at him.

"But you're forty-five years old ..." he stuttered, as if there was an expiration date on the age a person could have a wedding ceremony.

Diana's smile faded and she pointed at Anthony. "And you're fifty." She was well aware of her age. She found proof of it every time she looked at herself in the mirror. Straightening her spine, she asked, "What's wrong with being forty-five?"

"I just thought ... aren't we a little old ...?"

"I'm not talking about something extravagant with hundreds of people and a dress that makes me look like a marshmallow. Just a small celebration. A wedding with our closest family and friends."

"Your parents don't like me," he said.

Diana waved the truth away. "They like you fine."

"Our closest family and friends ..." He took another deep breath. "So, does this mean ... that you'll ..." He raised his eyebrows in question.

Instead of answering, Diana asked, "Did you really plan on proposing to me without a ring?"

A blush crept up his cheeks as he shifted in his chair. "I couldn't think about anything other than the question itself and taking you to dinner tonight."

Just then Rita Campitelli stepped forward. "I'm so sorry, but when Anthony was on his knees, I was concerned. So I came over to see if everything was okay and overheard your conversation."

Diana pursed her lips. Rita Campitelli didn't just *overhear* any conversation, she made it her business to overhear. She was an accomplished gossip.

Rita held out a ring to Anthony. "If you'll allow me to help. This was the ring my first husband gave me." She looked at the ring lovingly. "Perhaps you could use it until you're able to buy a proper ring for your fiancé?"

Wide-eyed, Anthony took the ring gently from Rita and gave her a nod of thanks, then holding it aloft between his thumb and index finger, he turned in slow motion and reverently held it out to Diana. His eyebrows pulled so far upward, his hope was tangible.

"Ask her again," Rita instructed.

"Diana, will you marry me?"

"Yes," she said, surprising herself a bit by the answer, but also finding strength in her reply. "Yes, Anthony, I will."

Rita clapped her hands together and waved the waiter over to bring the champagne. The tables nearby began to clap and Diana held out her hand toward Anthony for the ring. When it didn't fit her ring finger, she told him to put it on her pinky instead.

Once they were each handed a glass, they happily tapped them together. Anthony looked relieved and giddy. He was a good man, she thought as she watched him over the top of her glass. She enjoyed being with him and a thrill ran through her, realizing she was embarking on a new life, one of security and companionship. She wouldn't be alone any longer.

Anthony set his glass down and called out to the waiter, "Could we get the check please?" Giving an apologetic smile to Diana, he admitted, "If I had more courage, I could have asked you earlier and we could have enjoyed our meal. Now," he glanced at his watch, "I need to get going and the food …"

Diana shook her head. "I don't care. I'm so happy."

"You are?"

"I wouldn't have said yes if I didn't mean it."

His grin widened as he picked up his glass. He gently touched it once again to hers. "You said yes."

"I said yes." She grinned.

# Chapter Two

Anthony drove Diana back to her office where they'd decided to meet before dinner. During the fifteen-minute drive, he held her hand, and brought it to his lips several times to brush a kiss on her knuckles.

"I could have driven you to the airport," she said.

"I know, but the company will pay for the Uber and that way you don't have to deal with the traffic there and back."

"I wouldn't have minded." She squeezed his hand.

He pulled to a stop next to her car in the now empty parking lot, but didn't turn it off immediately.

"Anthony?" Diana called, asking after the still idling car.

He turned toward her, a gleam in his eye, and put his hand on the back of her headrest. "You make me a better man."

Diana felt a brief flutter twirl in her chest. "'Thank you."

He nodded and touched a finger to her cheek, shaking his head. "I'm a lucky man, thank you for saying yes."

She smiled and touched his hand. "I'm a lucky woman."

The alarm he'd set on his phone so he wouldn't be late went off. He turned off the car and climbed out.

Diana joined him by the trunk as he attempted to free his suitcase, yanking it, then frowning when it wouldn't budge.

She opened her mouth to say she could help just as he put most of his torso in the trunk to find the culprit. "The wheel's stuck behind the carpeted wheel well," he called. After freeing the case he stood and gave another forceful yank, but because the case was free from impediments, he lost his balance and stumbled backward a step.

Diana pressed a hand against his back. "Whoa."

He caught himself and let the case drop next to him with a thump before turning his attention to the car with a neon Uber sign on the dash pulling into the parking lot.

"My ride." He announced the obvious and closed the trunk.

Diana pulled Anthony's attention back to her. He slid his arm around her waist and lowered his lips to hers. It was a soft kiss, filled with sweetness and promise.

When he pulled away, they were both wearing a look of shock at the intimacy they rarely shared in public. Diana slipped her hands up to frame his face and smiled as she studied him.

Anthony said, "I love you," but the words came out a hoarse whisper. He seemed so astounded by the sentiment, as if they were a revelation he'd only just had, that he repeated them, "*I love you*," his emphasis making it sound like a sacred vow.

Diana blushed, feeling the words wrap themselves around her heart. She swallowed and brushed a kiss on his cheek, studied his eyes and opened her mouth to tell him how excited she was, how she was glad she had someone to share her life with. But the words lodged in her throat; and instead, she found herself spouting a lame fact and instructions. "It gets hot in Houston this time of year, so ... make sure you drink lots of water."

"I will." He nodded, then glanced over at the Uber that pulled to a stop next to them. The driver rolled his window down and called, "Are you Anthony Clark?"

"Yes," he nodded, "yes, that's me." Then he repeated his itinerary, "I'm going to be gone for three weeks." As if Diana had forgotten how long she'd put his mail and paper on hold.

"When you get back we'll start looking for a place together," she said.

"Together." He gave several jerky nods, which Diana had come to recognize was his way of comprehending the moment and what was happening around him.

"Anthony." She brought his attention back to her and he grinned. Taking her left hand in his, he studied the ring then kissed the finger where it rested. "I'm sorry I didn't think of a ring."

She offered a soft smile. "When you come back we'll look for a ring too. I don't need anything fancy."

"I can afford it," he muttered to the ring, "I have a good job."

He let go of her hand and pulled up several times on the suitcase handle in an attempt to unlock the extension. Diana reached down, pressed the button and wiggled the handle until the contraption released.

Anthony said, "You take care of me." Another revelation.

"I try."

"I'm going to take care of you." He seemed to like the idea; his chest puffed out as he said, "You make me feel powerful, and I haven't felt that way in a long time."

"Are you ready, man?" the driver interrupted.

"Okay, don't be late." Diana stepped close to him and ran her hands over the lapels of his jacket. "Your ticket is in your left breast pocket." She patted. "Phone is in the front pocket of your computer bag along with gum."

He kissed her once again then pulled away promising, "I'll call you when I land. Then we can start talking about wedding plans."

"Wedding plans," she repeated.

He straightened his shoulders and nodded happily. "Wedding plans." He transferred his bags into the open trunk of the Uber, then leaned in and brushed a kiss across her lips once more.

"Have a good flight." She patted his lapel.

"I'll talk to you soon." He climbed in the car and Diana closed the door, listening through the driver's open window as Anthony confirmed that the Atlanta airport was his final destination.

He held up his hand as the car began to move, and she overheard him tell the driver, "I'm gonna marry that woman."

# Chapter Three

On the short drive home from her office, she stopped and bought a small bottle of champagne because she was engaged and wanted to continue to celebrate. Traffic had thinned, and Diana couldn't hold back her grin as Frank Sinatra crooned about the best being yet to come.

As she double-checked for traffic in the rearview mirror, she caught a glimpse of her smile and had to do a double and triple take. It felt so long since she'd glanced in a mirror unsuspectingly and found a smile affixed to her face with the corresponding emotion pumping through her veins.

She rearranged herself and swallowed, but didn't stop the grin as she wound her way through the suburban tree-lined streets that would take her home.

But when she flipped the blinker to turn right, her mood faltered a bit. Diana felt like she'd been caught unaware by a wave. Like the times she'd been to the ocean; facing the shore, the water crashed around her, tilting the world and burying her feet in the sand while trying to push her over.

She pressed more firmly on the break as the continual blinker became a soothing metronome.

She gazed at the house. The word 'home' brushed past her, turning over a million thoughts in a matter of moments.

This wasn't her home. It never had been.

She lived with her sister, Lena – older by three years – and Lena's family. Well, Diana didn't necessarily *live* with Lena and her family, but in the one-bedroom guesthouse in the backyard of Lena's hugely opulent home.

Diana's occupation of said guesthouse was originally intended for only a few months; just so she could get back on her feet after her husband had passed away.

But somehow, a few months had turned into nineteen years.

*Nineteen years.*

The time had passed in a fog.

At first, Diana had stayed because she was heartbroken and didn't have any money. Diana married when she was twenty-one. She and her husband lived in a loft apartment in New York while she attempted to make a living as a writer and her husband studied and created art. They both showed promise, and at that point in their young lives, promise put a bit of food on the table and a bit of art in the world. They fully, wholeheartedly embraced the grappling life of artists, scraping together money for bills and food and school, the way you did as youthful artists in love.

Five years into their marriage, her husband was hit by a bus on the way to a gallery.

After that, promise was all Diana had left, along with a mountain of heartache.

She borrowed money from her parents to pay for the funeral, and with the bills piling up and no real-world skills to make a living, Lena stepped in and offered to help. In exchange for a place to stay, Diana could be a sort of nanny to her older sister's twins. And as an added bonus, Lena wanted to help pay for Diana to go back to school and get a degree, 'in a field that would help her make a living.'

Diana accepted the offer, became a CPA and helped Lena with the twins. The thin line of love and obligation to her sister and her niece and nephew – all whom she truly adored – blurred over the years. And Diana paid rent to stay in the guesthouse, convincing herself she had neither the time nor enough money to move, and because Lena needed the help.

The truth, however, was that her life died under a bus long ago. It'd taken so many years of going through monotonous day to day motions in order to finally feel human enough to make friends and find hobbies again.

The twins had graduated high school almost two years ago, and the year before that they'd both received their licenses. So the need to pick up and drop off, or even to remotely look after, had become a non-existent exercise.

Still, out of a now ingrained symbiotic relationship between herself and Lena, Diana stayed in the guesthouse, in which she'd been the only guest.

The other truth was that Diana was tired.

Not just tired; she was bone-weary haggard; *that* kind of exhausted.

Strangely, it was the exhaustion and wondering if there was anything monumental, or relatively fun, left in her life that made her agree to a date with Anthony in the first place.

A colleague at work set them up, and Diana had been pleasantly surprised when she had a good time. Anthony was subtly charming, caring and so very stable.

Now look at her, a year later and she was engaged.

Marrying Anthony was a good move. There was a polite respect they had for each other that held a strong enough foundation to build on. There wasn't any wild attraction or staggering passion. But that was fine. Diana had passion once. It wasn't something she wanted ever again. And after nineteen years she was convinced a person only got one chance. She had hers. It was short lived, but it was over and done with now.

At this point in her life, Diana had practicality at the forefront of her mind. She needed to think about her future. She didn't want to die in her sister's guesthouse. She finally wanted a bit more than being the family member people whispered about in wonder, always trying to figure out what was going on with her. *Didn't she want more out of life? What was she so scared of? Was she just going to live with her sister forever?*

Diana had heard the comments on several occasions over the years. She could have put all the whispers to bed, but every time *she* asked the question of herself, she was confronted with a deafening silence. Not even Diana knew what she truly wanted.

A car passing on her left jarred her out of the macabre thoughts.

Hand over hand she turned the wheel and pulled into the large driveway, past the big house, past Lena's Cadillac Escalade and her brother-in-law's midlife crisis red, Ford Mustang GT.

She continued down the driveway, onto a small lane that led to the guesthouse. After she parked, she sat and studied the small quarters that had been meant for out-of-town guests. Or for one nineteen year 'guest.'

"I'm getting married," she whispered, "this is good."

*Anthony* was good. They liked the same movies, they both liked reading the Sunday paper over coffee and croissants. And he offered the companionship and consistency she longed for.

She turned the car off then grabbed her purse and the small bottle of champagne. This time, when she unlocked the door to the guesthouse, she allowed the growing feeling of lightness to fully encompass her. She wouldn't be here very much longer. By this time next year (hell, by this time next month maybe) the door she would be opening would be the door to her own home.

Diana took her time going about her nightly routine. She exchanged her date night attire for a tank top and comfortable pajama pants. She washed her face and let her long brunette hair out of the bun. She gazed at herself in the mirror and ran her hand through her hair. There was so much gray showing. She'd thought about dyeing it over the years or opting for a dramatic cut, but she always came up against a hundred reasons why it didn't matter. Too many women were walking around faking everything about their appearance – that was one excuse she used. She liked looking natural and Anthony didn't seem to mind it. That was another one. Her sister Harper, younger by eight years, however, liked to insist Diana didn't want to do anything to her appearance because she was scared. To that, Diana stuck her tongue out at her reflection.

A knock sounded at her door. The only person it could be was Lena. She looked at the borrowed gold band on her pinky finger and thought about taking it off, but she actually liked it. She liked Anthony's nervousness, his sincerity and the promise that had worked its way into the ring.

And she was going to call her sister and invite her over to tell her the news anyway.

"Coming," she called as she got closer to the door. When she opened it, there was Lena holding a tray which had a cupcake with a lit candle and a laptop displaying their sister Harper (who lived in New York) on video waving.

"Happy Birthday to you. Happy Birthday to you ..." Lena began to sing along with Harper, but the two versions didn't match due to poor bandwidth. When they finished, Diana leaned forward and blew out the candle with a smile.

"Yay!" Lena beamed as Harper sarcastically called, "Ooh, she can blow out a candle. I would hope after forty-five years she'd figured that one out."

"Harper," Lena chided as she forced herself and her tray into the guesthouse.

"How you feelin' old lady?" Harper asked.

"Like my birthday was two days ago," Diana commented.

"I told you!" Harper screamed. "Lena, look at me. Lena, where are you?"

Lena moved the computer so it was on the counter of the kitchen. "I'm here. Okay, you were right, I was wrong. I was busy."

"Thank you both anyway." Diana said as she retrieved two champagne flutes and opened the small bottle she'd bought.

"What's she doing?" Harper asked and Lena turned the laptop so Harper could see Diana pouring two glasses of champagne. "Are we celebrating something?"

Diana nodded while moving to sit next to Lena at the counter. She turned the laptop so Harper could see them both, and held her glass aloft saying: "To me."

"Oh wait, damn. Hold on! Don't drink yet," Harper screamed, disappearing from the screen. She came back several seconds later and held up a beer. "To Luna." She used Diana's middle name, something the family had done her whole life.

Lena joined, "To Luna." She clinked her glass to Diana's and they all took a drink.

Diana smiled and held out her glass again. "Anthony proposed. And I said yes," she announced.

Lena was silent but Harper exploded across the internet, "No! Oh Lu, please tell me you're joking!"

"Settle down Harper, this isn't about you." Lena narrowed her gaze toward Diana. "Are you happy?"

Diana smiled with a nod. "He loves me and he's really nice."

Harper made gagging sounds and Lena pointed at the screen. "Keep it up and I'll turn you off."

Their younger sister stopped, but when Lena wasn't looking and Diana was, she put her hands over her mouth as if she were silently vomiting.

Diana rolled her eyes. "You don't understand," she started, "I had love. I had my chance."

"What chance?" Harper asked. "What chance did you give yourself?"

"I was married before and had my chance ..." Diana tried to explain.

"David ..." Harper referred to Diana's husband, "he died in an accident and it was horrible. Then you went into hiding to lick your wounds, but you never came out. You were a baby when all that happened and you never gave yourself another chance to do shit," Harper insisted.

Diana shook her head. "You're young, you don't—"

"Don't," Harper said. "Don't you dare tell me I'm young and you're some old biddy and that's why I don't understand."

"Harper," Lena warned, then she reached out and took Diana's hand. "Diana, if this is what you want, we support you."

"Speak for yourself," Harper said angrily.

Lena ended the call with Harper and emphasized, "*I* understand."

"The last nineteen years have flown by." Diana sighed.

A call came in from the computer, but Lena ignored it. Then her cell phone rang from her pocket, and after pulling it out to silence it, nodded for Diana to continue.

"Another nineteen years I'm going to be sixty. It would be nice to eat dinner with someone every night. To have someone to take care of me. It would be nice to not be alone anymore."

Lena smiled sadly. "I always hoped you didn't feel so alone with us nearby." She shook her head. "I'm sorry, I should have been there for you more."

"Lena, you've done everything for me. More than a sister should have to do."

Lena pulled Diana in for a hug, her voice catching as she said, "Congratulations, I really am happy for you."

The computer rang again and Lena answered, but before Harper could say anything, demanded, "Say congratulations to Luna or I hang up."

Harper took a deep breath and after a moment said, "If this is what you want, then it's what I want. Congratulations, Lu."

"I want a wedding this time. Nothing big or fancy … I just want to celebrate," Diana said. "So, I'd like you two to be my bridesmaids."

Lena nodded happily. "Of course. Whatever you need."

"Dad doesn't like Anthony," Harper offered instead, adding, "Mom's not a fan either."

"Harper …" Lena bit.

There'd been two introductions over the past year. Anthony's propensity for awkwardness in large groups of people didn't mingle well with her mother's continued work with various fundraising organizations. Diana had chosen to bring Anthony to a dinner supporting the zoo to introduce him to her family. He gestured strangely when he met her mother, spilling the glass of red wine she was holding down the front of her ivory dress. Then at dinner, he'd set his jacket on fire trying to offer bread to Diana's father. Harper wasn't lying when she said they'd not been impressed.

To smooth things over, Diana tried a second introduction over a small family dinner. Her father fell asleep halfway through Anthony's explanation of what he did for a living.

"So where's the lucky fiancé?" Harper sighed.

"He's headed to Houston. His company's been hired to work with a few manufacturers to see if new energy is a direction in which they want to go."

"Oh God, even his job is boring." Harper dramatically threw herself off screen.

Diana scowled. "It's green energy and it's going to save our damned planet one day."

"Whatever." Harper righted herself.

Lena patted Diana on the shoulder. "Tell us all about the proposal."

"Oh yeah," Harper dropped her disappointed sneer as her eyes lit up, "show us the ring!"

Diana looked down at her left hand and licked her lips. Her hand felt heavy, weighted down as she held up her pinky finger and the gold band.

"That's it?" Harper asked.

"It's lovely." Lena continued to pat Diana's shoulder.

"Actually, he was so nervous about the proposal he forgot about the ring." Diana twisted the band around her finger. "When he gets back we'll pick out a real one."

"So this is only temporary?" Harper asked, as if maybe Anthony was temporary as well.

"No, it's ... a placeholder," Diana responded.

"A placeholder for what? It isn't even on the right finger," Harper said.

"Say good night, Harper," Lena muttered angrily as Harper hurried a few more sentiments; "God damnit, Lena! You know she's—" The opinions died with the blackened screen.

Lena held Diana's hand in hers and squeezed it. "I love the ring. I love that he was nervous. When does he get back?"

"In three weeks."

"When do you want to get married?"

The question sent a thrill through Diana. She grinned as she sat forward and admitted, "Soon."

"Okay then," Lena clapped her hands together, "it looks like we have a wedding to plan."

# Chapter Four

Diana drank her coffee without any sugars, creamers or nonsense. It was something she learned to do when she lived in New York, had minimal funds and a need to caffeinate. A cup of strong black coffee became her favorite.

She finished getting ready for work while the water in the tea kettle heated on the gas stove. On Fridays she went in at eleven, giving her time to sleep in a bit and take a walk, or meet friends for breakfast. She spooned the coffee grounds into the French press and slowly poured the hot water in. There was a new way the hipster baristas were going about pouring the water atop coffee grounds and measuring everything with scales these days. Diana wasn't concerned with any of those new tricks, she enjoyed the comfort of her ritual that produced a good, strong cup of coffee.

She placed the kettle back on the stove, buttered a whole wheat English muffin, spooned out a portion of Greek yogurt and set it all with a coffee cup and the French press at the small table in the kitchen.

She opened the blinds and stacked the things she'd need for work – computer, various files and lunch – on the sofa. It was just enough time for the coffee to perfectly steep.

She pressed the grounds then poured the dark liquid. Holding her cup in both hands she took an appreciative inhale. When the engagement ring she wore on her pinky clinked against the white porcelain, she was transported into another life; a small coffee shop in New York, close to her old apartment, with a sturdy cup of black coffee gripped in her hands the same way.

And she remembered how it sounded to be married.

The sound of a ring tapping against her cup when she picked it up with both hands, the sound of a simple gold band as she gently hit it against the mug several times; to catch his attention, to annoy him, to accompany her thoughts.

Still holding the coffee, Diana glanced at her hands as if they were no longer her own. She then picked up her pinky and lightly tapped it against the cup, the sound bringing her out of the hypnotic time traveling reprieve.

She mindlessly put the cup down and held her left hand up to better examine her fingers.

After all this time, she swore she could still see the shadow of the ring she used to wear. It was an illusion, surely, but she could still see the indentation where the band had once graced her finger for such a short time.

The new ring, a promise, smiled at her from her pinky. She smiled back. It was good the ring didn't fit right, it was good this was going slowly. She needed a little time to move everything forward, to ease the ring to its rightful home.

She picked the cup up once more and clinked the ring against it, smiling at the loveliness of the familiar sound. It was a different pitch now, but that was good too.

Excitement was blooming all around her.

This new chapter of her life, this new promise, continued to wash over her with excitement. There was a definite bubbling of life in her bloodstream; one she hadn't felt since David.

The cup slipped out of her hand and landed with a thud on the table, brown liquid splashing out. Her eyesight having gone blurry, she blinked wildly, but instead of attempting to realign the moment, she found just enough courage to whisper, "David."

It didn't hurt.

Not the way it initially had so many years ago.

She'd locked his memories, and even his name, up for so long, it seemed like another lifetime. But now, as it all drifted past her, it was a welcome shock to see that it wasn't accompanied by pain.

Maybe nineteen years had finally healed her. Maybe nineteen years was enough time to give her past a soft, filtered quality. Now, all she had were foggy shadows at the edge of her memory. As if David had been someone else's ... everything.

"David," she whispered once more and nodded as her vision cleared.

She wiped up the coffee and picked up the cup once more, tapped the ring against it with more confidence and took a sip.

Her cell phone ringing from the sofa released the moment and when she saw Anthony's number blinking to life she liked the warmth that came with it.

"Anthony!" she answered.

"Diana, it's Anthony," he announced loudly above a din of noise.

"Yes, how are you?"

"Diana, can you hear me?" It sounded like he was in the middle of a construction zone. "I'm sorry, let me just close the door." A few seconds later and the sound was a low hum. "Diana?"

"Yes."

"Finally," he sighed. "I can hear you now, can you hear me?"

"Yes, how are you?"

"I decided to come in early this morning. I thought I would have some time to myself but there are so many people on site already, and there was so much paperwork and so many introductions ..." The noise started up again. "I'm sorry, they keep opening the door."

Once the sound dulled Anthony continued, "Diana, I have something I need to talk to you about."

She wondered if he was going to renege on the proposal, but before the thought could fully form he said, "There's been a change of plans with this job ... they need me to move here for the year."

"The year?"

"They're giving me a house. Fully furnished." He cleared his throat. "A fully furnished house and I talked to my boss. I told him ... well, it's all okay. You can move here. I'm sure you could find work. And tax season is over, so you could move if you wanted to?" he questioned, making it sound like asking her to marry him and move to another state was pushing his luck.

"To Houston?" she whispered.

"They're giving me a car, too," he said, as if that would sweeten the deal. "I understand this is going to be difficult for you, your family is all in Atlanta and this is so last minute. We can postpone the actual wedding or whatever would make you happy. But ... if you wanted to, you could move here. With me?"

"When ... when would you want me there?" Her head swirled with the details of moving. Though, if the house were already furnished, and it was only for a year ... She could store her stuff with Lena.

"I was thinking, if you want to, I could take a long weekend and we could get married. And then we can come back here together?" Another questioning statement.

Why did moving seem like a bigger commitment than agreeing to marry this man?

"Diana?"

"Okay." She glanced down at the ring, this was what clarity looked like. It was an adventure. The next phase of her life was going to be an adventure, so why not start now?

The only real problem would be finding a job, but Anthony had a good job and she wouldn't be trying to pay the bills by herself. This was marriage. She repeated her acceptance with conviction once more, "Okay."

"Really?" Anthony sounded surprised.

"You asked me to marry you. This is what married people do. If you're going to be in Houston for a year, I'm going to be in Houston for a year."

"Oh!" He cleared his throat again. "That's wonderful. What a week we've had."

"So I guess the question is, when can you come back for a few days?" Diana bit her lip as she glanced around the guesthouse and began to take inventory of what she would need to take with her and what she could leave behind.

"So we can get married," Anthony confirmed.

"Yes." Diana's stomach fluttered.

"Hold on ... let me look at ..." she heard him clicking around on his computer, "I just need to find my schedule." He swore under his breath a few times and finally yelled in triumph, "Here it is! I could take five days next month, around the twentieth?"

Diana opened her calendar and counted the weeks until the twentieth. It gave her about six weeks to plan a wedding and look at that, she'd be a

June bride.

"Is that enough time?" Anthony asked. "To plan everything? And what can I help with? Maybe I should come back a few weekends so you don't have to do everything yourself."

"It's just going to be a small ceremony. I was thinking we could go to St. Paul's with our families and a few friends then to Luciano's for the reception."

"Oh. Yes." He sounded pleased at the suggestion. "That sounds wonderful. Do I need to find a tux?"

"Your gray suit will be fine," Diana replied.

"My gray suit. Well, okay then Diana Barrett. We'll get married on June twentieth."

"Yes we will Anthony Clark. It'll be nice, I'll let you know what I need help with as I begin to plan things."

"Thank you, thank you, Diana," he said. "My heart ..." He cleared his throat. "I told everyone I talked to on the flight, and here in Houston, that I was engaged. And how wonderful you are. And how much I love you."

"Send me a list of who you'd like to invite, okay?"

"Okay, I'll think about that today and email you a list later tonight when I finally get back to the hotel."

There was another eruption of noise on Anthony's end of the phone and Diana heard several voices talking at once over each other. "Please, just a minute," Anthony said, and the voices stopped. "Diana, I'm so sorry. I need to go."

"Okay," she said. "Look, call me when you have time. Don't worry about anything."

"I'm not worried, I'm excited," he insisted as the noise began again; apparently whatever door he'd tried to shut was open again. He loudly called, "Diana, I'll call you later!"

She replied but wasn't sure he heard her.

She stared at her phone as Anthony's number disappeared and the screen went black. Married and a few months in Houston for a honeymoon.

This was good.

# Chapter Five

"So, Mr. Bennet over at Hill's Dry Cleaning said that his wife went into Merle's Hardware store and found Merle's son and the Hughs' oldest boy entwined in a rather desperate embrace. Isn't that romantic?!" Sybil, one of the five CPAs at Peachtree Accounting – where Diana had worked the past fifteen years – sat down heavily in the empty chair next to Diana's desk, sharing the gossip and twirling a pen in her hand as she watched Diana organize herself. Sybil was a spunky thirty-year-old, full of life and ready to take on the world. While she kept the office staff informed about the newest procedures, computer applications and programs; she also inflated the walls with vitality.

"You know Joe doesn't like us to gossip about our clients," Diana responded.

"They tell me!" Sybil defended. "Unprompted. Don't tell me when you're at a customer's office they don't just start telling you all sorts of crazy stories you didn't ask to hear."

Over the years, as clients got to know Diana, they loosened up around her and shared some of their stories. But she wasn't as open and welcoming as Sybil; the young woman had a superpower for putting strangers she just met at ease, pulling laughter and smiles from them.

Diana was trying to make a living and had forgotten the need for human connection. Working at Peachtree next to Sybil for the past three years, reminded Diana that perhaps, there was room for more.

Sybil tapped the desk with her pen. "It's like people get all weird about money and us looking at their books so they just start talking. A weird defense mechanism."

Diana gave her colleague a sideways glance as she settled herself, then admitted, "I suppose it's a lot like being a bartender; if our clients feel they know just enough about us to trust us with their accounts, they might as well trust us enough to unload a few other intimate details we never asked to know."

"Exactly," Sybil pointed. "Although, I'm just naturally a people person. I have the kind of face that causes people to trust me immediately and want to share their secrets."

"You're very personable. Just don't let Joe hear you gossiping."

"Joe's not in yet," was her defense. "And I'm not necessarily gossiping, I'm just passing on information."

"Well ..." Diana sat down and shrugged, "I'm glad the Hughs boy found someone. He deserves all the happiness. He's such a charming young man and that does sound very romantic."

Sybil continued to tap her pen happily on the desk. Diana fished her phone out of her purse, the last step in organizing herself, but the second she placed it on her desk, it began to buzz incessantly.

Sybil glanced at the caller ID. "It's Harper."

Diana grunted and swiped to ignore the call. A few seconds later, text messages began, vibrating the phone toward the edge of the desk. Diana frustratingly turned her phone off and tossed it back in her purse.

"What's going on?" Sybil asked.

"Nothing." Diana wasn't in the mood for Harper's opinionated, overbearing judgments. Even though her baby sister lived miles away in New York, the girl had a way of offering her blatant disapproval that could make the strictest of nuns squirm.

"I bet they make a cute couple," Diana changed the subject, "Merle's son and the oldest Hughs' boy."

"So cute!" Sybil twirled around in the chair a few times, then stopped and sighed. "So what do you have today?"

Diana looked at the calendar she'd just opened. "The Daily Grind coffee shop, Hillcrest Dry Cleaning, and Katie's Bakery."

"Oh, please bring back some of her madeleines."

"Regular or chocolate dipped?"

"What do you think?"

The creak of the front door called the women's attention as Joe, the owner of the company, walked in. He was tall and lanky, early sixties, with a full head of cloudy gray hair. A black satchel was hanging from his shoulder, and a pink box, with grease already sinking through the bottom, was held aloft in his right hand.

"Morning Joe! Where have you been?" Sybil asked.

"Tully's Pastries."

Sybil stood, thrusting a fist triumphantly in the air as she instructed Diana, "Forget the madeleines."

Joe opened the box, presenting five glorious almond croissants to them.

It was Joe who'd introduced Diana to Anthony a year ago, and as she took the pastry, she thought about telling him and Sybil about the engagement now rather than later.

"I have something to tell you both," she began just as Joe's cell phone began to ring. He glanced at the number and gave an apologetic sigh. "It's my mother, I've been trying to get her all morning."

Diana waved him away. "Take the call. This can wait."

While Joe's attention had been claimed, Sybil raised an eyebrow. "What do you have to tell us?"

Diana sat and took a bite of her pastry in reply.

Sybil followed Diana's example, twisting right and left in the chair as she ate, though her study of Diana took on a pointedness. After a few moments, she stopped and tilted her head, raising her eyebrows in expectation.

"Yes?" Diana asked.

"It's something big."

"What is?"

"What you have to tell us." Sybil narrowed her gaze. "You look …"

"Happy?"

"Yes, but it's something more."

"Maybe." Diana couldn't hold back the blush that crept up her cheeks; she was worried about telling her colleagues. Harper's less than thrilled reaction had stunted her.

"Just tell me," Sybil insisted.

Diana took a bite to delay the moment.

Sybil pursed her lips and after a beat, her eyes darted to Diana's hand. She grabbed the hand with the ring and excitedly declared, "This is new.

I should have been a detective. What does this mean?"

Diana whispered, "Anthony proposed last night."

Sybil squealed with delight, and still holding Diana's hand, jumped out of her chair, forcing Diana to stand as well. She then all but crushed herself to her friend, hugging the breath out of her as she called out, "Congratulations!"

Phillip, another colleague on the phone, holding his hand over the receiver, hissed, "Sybil, please be quiet."

"Diana got engaged!" she announced instead of apologizing.

He nodded at Diana. "Congratulations. Now please lower your voice." He went back to his call.

Sybil stuck her tongue out then picked up Diana's hand again to study the ring. "Why is it on your pinky finger?" she asked breathlessly.

The ring caught a ray of light shining in from the window and another rise of giddiness filled Diana. She began the tale of her engagement and ended with the fact that she was getting married in six weeks.

"Six weeks?!" Sybil said, a mix of shock and excitement.

Diana nodded; six weeks.

She didn't tell Sybil about the year-long honeymoon in Houston. She should talk to Joe about that first. Find out if there was a way for her to take a sort of sabbatical or if he had any connections in Texas.

"Well, tell me what you need and what I can do!" Sybil clapped, then hugged Diana once more.

"Just this; being happy for me means a lot." Diana dislodged herself and patted Sybil's arm.

"I am *so* happy for you. How exciting. How are you ever going to concentrate today?"

Diana winked. "I'll figure it out."

# Chapter Six

The announcement to the office resulted in everyone reworking their schedules and going to a celebratory lunch. Before they left, Diana talked with Joe who waved her concerns away. Taking a sabbatical was no big deal. "You've been more than an employee, you're family. You can work remotely for a year as far as I'm concerned. It'll all work out."

Diana's life opened wide with that comment. And feeling empowered by the conversation, she told the rest of her colleagues at lunch of her plans. A bottle of champagne was ordered and Diana blushed as she was congratulated. She took a photo of the table and sent it to Anthony with the comment: *Still celebrating!*

He texted back immediately: *Wonderful!*

Diana continued the celebratory day seated in the back office of Katie's Bakery. As she worked on the monthly oversights and payrolls, she found herself surrounded by corkboards filled with photos of wedding cakes, sketched designs for birthday cakes and trays of inspired cupcakes. Giving in to all the baked distractions, she asked Katie for a moment of her time.

"I'm engaged," she announced.

Katie clapped and excitedly declared, "Let me make your cake!"

"Great minds think alike." Diana laughed.

Katie hurried out of the room, returning with a plate of samples. She spoke quickly as she explained the different combinations she could do then pulled out a spiral binder to show some of the ideas she thought Diana would like.

Diana forwarded photos and descriptions to Anthony who liked every one she sent. In the end, he said: *I trust your judgment. I know the cake you choose will be as remarkable as you are.*

She read the text over several times before she thanked him.

So the day ended with Katie and Diana piecing together a tentative plan. Diana wanted to think about it – and finalize the number of guests – before she put the order in.

She floated home later than she planned, but in such high spirits she wasn't even deterred when she turned her phone back on to find three messages and twenty-five text messages from Harper.

With a deep breath she finally texted her sister: *Just home from work. Let me eat dinner and take a shower and I'll call you. Stop texting until then.*

Fortified enough to return Harper's call, and put her in her place, Diana sat on the sofa and called her.

"Luna Luna Luna Luna!" Harper excitedly screamed in place of a dignified answer.

"Yes," Diana answered, a bit leery. She'd been ready for more intense displeasure, not this excitement.

"I got you an engagement present!" Harper said excitedly.

Diana groaned, "Please no."

"You love my presents. And *this* is a good one." Harper's smile was tangible.

"The last 'good present' you got me was a stripper."

"*Everyone* wants a stripper at their fortieth birthday party."

Diana muttered, "CPA Gray," the stripper's stage name.

"He came highly recommended," Harper defended, "a lot of satisfied customers."

"Lena threw me a classy high tea ..." Diana started, but the flash of memory made her grin. The man had shown up in a suit, with a briefcase, glasses, and started going on and on about tax codes; then when he opened his briefcase, which held his sound system, he lost the glasses and became Superman to his Clark Kent. "It was so weird and before anyone knew what was going on, your little stripper was shirtless and grinding on some of Mom's hoity-toity friends she'd invited." Diana choked on laughter. "And then he was in nothing but this ridiculous thong and, dear God Harper, your *mother* was sitting on the edge of her seat, yelling at Lena and I to get her some ones."

"I wish I could have been there. Stupid work."

"And then everyone started whooping and whistling ... it was amazing how quickly a classy high tea turned into a gyrating madhouse."

"But you enjoyed it too, right?" Harper sounded genuinely concerned.

"It was ..." Diana snorted. "Yes. It isn't my sort of thing, it was embarrassing and weird but he was quite handsome and had some very nice ... moves."

"Like I said, *a lot* of good ratings."

"Harper, you are the life of the party, even when you aren't able to be *at* the party," Diana admitted.

"Did you want a stripper again? I'll get you a belated birthday present," Harper offered.

"No," Diana said too quickly then laughed, "thank you. I'm good with the memory of CPA Gray."

"Look," Harper cleared her throat and barreled ahead, "I'm sorry. About how I reacted and what I said about Anthony. I really am. It was insensitive and rude." She sounded properly contrite. "Can you forgive me?"

"I suppose."

Relieved, Harper let out a slow release of breath. "I love you, Lu. More than you know."

"I love you too."

"Good, because before you get married ..." She took a deep breath, so Diana decided to embrace the moment and get all of the latest developments out in the open.

"And move to Houston." Diana ripped the band-aid off.

"What?"

"Anthony's job in Houston is going to take a year, the company is paying for a house and car. We're going to move there after we get married. I'm thinking of it as an extended honeymoon."

"Oh."

"And we set a date. In six weeks. We'll get married on the twentieth of June. And I want you to be here for it."

"Well ... that's ..." Harper stopped herself from whatever she was going to say, "that's just great." She overcorrected. "I'm really happy for you,

Luna. That's just … I'll be there. Of course I'll be there."

Diana wondered what kind of chewing out Harper received from Lena to make her swallow her opinions so quickly. Instead of opening that can of worms, she prodded, "Okay Harper, tell me about this present you got me. Who's going to show up at my door to congratulate me on my engagement?"

"It's not who's going to show up on your doorstep, but whose doorstep *you're* going to show up on." The rushed announcement rebuilt Harper's original excitement. "Luna, we're going to Italy! Ten days. Me and you!"

Diana opened her mouth, but no words formed. Details about guest lists, finding a dress, packing and work swirled.

"Lu?" Harper asked. "Did you hear what I said?"

"I can't go to Italy," Diana said incredulously.

"Yes, *you can*!"

"I have work—"

"You don't, actually …" Harper interrupted, losing some of her steam. "I called Joe today and told him what I had planned."

So that's why Joe kept grinning at her and congratulating her and telling her not to worry so much about work before she left tonight.

"Did you know you have nine months of vacation time built up?" Harper continued.

"Yes, it's for an emergency. You know, in case I ever needed surgery or Mom and Dad needed me. I am saving it for a reason," Diana said between her teeth.

"You can afford ten days, you'll still be left with eight and a half months' vacation time."

"It's a nice idea, but Harper, you can't just intrude on someone's life and plan European vacations."

Harper took a deep breath before she barreled on, "Just listen to this itinerary. We land in Pisa, you know, the leaning tower? Then it's Florence, a cute little town called Orvieto, and finally Rome!"

"Harper, I have a wedding to plan."

"Lena has it all planned. You just want a small thing, so she is taking care of everything. All she's gotta do is plug in a date, and it sounds like you have one."

"What? When? I just got engaged last night."

"Do you seriously not know our big sister? She had the whole thing planned and organized by midnight," Harper said dismissively before demanding, "Italy Lu, focus."

"But ... flowers ... I wanted it to be colorful."

"Everything has a wildflower look. She can get the small chapel at the church pretty much whenever she wants and you told her you wanted the reception at Luciano's. That's easy enough. The way she figures it, the whole wedding party is only about fifty people."

"Even if I could go to Italy, I can't afford—"

"I'm paying for everything," Harper disrupted.

Diana looked around her, as if she could find a reason to not go just lying somewhere. "I need to pack up my things so I can move to Houston," she tried lamely.

"You'll still have time to pack. And I know this is last minute and scary, but you're so organized you could start packing right now and be ready to move by this time tomorrow."

Harper was right on that account.

Diana still stuttered, she wasn't one for jumping on planes and rushing to other countries. Paid for or not.

"Passport," she said, clinging to what seemed to be her last defense. Sure she'd gotten one years ago when Lena had taken the whole family to Belize for their parents' vow renewal, but it had to be expired by now, right?

"It doesn't expire for another three years. We still have plenty of time."

Harper was out of her mind. And apparently, had done her homework, ready to refute any of Diana's misgivings.

"What about Mom's fundraiser? I promised I'd help." *Talk about desperate ploys.*

"Jesus Diana, Mom's got a whole group of biddies that help with that thing. And if you're really worried, you'll be happy to know we'll be back about two days before, so you can still help."

"Anthony ..." she whispered at last.

"I called and talked to my future brother-in-law." Diana tried to ignore the slight hitch in Harper's voice when she used the term. "He thinks it's wonderful that you and I are going. He said it was a good idea. He said he won't worry about you being so lonely while he's working so far away." It was a direct quote, and it was working.

"If…" Diana said and repeated the word a second time, more harshly, "*If*…" she cleared her throat, "*if* I decide to go, when would we leave?"

"Monday."

"That's in two days!" Diana blinked wildly as she tried to take in the events from the past forty-eight hours and the monumental changes that were piling atop each other.

"I'll meet you at the airport in Pisa!" Harper exclaimed excitedly.

"I can't…"

"Why? Why can't you?"

"Because …" Diana had a handful of reasons but the biggest one was that the idea scared the hell out of her.

"Here's some tough love coming your way, Lu. You think you can't go because you've spent the past nineteen years hiding in that guesthouse convincing yourself you're no better than a poorly paid nanny. And while you've been hiding, you've gotten scared of your own shadow. And you went from being someone who was full of life and ideas and promise, to someone who's old before her time." Diana felt as if Harper had physically punched her, but her sister didn't stop; she was on a roll. "Well Lu, it's time to remind yourself that you've still got something to give the world. And we're going to jumpstart it all again in Italy." Harper's passion oozed out of the phone and into Diana's bones. "So we're going to Italy!" Harper held her breath.

Diana had so many thoughts running about. One was that it *would* be really nice to see Harper again. Not just through a video call. They hadn't seen each other since Thanksgiving. The whole family descended upon their parents' house over the holiday, but three days of loud family madness wasn't enough.

Diana and Harper didn't become close until Diana's junior year in high school. Then, since she lived at home to save money during the first two years of college, the two solidified their connection. Even after she moved to New York, Diana made sure to call and write to Harper. But when Diana's husband died, and Harper tried to comfort her, she shut her younger sister out along with everyone else.

It took several years for them to patch their relationship back together but by then, Harper was living in New York and Diana was helping with the twins and working on her certification. Then life got in the way and as the years passed, they tried their best, but never seemed to have enough time together.

"Diana?" The long pause must have been agony for Harper; she could almost hear her sister's crossed fingers squeezing together over the phone.

Diana allowed the honest pep talk to twirl around her until finally, with the same conviction she found to agree to marry Anthony, she said, "Let's go to Italy."

Harper screamed in Diana's ear. "Yes! Okay! Oh my God I'm so excited! Lena will take you to the airport. I suggest you start packing and talk to Lena since she has your wedding planned. I already told Mom and Dad you were engaged and that we'd tell them more later and that we'd send them postcards from Italy."

She took a deep breath and gave a gleeful sound, then added, "By the way, the flight actually leaves at nine on Sunday night." With that, Harper hung up so that Diana wouldn't have a chance to change her mind.

Which left Diana holding her phone to her ear, staring but not seeing any of her surroundings because her world seemed to tilt a bit and give a slight shake.

Engagement, Houston and now Italy.

Holy shit.

# Chapter Seven

T he plane shook as its altitude changed, the plastic overhead compartments creaking and the seats wiggling. A reminder to remain seated and keep seatbelts on dinged while flight attendants did a last glance around at all passengers on their way to strap in for landing.

Diana had only been on a handful of flights, none as long as this. She enjoyed the process; leaving late in the evening, the meals served while in flight and the movies offered on the small screen embedded into the headrest in front of her. She'd celebrated with a glass of wine with her dinner and smiled at the ridiculous relaxation of the moment.

She changed planes in Frankfurt, which was a tense experience. She was glad for both the signage in English that pointed the way to where she needed to go, and the Youtube video Harper sent of someone walking through the process. Diana hiked through the sprawling Frankfurt airport, stopping halfway to go through customs. As the frowning attendant slammed the stamp into her passport, a wave of excited nausea filled her.

After boarding her connecting flight to Pisa, she was relieved when no one sat next to her. It allowed her quiet for the next hour and a half to wonder at her current circumstances.

An engaged woman, winging her way to Italy with two days' notice. It was the most reckless thing she'd done since eloping.

She watched out the window as the plane descended through a white blur of clouds, like a screen was being pulled across the moment to reveal the blue of the ocean and the Italian coast.

Her breath caught as the reality of a foreign country, the reality of *Italy*, took form before her very eyes; out of the blue surf and sand, crawling into a seaside city of terracotta rooftops, transforming into a small forest of gorgeous green before stretching out into farming plots of dusty beige, sepia and wheat colors.

There was a sudden romance in the changing scenery and colors that brushed the landscape. The plane drew the scene closer, and just before it took a right turn, Diana spied the runway where they would land.

She never realized Pisa was so close to the ocean. Or maybe she did; she'd spent the day before she left clicking around the internet, and looking at maps of Italy, but it had been a dream then, not this tangible.

The plane smoothly slipped down the runway, and Diana watched the Pisa International Airport come into view. It was small. The size of a large department store, maybe. When comparing the 192 gated intensity that was the Atlanta International Airport, it was a fraction the size.

She wasn't sure what she was feeling beyond trepidation and worry. What was she doing? It was a question she'd asked Anthony when she talked to him before she left. He'd laughed and insisted, "It's good. A honeymoon before I can take you on an actual honeymoon. Maybe you can think of it as scouting out the country. Maybe we'll go back together."

So Diana tried to embrace the idea that this was a scouting trip in a foreign country.

At least there would be Harper. Harper, who'd never met a stranger and greeted the whole of the world with open arms, all for the experience.

The voice of the flight attendant came over the speaker, making an announcement in Italian then in English: the local time, 3:55 p.m.; temperature, seventy-one degrees; and the gate where their bags would be found, baggage carousel 'B.'

Welcome to Pisa.

*Italy.*

Diana felt light as she walked out of the plane doors onto the stairs, and took a deep breath of the fresh Italian air. It was musty and humid. Different. But she wasn't sure exactly how to describe it, and she didn't have much time to decipher it as the passengers behind her were waiting.

A ground crew member waved the passengers to a waiting bus that would drive them to the arrival gate at the airport building.

People had begun to shake off the exhaustion from their flights and a palpable excitement began to grow.

Or maybe Diana was projecting. Because no matter how scary she found this trip, it was all worth it to see her little sister.

Once the empty bus, that only offered standing room and a handful of seats at the front, was filled sardine style with all the passengers it could carry, it drove a few hundred feet to a door, where everyone climbed off and walked into the building that housed the baggage carousel with a giant yellow 'B'.

After collecting her rolling bag, she checked her phone for the time. The only messages were from Lena, asking how she was, and Anthony, who sent a photo of an animated teddy bear insisting that she have a good time. Nothing yet from Harper, although, there was still time before her sister's flight landed.

Diana's gaze followed red arrows that pointed to armed guards standing next to the sliding glass doors that exited the baggage claim into the greeting area. Diana clutched her purse to her chest nervously as she walked past them.

When the glass doors slid open, there was a sense of liberation. Diana wasn't certain if it was being past the armed guards or the symbolic crossing over into Italy, a real arrival, that caused her to feel that way.

There were a handful of shops and two cafés in the vicinity. She felt drawn to the café that had dark brown counters and walls with smoky yellow lighting. It boasted several free tables and a few customers in line. It would be the perfect place to hole up and wait for Harper.

When she entered, the smell of coffee swirled around her. Diana inhaled and her stomach did a flip at the possibility of a good coffee to help her stay awake and sooth her nerves.

She stood back for a few moments to watch how people placed their order. Each customer was presented with a receipt from the cashier, which they then took to the bar to hand over to the barista. One woman had ordered an 'espresso' and when the small cup of dark liquid was slipped onto the counter, the steam rising up, Diana knew that was exactly what she wanted.

At her turn, she tentatively asked for an "espresso." A sum of money was declared and she handed over the twenty euro Lena had given her, a leftover from a previous trip her sister had taken with her husband.

The cashier made change and handed the receipt to Diana, who then repeated what the previous customers had done, handing it to the barista at the bar.

The man glanced at it, set a saucer on the counter by the receipt, and with impressive efficiency, he completed the process and topped the saucer with a small espresso cup and spoon, then slid the offering to Diana with a nod.

She thanked him with a muttered "grazie," slightly nervous to use the phrase – it tasted strange on her tongue.

He gave an offhanded nod then moved to the next ticket presented.

Navigating the tight space, Diana found a small table in the back of the café, where she could see people exiting into the arrival area.

She wasn't sure where the thought or even the motivation came from, but she pulled out her phone, chose the camera app, held up the cup and took a selfie.

She carefully put the cup down and looked at the picture; actually thought about deleting it, but then on a whim, posted it to her account that Harper insisted she *needed* to set up for this trip. And why the hell not?

She wrote: *Pisa, Italy. First espresso,* and posted the picture.

She took a few sips, closing her eyes to savor the bitter hot loveliness.

Finally, a message from Harper came in, demanding Diana call her right away. This was why she'd activated an international calling plan for her phone.

Diana excitedly grinned when Harper picked up on the first ring and exclaimed. "You must be nearby!"

"Well ..." Harper drew out the word, "Lu, you have the itinerary, right?"

"Yes, I printed it off before I left and it's on my phone. Where are you?"

"Happy engagement!" Harper sang.

"Harper ..." Diana laughed and looked around the part of the airport she could see, as if her younger sister would appear at any moment.

"Look, if I told you the truth you wouldn't have gone, and you *needed to* go. Hell, if anyone needs a vacation it's you."

"Harper," Diana's heart began to thump wildly in her chest, "where are you?"

In almost a whisper, Harper answered, "New York."

Diana turned so no one could see her anger. She cupped a hand over the receiver of her phone. "What the hell do you mean you're in New York?"

"I couldn't afford to pay for both of us. But I wanted you to have something different ... I wanted to get you out of the house. I wanted you to see ... more, something bigger, something inspiring before you got married."

"Harper," Diana choked out in disbelief.

"I wanted to get you out of your fucking comfort zone," Harper admitted.

Diana was certainly out of her comfort zone now; that was for sure. And she'd be damned if she was going to stay in a foreign country by herself. "I'm not staying here alone," she hissed. "You got me into this Harper, you need to get me a return ticket and get me out of this. Now."

"No."

"Then I need to go, I need to figure out how to get home."

"No. Please. You have ten days paid vacation in Italy. Do you know how many people *dream* of something like that?"

"Harper." Diana's throat was closing with the urge to cry.

"Luna, if you can't figure out how to do this for yourself, then do this for *me*." Harper's voice hitched with the same emotion. "Please Lu, you *deserve* something like this. You deserve to see something beautiful. You deserve to ... to sit in a Piazza in a world-famous café and sip an espresso. You deserve to be moved to tears by a painting." It was Harper who was crying now. "Jesus, Luna, you deserve to stand in the middle of Rome and be inspired. I understand this is the scariest thing anyone has ever asked you to do, I get that it's a scary ass thing that *I* am asking you to do, but please ... *please*, if you can't do this for yourself, then do it for *me*."

Diana didn't know what to say, because even though Harper's begging was wearing her down slightly, Diana couldn't shake the overwhelming feeling of being betrayed.

She stared down at the espresso she ordered. Only moments ago, the act had brought her so much pride; but that pride had been dependent on the fact that Harper was nearby. Harper was the only thing on this trip that would have made Diana comfortable. She didn't have it in her to take on Italy by herself. She understood that this was a dream for a lot of people, but she hadn't asked for this.

"I don't know the language," Diana whispered angrily.

"You'll be in major tourist areas. *Everyone* speaks enough English for you to get around confidently. I read that on all the tourist websites."

"I can't–"

"For me," Harper begged.

The silence between them spanned the distance that physically separated them until Harper reeled Diana in with another plea. "Luna, please."

"So ..." Diana cleared her throat, "let me get this straight; you had almost three days to come up with a speech that would get me to stay in Italy. Alone," she growled. "And in all that time the best you came up with is a lame, whiny 'please'?"

Harper gave a slight laugh. "There's a lot more to the speech if you want to hear it."

"Save it for later," Diana muttered.

"What is this beeping ...?" Harper said as Diana heard the muffled sounds of the phone being manhandled. Harper squealed at whatever it was and yelled, "Luna! Look at the picture you just posted."

"I know what picture I just posted," she bit, annoyed.

"No, look at it. Really look at it. Right now."

Diana sighed and flipped to the picture on her phone. She nodded her head; yup, it was still a picture of her with an espresso at an airport café. "So?"

"Look at it again," Harper insisted.

She did, but looking at the picture again, *really looking,* she saw what Harper was referring to. Diana was happy. Her face was, dare she think it, glowing. She stared for several long moments before finally putting the phone back to her ear. "I see it."

"Please give yourself a chance."

Diana glanced around her and saw a young woman sitting by herself, a notebook in front of her, a backpack seated by her feet and a cappuccino at her arm. She looked so at ease and sure of herself. If the young woman could do it, then maybe...

"Okay." The word was a whisper.

"What?" Harper asked.

"I said okay. I'll stay," Diana said a bit more loudly.

"Yes! Oh Luna, yes! I'm so excited! I'm going to check every hour … no, every minute for more pictures of your trip that look like this one with the coffee!"

"You tricked me. Lied to me. *Abandoned* me in the middle of a foreign country," Diana scolded. "I'm not sure there are going to be other moments like that one."

"You're going to have so much fun!" Harper exclaimed.

"I don't know what I'm doing here," Diana muttered.

"You're going to go find the tram right by the airport and go to Albergo dei Sogni." She over pronounced the phrase. "Then tomorrow you're going to go see the leaning tower and have gelato and a glass of wine and maybe you're going to let your hair down."

Diana mindlessly touched the bun she preferred to keep her hair tucked into.

"Then what?" Diana asked, still angry and stunned.

"Then … anything." Harper said.

"Maybe," Diana muttered.

"You can do this, Lu."

"Does Anthony know you tricked me?"

"No."

Diana smiled. "Okay. I'll make you a deal, the first of many," she warned. "You tell Anthony you abandoned me; alone in a foreign country where I don't speak the language or know how to navigate anything."

"Okay," Harper readily agreed.

"Jesus, you really want me to do this."

"Yes. I really do. I just want you to … just be somewhere where you haven't been, *you,* for the past nineteen years."

"What is that supposed to mean?"

"I just want you to have a change of scenery. For yourself."

"Fine, you tell Anthony you abandoned me and tricked me and I'll stay."

"Okay," Harper agreed again.

"For two days." Diana threw the clause in.

"Two days?"

"Two days."

"Four," Harper countered.

Diana was quiet for a long moment before she agreed, "Four days."

"Okay." Harper let out a pent-up breath she might have been holding since she first called Diana with this ridiculous idea. "Four days. If after four days, it's not for you, I'll get you home."

"Okay," Diana repeated softly.

Harper gave a whoop of laughter.

"I'm still pissed at you." Diana sighed.

"That's fine."

"I'm gonna be pissed for a while."

"Fair's fair," Harper replied. "Have fun. Take a ton of pictures. Post everything."

"No."

"I'm sending you videos on how to use the metro thing there by the airport, and the address of the hotel and directions."

Diana sighed, the little shit might not be with her on this trip, but she was going to do everything she could to make sure Diana stayed comfortable enough to stay for ten days.

# Chapter Eight

Diana stared blankly at her phone as she watched the videos Harper sent. The first was a step by step guide on how to walk out the front doors of the airport, turn left, and follow the signs for the metro that would take her into the center of Pisa. Next, was a photo of a map that had been highlighted, along with a link to a map Diana could use in real time, which would lead her to her hotel, the Albergo dei Sogni (whatever that meant). It was her final destination for the night, and only an eight minute walk from where she would depart the metro.

There was also a stop along the route for a bank, and directions on how to take money out of an Italian ATM.

Within those instructions was a message that Harper had sent money to Diana's bank account. Lena had set up linked accounts years ago so the three sisters could easily pay each other when they split the cost of flowers and presents for their parents on various holidays.

Even with all that guidance, she didn't move to leave and instead searched for flights leaving Pisa, bound for Atlanta. There was one leaving in a few hours, but the whole flight and layover would take thirty-four hours. And it cost quite a bit more than the 'free' price tag Harper had hung on this outrageous plan.

So maybe it was better to sleep in a bed and see the leaning tower; *then* she could go home. Harper lied to her, she could lie about the four day pact.

But to execute even a few of these well-intentioned plans and begin this adventure, Diana had to first walk out the front doors of the airport.

*A journey of a thousand miles begins with a single step.* The old saying winked at Diana and she physically swatted it away with a frown.

"C'mon. This is nothing," she chided herself, then took the last cold swig of espresso, stood up, linked her purse over her shoulder and gripped her rolling suitcase overly tight. She paused only momentarily, then dared herself to go.

"Stupid Harper," she muttered as she finally left and followed the directions to the metro.

A whirlwind of emotions kept her heart rate up as she followed the instructions on the ticketing machine, thankful for the option to complete the process in 'English.' And even more grateful for Lena's money that helped purchase the ticket. She gripped the handrail, listening to the excited chattering in Italian happening around her. A roadway was off to the left of the raised tram tracks and on the right was chain link fencing that followed the course of the tram, littered with garbage and weeds.

At the exit, she followed the masses under a tunnel that took them to the main train station then finally out the front doors. She stopped, but was elbowed by several passengers who wanted her to continue walking.

She tightened her grip on her purse as she walked through one of the arches that decorated the front of the Pisa train station, moving toward the fountain in the middle of a circular structure. Cobblestones were designed in a fan shape, and on either side of her were matching plots of green grass with a small hedge. To her right flowers were planted in the design of a cross and on the left, the flowers spelled out Pisa.

The surrounding buildings showed off pristine red brick designs, and to her right, several orange buses hummed, waiting for passengers. Diana was prodded forward by the movement of so many people spilling out of the station behind her.

As if her purse was a physical representation of her courage, she hitched it up on her shoulder and pressed it against her body, looking both ways before crossing the street and continuing straight onto the covered walkway.

The shops were a swirling confusion of eye candy. She passed a small grocery store, a gift shop with racks of postcards in front to draw in tourists, cafés, a stationary store, a clothing boutique, and a newsstand. A handful of businesses had their dark gray roll-down gates already in place, closed for the day.

She found the bank, and was angry when the process was easy. She didn't plan on being in Italy for very long, but still took out a hundred euro. Just in case.

As she continued, the new and jarring smells – musk, humidity, perfume and espresso – reminded her she wasn't in Kansas anymore.

The noise was that of cars, an occasional high pitch beep of a scooter, a revving of a bus, laughter, and loud Italian that sounded so exotic, it was just a barrage of sound.

She pressed the purse harder against her side to dislodge the thought that laughingly screamed, *what are you doing?!*

Thankfully, the directions were easy: straight, the first right, then the third left. She pulled out her phone after the first right and followed the real-time map to make sure she was where she needed to be.

The narrowness of the road and the smaller cars that aggressively squeezed past each other made the street seem busy. She blinked at the umbrella-clad tables cuddled in front of small restaurants with names that started with words she understood; Trattoria, Bistro, and Ristorante.

The late day sun gave the three- and four-story buildings that lined the street a muted color scheme, ranging from dirty off-white, to yellow and peachy orange.

She turned down the last road that would lead to the hotel, and faltered when she spied a group of people illuminated under a neon light halfway down the street. Smoke rose from the middle of the group and Diana knew, with every fiber in her being, *that* was her hotel.

As she arrived at the Albergo dei Sogni, she cursed Harper who had failed to mention to Diana one important bit of information – it was a hostel.

The front steps of the four-story building were covered with a green canopy and the name of the hostel. The yellow walls had large chunks of stucco missing, and the windows were covered with aged dark green shutters, a few propped open with clothes hanging off fold-out laundry racks.

Diana gave a terse smile and cursed Harper's soul once more as she faced the group of young adults, *at least twenty years* younger adults. Two women were playing guitars and one of the young men happily greeted her by offering her the joint he was smoking.

*I'm too old for this shit,* she thought as she declined the offer, wondering if this was an omen while muttering a litany of "excuse mes" and playing Twister in an attempt to make her way to the front door. A tan, shirtless young man with fat brown dreadlocks and low riding pants tried to pick up her suitcase and carry it for her, but she tightened her hold, rejecting the help.

He shrugged and instead, held open the door. She nodded her thanks as she finally maneuvered into the uncrowded, muggy foyer. It was the kind of muggy that came from a number of people taking showers in quick succession, the kind of warmth and humidity that could only mean one thing: communal bathrooms and poor ventilation. A muggy memory from her college dorm days.

Harper be damned, Diana was heading home tomorrow.

A woman with black hair gathered loosely by a pink ribbon around the nape of her neck swept into the front room. She wore a light blue tank top and no bra, evident by the way her erect nipples pressed against the fabric. The shirt was accompanied by a full-length white cotton skirt belted with a length of gold rope around the waist. Without a greeting, she walked slowly around Diana, nodding until she came to a stop in front of her, the skirt swishing around her ankles. "You are American." Her accent was thick and her smile wide, revealing a row of perfectly straight teeth. However, years of smoking and wine drinking stole focus from their perfection.

"I have a reservation." It was more of a question.

The woman nodded and without looking at a registry said, "Barrett." Her voice was deep and smoky and she pronounced Diana's last name with a twirl of the 'r'. "Luna Barrett."

Really Harper? Diana cleared her throat as she corrected, "I prefer Diana." She held out her hand to the woman.

The woman took Diana's hand and pulled her close, kissing both of her cheeks in greeting and then, without letting go of her hand and obstructing her personal space, studied Diana. "I am Sofia. You are too uptight I think."

Diana tugged at her hand and once free from Sofia's grasp, moved back a safe distance and muttered, "It's been a long trip. If you don't mind,

I'd like to go rest in my room." She was worried what 'a room' meant in a hostel. From her limited understanding, which was television, she knew it often meant a large room with bunk beds and youths publicly exploring European free-loving customs.

"Certo. Of course." Sofia smiled and moved behind the front desk. She pulled out a key and produced a piece of paper. "You are paid for two nights in a single room. Just yourself."

Diana sagged a bit. *Thank God for small miracles.*

Sofia pointed to the stairs. "We have no elevator. You are on the third floor. Up. Then turning to right, you will find the room. Once you rest, come down. We have large room with many interesting people to talk with. And yes, a kitchen to prepare your own food, ma per favore, clean up after. And we have una macchina in the dining area with ... come si dice ... items of food for your convenience."

"A vending machine?" Diana offered.

The woman shrugged as if she didn't know those words, or perhaps it was an agreeable shrug. Sofia looked around as if she were forgetting something and then snapped her fingers. "You have towel and washcloth. Il bagno, bathroom, on every floor. Take your towel with you back to your room." She slid the key and a used map of Pisa across the desk toward Diana. "A free map of Pisa for you." She flashed another plaque filled smile.

Diana gave a quick draw of her lips together, hoping it was more of a smile than a grimace, then thankfully, was saved from further interaction when one of the patrons from the front stoop came inside and caught Sofia's attention.

Diana wavered before picking up her bag and heading up the stairs.

Sofia pointed at Diana, as if she were cursing her. "We will go to coffee tomorrow morning. We will talk."

Diana didn't even give a nod of agreement, just headed to her room. She passed unorganized groups of bright paintings that hugged the walls along the staircase. Each picture flaunted bold primary colors; no muted tones here. The walls down each hallway were a series of geometric primary colored shapes.

When she arrived at the third floor, she turned right and found more bold paintings against bright walls. A colorful cow, a collage of rubber ducks, an ad that looked like it belonged in a high school hallway. It was in Italian but she felt certain it was about seeking a degree.

An exhausted laugh at the ridiculousness of the situation bubbled over and when she opened her door, was glad the scene that greeted her was a fresh smelling, pastel, unemboldened room. One twin bed, one pillow, one towel, one washcloth, one side table, one lamp, one chair, one mirror hanging on the wall and one Ikea looking armoire.

"Okay." Diana whispered the sense of relief.

The furniture was light wood, the bedspread matched the sheets: faded polka dots. The bed had one thin pillow and a tired orange throw pillow attempting to add flare. It was warm, but not as stifling as it had been downstairs.

She sat down heavily on the bed and asked the leaning tower painting on the wall, "What the hell am I doing?"

If there was one thing she knew, it was that her sensible shoe wearing, gray-haired, tired self, did not belong in the land of colorful twenty-somethings trying to find themselves. She had not come on this trip to become some wise old advice giving aunty. What advice did she have to give? Marry for security. Life is difficult. True love will only hurt you.

"Okay, that's a bit much," she chided, "you're just hungry and tired and upset."

She retrieved her toiletry bag then grabbed her purse and the washcloth so she could wash her face. Maybe that would help her feel better.

Opening the door to the bright yellow and blue walls was another shock to her senses. She shook her head as she walked down the elementary school style hallway to the restroom, but the ridiculousness of it pulled a smile and then a laugh. She took out her phone and attempted to capture the dorm room feel of Albergo dei Sogni. When she found one she liked, she posted it with the intent to make Harper feel bad about what she'd done to Diana. But when it came to the tag, she grinned as she typed out: *Clown hell*. She liked it so much, she added: *College dorm, Elementary school or hotel? You decide.*

The bathroom was very functional. The toilet was in the shower and a thin curtain attempted to make sure the rest of the small bathroom wouldn't get wet, but as the curtain was six inches off the floor it was a sad assistant.

Diana hung her purse on one of the tarnished hooks on the back of the door then washed her face. Before she left, she took a photo, labeling it in her mind as she went back to her room. It was only six, but she was tired. And now, hungry as well. There was a small grocery store she recalled passing, but that was closer to the train station. She could go to a restaurant, but hated eating alone and was already so far out of her comfort zone, she didn't want to push it.

So it was time to patronize the vending machine downstairs, bring a picnic to the room and go to sleep early.

Maybe things would look better tomorrow. At least, once she got a little sleep, she'd be better equipped to argue with Harper.

# Chapter Nine

"It was just a tower, before it started the leaning." The thickly accented comment drifted toward Diana, but she wasn't sure it was meant for her.

A nonchalant glance to the left revealed an outline on a bench in the shade of a tree; just in front of the path that led visitors around the entire complex.

"Buongiorno," the shadow greeted.

Diana shaded her eyes as a smiling elderly man waved to her.

She nodded back then pointed to the scene before her. "I thought it was just a tower. I mean, I thought the tower was the only thing to see," she corrected. "You know, none of the pictures ever show the cathedral or the baptistery."

The Leaning Tower of Pisa was actually the bell tower of the Pisa Cathedral, a large, impressive Romanesque marble feat with black detailing. The two structures stood next to each other, the whiteness radiating in the morning sun. The entire complex, church, bell tower, baptistry and a cloister were surrounded by walls from the medieval days of Pisa and bright green, well-manicured green lawns.

"Our famous tower is bell tower of Duomo di Pisa, la Cattedrale." He paused for a moment and then loudly asked, "New York?"

One of the young women by the vending machine the evening before had asked her if she was from Hollywood and seemed disappointed when Diana said no.

She supposed, just like she received a lot of her current European geography from movies, Italians might be the same way. And a lot of movies were set in California or New York.

"Georgia," she supplied. And glancing at the man, opened her mouth to admit she once lived in New York, but decided against the direction that sort of conversation might take her.

The man leaned forward, a frown indenting his weathered forehead even more. Diana straightened her spine in answer; maybe she should admit to having lived in New York.

"Pesche!" he finally exclaimed, and then in English said, "Peach."

A smile soothed Diana's nerves. "Yes. Georgia peaches."

"I go to America when I young. Ho amici, I have friends in Oregon. We go all over the America. How you say ... from ocean to bright ocean?"

"From sea to shining sea?" she inferred.

"Brava, sì." He clapped his hands together then waved her over. "I tell you about her." He nodded toward the tower.

Diana stepped into the shade but shook off his offer to join him on the bench. "Is name is Campo dei Miracoli." He pointed and frowned as he slowly translated, "Field of the Miracles."

"Were there many miracles here?" Diana asked.

"No," the man shrugged, "is just name peoples choosing long long time. To be making place important."

"Why does it lean?" She made a tilting gesture with her hand. She would bet money that this man, sitting on the bench in front of the Field of Miracles, had been asked the question before. So it stood to reason, he'd also have a practiced answer.

"Is her nature." He grinned, then pointed to his chest. "My nature is to walking same path, drink caffè same bar, sit in same places ogni giorno, every day." He gestured toward the tower. "Is her nature to lean." He gave a wide toothy grin and tilted his head. "What is your nature?"

"I don't have a nature," Diana quickly dismissed.

The old man shook his head. "Even if peoples thinking they no have nature, is not true. Tutti, everybodies, we have nature." He studied her for a moment longer then narrowed his gaze, "Sometimes, maybe no so easy to be seeing, maybe you forget your nature?"

Diana cleared her throat. "So the tower leans because it's her nature to do so." She didn't want to think about her own lack of nature.

He clicked his tongue and sat back, unphased by Diana's reaction. "She is built one one seven three." He gave the year, 1173, as individual numbers. "Three levels men build. Then, she leans. The ground, is soft. So men try to fix her leaning. Non funziona. No work." He shrugged. "She sinks again. Is her nature."

Diana squinted at the tower; was it that simple?

"This is you first time Italia?" he asked.

She nodded.

"Good." He slapped his knee. "Then is good time to be finding what is you true nature."

"You think so?" Diana asked.

"Why not?" The old man grunted as he stood. "Now I continue what is my nature. Visit friend at bar, talk gossip ..." He winked at Diana before turning to walk a path that carried him away from the tower. "Enjoy Italia, bella. Is good for the soul."

Diana slipped her cell phone out of her pocket, thought better of her instincts and put it back; then re-thought her thinking, took out the phone and snapped a photo of the man's retreating form as he quickly shuffled away. She'd label this photo: *Italia is good for the soul.*

*If* she felt inclined to post such a thing.

"Good for the soul," she muttered, pressing her purse against her side as she glanced around at the early morning tourists meandering the grounds, and those attempting the typical tourist photo of either making it look like they were pushing the tower over, or holding it up.

Her phone rang, it was Anthony. She did quick math as she answered and made the comment, "It's so late," in greeting.

"Hi," he yawned, "yes, it's almost two in the morning."

"What's going on?"

"I have a presentation tomorrow, I wasn't happy with it so I started over."

"Oh, Anthony."

"It's fine. But I figured since it's this late, I could catch you in time for ... lunch?"

"Breakfast." She smiled.

"I'll get the time difference figured out. So, how are you? Are you still upset? Are you going to stay?"

She'd called Anthony the night before and complained with her mouth full of chips and chocolate. He'd tried to soothe her as best he could while his office phone rang incessantly and several people interrupted him. Finally, Diana thanked him for letting her vent then went to bed.

"I'm ... I don't know what I want to do," she said.

"Have you left the hotel?"

"Hostel," she corrected. "Yes. I'm actually standing in front of the Leaning Tower of Pisa right now."

"How wonderful!"

She supposed it was. She took the place of the old man on the bench with a sigh, admitting, "It is gorgeous."

"Did you walk? How close is it to the hotel?"

"Hostel," she corrected again, but this time she grinned. "I ... took the bus."

"You took the bus?" He sounded excited for her and she blushed at how ridiculous and exciting it was all at the same time.

She woke that morning with the intention of taking one form of transportation, a taxi, and heading for one place only: the airport. She'd decided she would buy a ticket and wait for her flight, no matter how long. Only after she'd showered and finished packing, there was a knock on her door.

"Well," Diana started, "the proprietor, Sofia, knocked on my door this morning and told me I was going to coffee with her."

"Told you?"

She rolled her eyes. "These people. She said she saw in my eyes I was going to run away and that if I was going to do that, I needed to have a real Italian pastry and see the famous tower before I ran."

"I've been thinking," Anthony said, "I know Harper put you in a bit of a situation."

"A *bit* of a situation."

"Well, it wasn't right. But, maybe you should just ... go for it."

"Anthony."

"Diana, I know you're scared of the situation. But I also know this is a trip of a lifetime. And you can still think of it as scouting for our honeymoon."

"I'm not scared," she defended.

Sofia had called her scared as well. At a café a block from the hostel, surrounded by bright white walls, white faux marble tables and modern white chairs. With the sound of clinking plates and silverware filling the gaps of chatting patrons at the bar where they threw back their espresso and headed off with a backward wave of 'ciao.' She and Sofia sat at one of the six tables, two pastries and two espressos in front of them (the best pastry Diana had tasted in her life). The whole time, Sofia nodded knowingly, like some hippie witch from whom no one had asked an opinion, and said these were the moments that defined a person; the moments a person decided exactly how they would face down their fears.

"I'm not scared," she repeated in a mutter.

"You're a very strong woman," Anthony agreed.

"I told Harper I'd give it four days. The room here is paid for two nights." Diana had slept off the shock of being left alone in Italy. The surprisingly restful night also helped with the initial anger and jet lag. But she didn't know what to do. She was frozen in indecision. But ever since coffee had turned from facing one's fears to a more causal history of Pisa being passed along to Diana; a very small, quiet voice had begun asking: *what if you just stayed?*

"That's very pragmatic of you." Anthony interrupted her thoughts.

"Pragmatic," she repeated; that was as bad as being called scared.

He yawned loudly and apologized, so Diana decided to put an end to the conversation. "Go to bed. It sounds like you have a long day ahead of you. I'll make a decision after breakfast tomorrow and let you know."

"So what else will you do today?"

She eyed the structures in front of her. "I think I'm going to tour a church and baptistery and ... there were these stalls set up all over the street where the bus dropped me off. I suppose I'll wander through those."

"Wonderful. That sounds like a good idea." Another yawn.

"Anthony. Get some sleep. I'll talk to you tomorrow."

"Yes, okay. We'll talk tomorrow."

She pulled out the used map Sofia had marked up and given her. After circling the hostel and the leaning tower, she then highlighted the roads Diana could take to get between the two destinations. Then, under the guise of needing to take the bus to the grocery store, she made Diana follow her to a shop beside the café. "You see that big 'T'? This is the shop you buy bus tickets. And le sigarette."

Sofia turned as she entered, to make sure Diana was behind her, then requested in English, "Three bus tickets." The small papers were produced and money was exchanged. With the simple transaction finished, the two women walked across the street to the bus stop. "Here is the numbers of the bus that stop. We will take four. It goes by la torre and l'albergo. The tower and hotel."

Diana didn't have time to argue as the bus pulled up and Sofia continued the education. "People exit in the back, get on in front." She led Diana to the center of the bus and handed over one of the tickets. She didn't explain, just put her own ticket in the machine. Diana listened to the mechanic scratching sound that signified the time stamp, then followed the example.

"It is good for seventy minutes. Any bus. Only need to stamp it one time." She handed over the extra ticket she bought. "You will need this to get home, or maybe you walk."

"I ... can I pay you?"

"No, just enjoy my city. Tonight we go to dinner together."

At this point, she'd seen the tower, had a bus ticket, the map, and a whole day to waste. Maybe she would do a little more sightseeing and window shopping. What would it hurt?

# Chapter Ten

Diana meandered through the opulent, wide open space of the cathedral and the surrounding outdoor market. The vendors had colorful purses, belts, scarves, t-shirts, pottery and other trinkets for sale.

There was a shop window where lace tablecloths and doilies created a delicate canopy, beneath which sat an abundant tea party with pastel cups and plates and napkins and sparkling silverware.

Her feet carried her in the store before she understood what was really happening. She reached out and let the tickling wisps of homemade lace trace her fingertips.

"Buongiorno," a woman called as she crossed the small space. It was clean with floor-to-ceiling shelving of different sizes. The dark wood held stacks and stacks of folded tablecloths and lacy things, and every other eye level shelf had artful displays of gathered fabrics.

In the middle of the store, two long, thin tables were strewn with table runners and lace doilies. Diana stopped and gazed up at a circular, off-white tablecloth edged with lace roses. The border was echoed in the center of the tablecloth.

As she reached out and touched it, the saleswoman came and stood next to Diana. "Is very beautiful."

"Yes, it is." *But I don't have a round table.*

The woman produced a step stool and made quick work of taking it down. Diana tried to protest, but when the woman laid it out on a table off to the side – cleared for such things as demonstrating how simple fabric lay – Diana was enchanted.

"I could buy a table to match," she muttered. "That's not ridiculous, is it?"

"It's beautiful and strong," she nodded to Diana, "like you."

Diana blinked at the comment and gave a slight shake of her head as she said through her teeth, "This place." She cleared her throat. "I'd like to buy it. At least it will have an interesting story."

"Certo." The woman nodded and folded the cloth expertly before wrapping it in tissue paper, then brown paper, and placing a sticker with the logo of the shop on the folded closure.

Feeling high on the interaction in the store and her purchase, Diana decided to indulge in another coffee. She successfully ordered herself an espresso, but instead of a pastry, she couldn't resist the fresh focaccia bread that glistened in the case with oil and salt. She thought the snack would perk her up a bit, but after leaving the café, she gave a surprised yawn; maybe she wasn't quite over her jet lag just yet.

The youthful crowd was still gathered on the front stoop of the hostel, smoking and singing. This time, she didn't feel as awkward as they parted, creating a path for her in greeting.

She thought she might sneak in, but somehow Sofia rounded the corner like an oracle and called a greeting.

"So you found your way back, and you've had an adventure?"

Diana nodded. "I'm just feeling a bit tired. I was going to have a nap." *Have a nap?* She'd never put it that way in her life.

"Perfect, then you will be rested for dinner. The trattoria is close. We leave at eight."

"At night?" Diana asked incredulously.

Sofia laughed as she crossed the space between them. "You are funny. Here," she handed over a copy of a travel book of Italy, "people leave these books all the time. You should take this one."

"Oh, I couldn't ..."

"You'll need it." Sofia turned and walked away, calling back, "Have a good nap."

In her room Diana ripped open the bread and put a slice of meat and cheese inside, took a bite and opened the book. A note was scrawled on a piece of paper sticking out saying: *Your adventure begins.*

"We'll see," she told the note as she began to flip through the pages, stopping on the Florence chapter that began with a message from the author touting the glories of the Tuscan countryside; the historical significance of the Renaissance and the stamp it left on Italy.

Diana was supposed to leave for Florence tomorrow, according to the itinerary. Though, she still hadn't made up her mind.

Just for fun she read a bit more:

*Florence, the home of the Renaissance and birthplace of our modern world, has the best Renaissance art in Europe. In a single day, you can look Michelangelo's* David *in the eyes, fall under the seductive sway of Botticelli's* Birth of Venus, *and climb the modern world's first dome, which still dominates the skyline. Of course, Florentine art goes beyond paintings and statues — enjoy the food, fashion, and street markets. Sure, Florence is touristy. But where else can you stroll the same pedestrian streets walked by Michelangelo, Leonardo, and Botticelli while savoring the world's best gelato?*

"Well ..." She tossed the book aside.

# Chapter Eleven

Sofia wore a long, straight purple skirt and a blousy white cotton shirt; a new layer of jewelry jingled happily around her neck and on her wrists. They walked around the corner to the trattoria where Sofia was greeted by the maître d' with a happy hug and traditional cheek kisses.

Diana watched the scene unfold, the unabashed friendship stirring up a brush of unexpected jealousy. But she wasn't given long to contemplate the emotion as she was introduced, then received the same cheek kisses. The warm breath of the maître d' and his well applied cologne filled her nose.

He led them through the restaurant to the back room, where walls made of a light red brick held dimly lit sconces. There were several black and white photos hanging of the leaning tower and Italian countryside. The tables were set with white cloths, mustard yellow paper placemats and copper napkins under the silverware.

Before Diana had a chance to sit down, the trio was joined by the waiter who repeated the host's greeting.

After a laughing, quick exchange in Italian, everyone gestured for Diana to sit down, then left her and Sofia.

Diana glanced around the busy restaurant, at the food adorned tables, and took an appreciative inhale; fresh baked bread, sauce and herbs filled her nose. More authentic than Luciano's, which normally possessed a frozen and canned smell. This was a fresher scent. "Everything looks so good."

"I ordered for us." Sofia waved a hand just as the waiter returned with two glasses and a bottle of wine. He made a grand gesture of uncorking the bottle of red, pouring a taste in Diana's glass and waiting for her to take a sip. The bold red warmed its way to her stomach and widened her eyes with appreciation. She nodded her approval.

Two glasses poured, Sofia raised her glass toward Diana before she took a drink. "So, you are thinking of staying," she started, sitting back and cradling her glass.

"Maybe."

Sofia shook her head at the reply as if it wasn't good enough. "You'll stay."

A grunt of a laugh accompanied Diana's question. "What makes you think so?"

"You are so … ragionevole. Sensible. It makes sense to stay. You don't want to waste the money."

It was a dagger; for some reason, this free spirit who was the face of the Albergo dei Sogni, stung Diana by calling her sensible (even if she *was* most of the time).

"I'm not that sensible," she argued. "I just got engaged, I'm moving to Houston and in two days I rearranged my life to come here."

"I didn't mean any harm."

Diana glanced around the restaurant, then sitting up straight in her chair, asked Sofia, "How old are you?"

"Thirty-seven, the same as you, no?"

Diana snorted. "No." Sofia raised an eyebrow in question and after another sip Diana muttered, "Not that it matters, but I'm forty-five."

"It doesn't matter."

"Look, I'm just trying to say, when you get to a certain age, you *have* to be sensible."

Sofia shrugged in reply.

Diana continued, "I'm grateful for your time, truly. Thanks for the book, and taking me to breakfast and showing me how to use the bus. And for bringing me to dinner; but I'm not some … lost charity case …" In truth, Diana wasn't sure what Sofia thought she was.

"I know."

"So you are this nice to everyone at the hostel?"

"Only the wayward travelers."

"Wayward …" Diana sputtered, "I don't think that means what you think it means."

"Strong wanderer," Sofia gestured to Diana along with a stained toothy grin, "who perhaps, she forgets herself."

The waiter interrupted with a plate of sliced meat, several crostini rounds of bread and a softball size cheese that looked like mozzarella.

"You will like this. Il formaggio is burrata, and prosciutto, of course, is the meat." She used a knife to scoop some cheese onto the bread and topped it with a slice of meat before handing it over.

Diana held the bread aloft, a deepening frown on her face. She glanced at the food in her hand and back at Sofia as she made a crostini for herself.

In a soft whisper, Diana said, "I'm not some lost, hopeless, *sensible* woman. I'm reasonable," she licked her lips, "and loyal and smart. And sure, I might be down to earth, but there's nothing wrong with that."

"Ah," Sofia pointed at Diana with the new crostini she'd made herself, "I never said anything was wrong with you."

"What am I doing here?" That question was more rhetorical than anything else, and she wasn't certain who she was asking: herself, Harper, Sofia, Anthony ... "I don't need a babysitter."

"Who said baby?" Sofia tilted her head. "I think you need to talk. You needing a friend."

Diana took a bite in reply, and even that made her slightly angry. The taste was delightful. She didn't know there was cheese that could melt in your mouth.

"É buono, no?" Sofia asked, fixing another bread for each of them.

"Buono ..." Diana tried on the word.

"It means good, when you speak of food."

"Your English is very good," Diana offered.

"I studied three years in America. In California."

"That's wonderful. That would have been fun to do when I was younger. To learn a new language."

"There's still time."

"Hmmm ..." Diana grunted softly in reply.

Diana sipped her wine and ate her share of the cheese as she tried to come up with a defense or a way to talk to Sofia. The woman was pushy, in an annoyingly awkward way. Like a corn on the cob kernel that sticks in the teeth and won't go away.

"What's the cheese name again?" Diana figured talking about food was as safe as talking about the weather with strangers.

"Burrata."

"Like butter?"

"Ma, burro is Italian word for butter. So this cheese, meaning burrata, like butter. Creamy."

"Burrata," Diana repeated and smeared another healthy bit onto the bread.

"Risotto con asparagi," the waiter announced as he set a shallow bowl in front of Diana. Steam rose from the perfectly portioned rice and stalks of asparagus, and a large swirl of cheese, most likely parmesan.

Diana took a bite and this time, let the appreciation show on her face. Sofia winked in reply.

They ate in silence and drank their wine as the music and hum of conversation and warmth of the restaurant smoothed out the evening.

"Okay, I can admit that I might be in shock still," Diana said after several bites. "I *am* sensible and my life the past few years has been very—"

"Calculated," Sofia interrupted.

"Organized," Diana offered instead. "My birthday was last week, Tuesday. I got engaged last Thursday, then Friday I agreed to move to Houston for a year, ordered my wedding cake and was surprised with an all-expense paid trip to Italy. My sister was supposed to be meeting me here, but when I arrived she called to tell me that the all-expense paid trip was only for one. So, if I seem uptight, it's because I haven't had enough time to properly process everything that's happened."

"Perhaps I can understand." Sofia emptied her wine glass, poured herself another, then topped off Diana's. "So you understand why I too say you are sensible? Your hair is in a clean, tight bun. Your clothes show no womanly curve, just straight ..." She gestured across the table at all of Diana.

"What does it matter how I choose to dress?" She took a drink of her wine for fortification and started again, "I don't care to have my clothing and hair choices picked apart by someone who doesn't know me. I like how I look. And my *fiancé* likes how I look."

"You misunderstand, you are *gorgeous*."

Diana frowned and shook her head several times. "I feel like I'm losing my mind. How much is my part of this bill? I think I'm gonna go."

"Ah," Sofia straightened, gave a snap of her fingers and gestured to Diana, "yes. There you are."

Diana pursed her lips angrily as she pulled her purse off the back of her chair to search for her wallet.

Sofia continued, "You are doing what you want, but it's only because I'm pushing you."

Diana stilled. "Pushing me? You're making all these crazy comments on purpose?"

Sofia shrugged and fell back in a slouch against her chair as she raised her glass. "I told you. I help people."

Diana let her purse fall back and leaned across the table. "How is this helping?"

"Why don't you stay all'aeroporto when you hear your sister is not here? Why did you come on this vacanza at all?"

"Because …"

"You just say, you only have two days to prepare for a trip to Italia. Many people need more time to prepare."

"I am organized …"

"I think there is so much changing to your life, perhaps now you, Diana, opens up herself to changing more."

"Oh, is that what this is?" Diana mocked.

"Yes. And you are thinking the same." Sofia narrowed her gaze. "You want the change and the adventure."

"I wanted a free trip to Italy."

"You will stay," she nodded, "you will continue to finding yourself."

"I know who I am," Diana refuted.

"You *think* you know."

"Oh my God, you're like a confusing oracle that no one likes. Or are you a witch?"

Sofia laughed and clapped her hands at the idea. "Una strega? No, I am just … a woman who watches and sees the truth."

"I suppose that's very handy for running a hostel." Diana meant the comment to be biting, but instead she found herself laughing.

Sofia's smile widened. "Yes, is very helpful."

"Well, if you're so observant, you'll be happy to hear that I *have* decided to stay and continue the vacation. But not because you said I was going to."

"I know."

"You did not."

Sofia picked up her glass and touched it to Diana's. "Sì, certo. Of course I know. You want to let that hair down."

Diana touched a hand to her bun. "What's wrong with my hair?"

"Is a reflection, bella. Of how you viewing yourself. You are hiding, tight in a ball so no one can ever see you true desires. Or see you. You make sure, no notice to you. Bella, even you clothes, you dress to disappear."

Diana rolled her eyes, because her other option was to start crying. She opened her mouth with the intention of biting back that it *was* her nature to be wound tight, to keep her dreams and herself hidden. But the shock of the sentiment froze in the back of her throat.

Instead, she hurriedly focused on the fact that this was a ridiculous dinner, with a ridiculous woman, with the best bottle of red wine and the most wonderful food she'd had in a long time. She took a drink and cleared her throat.

"I'm an interesting person." She hated the muttered, childish defense.

"Ah, yes, there is the spark in your eye and the light around your head."

"Are you going to read my aura?"

"I could."

"If I were to turn the tables on you, I would say you were a witch, oracle and hippie." Diana frowned. "Do they have Italian hippies?"

"I am more similar to the bohémien."

"A vibrant bohemian," Diana muttered before sighing. "Are all those prints in the hostel yours?"

Sofia nodded, puffing out her chest a bit. "All mine."

"Well, they are very vibrant."

"Lo so. I know."

"Oh, what does the name of the hostel mean?" Diana asked.

"Albergo dei Sogni. The hotel of dreams."

Diana snorted, "Of course."

After the waiter cleared their plates, Diana sat back and admitted to Sophia, "The food was all wonderful."

"Good."

Just then the waiter returned with two more shallow dishes, giving a nod after placing them in front of the women.

"What is this?"

"Costolette d'agnello."

"I thought ... what is this?"

"Lamb, grilled with herbs and patate. It is i secondi, the second course."

Diana looked at the gorgeous plate; three small lamb chops seared to perfection, the scent of herbs rising to assault her nose.

"How many more courses will there be?"

"He will bring out vegetable and then we talk. You tell me your life, I tell you mine and we drink wine and finalmente, a dessert."

As full as Diana was, the smell of the meat was enticing. She took a bite and nodded. She'd figure out how to finish the meal. As for airing out her life story to Sofia, she wasn't so sure she was going to be as open to that.

# Chapter Twelve

Diana's cell phone screamed to life with a call. She fumbled it off the bedside table and squinted at the screen. It was Harper and it was six in the morning.

She answered the phone to shut it up and grumbled, "It's six a.m."

"I know. I thought you'd be up because of jet lag."

"I'm asleep because of jet lag. And a bottle of wine."

"You drank a bottle of wine?"

"No, I shared a bottle," she mumbled, rolling onto her back and blinking her eyes wide a few times, the dim morning light creeping into the room between the shutters she'd left open.

"*Shared* a bottle?" Harper happily drew out the word.

"With Sofia, the landlady of this place, who you told to babysit me."

When Harper didn't defend the accusation, Diana clicked her tongue. "I knew it."

"I'm trying to help you. If I can't be there, I'm trying to make sure you feel comfortable enough to keep going."

Diana sat up and scrubbed her face with her free hand. "I'm not some elderly invalid who needs to be minded at all times of the day."

"I never said you were."

"Well, I'm tired of people thinking they know me."

"I do know you," Harper said matter-of-factly.

"You *did* know me." The angry retort rushed out before Diana had a chance to check herself. "I'm sorry. Harper ... I didn't mean it."

"You're right though," Harper sighed, "I did know you. And what *I* know is that the woman I knew would not enjoy who you've become."

"Don't start with me. I'm in a foreign country because of you and continuing on this trip because of you, so don't throw what you think you know around when you don't have all the facts."

"Luna—"

"Harper."

There was a long silence, and for a moment Diana thought maybe she'd truly hurt her sister's feelings, until a deep gulp of breath signified that she hadn't hurt Harper; she'd lit her up. Before she had a moment to call out a defense, Harper began, "You were a writer once. You were unstoppable. Not because of David, but because you were just ... *unstoppable.* You used to love talking about words and how to create a beautiful sentence. It was like poetry just listening to you talk about writing. And you were vivacious, Luna. Always laughing and smiling. Then you got dealt a bad blow, but never got up again. You hid that girl away under some boring, uptight woman. You are in Italy. Birthplace of the Renaissance. Where the words of Dante were so renowned, the whole Italian country decided *his* dialect would be the *official* dialect."

"You don't think I know that, or that I haven't thought about that?"

"Luna, I don't know what you think anymore. I don't know if you have any more creative ideas left. I don't know what you did with my sister, but I know she wants out and I want her back out in the world."

"Harper." Diana whispered the name, her only defense as tears gathered.

"The world needs that vivacious Luna back."

"I'm not the same. Life changes us and you can never go back. You know that Harper."

"I know I do," she soothed, "but you can go forward. And from where I'm sitting, forward, into the future, holds so much potential for you."

Diana was openly crying now. "I don't know how."

"Why do you think I sent you on an odyssey?" The bright smile was evident in Harper's voice. "To figure it all out."

"In ten days?" Diana let lose an unladylike snort.

"Not in ten days," she corrected. "Ten days is just a starting point. No work. No Lena. No Anthony. No obligations. Just time."

"I'm still, so mad at you."

"Tell me what Pisa is like."

"No," Diana muttered, then after a long silence between them, said,

"Pisa is more than just a leaning tower. She is a meandering bohemian, edged with roses, walking into the modern age through gates of the high medieval walls that surround her." She gave a dry laugh and was going to comment on how clunky and lame the sentiment was when she heard a true sob sound from Harper. "I'm sorry."

"Luna, just be open to experiences, okay?" Her voice caught and a loud blow of her nose caused Diana to pull the phone away from her ear. "Luna?" she asked when there was no answer.

"I'll try."

"That's all I want."

Wide awake now, Diana reached for the guidebook to find out what time the cafés opened. The book noted several local coffee shops that opened at 6 a.m., and also gave the sage advice that when one found themselves in Pisa, they should take a walk.

"Okay then, let's take a walk."

She dressed quickly in a pair of gray slacks, a patterned button-down blouse, and navy sweater, then twisted her hair back into its bun. Slipping on her walking shoes, she rolled her eyes and muttered, "Sensible walking shoes."

Purse, book and map in hand, she double-checked her reflection in the small mirror that hung by the door of her room. Her face was clean, her eyes looked tired, but not a hair was out of place. She gently touched the bun, her fingers lingering before she shook her head and straightened.

Before she rounded the last few stairs that would lead to the foyer, she paused and peeked. No Sofia. Diana felt some small relief; she didn't need company this morning. She hurried out the door, where the early dawn streets of Pisa were washed in soft gray.

Diana lingered for a breath, only a blink really, on the front stoop of the hotel of dreams, then took another proverbial step on her adventure of a thousand miles. Of course she wasn't sure exactly how many miles there were between Pisa and Rome, but on the map, it didn't look like a thousand.

Still ...

With the map in hand, she turned in the direction of the river. The street was wet from overnight washing. The walls were faded, some spray-painted with graffiti, others with stucco peeling, and most had a build-up of dust and soot from car exhaust. But if she looked just a bit higher, the Italian hues of the buildings seemed to preen a bit, to open up like a peacock's feathers toward their flourishing flower boxes, up to their terracotta topped roofs.

She turned right, and this street was an intricate design of old cobblestones. An older man and woman were busy setting up a fruit and vegetable stand. Diana slowed, under the spell of all the vibrant colors. Was produce this appealing in the states? The man put bunches of celery in a stack, but the woman picked them up and waved them around in the air as she explained where they were supposed to go. Even Diana, who didn't understand the language, knew the man was being scolded for doing it wrong. The scene was brought to a halt by the passing of a priest who called out a greeting to the couple.

Another turn encased her in the smell of fresh bread being baked. She slowed and breathed in deeply. Warm scents of yeast and salt and cinnamon mingled. She glanced around and found the source of the smell. Across the street a door was propped open, and in the doorway a box fan pulled the cool air in and allowed the smells out. She crossed for a closer view. A man with a baking cap was pulling out poster board size sheets of focaccia from the oven. She watched as he turned the sheet he'd just removed on its side then placed it on a slender cart with bars that keep the bread upright.

The steaming sheet joined at least ten more of its kind, all shining glorious and golden.

The man saw her and nodded in greeting. Diana gave a quick nod and backed away, sorry to interrupt his work, embarrassed to be caught gawking.

Another block away, she realized she forgot to look at the name of the bread shop. She would've liked to stop on her return and buy some of that focaccia. Reaching the corner she looked around for the street signs and when she found them, gave a little laugh. The names were long, intricate, almost unpronounceable. Locating them on her map she pulled out a pen, circled the corner then patted the nearest wall. "If it's meant to be, I'll be back."

Another turn and the Arno River was before her. She crossed the street and smiled as she rested her hip against the low wall that separated the sidewalk and the river, flowing several feet below where she stood. The waters were dark and meandering; the glow of the coming sun hadn't touched them yet. However, it had begun to illuminate the buildings that lined either side, giving a soft morning polish to the old structures. It looked like their muted colors were born again in the spring sunlight.

She took out her phone and snapped a few pictures before continuing. She walked the river path until she spied, down one of the streets, a small piazza with a group of open umbrellas; a physical advertisement that the café was open for business.

Yellow light from the café filled the gray streets where the sun still hid behind the buildings. The door was open and the clinking of dishes and conversation of several early morning patrons drifted out. She stood for several heartbeats at the door, the insecurity of the moment capturing her.

"C'mon." She whispered for her feet to move.

"Scusi?" A voice behind her made her jump. She turned and found an older couple, short, and bent at the shoulders with the weight of their years.

"Oh, I'm sorry." She moved aside.

They nodded, but waved for her to go in first. She had no choice now, so she stepped inside then gestured for the couple to order before her. Even in her uncertainty, the delectable smells of coffee and pastry solidified that this was a very good decision. She waited patiently behind the couple, using them as a study guide on how to order.

Once she had an espresso and beautifully plated pastry, she sat down at a table in a corner offering the perfect vantage point to watch the morning ritual of the Italians at their café.

She picked up her cup, but before taking a sip, thought better of it and put it down to snap another picture. She would post these and maybe use some of the lines from the guidebook about how there was more to

Pisa than the tower. After all, it was here that Galileo studied the solar system, and Andrea Bocelli attended law school before embarking on his musical career. Or she'd quote the old man in the park, and explain that the tower leans because it's in her nature to do so.

Or maybe she'd just supply her own observations, that Pisa was a great jet lag city; the perfect place to rest after a long flight, find some good food, see a remarkable sight and begin a journey.

She picked up the pear filled tart she'd ordered and took a bite, smiling out at the streets of Pisa.

# Chapter Thirteen

"Signora." The taxi driver called Diana's attention. She was staring out the window at the Pisa train station. Had been for the past few minutes.

"Oh, Signora ..." The man had a begging lilt to his voice.

She shook herself, pulled the money that was requested and climbed out as the driver did. They met by the trunk where he handed over her suitcase with a mumbled, "Arrivederci."

Diana nodded as she pressed her purse to her side and stepped up onto the sidewalk.

She decided to stay.

*She wasn't scared.*

"It's not fear," she whispered.

It was being out of her norm. There was a rhythm to her life. A schedule she could count on. Sure, a hundred years ago she hated the monotony of consistency; so maybe, if she was going to open her life to a new schedule, she needed to pull that part of herself out again.

To prolong the internal battle, she pulled out her itinerary; the deep folds exhibited the number of times she'd studied it so far.

And she'd already watched the video Harper sent her that morning on how to pick up her ticket from the self-service machine. And Sofia had added her two cents worth of instructions when Diana declined the offer to have the woman accompany her to the station.

She read through the itinerary. She'd take the 2:40 p.m. train from Pisa which would put her in Florence at 3:42 p.m. It was a ten-minute walk to the next hostel from the station.

She would text Harper from the train and ask if she had another single room. If not, Diana was going to tap into her savings and find a new hotel.

Of course, if she didn't like it, the Florence airport was just a fifteen-minute ride from the hostel. (Not that she'd already looked up that bit of information.)

The never-ending possibilities of escape soothed her, so she slipped the paper back in her purse, straightened her shoulders and headed into the train station.

Voices echoed and mixed with the squealing of train breaks. Diana shuffled around trying to read the various signs and make sense of the numbered train tracks and her departure time, none of which seemed to be matching up.

"Allo," someone called fairly close; so Diana moved out of the way of the conversation. But the greeting came again, "Allo." This time Diana gave a discreet glance in its direction.

A young woman, early twenties perhaps, was indeed waving happily at Diana. "Allo," she called again from the arm of her boyfriend.

"Oh, hi?" Diana replied.

"You stay Albergo dei Sogni." The young girl gave the name of the hostel in a thick Scandinavian accent. Diana wasn't certain it was Scandinavian, but the young girl's long blonde hair, blue eyes and height had Diana leaning toward the stereotype.

"Yes. I ... yes."

"You need assistance?" the girl asked. The boy she was with pulled out a camera and turned his attention to the line-up of trains and began taking photos.

"No ... I just, I'm supposed to ... I need to find a self-service machine. And then find the train platform." So yes, in a sense she did need help.

"Oh ja, is difficult at first, no?" The girl nodded in the direction of a ticketing machine against a gray wall. Diana followed, dodging other passengers swarming through the station.

The girl had begun talking the moment she reached the machine; Diana caught up to her a few words in, "... the place you will go."

"Oh, Florence."

"Ah, Firenze. But, you have a code?" The girl pointed at the machine and the spot where the code was required.

Diana held out her phone with the code Harper had sent.

"Ah, this is good. You take the train that goes direct. No stops will be required."

She pointed to the options and talked quickly, punching in the numbers when it was time. Then a printed ticket was spit out of the machine. The girl collected it and studied the numbers, then handed it over with a nod and glanced up at the station. Finally, she pointed. "Just there, Track five. It departs in twenty minutes."

Diana looked at the ticket. "The seat?" she asked.

The girl peeked over her shoulder. "This here. Is seat number."

"Thank you." Diana stood frozen, still looking at the trains.

"You understand?" the girl asked as her boyfriend came back to join her.

Diana nodded. "Yes. Yes," she cleared her throat and smiled, "thank you for the help."

"Of course."

"Where are you going?" Diana asked.

The young girl's eyes sparkled as she said, "We go to Venice now."

At the mention of Venice, the young man slipped his arm around the girl's waist and leaned toward her. When he was a breath away from her neck, she tilted her head ever so slightly so he could brush a soft kiss there.

Diana took a step back, so jarred by the simple, quick, public display. It was nothing really, just a kiss. But the young man's eyes, alight with love for the woman next to him ... alight with life, and the raw power and need that was exuded in such a simple action, unseeingly pushed Diana back.

The flash of romance blinded her; pulling up a memory of her own youth, of the life she'd once lived.

What would it be like to be with a man who kissed her on the neck at the mention of Venice?

Anthony was lovely, but he was as sensible as she was. "Well," Diana cleared her throat, upending old memories and current personalities before they could shake her up any more, "thank you for the help. And have a good trip." She smiled.

The young girl, still smiling, wound her arm around her boyfriend's waist. "You too. Firenze is glorious. You will love it," the young woman promised.

Diana gave a nod of her head and convinced her feet to carry her to track five.

The train pulled itself slowly, exhaustedly out of the station. It took several minutes for it to finally shake off its lethargy and pick up speed.

The landscape passed in a mirage of images. The famous Tuscan countryside was abundant beyond the window. Rolling hills, tall stately cypress trees hugging dirt roads, terracotta rooftops peeking from among a sea of green and brown fields. The train rocked rhythmically once it reached its top speed, lulling Diana into a dreamy state.

She stared out the window, not seeing the scenery but rather the kiss the young man pressed to the girl's neck. The whole scene continued to repeat in a foggy etched haze just where Diana's eyes obscured the horizon with the memory.

She'd had that once. That lightness of being young and in love. Young and in lust, she corrected and allowed the smile that tugged at the side of her mouth to widen. She'd been so passionate when she was younger … no, that wasn't right.

They.

*They*. The two of them, Diana and David.

They had been young and passionate and ready to take on the world.

Had he kissed her like that? In the middle of a conversation, had he slipped his arm around her waist and lowered his head to the side of her neck?

Diana tilted her head to the side, just slightly, reached up and traced the part of her neck that the young man kissed on the girl.

She must have been kissed there, but how many hundreds of times and how had she forgotten?

"Signora?" a voice interrupted.

Diana dropped her hand and glanced up at the woman standing next to her seat. She wore the uniform of the ticket agent.

"Ticket?" she said in a thick accent.

"Oh, yes." Diana pulled the ticket out of the front pocket of her purse and handed it over. The woman studied it and with a nod, punched the ticket, handed it back and moved on.

Diana glanced out the window and whispered, "Anthony's a good man." What he lacked in passion he more than made up for in stability.

"It's Harper," she added. It was Harper's judgmental tendencies, and how disjointed this trip was making her feel. "I know what I'm about," she whispered to her reflection. Passion was for the young.

She pulled out her phone to distract herself and took a picture of the passing scenery. *Headed to Florence* she wrote as she posted it. Then she turned her gaze once again and tried to settle into the seat and forget that kiss that replayed again, taunting her with memories of another life.

# Chapter Fourteen

Arriving in the late afternoon, Diana found Florence alive with movement and sound. She followed the exit signs, pulled out the map in the guidebook and easily found the hostel. The ten-minute walk from the train station became a time warp, going quickly while the number of stunning scenes of the ancient Renaissance city overwhelmed her senses.

She walked down crowded streets of four- and five-story buildings, where small cars littered the curbs and scooter parking zones were tightly and impressively packed.

She was passed on the sidewalk by tourists and locals. The tourists had an exhausted look of excitement, and comfortable clothing with fanny packs or backpacks worn against their chest. The locals looked exhausted but lacked the excited look, and they were dressed stylishly with shoes that made Diana wonder about their comfort.

She passed pastry shops, chocolate shops, boutiques, a cell phone store, jewelry shops, tobacco shops and more small cafés; all of which were tucked into small spaces, almost on top of each other. It seemed each doorway she passed, every fifteen steps, was a new business.

Birds chirped loudly to be heard above construction taking place inside one of the buildings she passed. The conversation from cafés with umbrella-covered tables set up precariously close to the street, and locals calling loudly to each other, mingled with the hum of cars as they passed.

When the large orange buses came wobbling down the road, she stared wide-eyed at their ability to make themselves thinner and miss the parked cars on either side of the narrow, aged street. She herself sucked in and stepped closer to the building as they passed, as if that would help.

It was contagious, the busy movements about the city. Diana decided to check in and go for a walk. According to the guidebook, she was rather close to the oldest cathedral in Florence, San Lorenzo, which was also home to several pieces of art by Donatello.

*Donatello.* She shook her head at the thought. This was the city of all the greats. Diana whispered their names under her breath, "Michelangelo, Botticelli, Leonardo da Vinci, Titian, Raphael ..." Goosebumps formed on her arms.

All the greats started here.

The hostel was more of a two-star hotel than an experiment in a college dorm, and Diana thankfully found she not only had a room to herself, but her own restroom.

Once she had her luggage put away, she headed back out on the streets.

The woman at the front desk stopped her, gave her a map, circled restaurant suggestions and a grocery store as well.

"Grazie," Diana murmured, grateful the woman wasn't as interested in her as Sofia had been.

She wandered the streets slowly and easily found the Basilica of San Lorenzo with its imposing, yet unfinished façade, a slab of brown stone. Paying the entrance fee, she walked into the cool, dark, open space and had a difficult time marrying the drab exterior with the inner lavishness; such an abundance of color and elaborate decoration that stretched so far.

The quiet shuffle and hushed tones of visitors, staged throughout the large area, added to the sacredness the church was intended for.

She meandered from the back of the church, then along the side, and when she was close enough to the front to turn to the left, her whole body reacted as a flash of memory petrified her.

It was just a piece of art by a priest from the Renaissance.

She knew the name, Fillipo Lippi. She knew the piece. David had explained it to her several times, always excitedly claiming, "This piece, *The Annunciation*, is a masterpiece of the Renaissance."

There was more he would go on about, particularly geometric perspectives, but what Diana had always been taken with was the blue of Mary's dress and the red of the messenger's cloaks.

Diana stepped back and tripped, finding it difficult to breathe. She felt dizzy and flailed to catch herself.

"Are you alright?" A man nearby caught her mid fall and she frantically grabbed for his arm as he tried to steady her. "You're very pale," he offered and helped her to a nearby bench. Once she was seated he knelt in front of her and took both of her hands in his.

It took several long moments before Diana realized he was gazing intently into her eyes and she had been looking through him. She looked over her shoulder at the art piece and then back at the man, coming back into her body.

"I'm sorry," she muttered confused, "it was just a shock."

He squeezed her hands. "I think some color is coming back into your cheeks now." His voice was deep with a touch of an English accent.

She glanced into his green eyes, then noticed his dark hair with a slight curl and a touch of graying. She blinked several times as she tried to collect herself and pull her hands away. "I'm feeling better, thank you."

He nodded and sat next to her. "It happens all the time."

"What does?"

"The art of Firenze, it causes people to feel faint."

She gave a scoffing laugh but he insisted, "No, I promise, it is a real affliction. There was an author who visited this city and was so overcome by the artwork he felt faint. It's named after him, the affliction ... Stendhal, I think that was it, Stendhal's syndrome."

"That sounds made up." Diana laughed.

"I promise it is one hundred percent true." His smile wrinkled the skin around his eyes.

"Or maybe I'm just dehydrated," she offered.

"Well," he glanced at his watch before saying, "we can't have that. Can I buy you a coffee, and water?"

Diana glanced back at the painting.

"I have no ulterior motives, I promise." He smiled. "There is a café right across the street. Actually, we're in Florence, there are cafés everywhere."

"Are you meeting someone?" Diana asked, nodding to the way he checked his watch.

"Yes, I am meeting some colleagues for dinner."

"Oh, then I don't want to keep you."

He stood and held out his hand. "You aren't keeping me. Dinner here starts late. I was just killing time. And now I'm concerned about you."

Diana pulled out her cell phone and before she knew what she was doing, took a quick photo of the man. He tilted his head with an interested smile at what she'd done. She tried to hide her smile as she said, "I don't really go places with strangers in foreign countries. I'll send your picture to my sister. Just in case."

He laughed and covered his mouth, glancing around at the employees who were giving him terse looks. He held out his arm to Diana. "I understand. Let's find a café and you can tell me why Fra Fillipo's art caused you to almost faint and what your sister will think of a stranger buying you a drink."

Harper: *Oh my God, you met a man! Go Diana!*

Diana: *I didn't meet a man. I almost fainted. He was being nice. (I think.) I'm sending you his picture so if I end up dead in an Italian ditch you can show this photo to the authorities and tell them you were the one who really got me killed.*

Harper: *Dramatic much?*

Diana: *Yes. Because you ditched me in Italy.*

Harper: *Get some!*

Diana: *I'm engaged.*

Harper: *Get some!!!!*

Diana rolled her eyes as she put her phone away. Greg, the British gentleman, who was fifty-two, in Florence on business, widowed but dating a very nice woman named Kay – all information he gave her on the short walk to the nearest café – was returning from the restroom.

The other thing she learned on the walk was that after five, most cafés become a bar where you stop after work to have a before dinner drink and snack. And it was the reason they forewent the coffee and settled for a glass of wine outside. It was a warm evening, and perhaps having a glass of wine was something a person *should* do outside when in Florence.

A waiter delivered two glasses of red, a plate with cantaloupe wrapped in prosciutto, four crostini with tomato, a few slices of hard cheese, a bowl of olives and another bowl with broccoli that looked to be drowning in olive oil.

"So how long are you in Florence?" Greg inquired.

"Two nights, three days, though two of the days are kind of travel days … How long are you here?"

"A week," he said as he picked up a melon and took a bite.

"Do you work in Florence often?"

"Well," he shrugged, "I work as a conservator of art in London. I was hired by a non-profit organization several years ago. We restore artwork around Florence."

"That's … impressive." She picked up her glass and before she took a sip said, "Please don't ask me what I do after an introduction like that."

"Well, I won't, but I can tell that what you *are* is a lover of the arts. Why else would you have the reaction you did?"

For courage she took a long drink before admitting, "My husband was an artist. Among his top million favorite pieces of art, the *Annunciation* was one of them. I haven't thought about it for many years and it caught me off guard."

It was the most she'd ever told a stranger of her former life or former husband.

Greg nodded and studied the food for several long seconds before he met Diana's eyes. "You said was."

"I did." She swallowed the heavy feeling growing in her throat so she could continue. "He passed away about nineteen years ago."

He nodded and sat back in his seat. "My wife passed ten years ago."

"I'm sorry," Diana offered.

"So am I." His smile crinkled around his eyes and Diana returned the gesture. He tapped the table lightly with his fingers. "So, you understand art as well then."

"I understand art as well," she agreed, thankful that he didn't ask more questions about her husband, nor offered any more information about his wife.

"The nonprofit I worked for recently returned Fra Fillipo Lippi's work. It was the last large project that I helped on," he held up his hand,

"and before you think I had more to do with it than I did, I just made sure the piece was handled properly from the church to the lab."

"I think you're being modest."

"How can you tell?"

"You wouldn't be sent to Italy just to watch a piece of art take a ride."

He tilted his head, giving into the fact that he was indeed being modest.

"Well, it sounds like an amazing job," Diana said. "And were you just checking in on the piece?"

"I was."

"Then remind me why it's one of the important masterpieces of Renaissance art," she said and popped an olive as Greg launched into the life and techniques used by the Florence friar in the early 1400s.

They parted ways when the wine and aperitivo was finished. No exchange of numbers or social media accounts. Just a thank you and a hug. When he was a few feet away, Greg called out to Diana, "Look up Stendhal's syndrome tonight."

She laughingly waved that she would.

Properly exhausted and still jet lagged, Diana decided to go to a grocery store and buy some more picnic food for the rest of her evening.

The small store she found was bloated with goods. A colorful array of fruits and vegetables in yellow crates surrounded the front door. Hard salamis hung across a chain, an Italian garland of goodness setting off a fresh meat and cheese case. There were crackers, canned goods, a selection of black and white postcards of Florence and a display of trinkets all touting 'Firenze' on them. Diana grabbed four postcards, a set of stationary paper surrounded in a blue and green filigree pattern, and a keychain – a pink Vespa that said Italy on the side. In another life, she thought, it might be fun to ride around Italy like Audrey Hepburn.

The proprietor of the shop spoke enough broken English to help her, and as she walked back to the hostel with a yellow bag of snacks, she felt light; like she was in a walking dream.

Tomorrow she would make plans to follow in the footsteps of Dante and Michelangelo; a thought that reverberated up and down her spine.

Once she had her picnic laid out, she took out a piece of stationary and opened the guidebook so she could make a list of the things she would like to explore. But before writing anything, she stopped, took out her phone and opened up her search engine. After a moment she began to laugh. "Well hell, it *is* a real thing."

# Chapter Fifteen

*What the hell is this? A spinster's guide to Italy?*

Diana tossed the phone, irritated at the message Harper had posted under a set of her Florence pictures. "Thanks, great way to wake up, Harp," she snarled at the phone. "The only reason I'm posting anything anyway is so you can see it." *Ingrate.* Didn't the little shit want to see what she was missing?

"Little shit." She retrieved the phone then pulled up the conversation between her and Harper, tapping out a message as angrily as she could: *You little shit! You could have come with me, but you're the one who stranded me here to eat alone and sightsee alone and walk through strange streets alone and you know what else? Sometimes Italy isn't all it's cracked up to be.*

Her finger hovered over the send button, but she couldn't bring herself to hit it. Instead, she deleted the message and tried: *You are selfish and rude and I only came on this trip because I didn't think I was going to have to do it alone.* She thought for a few seconds and ended up deleting that one as well.

She opened the app and scanned Harper's message under her post once more: *What the hell is this? The spinster's guide to Italy?*

Diana angrily punched three letters and posted a reply: *Yes.*

She dropped her phone and threw herself back onto the bed. "Little shit."

While Pisa had helped Diana with her confidence, a full day in Florence deflated her.

Diana woke early, excited to get started. She had the complimentary breakfast of coffee and a pastry then stepped her sensible walking shoes onto the cobblestone streets to follow the itinerary she'd made herself.

The first stop was the Academia Gallery, the art school and museum that housed, arguably, the most famous piece of art in Florence: Michelangelo's *David*.

She waited in the long line of tourists who, like her, weren't aware that reservations could be made beforehand. But she didn't mind the waiting; being surrounded by so many English speaking tourists put her at ease and she appreciated the time to listen in on the swirling conversations. The couple behind her couldn't stop talking about a place they'd been where they could view the whole city of Florence. The group of women in front of her were stuck on the fact they couldn't get ice in any of their drinks. A loud whisper from another couple complained about the smell of BO so early in the morning. And still, the wind carried the comment of a lilting voice reminding someone that when Michelangelo sculpted *David,* he took into consideration every angle from which the statue would be viewed.

Finally, the wait was over. She entered the museum slowly, allowing those in a rush to fan out and hurry past her. Curious at their speed, as if sightseeing was a competitor sport; those who saw the most in a minimal amount of time won.

Diana meandered into a long room lined with unfinished statues carved by Michelangelo. Fragments of half men were straining their taut muscles, attempting to climb out of the marble and fully realize their complete form; fighting to be free from their marble tombs with no relief in sight. The tortured men, each individually lit by floor lighting, created a runway leading to the opposite end of the long room where a high arched doorway eloquently framed Michelangelo's masterpiece: *David*.

The name was a strange shock. She had been thinking about seeing this, listing it on her paper last night, but there was something about standing before him that brought her old David to the forefront once again. Something that she would have to think about later. But not today.

She couldn't keep her eyes off the statue. As she got closer she thought he'd moved several times; that perhaps the veins that stood out on his arms did indeed have blood flowing through them.

A rotunda room had been built to showcase this giant statue of a man. Seating lined the walls, and as Diana sat she became aware that she should close her mouth that had fallen open, but somehow just couldn't yet. There were several security guards roaming an endless circle around *David*, encouraging people to follow the posted rules, which was no flash photography. Two school groups were huddled in opposing corners while their teachers attempted to shush the youthful irreverence so the hired docents could expand on the lecture they'd been paid to give.

She shook her head as she recalled what she'd read last night, that this statue was the number one offender of Stendhal's syndrome. It was something she couldn't understand, even after the shock she'd received so recently. But now, face to face with the stony hulk, she was sure that she'd already seen his hand twitch once or twice.

As she gave herself over to the syndrome of Florence, another memory flashed. David, *her* David, had told her about coming to Europe his senior year of high school with his art class. He always wanted to come back, to bring Diana. He promised they'd stay up all night and drink in cafés and sleep at the feet of statues and he'd sketch it all while she found so many new worlds to write about.

Diana's mouth dried and the room began to spin because of two Davids. Until this moment, she never realized she would be checking off destinations David once planned to show her.

Desperate to leave the museum, she ignored how shaky and dizzy she was, and used all her energy to leave. When she was finally out in the fresh air, and had a little distance between herself and the museum, her emotions seemed to regulate. "You're just hungry," she reasoned.

As she pulled out the map, her phone rang.

"Hi, Anthony," she greeted.

"Hello," he said with a yawn.

"What time is it there?"

"Five. My alarm just went off." He gave another loud yawn. "I'm going to be so busy for the next few days, I wanted to call you when I could."

"Oh, well thank you."

"How is it?"

"I just saw Michelangelo's *David*."

"Imagine that ... well no, you don't need to imagine that." He gave a soft laugh. "Was it wonderful?"

"It was." She gave the honest simple answer. The larger, more complex answer still needed a little more thought and time.

"You'll show me. One day, you'll show it all to me. What else are you doing?"

"I'm going to see the Duomo and I wanted to go to a museum called the Uffizi. Then I'll see the Arno River and the famous bridge that crosses it."

"That's quite a day. Sounds perfect."

See, she could do this, though a strange pang of guilt rose up. "It's okay I came here, right?" She wasn't asking for permission, not from Anthony. She was asking it of herself.

"Of course. You can do whatever you like. I'm happy you went. I'm so busy. I didn't realize how busy this project would make me. I suppose it's good we won't move in together for a few weeks. The house they put me up in is already a mess. I'll need to find a housekeeper before you get here," he joked.

"It's okay, we can take care of that later."

He gave another loud yawn and apologized that he needed to get ready for the day.

"Have a good day," she called.

"You too," he said happily, then repeated, "You too. I'll ... text you or call when I can."

She said her goodbye, but she was already sidetracked by the large display window of a bookstore with a sign touting books in English. She bought a guidebook for Florence and Rome, and she thanked the cashier with a "grazie" – the one phrase that was growing with conviction the more she said it.

A short distance from the bookstore was a restaurant, with ample outdoor seating and an abundance of tourists, many of whom were single diners. Diana gathered her courage and asked the maître d' for an outside table for one. She ordered a glass of wine and pasta, then retrieved the book about Rome. Opening it at random, she was met with a vibrant photograph of the Colosseum. "I'm going there," she whispered running her finger gently over the glossy page.

When a heaping twirl of pasta with red sauce was placed before her, she closed her eyes on the taste. It was delightful and hardy. The second hot meal she'd had since she landed.

Such a simple day, some good art, some good food. What must it be like to live in this city?

She ordered an espresso after her meal, a little pick-me-up to help as she continued to wind her way around the cobblestone streets and throngs of tourists.

She was in awe of the many intricate details she passed. Old wrought iron rings left bolted in walls where horses were once tied. Bells of churches that rang the time throughout the city. The coat of arms hanging on the side of a medieval looking building that she overheard a tour guide explain was the Medici family coat of arms.

She clutched her hands to her chest as she turned a corner and came face to face with Florence's Duomo. The grand dame who stood stoic in her centuries old gothic attire. Diana craned her neck as her vision tried to comprehend the spectacle spread out before her, and though she was content enough to see the edifice, she dreamily got in the line of people waiting to enter.

Once inside, she marveled at the height of the ceilings and the intricate paintings and decorations on the arches above her head. The soft murmur of voices echoed off the stone walls. There were pews set up for weekly attendants, the pulpit where the priest would say mass, and behind that an area for a choir. All knowledge gained from being brought up Catholic.

In the center of the church was a stairwell leading down, which required an extra fee; but it held the ruins of the church the Duomo replaced. Another fee would take her up, to the top of the dome. Diana chose neither, and instead sat down on a bench and tried to grasp the enormity of such beauty. "Years," she muttered to herself. It would take years to comprehend it.

The hushed arguing of a family, exhausted and at odds with what do do next, broke up Diana's reprieve. She said her good bye to the glorious structure as she made her way to the exit.

No more had she shaken off the dream of the Duomo than her feet had led her to a piazza filled with iconic buildings from movies she couldn't recall. Each new piazza and building was a siren's song pulling her into their embrace.

There were more groups of tourists here. Many surrounded a guide speaking and pointing out various areas in the piazza. Any place there was a seat, was taken.

She saw a reproduction of the *David* at the opposite end of the piazza, and headed over to look; it didn't move her the way the original did. Still, she took a photo because he was impressive.

Just as she lowered her phone, an English speaking tour guide parked a group beside her. "The Piazza Signorina. This is where Savonarola incited the Bonfire of the Vanities. And where he was later hung for treason and heresy. The sculpture garden you see before you was built in 1376 as an open-air gallery for antique and Renaissance art."

Diana drifted away from the group. Glancing around the square, there was no imagination needed to date this piazza back to the days of the Medici and Michelangelo. She wondered if it had really changed much at all. She took pictures of everything and when her eyes focused on a sign that pointed out the entrance to the Uffizi Gallery, she smiled proudly.

The entrance was in an alley of sorts, not really an alley as it was a small piazza surrounded by the gray stone building that housed the museum; two sides with a connecting, covered hallway at the far end, but with an open arch that led beyond the alley. And setting off the area were columns, each with an arch that housed a sculpted representation of Renaissance movers and shakers: Dante, Machiavelli, Galileo, Leonardo da Vinci ...

While her attention was on the statues, men selling posters, sunglasses and jewelry vied for tourists attention; one of the men zeroed in on her. "Hey pretty lady, you want buy? I make good price," he called, shocking her out of her study.

She shook her head and stepped away from him.

"Yes, you look like rich pretty lady. You want Italian sunglasses?" another man joined.

"No." She pressed her purse against her side and tried another step backwards. But the man with chains and necklaces hanging from his fingers encroached and gave her a leering smirk. "Yes. You have money. Want pretty necklace for pretty neck."

She frowned. "I said no."

The man with the sunglasses tisked and laughed. "We help you. Nice sunglasses for pretty lady."

She was pressing her purse hard against her now, and began to try and outwalk the men, but they kept pace with her.

"Go away," she said angrily.

"Go away," one of them parroted. "You buy then we go," he continued.

Diana felt like she was the only woman, the only tourist in this corridor. The line for the Ufizzi was so long, if she joined it, these men might not let up. She was so rattled, she didn't even try to make eye contact with someone who might help her.

Instead, her heart raced, her pulse pounded in her head.

"You buy," another man said laughingly. He was holding posters, and seeing his friends having all the fun, decided to join in.

Only none of it was fun for Diana.

"Stop," Diana hissed just as one man reached out and tried to slow her down. "You are alone here? All alone?" The voice was too close.

She pulled away and glanced around, three men surrounding her now, but she could still retreat. "Leave me alone," she bit with all the anger she could muster through the fear. And this time, they let her escape but not before one of the men laughingly called after her, "Bitch," while another said, "We find you tomorrow." And they all laughed.

She didn't run. She wanted to, but she figured if she just kept up a quick pace and got out into a crowd, she would be okay. She kept her eyes fixed on the end of the corridor, where large groups of people were traveling by.

The laughing seemed to keep pace with her until she reached the end and thrust herself into the crowd of tourists. She didn't excuse the way she bumped into other people, she just gave a glance over her shoulder as a new arrival of tourists caught the men's attention.

She gasped for air when she found that she made it to an overlook along the Arno River. She should have cared how beautiful the sight was, but she didn't. Her increased heartbeat thumped loudly in her head. She continued along the river until she found a taxi, shakily climbed in and gave the address for the hostel as she tried not to cry.

Harper had been right about one thing; everyone in Italy spoke just enough English.

# Chapter Sixteen

Her phone rang. The third call in five minutes. Harper again. She was probably feeling bad about the spinster comment.

Diana's finger hovered over the ignore button once more, but instead, she answered without saying anything.

"What's wrong?" Harper demanded.

"Nothing's wrong. You don't like how I'm exploring Florence, it sounds like you have the problem."

"Something's wrong."

"Other than your snarky comments?" Diana pursed her lips.

"I'm sorry."

"You know, I've seen some pretty amazing things and I think the pictures I'm sharing are really nice."

"They are. And I shouldn't have made the comment."

"You know, I'm not gonna be dancing at clubs or going for drinks and staying up all night at bars with strangers," she defended.

"I realize that. I'm sorry," Harper said and a laugh escaped from Diana's diaphragm. In fact, it felt so good, she continued to laugh.

Harper grumbled, "What?"

When she could take a full breath, Diana stuttered out, "Lena got to you, didn't she?"

"Maybe ..." The mutter was the only verification Diana would get and it made her laugh even harder, though at this point she was sure it was a release valve she didn't know she needed. The fear she experienced the previous afternoon had burst her good mood, her courage and her self-esteem. She wished finding attributes of one's youth was a tangible exercise. It would be so convenient if there was a store where you could go buy your old courage and put it on like a t-shirt.

A knock came at the door then, and Diana knew it was the staff asking her to leave; she should have been checked out thirty minutes ago.

"Hold on," she told Harper as she opened the door.

"Signora?" The young woman who'd checked her in gave a slight smile. "I am sorry to disrupt, however, it is time for checking out. We have need of this room."

"I'm just finishing up," Diana said. "I'm sorry. I lost track of the time." She gave the white lie. "I'll be down in a few minutes."

"Do you require a taxi?"

"No, thank you. I'm going to the train station." She was surprised when the words came out, because last night over another picnic dinner, she'd spent her time looking into flights home from Florence. At this point, there was a five-hundred-dollar change fee. And Sofia's fortune telling, annoyingly whispered in her ear: *It makes sense to stay. You won't want to waste the money.*

So she would stay, but not because of money.

"Very good." The woman retreated.

"Okay," Diana smiled as she sat on the edge of the bed, "I had an amazing time when I first got to Florence, and yesterday morning was wonderful. Then I had the shit scared out of me and it threw me for a loop."

"What? What happened?"

"Nothing important ..." Diana needed to hear herself admit that. "Nothing important, but I feel like I took two steps forward and five back."

"I'm sorry," Harper whispered.

"If you're thinking this is all your fault and you should have figured out how to come with me instead of pulling the trigger on this hairbrained idea, you're right," Diana said sternly.

"Luna ..." Diana could hear her sister rolling her eyes.

"If you're thinking I'm not having a good time ... well, you'd be wrong to think that."

"Really?!"

"But, be nice to me. I'm trying." What she was *trying* had yet to be seen, because there were so many levels to what Diana was trying to do for herself; old and new.

"I am. I will. Lena ripped into me."

"Good."

Harper muttered in reply.

"Okay Harp, I need to get going. I'm late for checkout which means I have less time to get to the train station."

There was a muffle of noise before Harper confirmed, "Your train leaves in two hours."

"I know."

"Will you get there in time?"

"Cake of piece," Diana joked and Harper's instant tears were audible. "Now what?" Diana asked.

"You sound like you."

"Of course I sound like me."

"No ... don't you remember? Everything that was challenging that came your way, when we were kids, well, when I was a kid ... I'd ask you how you were going to figure it out, you always shrugged and said 'cake of piece.'" More tears.

"I remember."

"You sound like you."

Diana nodded a few times and had to clear her throat; she knew what Harper was saying. "Okay, Harp, I need to get going."

"I know. Okay." She noisily blew her nose. "Have a good day. I'm sorry I called you a spinster and I love the pictures. Please don't stop posting."

"I won't."

"I love you, Lu."

"Love you too." She hung up and muttered, "Even though your love is sometimes difficult to take, kid."

Diana turned in her key at the front desk, apologized again and asked the receptionist, "Have you been to Orvieto?" She said the name of the next stop on her itinerary slowly, hoping she wasn't butchering it.

"Is bellissimo. Very quiet, very small, but the city, all of it is on mountain. They are famoso for pottery."

Diana nodded, hoping small and quiet equaled safe.

"You should go to Roma." The girl smiled. "Roma is molto molto bella."

"I'm supposed to go to Rome."

"I *love* Roma. Everyone should go." She reiterated her stance on the city.

Diana nodded. "Then I won't miss it."

"Buon viaggio."

"Grazie," Diana said as she stood and looped her purse over her shoulder and grabbed the handle of her luggage. She stepped outside and took a steadying breath, then glanced to her right at the café across the street; there was time for coffee and a pastry. It had six tables outside, three of which were taken. That's what she'd do to ease herself back into Italy. "Baby steps," she muttered as she crossed the narrow street.

After a decadent pastry, she still had time to waste and decided to stop at the large department store on the corner. There was something soothing about the idea of being in an enclosed space where the goods for sale wouldn't be hoisted aloft on arms and forced upon her.

She took her time walking through the Macy's knockoff. The smell of over-sprayed perfumes mingling with the bright florescent lighting was strangely comforting. She ambled through each of the four stories, finding a slight injection of courage. She wondered if she wasn't soaking up power from the fluorescent lights.

See, she told herself as she watched single women shopping and leaving the store, there are plenty of women who are by themselves in this city, not scared, just going about their lives.

The immature pep talk actually helped.

After purchasing a light blue scarf that declared it was made in Italy, she continued to the train station, studying each of the shop windows as she passed.

She slowed to a stop in front of a leather shop where leather bound journals of all colors were displayed; some held blank pages, some dotted graph paper and others lined paper begging to be written on. She opened the door and found a red leather journal sitting on a table just inside. A fleur de lis, the symbol of Florence, was stamped into the cover along with the word 'Firenze' beneath that. She picked up the book, the soft material caressing her hands. She flipped through the handsewn pages and nodded, this was her book. It had been waiting for her.

The thought weakened her knees, but she swallowed the feeling and handed the journal over to the shopkeeper to purchase. He wrapped it in a dark mustard yellow paper and tied it with a ribbon before handing it back. Diana had made two special purchases so far, and if this was the ceremony that went along with it, she was tempted to buy more; because the care taken made her feel just as precious.

She cradled the wrapped book in her free arm as she continued to the station and Orvieto: a small, quiet town for one night. Then she would go to Rome.

After all, she'd come this far.

# Chapter Seventeen

Laughter woke her.

Diana stared at the light from the hallway spilling in from under her door. Half awake, the chair she'd propped under the doorknob looked ridiculous now. The door had a lock and a latch on the inside. And Orvieto had been gloriously calm. She'd leaned into it, a reaction caused by the number of women she saw pulling foldable shopping bags behind them, filled with the groceries and goods they needed for the day. Single older women, who she was certain, wouldn't take any shit from anyone. She'd placed this attribute on their shoulders, partially because the short heels many of them wore to traverse the cobblestoned city made them seem badass, but also because she needed an infusion of stalwart determination.

More laughing followed by a round of shushing. She shook her head, annoyed at people having fun.

"No," she muttered to the dim room, she was annoyed that she couldn't recall the last time she had fun that way.

Diana rolled over and glanced out the window she'd left open, the irony not lost on her. But the pensione – which she'd learned was a type of Italian Bed and Breakfast – sat on the edge of the city. And as Orvieto was built atop a large mesa, it meant her room was on the edge of the building, on the edge of a cliff, with a drop-off below the window. Only invading forces would be attempting to climb the mountain walls tonight. So, she was pretty sure the open window was safe.

It was a cool evening, but the room had been warmed from the setting sun, and offered a stunning view of the Umbrian countryside. The proprietor of the pensione explained that she was no longer in Tuscany, but now in glorious Umbria. A fact, she feared, that was lost on her, but the view out her window, made up of gorgeous greenery, open spaces of farmland, and tree-lined roads, was not.

Another round of laughter and shushing.

She sat up and glanced out the window at the lights from small homes dotting the countryside.

Orvieto had been more than she'd imagined. Exiting the train, she walked through the small station, crossed the street to catch the mountainside railroad that could travel steep inclines and take her into the heart of the small city. She'd watched another of Harper's instructional videos, purchased a ticket and stood toward the front of the car with a view of the tall, tree-lined tracks that pulled the clickety-clacking car upward.

Diana followed her fellow passengers to the beginning of the hilltop town. It was a fifteen-minute walk to the pensione. But time, yet again, was relative as the perfectly preserved medieval city rose up around with brick buildings, blooming bougainvillea and geraniums. On a narrow street she watched in awe as the driver of a smallish van crawling along the cobblestones, reached out to pull in his rearview mirror to help make more space.

Once she had her room key and freshened up, she was eager to explore. She passed restaurants brimming over with lunching tourists and shops filled with wines, olive oils, pastas, and pottery.

The young woman who'd said Orvieto was known for pottery hadn't been lying. Diana thought she hadn't made enough of the fact. Most storefronts were covered with colorful displays. Serving platters with bright lemons and leaves; plates with red, yellow and blue flowers chasing each other around the rim; and pasta bowls in orange, with hints of deep blue and maroon, held graceful dragons in arabesques. She overheard one of the busy shopkeepers explaining about the traditional Italian patterns, but the centuries-old techniques and tradition was such an in-depth conversation Diana decided to just appreciate the colorful displays. She purchased a small creamer pitcher, the decoration done only in a soft maroon, but it was the fleur de lis that charmed her.

She was jarred out of her memories by muted, snorting amusement, followed by dramatic hushing that swirled again.

Diana rolled back onto her side and closed her eyes as a soft gust of air pushed its way into the room; Italian air, sweeping past the cypress trees and crops, over the Italian earth.

# Chapter Eighteen

If Pisa was a jet lag city and Florence was the test of a woman's courage, then Orvieto was a lovely history lesson in perseverance.

Diana blinked her eyes open to dusty Umbrian light filling the room, and the morning song of birds wafting in.

Visions of Roman ruins prodded her into action. Her train for Rome departed at ten and the trip would take a little over an hour. With the early start this morning, she would be able to take in more of Orvieto before she left.

She readied herself and went to the breakfast room, a space consisting of five tables and full-length windows overlooking the countryside. The proprietor was putting the finishing touches on the breakfast bar. "Buongiorno," she called.

Diana tentatively returned the greeting.

"You are first awake," she picked up a plate and handed it to Diana, "sit where you like."

"Thank you."

Diana inspected the breakfast offerings. There were rolls, croissants, butter and individual jams along with small glass jars of local honey. Also fruit, dried salami, and some hard cheese placed prettily on plates, and bottles of sparkling and regular water.

"Caffè?" the proprietor asked. "Posso preparare un espresso o un caffè americano."

Thankfully Diana understood the two offerings: espresso or caffè americano. As Sofia had explained, caffè americano was a shot of espresso and a small pot of boiling water served together.

"Espresso, please."

"Certo." The woman patted Diana on the shoulder as she went back into the kitchen. "Sit, I bring."

Diana sat with her coffee and marveled at the view. The sky created a blanket of white and blue patchwork, and she took a photo but wanted to know how to bottle the fresh green spring colors that created a plaid against the rolling countryside. She wanted to linger, but the alarm she set to allow herself enough time to retrace her steps, explore and get back to the train, chimed. This was her goodbye to Orvieto.

She let the echo of her footsteps on the cobblestones become a rhythm through the medieval town, as if she was shaking off some of the invisible fear that should have been shed long ago. A release as her foot thudded down, and with every lift, a gathering of confidence.

She'd come back with Anthony and maybe do a real trip with Harper.

But she'd never return for what she was leaving behind.

Diana boarded the train, found her seat and offered a polite smile at the four young women across the aisle as she stowed her bag. Once seated, she checked her messages from Anthony, Harper and Lena. All wished her continued success and fun on her trip, and all three had gotten the timing wrong between the states and countries.

Settled, she glanced out the window and readied herself for another episode of Italian countryside watching.

At the back of her mind, she still had her backup plan. After she saw the Colosseum, and maybe the Vatican, if she still wanted to change her plane ticket and go home, she could. At that point she would have accomplished a lion's share of both sightseeing *and* getting out of her comfort zone.

"Excuse me," one of the women across the aisle caught Diana's attention, "sorry to bug you, but weren't you in the same B&B as us last night?"

Diana gave a quiet nod before turning her attention back to the passing scenery. *This must have been the giggling crew.*

"Are you going to Rome?" The questioner didn't take Diana's polite dismissal.

Harper's comment swirled: *What the hell is this? The spinster's guide to Italy?* Diana frowned at it and turned her attention to the blonde with short hair, naturally curled into a cute mess. Her youthful eyes were sparkling blue, though it was difficult to make focused eye contact as the woman's chest was so abundant; and the way she was leaning across her armrest, not to mention the tank top she was wearing, made a parade of her cleavage.

"Yes, headed to Rome," Diana replied.

"We are too. Where are you staying? Wouldn't it be a hoot if it was the same place again? We're staying at the Yellow something hostel."

Diana pulled out her itinerary to give herself more time to answer, because she was indeed staying at the Yellow Door Hostel. And while she held no grudges against youthful exuberance, she wanted to get a good night's sleep.

Or maybe Diana didn't want another event where her forty-five years were on display in a place that was clearly not meant for lonely women over the age of thirty.

*Lonely?*

"I'm there as well." She interrupted her own train of thought this time by answering the well-endowed blonde.

"Oh, cool," the blonde said. "Hey, I hope we weren't too annoying last night," she went on.

Diana shrugged her shoulders.

"It was all Michele's fault, for bringing us to this magical land to begin with." The blonde elbowed the friend sitting next to her, a stately brunette, straight-backed, sharp facial features and dark purple streaks throughout her hair; the sun shining through the windows brought out the highlights. "We went to see an opera at this place ..." The blonde looked at her friend for confirmation.

"Teatro Mancinelli," the brunette, Michele, supplied in a rather lovely sounding Italian.

The young woman sitting directly opposite the blonde, with chestnut hair twirled in a messy bun, joined in the conversation, explaining, "We saw Andrea Bocelli in concert."

That was a shock. Diana assumed their antics had been alcohol-induced. Andrea Bocelli-induced was … intriguing.

"How was the concert?" she asked.

The last of the quartet, sitting across from Michele, with a short bob of straight dark hair, a piercing in her nose, and a tattoo of a lotus flower on her exposed shoulder, leaned across the table with a smile and added, "He was amazing. Seeing him was bucket list stuff." Diana couldn't keep from raising an eyebrow in interest as the young woman continued, "You could feel each note in your chest." She pressed her hand on her chest as if to exemplify what she was trying to convey.

The blonde nodded. "There are no words."

"But Orvieto is such a small town … was there a big crowd? Sorry," Diana apologized, "did you go to Orvieto to see him in concert?"

The blonde's eyes sparkled. "No, we were just visiting to visit. But we went to this really cute trattoria for dinner."

"Trattoria la Palomba," Michele offered.

The blonde waved a hand toward her friend. "Michele remembers all the names. So, we were at this cute trattoria, great food." She was animated as she talked and Diana had the urge to pull out the scarf she'd bought and cover the girl's assets, to keep them from spilling out. "So we're halfway through dinner and talking about dessert and our waiter is totally flirting with us, but that's fine because that's what waiters do."

"I was a waitress in California," the girl with the nose piercing said, "and I admit, the guys who visit from out of town with the accents, there's just something about it that makes you get your flirt on."

"Right?" The blonde nodded. "Oh, that's Sabrina." She introduced the girl with the nose piercing sitting next to the window. "And next to her is Tasha."

"This is Michele next to me and I'm Renee." Renee held out her hand as if she would be shaking hands for the whole group. Diana returned the greeting and supplied her name. "Diana."

"Where are you from?" Renee asked.

"Georgia."

"We're from California. Well, we grew up together in Southern California. Sabrina moved to Texas during college and never came back. Tasha moved to San Francisco, but Michele and I still live in SoCal,"

Renee explained.

If there was an ambassador for goodwill for the little group, Renee was it. Diana glanced at the other girls, curious what they thought about their friend offering their life stories to a stranger on a train. But they didn't look overly concerned. It must be something they were used to.

"How nice that you can travel together." Diana cringed at the lame sounding comment.

"Michele lived in Rome for three years, she came here for school." Renee's pride in her friend was apparent. "We always said we'd come to Europe together and travel and I don't think any of us ever thought it would really happen. But life's funny and here we are on our way to Rome." She was bursting, literally and figuratively.

"How long have you been in Europe?" Diana asked.

"Seventeen days. We have ten more days left." Renee sighed.

"Wow, where have you visited?" Diana wouldn't say she was captivated, but she was curious about these girls whose midnight carryings-on were caused by Andrea Bocelli.

Renee took a deep breath, as if she had been asked to recite all the American presidents in order. "We started in Paris, then to Copenhagen, Berlin, Prague, Salsburg, Florence, Orvieto and now Rome."

"That sounds like quite a trip."

"It's been life changing." Renee shot a grin in her friend's direction, then turned back to Diana. "So, are you here on business?"

*That* would be a very 'sensible' deduction.

Diana's outfit did look a bit on the business side. She definitely didn't have the carefree tourist look the way the young women did.

"No. I'm on a tour of Italy. My sister ..." she trailed off, then started again. "I recently got engaged and my sister surprised me with a trip to Italy."

"Oh, that's so cool!" Renee exclaimed.

Encouraged by the reaction, Diana continued, "I thought she was coming with me, but when I landed in Pisa, she called and said she only had enough money for *one* all-expense paid trip."

"Free trip to Italy? Sign me up," Renee said.

"I thought ..." Diana started and then sighed. "I didn't expect to have to see Italy alone."

"Oh." Renee looked contrite for Diana then in a flash her face changed. "Oh! Come see Rome with us."

Diana shook her head, politely declining the offer. There was no way she was about to play den mother to a group of twenty somethings.

"Yeah," Tasha nodded, the bun on her head bouncing. "We're going out with a few people Michele knew from when she lived here tonight. You should come with us."

"You don't need a spinster cramping your style." Diana used Harper's words, cringing as she said it aloud, then quickly tried to turn the spotlight back on the women. "You never finished your story about getting tickets to see Andrea Bocelli."

"Age is relative." Michele offered instead of taking the bait. "We're all twenty-eight. I act like I'm thirty-eight, Renee acts like she's sixteen." She waved toward Renee who nodded her head happily in agreement then asked, "How old are you?"

Diana raised an eyebrow at the question. She thought about not answering, then with a sigh said, "Forty-five."

"But that's not the question," Michele corrected Renee as she sat forward, leaning across her friend toward Diana. "How old do you *feel*?" She emphasized the word.

Diana *felt* as if she'd been punched in the gut. "Seventy-eight." She whispered the age so quickly she realized the truth of what Michele had said. Age was relative, and Diana had felt old and tired for so long. She was haggard. She swallowed the sudden tightness in her throat.

"I don't mean to be rude," Sabrina, the girl with nose piercing, interrupted, "but you should come out with us tonight; maybe we can help get that number down to something reasonable."

"Look," Renee waved a hand, "you don't have to answer us now. I know I come on strong, but you'll have a blast with us. But let's get to Rome, get checked into our rooms and then we'll revisit you going out with us tonight."

Diana nodded, that she could do. It gave her enough time to come up with an excuse.

Renee smiled. "Okay, now I'll tell you the rest of the story from last night. So, we're at this cute little trattoria and this older couple stopped by our table and asked us how we were enjoying our trip and where we'd been and what kinds of things we'd done. He was a farmer."

"Winemaker," Michele corrected.

"You gotta grow grapes and they're a crop," Renee argued. "You say winemaker, I say farmer." Renee patted Michele's hand. "So they were super nice and we had a great conversation, and then they asked if we had any plans for the evening. Of course we didn't, so the wife tells us she's on the board of the opera house and they have some extra tickets to see this opera singer. Do we want them? We agree, because it would be fun to hear opera in Italy. But when we get there and find out it's Andrea Bocelli, we freak out."

"To say the least," Tasha added.

"He was amazing," Renee continued. "Afterwards, we tried to find the couple to pay them back for the tickets, because we're pretty sure they weren't cheap ..."

"We never found them," Michele finished.

Renee grinned. "But we were so high on Orvieto, and cobblestone streets and opera and Andrea Bocelli ..." She sighed as if just saying the words mixed together created a magic spell that would take her back to the moment.

"That would be lovely. To hear an opera in Italy," Diana said.

"So you see? That's why you should come out with us tonight," Renee reasoned. "Who *knows* what's going to happen when you hang out with us. Maybe we'll get free drinks or end up with tickets to see a circus in the Colosseum."

"They don't do a 'circus' in the Colosseum," Michele said.

At the mention of the Colosseum, Diana felt her heart rate rise. *What is this the spinster's guide ...?* She shook off the rest of the sentence. If she accepted the offer, at least she wouldn't be alone at dinner.

The hour train ride flew by as Renee, Tasha, Michele and Sabrina continued to engage Diana in conversation.

"Tasha teaches second grade." Renee started listing her friends' credentials. "Sabrina is a massage therapist and yoga instructor in Texas. She keeps making us do yoga every morning," Renee complained.

"And how have you been feeling?" Sabrina asked.

Renee laughed. "Good, okay? I feel pretty damn good."

Sabrina aimed an 'I told you so' smile at her friend. Renee waved her away.

"I'm moving to Texas in a few weeks," Diana said.

"What part?" Sabrina asked.

"Houston. My fiancé is working there for the year and I'll be joining him."

"I'm in Austin," Sabrina said.

"Oh, another adventure," Renee cooed.

Diana nodded and her smile widened at the idea of another adventure.

Renee continued, "Michele works for an import export company in California, but the company is in Rome. She gets to use her Italian every day."

"Not every day," Michele corrected.

"Can you imagine, speaking Italian fluently? God, I need to actually start working on a goal like that." Renee sighed.

"What language would you learn?" Diana asked.

"French," she said immediately. "The French men were dreamy and the whole country was dreamy." She sighed and her eyes fogged over as if she could still recall the dream. "What language would you learn?"

"I think Italian." Diana glanced out the window as the train rumbled through rolling spring hills. "Yes, I think I'd learn Italian."

"That would be wonderful." Renee joined Diana in watching out the window for several minutes.

"I'm a beautician," Renee continued after her slight reprieve to dream about other languages, "and you're going to let me update your look."

"Oh," Diana shook her head, "I don't think that's necessary."

"Do you like how you look?" Renee asked.

"Renee." Michele's tone was a warning that her friend should mind her own business.

"Of course." Diana wanted to explain that there were fine lines when having polite conversation and even Renee's friends knew she had just crossed one. But Diana also suspected Renee was such a free spirit, she just jumped in with both feet no matter what the situation.

"Really?" Renee prodded.

"I think I look respectable." Diana straightened in her seat.

"Renee ..." Michele tiredly tried to stop her friend, but that didn't deter the bouncing blonde who tilted her head and narrowed her eyes as she studied Diana. "Do you keep it in a bun every single day?"

Diana nodded and touched a finger to her hair.

"Do you ever let it down? For special occasions?" Renee asked.

Diana didn't answer.

Renee nodded. "That's what I thought." She pursed her lips and after a moment said, "Maroon highlights, nothing drastic, but classic. And a bob."

"I don't ..." Diana didn't know what to say.

Renee waved a hand. "I think we need to lose the travel suit too. I'm not talking about a total makeover that would make you feel uncomfortable; I'm just talking about a few little things, tiny updates. You know, let out all that beauty you've got trapped inside."

"I really don't think—" Diana started, but Tasha leaned across the aisle and patted Diana's hand. "She's got it in her head now. She won't give up and she always gets her way."

Diana raised an eyebrow; well, the busty thing wasn't going to get her way this time. Diana wouldn't be a willing participant and what would these girls do, hold her down and force her?

Tasha tried to soothe the situation, "I will say this about my dear friend, as intrusive and crazy as she might seem at first blush, beneath the big boobs she's a genius."

"Thanks." Renee slapped Tasha's hand. "Diana, you're probably worried about it, but don't be. We're in Italy, no one knows you here. You'll never see any of these people ever again. What better time to do something a little different and daring than right now?"

Diana began to formulate her plan of escape. She would follow the girls toward the hostel, find the nearest alley and run until she found a new hotel.

"Do you believe different people are brought into our lives at different times for a reason?" Renee was unrelenting.

"I believe ..." What did Diana believe? The only thing she seemed to believe in lately was security. Security and old age. She looked at Renee who was studying her, the young woman was right. She was in a foreign country. She was also engaged. She was going to move to Texas. She was changing her life and shaking things up anyway. So why the hell not *really* shake things up? "How drastic of a change?"

"I see some gray, so that's where the dark maroon highlights will come in. It will look really natural. I promise." She traced an 'x' on her left breast. "The cut will be short, but with your bone structure, it will look *darling*. And it will be just as easy to manage as a bun." Renee smiled reassuringly.

It sounded so easy, as if it should have been something Diana thought about a long time ago. She opened her mouth to say something but couldn't get the words out so settled for a quick, jerky nod.

Renee clapped her hands. "I know you don't know me, but I *promise*, this is going to be *so* much fun and it won't be painful at all and you'll feel at least sixty when I'm done."

Sabrina leaned over this time and said, "You really can say no and we'll stop her. But she truly has a gift. She can see the end result with such clarity and she's never wrong."

Diana looked at Renee who was nodding her head in agreement with her friend's assessment of her personality.

"You're going to have so much fun!" Renee insisted.

# Chapter Nineteen

The women kept up a steady diatribe of conversation once they were off the train, leaving Diana without the appropriate opportunity to make an excuse or attempt a dead run. Of course, the real reason she didn't tuck tail and bolt was because she was in awe of how large the train station was in Rome, and impressed with the effortless way Michele calmly and masterfully navigated the group from the train to the metro, and finally up from the underground into the busy late morning streets of the city.

While on the metro, Renee had rummaged through beauty supply store listings, showing the locations to Michele for approval, until finally they found one that was – depending on how you looked at the five-block detour – on the way to the hostel.

Surfacing from the underground onto a busy corner of Rome, Michele smiled and took a deep breath. Diana watched the woman close her eyes, a contentment taking over, as if that one deep breath was filled with fond old memories. Diana took an experimental sniff, getting that note of foreign humidity along with a scent she'd been trying to pinpoint since she exited the plane in Pisa, but continually failed because it was unlike anything she'd been privy to.

"Okay Renee," Michele motioned, "let me see that address again?"

Michele nodded the women in the direction they were headed as their suitcases clicked behind them on the pavement, conversation rose among them, and Rome blossomed all around.

Diana's stomach did a flutter as they continued. Sure, she was intrigued at the *idea* of a haircut. Not that she had a lot of faith in the blonde, but Renee's excitement and nonchalant attitude about how this wasn't a big deal put her in the mood to be open to the possibility of a slight change.

And she was an adult. She didn't owe these women anything, they had each other and at any point and time, Diana could just walk away.

Renee held up swatches of synthetically colored hair against Diana's, frowning as she attempted to pick the perfect maroon. Of course, Diana was apprehensive about the brightness of the shades, thinking Renee had been joking when she'd mentioned the color on the train.

"I don't know," Diana politely debated, "maybe it's a bit too … dramatic."

"I know it looks like too much now, but we're not dying your whole head this color. We're taking out the gray and adding a slight highlight. You'll see."

"Are you sure it isn't a little too …" for lack of a better word, Diana let loose, "too young?"

"It's perfect." Renee shrugged.

"I'm not in my twenties anymore." Diana was letting go of politeness. Next stop was fearful refusal that was bound to come off as bitchy.

"And you aren't in your seventies either. And fashion's changed, there are no real age rules for women anymore." Renee winked. "I know it's asking a lot; I'm a complete stranger, but *please*, trust me. When we're finished, you're going to be so glad the fates introduced you to me."

"You truly have a healthy sense of self," Diana muttered.

Renee's smile widened. "I know. Isn't it great? In this day and age, I'm a strong woman with a strong sense of self. Come on, let's go look at makeup."

Diana glanced back at the store clerk, her hair tied up in a messy bun, a maroon bun similar to the shade Renee picked out. Her makeup was reminiscent of a style made popular by Adam Ant in the eighties. She had a white stripe across her left cheek, bright red eyeshadow and purple sparkle fake eyelashes that could be seen from fifty feet away, where Diana was standing.

Diana knew her eyes had grown as big as they could get when Tasha passed by and touched her gently. "She'll never let you look like that."

Diana nodded and Sabrina added, "The kid's good at what she does. She cuts all our hair. She just doesn't hear the word no."

"How about 'I don't want to,'" Diana mumbled under her breath. "Aren't we living in a time when 'NO' is supposed to be a complete sentence?"

Sabrina let loose an unexpected laugh.

"Diana? Could you come here for a second?" Renee was holding three items, all very tame looking. Diana's sense of relief slowed her erratic heartbeat as Renee asked for Diana's hand and touched a dot of the concealer to it then rubbed it in. "Perfect."

Carrying the items, Renee went up to the counter. Diana followed and tried to intervene as Renee reached for her wallet.

Renee shook her off. "I'm not gonna make you pay for something you're not convinced you want to do just yet."

That seemed fair to Diana.

"Listen," Renee faced Diana and reached for her hands, giving them a squeeze as the items were rung up, "if you don't like this, I can put everything back to the way it was."

"Not if we cut my hair."

Renee waved that away as she turned back to pay. "Hair grows back. But trust me, you're not gonna want it to, because you're gonna love it."

The contents of the bag were minimal, a pair of scissors and seven little bottles. How much damage could one busty blonde do with such inconsequential items?

# Chapter Twenty

"**D**iana?"

"Anthony, how are you?" she answered, dripping from the shower.

"Did I catch you at a bad time?"

"No, I'm just getting out of the shower, but I didn't want to miss your call."

"Oh, then ... we'll talk later. I don't want to bother you."

"I ... I met some interesting young women on the train. We're staying at the same hostel." She swallowed the half truths; not explaining that somehow the little sirens had convinced her to stay in their room with them as it had two extra beds, and now she was getting out of the shower because she'd agreed to a haircut.

"Oh, that's nice. Very good."

"They asked me to dinner."

"You won't have to eat alone."

"Yes, I just ..." She covered the receiver with her hand as she whispered, "They're young and I don't want to be their girl scout troop leader."

"But you were a girl scout troop leader to your niece."

"Exactly," Diana laughed, "I've already done that."

"Go to dinner, then you could always fake a migraine."

"That's what I was thinking." She nodded as she stared blindly across the room. "What does your day look like?"

"Busy, so busy. I need to find a housekeeper. And I need to figure out how to keep more reasonable hours. I've been a bachelor for so long ..."

"Are you pulling out of the proposal?" she asked jokingly. He was quiet for so long, she frowned and thought about repeating the question when Anthony's voice said, "Diana? Are you there? I lost you."

She cleared her throat. "Okay, well, we can figure that kind of stuff out later."

"Yes, later," he agreed and then gave a large yawn. "I should go make coffee and get to the office."

"Okay, have a good day."

"You too." He ended the call and Diana stared at the phone in her hand but didn't have too much time to contemplate the conversation as a knock came at the door. She hurriedly finished drying off and solidified her game plan for the evening, just in case; she could always fake a migraine.

"Smile!" Renee sang as she held Diana's phone out in front of her, trying to get the whole group hugging in on her sides in the selfie. After, she turned the phone and studied the picture and exclaimed, "Nice!" but didn't hand it back to Diana right away. Instead, she proceeded to swipe and type. Diana stepped toward her, glancing over Renee's shoulder. "What are you doing?"

"I posted it and tagged us all," Renee replied, handing the phone back.

Diana gazed at the picture, five smiling faces with the tagline: *Fun in Rome*. It was nothing horrible or weird, only that the woman that was supposed to be Diana, didn't look like the woman she'd been staring down in the bathroom the past few years.

"I still can't believe it," she whispered, reaching out to touch the photo. She felt like herself still, but lighter and fuller.

Most likely it was the ton of hair she'd shed, but it was more than that. She shook her head and the short slight curls she didn't know she had, brushed against her cheeks.

That one, tiny little bag Renee swung out of the beauty shop ended up holding a multitude of miraculous changes.

While Renee worked, she didn't allow Diana to look in the mirror, saying she wanted a big reveal. Though Diana believed it was really

Renee's way to keep her calm throughout the process.

She expertly cut Diana's hair, standing back and nodding thoughtfully as she studied her work. Then she did some kind of wash that took out the gray, and finally using sheets of foil she'd also bought at the beauty supply, brushed the maroon in various areas. Diana didn't feel like her hair was being highlighted, she felt like her entire head was covered in foil. And the color she spied was brighter than it had been at the shop and the one time she glanced down at her feet, the amount of hair was shocking. So she had to breathe through a building panic attack.

Renee sensed Diana's hesitation and called in reinforcements. Michele promptly picked up the hair and Tasha pulled a chair into the bathroom, sat facing Diana and began to chat her up; asking questions about her trip so far and Atlanta and her family.

"You're very good at distraction," Diana told Tasha.

"I have to be, second grade kids are usually an emotional wreck."

"You're not saying I'm an emotional wreck, are you?"

Tasha winked. "It's Renee; everywhere she goes she causes emotional distress."

Renee muttered as she cleaned up the sink and readied it for the next step.

Diana addressed Renee, "I'm trying to trust you."

"Of course you are, but I'm trustworthy. And I know this seems stressful but just wait, when I'm done, we're going to exchange phone numbers and addresses and be friends forever."

"I'll hold you to it," Diana mumbled.

Renee moved Diana into the room as they waited for the color to set, and Sabrina and Michele took showers.

Renee brought out a piece of thread and pursed her lips. "Have you ever heard of threading?"

Diana hesitated. "Threading, as in plucking your eyebrows?"

Renee shrugged. "So, how 'bout it?"

Diana shook her head, making the foil flap.

"The thing is, I could pluck your eyebrows, but this is so much quicker. And easier," Renee reasoned in an attempt to sell the process.

Tasha stepped in. "How about you watch Renee do mine first?"

That's how Diana ended up with her eyebrows cleaned up before it was time to wash out her hair.

Renee had to use the shower with Diana kneeling next to it and her head upside down, to wash the color out.

"Just ... keep your eyes closed," Renee muttered. "And if you do open them and think the color being rinsed out is too much, just ... it's supposed to be that way." She pointed Diana into position.

Even though she was on a folded towel on her knees, head awkwardly upside down in the shower of a Roman hostel, Renee's fingers were working some kind of magical head massage that pulled out more layers of stress and worry.

Diana kept her eyes closed and breathed in deeply, allowing it all to slip away, down the drain.

After a comical argument about the hair dryer that Sabrina brought and the adapter usage, Diana's hair was dried. Renee grinned widely and clapped. "Damn girl, you look modern and sassy and sexy as hell."

Diana gave a test shake of her head, it felt so different.

"Makeup time," Renee said, arranging the next steps beside her. "Okay, we're going for subtle. To bring out your inner glow."

"Mmm hmmm."

Renee explained about current trends in makeup as she applied it. "These days, you can get away with a good quality, all-in-one coverage. This has SPF, moisturizer and a tinted color matching foundation that'll smooth you out."

Next she held up a berry toned blush. "Use this on your cheeks and as eyeshadow."

The last steps were mascara and tinted lip gloss.

"That's it?" Diana asked, still in shock at the process.

"A makeover needs to leave you comfortable but excited. Think of this as the first step in trying new things."

The sentiment was reinforced as Renee pulled Diana out of the bathroom and asked to see all the clothes she brought with her.

Diana laid out her clothing, realizing that, along with a few white blouses, she basically only had three colors; gray, black and navy.

She was grateful that Renee didn't even balk at the sensible selection, but simply started looking through everything as she explained, "We'll use your own clothes. If I tried to change too much right away, you won't feel comfortable and you won't like anything. Later, when you get used to this idea, you'll be willing to experiment more and look outside your comfort zones."

Tasha was pulling on her jeans as she commented, "She's a makeover whisperer, I'll give her that much."

Renee laid out Diana's black slip-on shoes, black cardigan and held up a pair of cotton black capri pants. "You said you trust me, right?"

"I said I'm *trying*," Diana said slowly. Renee retrieved the hair cutting scissors. "Hold the pants up to your waist, so I can see where they land."

Once Diana did, Renee bent and made a small cut on each side of the bottom of the pants. Then she took them away, cut off the excess fabric, and added a two inch cut up the outside seam and the inside seam. "Just a little flare."

"A little flare." Diana's mouth was dry.

Renee nodded at the final product then snapped her fingers. "I know which shirt." She pulled out a shirt from her own bag, a new white t-shirt with 'Italy' written in cursive silver lettering across the chest and a silver Colosseum beneath that.

"Are you sure I should be the kind of woman who wears the shirt of the country she's in?" Diana tried to joke.

"Put it all on, and tell me how it feels."

When she had the shirt and pants on, Renee took the hem of the t-shirt and knotted it on the right side.

"How does it feel?" Renee asked.

Michele's words from the train floated back to Diana, about asking the wrong question. *Had* she been asking the wrong questions all along?

Diana cleared her throat. "It feels good," she admitted.

As the other girls were finishing their own makeup and clothing, Renee called out for a collection of silver, dangling earrings.

She dug through the offerings, settling at last on a pair of long, delicate dangling silver earrings.

"Are you cold?" Renee asked.

Diana shook her head and Renee nodded, tied a sweater around her waist, then finally stood back to study her work.

The other women joined in, all grinning at various intervals.

"Well?" Diana muttered the question.

"Amazing." Sabrina nodded.

"Look out Rome." Michele gave a low whistle.

"Look out Italy," Tasha added.

"Diana's in the house," Renee finished then moved and turned Diana so she could help her into the bathroom, facing away from the mirror. "You ready?"

"I hope so."

Surrounded by all the women, Renee turned Diana around slowly for the big reveal.

Diana's mouth dropped and had she not seen the mouth in the reflection drop as well, she wouldn't have thought it was her.

The effect of seeing herself so different began in the back of her throat, rendering her speechless. The weight of her hair was gone, unearthing a magical wave; the gray had been replaced with color, and her hair was full and thick and fun. She turned her head right and left, as the subtle highlights winked at her. The makeup was subtle and did make her glow, muting the sun damage and filling in her pores. Her eyes welled with tears and Renee touched her arm. "I thought … it's too much, isn't it?"

Diana shook her head several times, trying to find her voice, and when she did, it wavered through the tears. "I remember her." She crossed the distance between herself and the mirror and tentatively reached out her hand, shocked and thrilled that the reflection did the same. "I *remember* her," she said again as another sob caught in her throat.

Diana took a Kleenex Michele handed over and wiping her eyes, gave an apologetic mutter, "I'm ruining the makeup."

"It's an easy fix," Renee assured, and when Diana could tear her eyes from her reflection, she saw all four women were crying as well.

She smiled at them, nodded her head and glanced back at herself; a self who seemed to beam her relief that she was finally free.

"What's the biggest shock?" Renee asked.

Diana gave another shake of her head, it really was her. The words were difficult to get out. "I forgot about her." That was the biggest shock. She didn't see the forty-five-year-old woman who was haggard and lost, but instead the young woman who had been so full of dreams. "I forgot about her," she sobbed. How in the world could she have forgotten? Diana owed that girl in the mirror an apology. She owed the girl looking back at her a *life.*

"How …?" Diana couldn't finish the question because that one word held nineteen years of questions.

"You were ready." Renee shrugged. "If you really weren't, you would have said no and meant it."

"Didn't I tell you no?" Diana couldn't truly recall.

"You said maybe. An indication people are usually ready for a change."

"Who are you?" Diana asked.

"Magic." Renee laughed and wiped her own eyes. "But just so you know, this is the normal effect I have on people."

Diana took a deep breath, still staring at herself, still shocked. "I believe it."

Sabrina gave Diana's arm a squeeze. "Who knew that was hiding underneath, huh?"

Renee clapped her hands and handed over a few makeup removing towelettes to everyone, then turned Diana back toward her. "Okay. We can cry some more later, but now we need to show Rome this new you."

"I'm … thank you." Diana swallowed the second round of tears that were trying to unleash themselves.

Renee reached out and patted Diana's cheek, then went to work taking off the makeup so she could apply a new coat. "You know, it's too bad we didn't meet up with you in Florence."

"Why's that?"

"Florence is where the Renaissance began, the OG rebirth. It would have been the perfect place to have your rebirth."

That's what this was, a rebirth.

Diana shook her head slightly as she took a deep breath. "No, I think it had to be Rome."

# Chapter Twenty-One

As the women began walking, Diana stood with her phone in her hand, still staring at the photo, trying to shake off the bombardment of regrets and memories rising to the surface. She put the phone away with a definitive nod and blew out a breath. Time for the evening's main event: dinner. Which was accompanied by it's own set of insecurities. But she tried to wave those away and lean into how she was *feeling*. She felt good. She was enjoying the company and she felt Rome deserved her attention.

"Diana," Renee called, trotting back and linking arms with her. "C'mon, Michele started explaining the history of the place we're headed to."

Michele led them through the city streets lit by early evening and doused in brushes of honey tones, while neon lights shone amber.

"We're meeting everyone at a restaurant in the Piazza Navona," Michele explained.

"Isn't six early for an Italian dinner?" Diana asked.

Michele's grin grew. "It is, but we've got a long night ahead of us and it's been a few years since I saw my friends, so we decided to meet sooner rather than later."

Diana nodded, giving the sweater around her waist a worried twist.

"So the piazza we're going to is oval shaped and was actually built for chariot races and mock naval battles. Navona means big ship."

"Mock naval battles?" Sabrina asked. "They did that in the Colosseum too, right?"

"That's what they say," Michele offered.

"How?" Renee asked.

Michele shrugged. "Not sure, but I know just the people to ask tonight." They rounded a corner and the Piazza Navona opened before them. A large space of cobblestone was surrounded on both sides with three- and four-story buildings in coral and beige, yellow and peach. It wasn't difficult to imagine chariot races being held here. There was an outer road, wide enough for two cars, or maybe three chariots to race around. In the center, divided by a brick edging, was a smaller oval with two visible fountains; one close to the end where they stood, and one in the middle with an obelisk reaching into the sky from the center.

The area was encircled by restaurants and gatherings of people, sitting on the available benches, the small raised curbs, the edges of the fountains, and meandering through all points in between. Noise rose and bounced off the surrounding buildings, creating an inviting atmosphere.

"Oh wow." Tasha pulled out her cell phone to take a picture, which led to everyone doing the same.

They walked slowly, soaking up the atmosphere. There were merchants selling trinkets and photos. A man with jewelry, strung on the length of his arm, walked up to Diana and said, "You buy?"

She sucked in a breath as the memory of Florence assaulted her; but before it could take hold, Michele stepped between the man and her, waved him away like he was an apparition of smoke, and ushered the group to the right.

"It should be ..." she was reading the restaurant names, "there." She smiled and, excited, hurried in the direction she'd pointed.

It was difficult to tell the difference between restaurants at first. They all flowed into one another. Tables were set in front of the buildings with umbrellas, adding an extra touch of décor. However, after the first blush, it seemed the colors of the umbrellas differed depending on which restaurant they belonged to; as did the shapes of the tables and chairs. Where one had round tables, the next had squares. Where one had red umbrellas the next had green until the different restaurant color schemes were properly represented.

"Oh!" Michele gasped, hastily finishing the steps that would carry her to the friends she must have just caught a glimpse of.

"I think we're going to meet a mix of people from when Michele was here for college," Renee explained.

A flash of this group quadrupling made Diana feel like an old third wheel. But as that trepidation passed, another flash; a heightened feeling of security and confidence. Being around these young women was slightly addictive. She liked how they made her feel; no longer seventy-eight, but maybe more fifty-eight now. She was untwisting, like all her hair had done, having been twisted up in a tight knot atop her head for so many years. *The question isn't how old you are, it's how old you feel.*

Diana's eyes followed Michele, but when she saw the young woman embrace an older woman, one that actually might be seventy-eight, she was shocked. After they exchanged kisses on both cheeks, Michele moved to a couple standing next to the old woman, an older couple that looked to be Diana's age.

The girls finally came to stand behind Michele who was now talking animatedly with a motley group of people. Motley, Diana thought, in age and appearance. Her fake migraine completely dissipated.

Michele began the introductions. There was a professor of Italian literature who had taught Michele, and a college friend who had married a Roman man and become an expat. A colleague from Michele's current job that she spoke to regularly and her spouse and finally, the older woman, Angelina, who Michele had rented a room from.

Michele introduced Renee, Tasha and Sabrina, then she took Diana by the hand and introduced, "This is our new friend Diana. Her sister gave her an all-expense trip to Italy and she's been bravely exploring the country on her own."

*Bravely?*

It was a shocking thought and a lovely one that she could be brave; that it wasn't out of the realm of possibility. The number of emotions these women unearthed in such a short amount of time continued to keep her off-kilter. Maybe bravery was part of her nature. If it wasn't, she would have gone home from Pisa the second Harper called.

The idea fluttered in her stomach and she was glad for Michele's hand, holding her in place.

A waiter came and showed the group to a collection of tables that had been pushed together on the patio. Conversation at the beginning was stuttered, but it was Angelina, Michele's obvious, beloved landlady, who put everyone at ease. She was lively and gently commanded attention as she seamlessly steered the conversation in both languages. And after the wine relaxed the group, and the sun set, leaving everyone bathed in the light of Roman fluorescence, they fell into warm, affable conversation.

The dinner was another five-course affair. Diana asked Michele to order for her, enjoying the unexpected. When various plates were brought out, however, everyone ended up taking a bite and then exchanging plates with excited declarations of, "You *have* to try this."

The conversation floated between travel, Rome and politics; to life, food and art. The meal was jovial and delicious and it lasted almost four hours. Though, it felt like they'd only been visiting for thirty minutes.

It was ten when Angelina suggested the group move on. In a thick accent she offered, "How do you all feel about a little jazz in a delightful antique building?"

Angelina promised the establishment was within walking distance and she could use a passeggiata, a little after dinner walk, herself.

They strolled, following Angelina and Michele. Various conversations circulated, echoing among dimly lit streets, until they came to a worn, brown door with a neon sign above it. The professor held the door as they all walked down two flights of stairs that opened into a large room in the basement.

"When she said antique building, I forgot just how old buildings could get around here," Diana murmured to Renee who had linked her arm with Diana's as they walked into the bar.

"Told you to stick with us. We get ourselves into some wonderful adventures," Renee said. "According to Sabrina we have to be open to the excitement and wait with baited breath, and then the universe will supply the adventure." She waved her hand. "At least that's the yoga bullshit she always spouts. But hell, who can argue with her? Look at us!"

"I never thought ..." Diana shook her head as her chest tightened again. She never thought a group of young women could change her outlook so quickly, so seamlessly. She never thought she'd sit among a group of strangers and feel like she was home as she talked about art and travel and music and the world.

"I get it." Renee squeezed Diana's arm and they walked further into a dim, stone-walled bar.

"It's something out of the prohibition days," Diana observed.

"Yeah, Roman prohibition." Renee laughed.

It wasn't a large bar by any means. The words 'quaint' and 'out of the way' came to mind. It was big enough for twenty tables of various sizes and a dark wooden bar that sat about ten.

A jazz trio was playing something sultry and sinful on a small stage in the corner of the room, adding to the ageless ambiance of the space.

"Angelina!" Their group had no more touched their feet to the bottom step when a man came rushing toward them. "Angelina mamma mia! Che fai? Sei qui! Davvero?"

"That's Carlo, the owner," Michele whispered over Renee and Diana's shoulders. "Angelina would never admit this, but she helped keep this place afloat. Her mother was a jazz pianist and made it popular after the Second World War and then Angelina acted as beneficiary. Now, there is a sort of cult following that keeps this place in business."

"You've been here before?"

Michele smiled. "I spent some good nights here with Angelina and whatever friends she felt needed some good music and a night out."

The man gently took Angelina by the shoulders and kissed both of her cheeks.

Diana watched Angelina speak animatedly to the man and waved toward the group. He nodded to everyone and was introduced to a few who were standing nearest.

While this meet and greet was happening, a waiter was shooing several patrons away from a large table diagonal from the stage in the opposite corner. He added chairs and even as the owner, Carlo, helped seat the group, the waiter returned with glasses and three bottles of wine.

Michele said something to the waiter and two more chairs were added. "Who's that for?" Renee asked as she sat down.

"My friends Giovanni and Elsbeth were going to try and come by after work," Michele explained.

"Where do they work? It's almost eleven," Renee said.

Michele wiggled her eyebrows. "They work in the sewers of the city." She tried to sound eerily ominous.

"Oh, are those your archeology friends?" Renee said.

Michele nodded.

"You are fascinating," Diana told Michele.

"You can tell a lot about a person by the company they keep." Michele shrugged and then bit her lower lip in concentration. "Who said that?"

"You," Renee replied letting out a hoot of laughter.

Diana thought about her sisters, her niece and nephew. Anthony, and her work colleagues. Good people, but that was all the company Diana kept. If it said anything about Diana, it just reinforced that she truly did give up when David died.

"Sit here." Renee patted the chair that was pulled up to the table nearest her. Diana sat with Renee on her left and one of the open chairs on her right. Angelina sat opposite Diana. The professor of Italian literature, whose name Diana continued to forget, poured a glass of wine for everyone. Once they were all filled, Angelina held her glass gently aloft. "Ai vecchi amici e ai nuovi amici. To old friends and new friends. Cin cin."

Everyone happily chimed in with 'cin cin,' which Diana had found out at dinner was the Italian version of 'cheers.' They laughingly touched their glasses together before taking their first sips.

The wine was wonderful, and Diana had begun to feel as if her bones were less dense; her head was already threatening to detach itself and float away from its new lightness, but her body was now buoyant.

She pulled out her phone and leaned toward Renee. "Smile." Renee cooperated, making a kissy face. After Diana stared at the picture, still unable to believe it was her, she posted the photo and wrote: *Out past midnight on a school night.*

She was about ready to turn her phone off when she saw there was a comment on the previous post. It was Harper.

*Jesus Mary and Joseph and all the saints in heaven!! That's exactly what I'm talking about!!! You. Look. FUCKING AMAZING. A. MAZE. ING!!! Who convinced you to do that? I want to send them a thank you note. I want to send them gift baskets for the rest of the year! That is exactly what you should be doing in Italy! I'm in tears here, you are so beautiful. You've always been beautiful. But now you look like YOU again. Send more pictures. I want a thousand pictures! All the pictures!!*

Diana wiped away a tear as she put her phone away.

"You okay?" Renee asked.
"Yes," Diana replied. And she meant it.

# Chapter Twenty-Two

The added noise of the jazz trio caused the group to converse in pockets with whomever was closest.

Angelina sat back in her chair, a serene look on her face, looking as if she were holding court and this was her preferred room for such a queenly task. She sat forward when someone said something of interest, asked questions and carefully offered her opinion when required.

Diana tried to memorize everything about this night. She wanted to make sure she could recall it with such clarity she'd be able to once again touch it, taste it and smell it. There was still a surrealness to it all, as if she were someone other than herself. Other than the woman she'd been last week. Hell, she felt different than the woman who boarded the train this morning.

*Had it only been this morning?*

She felt the smile rise in her chest again, that same smile had continued to ruffle up and down her spine all night.

Michele and Tasha were talking animatedly with Angelina, Sabrina was talking with the expat and her husband, while Renee spoke with the professor. Diana was happy to study the bar around her as she sipped her wine.

Some patrons were leaning across tables, deep in conversation. Some laughing, some touching, some desperately in love. Some intoxicated by the music and the evening, she thought.

The jazz was sultry. Not the mad, passionate riffing kind. This was jazz used to woo a woman. The few couples on the dance floor pressed their bodies together, slowly moving in each other's arms; exemplifying what the music was for. She watched as Michele's colleague from work and her husband excused themselves to make the most of the music.

"They get it," Diana whispered to herself as the low whine of the trumpet expanded in her chest. The undercurrent of the bass line became her heartbeat. The piano romanced her with the melody of a song she was certain she'd never heard before, yet it felt like a memory from another life. A spell had been cast, she easily gave over and was lost in a dim, jazzy forest.

"Buona sera," a voice greeted. The form of the man appeared before her, she slowly raised her gaze up the length of the sturdy apparition to rest on a face of an olive skinned, handsome man that might have been chiseled by one of the famous Italian sculptors.

"Hi," she sighed. He was just the kind of man a woman should meet when a song like this was playing in a bar like this, when it felt like the world would bend to her very will whenever she wanted.

The creature reached out his hand, so she took the offering and floated out of her chair. Later, she would try to recall this moment and wonder how she stood up; what muscles did she use? How had her body helped her upright? She had a better view of the strapping vision now. The shadow the slight stubble created, his soft smile, thoughtful, light brown eyes that caught the low light, and rumpled short dark hair.

Still holding her hand, he slowly leaned toward her, his face inching closer, his lips slightly parted in an intriguing smile, Diana's breath caught in the back of her throat at the prospect of kissing him and she wondered if she should stop him. But she was in a dream. And this was the kind of man you kissed in dreams.

Yet instead of melting his lips against hers, he pressed a warm kiss against her right cheek. He smelled warm, of breath mints and soft cologne. He repeated the kiss on the opposite cheek, finishing what Diana thought of as the traditional Italian greeting.

When he pulled away, she could still feel the kiss singed against her cheek, still smell his lingering scent. She longed to feel that heat again, but took comfort in the fact that he was still holding her hand. His smile spread, pulling at the corners of his eyes.

"I'm Renee." Renee's voice broke through the fog and her hand extended between Diana and the man, breaking the trance.

So, he wasn't a vision.

The room that had faded into this man, opened back up.

"I'm Giovanni." He smiled.

Diana turned to see Michele making introductions and realized these must be her friends who were arriving late. Still, Giovanni held Diana's hand, and as the earth touched the bottom of her feet and she comprehended what was happening, she let her hand slip away from his. Only then did he turn his attention to Renee, and the enchantment that had been created by his intense brown eyes fell in a fine dust to the ground.

*Good Lord, what was that?*

Diana moved so Giovanni could be introduced to the professor after Renee, but she couldn't stop staring at him.

Giovanni was a head taller than Diana, probably about six three. He wore a blue, slightly loose, long sleeve button-down with the cuffs rolled up a few times, black slacks and the European shoes Diana had spotted in shop windows. She liked them – it was strange, as she'd spied other men wearing the shoes, she thought about how they looked so confident. Anthony would look ridiculous in a pair of shoes like that.

*Anthony.*

The thought of him had a sobering effect. As did the pretty blonde that was introduced to Diana next.

Michele introduced. "Diana, this is Elsbeth."

Elsbeth – petite, pixie cut blonde hair, bright green eyes and a sweet smile that made Diana like her immediately – went in for the same Italian kiss saying, "Diana it's a pleasure. I'm so glad we could make it tonight."

"England?" Diana commented on Elsbeth's accent and felt like an idiot for stating the obvious.

"Born and bred on the Queen's tea," Elsbeth smoothed the moment over, "though I've been in Italy for six years now."

"How wonderful."

"It is, though my Italian is bloody rubbish, but at least I can get by and it doesn't matter anyway. I'm part of an elite boys' club and I'm here to prove a woman is just as good as any of them. So long as my work is brilliant, that's all that matters."

Giovanni, having caught the end of Elsbeth's tirade, nodded. "Hear, Hear!"

Elsbeth rolled her eyes at the comment as the gathering arranged themselves once more around the table with the newcomers. Diana kept her same seat and watched Giovanni pull out one of the empty chairs for Elsbeth; the seat farthest from Diana. Which meant he was about to sit next to her. She chided herself for the adolescent thrill that ran up her spine in reaction.

Once seated, Giovanni turned toward Diana. Her knees weakened with the force of his full attention.

"I'm sorry, we weren't properly introduced," he started. "I was ... distracted." He studied Diana for a moment before he remembered himself. "I'm Giovanni. Giovanni Donato." His name, whispered in a deep baritone, put Diana back in her trance and she swallowed several times before she was able to say, "Diana Barrett."

"Diana." She wondered if her name had ever sounded so good. The left side of his mouth turned up as he commented, "The goddess of the hunt and the moon."

Diana raised an eyebrow at his words.

"Don't mind him," Elsbeth leaned over Giovanni and explained, "it's an occupational hazard. We work in the past and study the past and sometimes," she gazed out of the corner of her eye at him, "it seems as if we live there as well."

"She's right," Giovanni said, "names were such an important part of the antiquities culture, it's difficult to not think of their historical meanings. But Diana really was the goddess of the hunt and the moon."

"Actually ..." she started, then thought better of the comment.

"Actually?" Giovanni encouraged.

Diana took a deep breath and offered, "My middle name is Luna."

He raised an eyebrow and his interest and study of Diana seemed to grow in intensity, causing every atom of her skin to spark.

He was sitting so close she could feel the heat radiate off of him, so she tried to focus on the way his other arm rested comfortably against Elsbeth's. Which wasn't easy as his deep baritone rumbled "la bella Luna," disrupting all sensible thoughts.

Thankfully, it was Renee to the rescue, leaning over Diana. "I could listen to you speak Italian all day."

*All day.* Diana cleared her throat as Giovanni laughed and Elsbeth confirmed, "It *is* dreamy, isn't it?"

"You two make a darling couple." Renee pointed between Giovanni and Elsbeth.

It was good the fact was on the table. This man was doing strange things to her insides, no matter how engaged she was. Again, she silently thanked Renee for her exuberance and tried to focus her attention on Elsbeth; so she was privy to the wink Elsbeth gave Giovanni just before they both laughed.

"What am I missing?" Renee asked.

Giovanni explained, "If you met Elsbeth's husband, you would see that he is better suited for her."

"Oh, I'm sorry. I didn't mean to assume ..." Renee said.

"It happens all the time," Giovanni reassured, "and we did date for at least five minutes at university."

Elsbeth gave an exaggerated shiver of her body. "The first kiss was like kissing a brother. It was ..." she twisted her face with a cringe, "we are better friends." She punched him in the arm. "Besides, God love him, I found someone better."

"Better than him?!" Renee laughed and gave Giovanni the once-over before looking back at Elsbeth. "Is it rude to ask if I can see a picture?"

"Sure!" Elsbeth pulled out her phone.

"Since I'm already making an ass out of myself," Renee continued, "got a girlfriend, Giovanni?"

Once again Diana silently celebrated Renee's youthful willingness to ask the questions she so desperately wanted to ask.

"I'm single," he answered with a smile.

Diana laughed with everyone else and tried to ignore the new electric shocks racing around her nerve endings.

Even though his single status didn't matter to her.

"How old are you?" Renee asked next.

*I love you, Renee.*

"I'm thirty-nine," his grin increased as he teased, "I'm a Capricorn and I like long romantic walks in the Colosseum; but only under the light of the full moon." His voice dipped at the end of his introduction, and when Diana looked at him again, his eyes were intensely watching her. She blinked, feeling pinned to her chair.

"How do you feel about younger women?" Renee asked, the joke in her voice.

*How do you feel about older women?* Diana felt like she was on a roller coaster that just plummeted, so she righted herself as she quickly searched for any topic of conversation other than the moon. Or Giovanni's single status.

"Michele mentioned you were her archeologist friends." Diana nodded, this was good, a good topic. "That sounds intriguing."

Giovanni's eyes lit up at the mention of his job, and she felt a flutter in her stomach at finding a foothold in which to have a conversation with this single, attractive, Italian man.

*Who was six years younger than her.* But just as soon as the thought wafted by, another shot it down. *Who cares?*

"My degree's actually in Classical History, Ancient Romans and Greeks. After I finished my doctorate program, I meant to teach, but then Elsbeth called me and asked if I wanted to come work with her. So for the last five years I've been working for Rome's Archeological Ruin and Excavation Team."

Was it possible that someone could love their job *and* be passionate about it? While she was impressed she also felt suddenly intimidated.

"Mi dispiace," the professor leaned across Renee so he could be heard, "you say archeologia di roma?"

Giovanni nodded his head in reply and the professor leaned over the table to be better heard as he began talking wildly in Italian and Giovanni laughed and replied in kind.

"I don't know what they're talking about, but I could listen to this for the rest of my life," Renee admitted, not worried about who heard her, even though the comment was meant for Diana.

However, it would seem Renee wasn't about to have time to listen as a young man approached their side of the table, asking her to dance.

Renee scooted out of her chair saying to Diana, "I was wondering when he would finally get his courage up."

A pang of jealousy radiated through Diana as she watched Renee bounce away. She missed being that outgoing and open to the possibilities of the world.

"He asked me about a recent dig." Giovanni brought Diana into the conversation as the professor scooted into the spot Renee abandoned. "We found a home from around 600 BCE and it was impressively intact." He shook his head as if he were still trying to believe the find. "It was covered in ash, just like Pompeii. There is some significant detail in the frescos on the walls, still colored a vibrant red. The wooden roof was preserved along with an extraordinary amount of goods within the house; pottery, utensils, a table and chair."

He continued the conversation in Italian.

Diana was grateful to know what they were talking about, but Renee was right, just listening was delightful. It sounded exotic when she first landed in Italy, but it affected her differently now, sitting at a table with a group of people who were no longer strangers, but fast friends made over the simple act of sharing an evening together. Of course, it could also be the wine, deep reds that were smooth as she sipped them; or the music; or her bones, that had eased as she grew comfortable; or the fears and past woes that were washed down the drain in a bathroom at the Yellow Door Hostel. All of it was romance now.

*And the good-looking Italian man who continued to brush your arm with his as he spoke couldn't have anything to do with it, could it Diana?*

"He teaches literature at the University of Rome, La Sapienza," Giovanni said. "The professor is of the mind that if the Roman Empire had not insisted on its people being literate and had instead chosen to rule by illiteracy and barbarism, then the cornerstone of a rich empire would have fallen. And he's also of the mind that such forward thinking in the Empire accounts for the many, many artifacts that remain today."

Diana grinned. "Is he saying without literature you wouldn't have a job?"

Giovanni laughed and translated what she said for the professor. "That is exactly what he's so eloquently trying to say."

Diana nodded. "It's the chicken and egg theory then, isn't it? Which came first?"

Giovanni inclined his head. "Of course, I argue that even without a literate society, they still needed roofs to sleep under and pots to cook in, and men would still have painted pictures of women on vases; so I would still have a job." Giovanni translated his stance.

The professor laughed and responded. Giovani translated, "He said if only velum had the sturdiness of marble."

"Your English is very good," Diana said, then excused herself, "I'm sorry, I'm assuming English isn't your first language and ... I don't mean to interrupt your conversation."

"No, it's not an interruption. My parents are from a small town south of Naples. When I was six we moved to New York. So, between visits to see grandparents and cousins my whole life, I learned both languages. But sometimes I feel like I'm not very good at either one."

There was something about the way he waved off the little bit of history that made Diana suspicious. "You know more than two languages, don't you?"

"None that would do me much good," he offered with a chuckle.

"So more than three?"

He sighed, and even in the dim light she caught his blush as he muttered, "Greek and Latin."

"A true Renaissance man."

He shrugged but was saved by another comment from the professor. Diana caught the word Napoli.

Giovanni gave a groan. "Ah, here we go. He asked if I said I was from Naples." He nodded his head and answered the professor.

Their conversation became a bit more passionate, a bit more animated. Had it not been for the smiles on their faces, Diana thought they might truly be growing angry.

"Our good professor here is from Milan," Giovanni explained, "I am from south of Naples. In Italy, there are certain stereotypes of the different areas where people live. In my case, the southern Italians have a very distinct stereotype."

"Like ...?" Diana asked.

"Southerners are lazy, not interested in doing any real work and are often misconceived as ... obtuse."

"I think I get that. I was born and raised in Connecticut, but when I was ten we moved to Atlanta, Georgia. The accent there is often mistaken for ignorance."

"Exactly, it's similar here. The professor jokingly asked how I managed to get a full day's work done without wasting the resources of our country."

"What did you say?"

"What I normally do, that I lived so long in the United States and England, my lax work ethic was compromised."

Diana laughed.

The professor put his hand on Diana's arm and said, "Mi dispiace," before turning his attention to Angelina who'd asked him a question.

"What does ... mi dispiace mean?" Diana asked, hoping she hadn't butchered the phrase too much.

"I'm sorry, or excuse me." Giovani smiled. "Che vuol dire." He said the words slowly once more (*kay vowl dee-ray*), then nodded for Diana to repeat what he'd said.

After she did, he explained, "That's how you ask what something means. Che vuol dire mi dispiace?" He referred to her previous question, "What does mi dispiace mean?"

She repeated the phrase again and tried to hold back the radiant feeling spreading throughout her whole body. "I shouldn't be so impressed with myself, but I just never thought ..." She let her explanation peter out, not interested in admitting to this highly educated man that she never thought she'd be able to learn something new this late in life.

*The question isn't how old you are, but how old you feel.*

Well, given the new question, as the minutes and hours ticked by, she wasn't feeling all that old.

"What?" Giovanni asked.

Diana shook her head. "You're quite an impressive young man."

"Young man?" He raised an eyebrow.

*God damnit, Diana.*

She swallowed an embarassed lump. She hadn't meant to say anything about age. Six years wasn't anything. But forty-five seemed so far away from thirty-nine and his continued provocative interest in her was releasing a few unrealized insecurities.

Not everything had been washed down the drain with the hair color.

The new Diana that wasn't in the mood for this bullshit stepped in and demanded to turn it around. *Go big or go home.*

"I'm forty-five ..." she forced. "These days everyone feels younger than me."

Giovanni studied Diana for a moment; those eyes, intense and narrowed, made her nervous and seen and scared. He leaned closer to her and she had to dare herself not to pull away.

"Bella Luna …" his voice rasped, and when no more words came, he shook his head and shrugged, reaching out instead to touch a stray strand of her hair. He sat back in his seat and Diana sucked in a deep gulp of air, unaware she'd been holding her breath.

"So, what do you think of Rome?" he asked.

That since she'd been in the city, her whole life had changed. Her look, her *outlook*, her social circle …

"We just arrived today." She decided to start there. "I haven't seen much. After we arrived, we walked to the hostel and … rested." *After the trauma of cutting a hundred inches off my hair and dying it and trying to explain to the pert Renee that my sagging boobs didn't do perky things like hers …*

She ran the thoughts off with a wave of her hand and continued, "I've only been to Pisa, Florence, and Orvieto. So I can speak of those places. But I think, so far … for the very little I've seen and experienced," she justified, "that Italy is extravagant."

He tilted his head. "I don't believe anyone's ever used that adjective to describe my country."

*His* country?

When did a person gain ownership of a country? Was it inherited because of DNA? Was it time spent in a place? For instance, did he refer to New York as his too? Did he claim the US? Or, perhaps an area of study enabled him to claim a country, and such a field as archeology gave him Italy.

So many paths of questioning she wanted to go down, but instead, she tried to focus on explaining her word choice.

"Italy is prolific," she began, "in its art, and houses, and history. *And scenery.*" She shook her head as visions of her trip so far danced before her eyes. "It's not fair that one country should have such an abundant culture. Richness and extravagance kinda oozes into everything here. The food, the color of the fruit in the farmers market. The way store owners wrap purchases. The way the sun shines on the Tuscan countryside. The recreated frescos painted on the pottery in Orvieto." She blushed and waved a hand. "I'm gushing." She had trouble catching her breath, mainly because after the strange attack of the vendors in Florence, she hadn't felt that way about Italy. She'd felt scared and small. But after meeting the girls, after seeing the old part of herself, all the events seemed to have released the beauty of Italy, overshadowing the fear.

"Please, don't stop," he begged softly, but she couldn't go on even if she wanted to, his interruption, fueled with such an impassioned plea, disrupting her train of thought.

"What?" she whispered.

"You were telling me what you thought of Italy." He leaned closer, biting his lower lip between his teeth.

*What was happening?* She resisted the urge to lick her own lips.

"Italy?" he prodded.

"I'm impressed ..." she forced, "by *Italy*. And I truly do find it extravagant. And enchanting. And enthralling ... and a whole bunch of other 'e' words."

"What do you do?" Giovanni whispered the question.

"My job?"

He nodded.

"I'm an accountant."

"No," his face became a shock of confusion, "but you have the soul of a poet."

Diana sat back heavily in her seat.

"Sorry. I didn't mean ... did I say something wrong?" Giovanni asked, reaching out to touch her arm. "I just meant that no one describes my country that way. When I ask them what they think, they say it's wonderful, spectacular, beautiful. But no one has ever explained it the way you have. So accountant or not, you have the soul of a poet," he repeated.

"It's been a rather long, odd day," she admitted. "In another life ..." She thought about not finishing that sentence, but she wanted to say the words aloud. "In another life, I tried ..." She shook her head because that wasn't the truth either. "I was a writer." She hadn't admitted that out loud or even allowed herself to think the sentiment since David.

"Would it be presumptuous of me to ask about that other life?" Giovanni asked.

She nodded her head. "I think it would be." She gathered her courage and continued, "There's magic in the air tonight and if you wouldn't mind, I just want to be Diana from nowhere in particular who has pretty words and wonderful conversations with fascinating people while I drown in it all." It was more of a question than a statement when she finished.

Giovanni stood up and Diana was worried she'd somehow offended him, until he held out his hand to her, his deep voice a questioning insistence, "Dance with me."

She took his hand and followed him to the dance floor, happily swept away in the enchanting current.

# Chapter Twenty-Three

As glasses of wine were slowly enjoyed and new patrons replaced those who left, Giovanni held Diana's hand to his chest, between their bodies, while his other rested possessively on her waist. The dim light and jazz bewitched her, seamlessly submerging her into the unexpected intimacy. When was the last time anyone held her so confidently? She inhaled him and knew, whenever she thought of Italy, she would think of jazz and the best red wine she'd ever had; and how a man she danced with smelled of musky aftershave with a hint of breath mints, wine and possibly the indentation of Roman history. He smelled like the dust of history.

He'd appreciate the sentiment if he knew what she was thinking, but this was a sense memory she was creating all for herself, so she leaned her head against his shoulder, drinking in another deep inhale.

After a while he whispered in her ear, "What do you want to see the most in Rome?"

She smiled as the question brought the memory of how he'd introduced himself, so she laughingly said, "The Colosseum. In the moonlight."

He stopped moving, pulled away slightly, and looked down into her eyes. After a moment, he glanced around the room, and as if making a decision, led her back to the table, touching Renee and the young man she was dancing with on the shoulder, gesturing for them to follow.

When he got to the table, he leaned into the center so everyone could hear him and asked, "Who wants to go to the Colosseum?"

"What?" Diana asked as he repeated the question in Italian.

"When? Now?" Renee asked excitedly.

He nodded with a grin and sent Elsbeth a questioning look.

"Taxi?" she suggested, probably reading his mind, holding the question: What's the best way to transport this crew to the historical monument?

"Just to see the outside, or are you really getting us inside?" Michele asked.

"Let's go inside." Giovanni's face brightened with the announcement, Diana was secretly wishing that was what he meant. There was a long pause after his announcement, and then a giggle from Renee launched the group into action.

Angelina waved over the owner and explained what was happening as wallets were drawn to pay equal portions of the evening's tab. But Angelina waved everyone away; she'd taken care of it earlier.

The cool night air was a welcome reprieve from the warmth generated by the club, but the energy of the evening hadn't been lost with the change in atmosphere. Giddily, the group followed instructions to the nearest taxi stand where several white cars were awaiting late night bar patrons. Without breaking the connection that had been created between them, Giovanni took Diana's hand while they walked, like they'd been holding hands for years.

The group separated into various fractions, four in one car, three in another. When one driver only had room for two, Renee insisted Diana and Giovanni take it. "You need to get there first, this was your idea."

Giovanni held the door for Diana, then rounded the car to the other side. When he got in he was on his phone; happily talking, giving Diana time to continue her curious study of him. There was more light from the street and the neon dash of the car, so she could make out the faint outline of a sunglass tan; and on his right temple, just next to his eye, was a scar from a poorly stitched wound.

His brief conversation ended with him repeating "grazie, grazie mille."

"Is this ..." Diana checked the time displayed on the driver's dash: two-thirty in the morning.

"What?" he asked.

"Are we really doing this?"

"You said you wanted to see the Colosseum in the moonlight. So I'm going to abuse my powers to impress a woman," he admitted.

"Your powers?" Diana's voice wasn't even her own, it was such a breathy thing.

"A few times a year, I work with archeological students who come to study in Rome. And recently, quite fortuitously, I've been working with them at the Colosseum."

"Oh."

He tilted his head a bit and shyly asked, "So does this impress you?"

"We'll see," she flirted.

He took a deep breath, those eyes bearing down on her, trying to see into the depths of her soul, and when he couldn't seem to find what he wanted, he pulled her hand to his lips to brush a kiss across her knuckles. The gesture unleashed an army of shivers and yearnings.

"I don't know what it is about you."

"I just got a new haircut," she said in an almost inaudible whisper.

"That must be it." He smiled and Diana wanted to tell him how much she liked his smile, the way it wrinkled the corners of his eyes and how the left side of his lips rose slightly higher than the right.

His fingers were slowly, gently twisting and twirling around her own. Or were those her fingers examining his, trying to read and memorize him by touching the one area that seemed safe for strangers to explore in the twilight of an evening. She imagined this was what Shakespeare had been trying to convey when he had two characters pressing their palms together, fingers entwining; searching and studying.

"What are you thinking about?" he asked.

Diana's smile widened and she warned, "Be careful or I'll tell you."

The driver interrupted them as they arrived at their destination.

"That was quick," she sighed.

"We were fairly close."

The Colosseum was emblazoned against the dark night sky drawing the group to her gates.

"Dear God," Diana whispered as she craned her neck to take in the spectacular site glowing sandstone beige and heady earthen tones; radiating pockets of that Italian lighting while the stars winked in the background and the moon, still a few days away from being full, drenched the scene in an ethereal glow.

Giovanni called everyone to follow him and Elsbeth, just as a security guard came meandering toward them. The three greeted each other and Diana thought maybe Giovanni was overexplaining their credentials and giving their life stories. Either way, the guard turned to the group and offered a "benvenuti a tutti," then opened the gate they'd gathered around. He waited until everyone was in, then proceeded to open another gate set into the first arch of the Colosseum. To the right, sets of ropes to keep lines of tourists organized had been gathered to sag against each other now that they were off duty. An agonized squeal, and the final barrier between them and the majestic site was opened.

A few words were exchanged among Giovanni, Elsbeth and the security guard, then after thankful handshakes, the guard waved the rest of the group inside before locking the gate behind them.

"This way." Elsbeth smiled, standing to the side of a large entrance and pointing in the direction they were to go.

Renee took the hand of the young man she might have abducted, and skipped happily forward. Michele followed, arm in arm with Angelina; while Tasha and Sabrina mixed with the rest of the group, talking in excited, hushed tones.

Giovanni led Diana up a wide walkway, dark at first, but the moonlight beyond beckoned them forward. She lost all ability to comprehend or react as her feet floated her onto the recreated arena floor of the Roman Colosseum that now rose up around her, echoing and humming with a lifetime of cheers and defeats; weathered by political regimes, world wars, art movements and philosophies.

Renee's laughter radiated off the deteriorating rocks as she did a twirl then danced over to Diana, hugging her and Giovanni from behind. "I *told* you we find ourselves in the coolest situations! Bucket list stuff, I'm telling you." She danced away, back to her young man.

Diana suddenly had something worthy of a bucket list. *The Roman Colosseum in the moonlight: Check.*

"Okay Mr. Tour Guide, you got us into this mess. Tell us something," Michele called out.

Everyone gathered around the railing at the edge of the recreated floor, where below them the moon shone on the dark gray ruins of a maze.

The smile could be heard in Giovanni's voice as he began, "The

Roman Colosseum is over two thousand years old and It's one of the few intact structures from the peak of the Roman Empire. While we know that this amphitheater saw some ruthless games, it also stands as a symbol of Rome's genius and power."

"Now who's the poet?" Diana whispered softly.

He squeezed her hand in reply. "We're standing on a re-creation of what would have been the original main level. The arena floor." He pointed in front of them. "Below us are the underground passages where the gladiators, wild animals, criminals and enslaved people were kept. The behind-the-scenes arena, so to speak." He repeated the information in Italian.

"What's the most important thing to know about the Colosseum?" Elsbeth asked. When Giovanni sighed, Diana thought maybe the question was more baiting than anything else.

"Well," Giovanni started, "I could explain the respect of all things Greek that can be found in the design of this place. I could talk about the marble and stone used to create it. I could talk about how the Romans built on a larger scale than the Greeks ever did and I can spout the number of spectators the seats held, the number of lives lost, or the date of the last games played here." He was thankful that Angelina had taken up the translation, and took a deep breath so he could continue. "But I think, when you're here, while *we're* here; without tourists or the heat of the day, maybe it's important to just appreciate the stories of so many men and women whispered around us; and maybe think about the fact that this structure was referred to as Colossal for a reason." He paused and after a moment added, "The ancient Romans could be brutal and hard, but they also pushed for modernization and valued intellect. This land we're standing on was the heart of a once great civilization and a lot of their innovations are still with us to this very day."

The group kept a respectable silence as they washed themselves in moonlight and history. Diana was, completely and utterly afloat on the sea of enchantment created by it all.

After a few moments, the professor interrupted the quiet with a question. Other's added their own curiosities. Elsbeth answered some, Giovanni others. Then the group merged and parted, walking different areas closest to them, no one wanting to be troublesome and going too far afield, all aware of the gift this tour was. Angelina sat on stone benches on the outer edge and Diana leaned her elbows on the metal railing, trying to grasp the levity of the moment and memorize each element.

Giovanni copied her pose and elbowed her gently. "Now are you impressed?"

She glanced at him out of the corner of her eye. "It's pretty good."

He nodded. "I think so too."

Diana was sure there was no way Italy could ever outdo this evening.

# Chapter Twenty-Four

*How was a person supposed to sleep after such a night?*

A night Diana wasn't completely sure had actually occurred.

She looked up from her notebook and out the window where she could just make out a sliver of the Pantheon.

*The Pantheon!*

The morning sun was yawning, peeking several rays of light, dusty from her long night's slumber, down upon the Pantheon, bathing the ancient building's domed roof. The worn brick backside of the structure took on a faded peachy hue; a color Diana thought she might paint a kitchen if she lived in Rome.

Pantheon peach. That would be something. Or maybe the color would be called Pantheon sunrise.

Streaks of sun across the front of the columns, which stood at perfect attention in soldier-like rows, bloomed with the dawn of a new day. Their color: a romantic, historical gray. Another accent color she could use in her Roman apartment, historic gray.

Imagine if such colors existed.

*Imagine ...*

When was the last time she sat daydreaming in the early morning light? When was the last time she wondered about the existence of such colors?

As she let her eyes unfocus, particles of dust swirled in the morning light, a representation of the whispers from a million people whose dreams and fears had come before her. All mingling together now for the rest of their days.

Diana wiped a tear from her eye and swallowed the thoughts that tightened her throat. She was riding the residue of emotions from the previous evening and loving every inhalation and exhale.

It was 5 a.m. when the group regretfully parted ways. Giovanni kissed Diana on the cheek, his lips lingering as he held her hands in his.

"I've enjoyed meeting you," he whispered.

"Thank you for the Colosseum." She wanted to say more, to continue the evening, but how? She'd asked for magic, she'd asked to be left adrift in the current of it and he'd honored her wish.

He slipped his hands down her arms, to the tips of her fingers, holding on until the very last second before they fell to their respective sides.

"Buonanotte, bella Luna."

"Good night ..." She sighed as Renee linked her arm in hers, pulling her away.

The girls tiredly began the journey back to the hostel. Only, Diana wasn't certain they were actually walking, she felt like a petal dancing on the wind.

"So Renee," Tasha asked with a yawn, "who was the cutie?" Since she'd sat farthest away from Renee all night, she hadn't caught the whole story.

"Paulo. I think." Renee swayed as she walked. "Or maybe it was Raul."

"Seeing him again?" Sabrina asked.

"Of course not." Renee smiled tiredly and said to Diana, "I'm playing the field on this trip, but I'm not interested in one-night stands or relationships."

"What does that leave?" Tasha asked.

"Sweaty groping on a dance floor." She sighed and began to hum.

"Giovanni is nice," Sabrina said in a sing-song voice, giving Diana a playful nudge.

"Giovanni is *hot*," Renee amended. "And he wants Diana bad."

"Couldn't tear himself away," Tasha added.

Diana waved her hand at the idea.

"He really is a nice guy," Michele chimed in. "Want his number?"

*Yes*, she thought, but said, "I'm engaged."

Renee shrugged. "Engaged isn't married."

Yeah well, engaged is almost to a place where security lives. The old humdrum views of American Diana interrupted. Italian Diana swatted the thoughts away.

*Italian Diana?*

Yes, Italian Diana, who could be attractive and interesting to the Giovannis of Rome. And Italian Diana would bask in such things. She'd take the magic of Rome, the magic of new friends, and the magic of a night that was still afoot.

Back in their room, the girls gave exaggerated yawns and information as to how long they wanted to sleep then flopped down on their beds.

Sleep was the last thing Diana wanted. She wanted to continue floating, buoyant in the remaining magic of the evening.

"I can't sleep," she whispered. "I think I'm going to go get coffee and write." Goosebumps formed at the declaration.

*Get coffee and write.*

Her legs wobbled, so she sat down on the edge of her bed for a moment, bracing herself with her arms. She bunched the comforter beneath her hands, to make sure it was real, all of it. This trip, these minuscule changes that had come upon her, this evening, she needed to touch it somehow, make it all tangible. Because the culmination of it all seemed to be the urge to have coffee and write. It had been a lifetime since such a thought brought her this much joy.

Renee pushed herself out of her bed, shuffled over to Diana's suitcase, pulled out a pair of jeans and tossed them at Diana. "Keep the shoes, change the pants, roll the hem twice." Then she went to Tasha's suitcase and began rummaging through it.

"What do you want?" Tasha sat up and slapped Renee out of the way.

"Pink sweater," she said,

Tasha found the sweater and handed it over.

Renee took it to Diana who was just zipping up the jeans and instructed, "Leave the shirt." Though she unknotted the bottom of it and did a French tuck into the jeans now. "Wear this sweater. Put on my dangling pearl earrings, they're in the bathroom." She looked at Diana's face. "Makeup is holding strong and your hair looks fantastic." Renee nodded and returned to her bed, throwing herself down. "Have fun," she muttered from her pillow.

Diana went to the restroom and jumped at her reflection. It was still shocking to see the girl who'd become a stranger over the past few years. She wondered if she would ever get used to it. She stepped closer to the mirror and studied herself. That girl was older now, the signs were there; some spider veins on her legs, the wrinkled creases in the corner of her eyes. Her stomach had the slight pouch that came with age and no kids. Her muscles were softer and her eyesight wasn't what it used to be. Her back ached when she woke up in the morning and she'd begun to take multivitamins and eat healthier because her doctor had suggested a heart healthy diet. But even with all those changes in her physical body, she was overwhelmed to find that the soul of that girl was still intact. After all these years ...

She smiled at herself in the mirror, at all of herself.

Teeth brushed, she reapplied deodorant and perfume then tiptoed back into the room. The girls had all donned some sort of sleeping attire and were already breathing heavily. She slipped the leather notebook she'd purchased in Florence into her purse, stepped out of the room, down the hallway and back into the early morning.

She pulled out her phone and typed in the name of the café Giovanni said she should try if she had time. Doing so felt akin to stalking a schoolgirl crush; but who cared. She was going to the place he recommended not in the hopes that she would see him again – he'd said he was headed home to sleep – but to merely *be* in a place he liked.

It was a safe daydream.

She followed the suggested route, rounded a corner, and coming face to face with the Pantheon, shuffled to a stop so she could soak up the whole effect the structure was having. It hummed with energy, or maybe that was her. She walked over and touched one of the pillar's cold marble to see if the vibrations of history could be felt.

"Possibilities abound," she whispered, then gave a laugh. "Jesus Diana, you're drunk."

And she was; she was drunk on Rome.

Standing on the steps of the Pantheon she was aware of the way the blood flowed through her veins, the way the gray dawn sky kissed the surrounding buildings, and she decided it was a glorious thing to be drunk on Rome. She closed her eyes and with her hands still on the night cooled marble, realized it was indeed humming.

Her destination, Caffè Vita Nuova was just a few feet away from the Pantheon and they'd just opened; so other than herself, there was only one other patron and the staff this early.

Espresso at her elbow, partial view of the glorious Pantheon before her, she opened the notebook. The spine creaked its newness and the smell of the blank page filled the air. She remembered this too, this girl who'd filled so many notebooks.

She wrote about the night, how the conversation had moved fluidly from art to theology. From politics to romance. From history to favorite films. Italian was the first spoken language, but between the English speakers, things were translated seamlessly for those who needed it.

She became flushed when she shared her views on art and how to interpret it. They were thoughts she hadn't spoken out loud since David.

*David.*

She wrote his name and it felt so good, she did it again and again.

*David.*

And that was how he slipped back into her life so effortlessly. Through one of the many cracks that had developed in the past few days. The wall she had so carefully constructed all those years ago was ash crumbling, the final bit of dust blowing away with her breath when she spoke of art forms and theories she and David had spent so many long evenings debating in their youth.

And she found, as she laughed with the group, she didn't desperately miss him. She was celebrating him. She didn't mention him; she didn't need to. She felt the way she had when David was alive and they would spend long nights sipping crappy cups of Folgers at some dive bar, debating artistic interpretation and life and love and all its phases.

*David.* She wrote it again.

What she thought would hurt to remember became a strange joyous memorial.

A tear fell, not from heartache, but delight.

She turned the page; a new, clean lined sheet smiling brightly up at her. She touched the page and wondered if her imagination still held any stories.

Diana glanced around the café and thought of Giovanni. She thought about him sitting at any one of the tables or standing at the bar. She looked out the window and imagined the generations of men and women, Romans and tourists, who had come before her. She thought of the thousands of people who had imprinted their stories on the very table she was sitting.

And like she was strengthening a muscle that had been hidden in a cast, she began the therapy of writing once more.

And the world disappeared as a new one opened up in the form of sentences and paragraphs and full pages, dripping with words.

# Chapter Twenty-Five

Diana shook her right hand, wiggled and stretched the cramp out of it. She'd written twenty-some odd pages and found a story. Nothing spectacular, but she'd *found* a story. She went back to work; her mind buzzing with the words, ink flowing, her shoulders hunched over the notebook as she lost herself in lined pages. The noise that surrounded her became a symphony to work by. She smiled as she wrote, then a laugh moved her and she looked up, across the table, so she could tell David.

How many times had she been lost in the words, only to look up so she could share something with him? The empty seat was a shock, but not painful. She didn't lose her smile, just turned the page and wrote: *"David, I'm sorry. I thought forgetting you, and us, and me, was the best way to deal with everything."*

Her pen hovered over the paper because she wanted to write that she was back now. That she would never forget again.

She looked at the seat across from her, as if he were there with her. *Did you see what I did? What I'm doing?* She directed the silent words at the chair, like David's ghost would materialize any moment and answer back.

But as she thought about David her thoughts turned to Anthony. David would hate him. He would hate that she decided to settle for Anthony.

*Settle?*

But David would hate Anthony for a twenty-four-year-old girl. He wouldn't understand the security and companionship the forty-five-year-old woman needed.

*I was scared and I hid,* she thought, in answer to the imaginary question.

'*And are you still hiding?*' David would have asked. '*Because Anthony is a safe bet. And that safe bet looks like hiding.*'

"What do you want me to do?" she whispered.

Then, even though she was arguing with her dead husband in her mind, she smiled because it was absolutely delightful to have him back.

What inadvertent issues had she caused by insisting no one ever speak his name so that she could get over his death? They say you die twice, once when a body is buried, and the second death comes the last time someone utters your name. So had she killed David twice?

It didn't matter. It was time for his resurrection. Along with her own.

"You would have loved it here," she said quietly as she glanced out the window.

'*We would have slept on the streets, there's too much to sketch and paint. Too much to see,*' he would say.

She grinned at the empty chair and suddenly found the end of the short story she'd been writing.

Diana picked up her pen and disappeared again; drowned in the motion of looping words and enveloped by notebook paper as the story continued to feed her.

"Buongiorno." A deep voice penetrated her writing. Diana raised a dreamy smile in its direction.

"Giovanni," she whispered, "I was just writing about you."

He raised an eyebrow, and a smile pulled at the corner of his mouth.

She looked around as the café came back into focus, gazed out the window at the Pantheon for the hundredth time and wondered how long a person would need to stare at the structure, take pictures of it, sit across from it, ponder its beauty, until it was no longer sigh-worthy.

"Bella Luna?" The endearment caught Diana's attention, and she absently searched for the sound as Giovanni came into focus.

"Giovanni?" she asked, surprised. Was he really here? She thought it had been part of her daydream.

"Buongiorno, bella Luna," he repeated softly.

She ran through a succession of nervous ticks to dislodge the dream state and find reality. Had she somehow summoned him?

"Are you okay?" he asked.

"Yeah. Yes, I'm fine." She cleared her throat as the excitement of seeing him mingled with embarrassment of being caught in the place he'd suggested. "I couldn't sleep, so I decided I'd try the café you recommended." She internally cringed, hoping the admission sounded nonchalant and not as adolescent as her ears insisted.

"Would you mind if I joined you?" He pointed to her open notebook. "If you're busy, I understand."

"Oh, no. Please." She set the notebook to the side and gestured to the empty seat.

"I am waiting for my cappuccino, would you like anything?"

Diana glanced at the half drunk espresso. "I let mine get cold." She stood abruptly, and swayed. Giovanni was quick to steady her with his hand around her waist, and she grabbed for his forearm for balance.

"I'm not still drunk." Another cringe.

"I didn't think you were."

She wanted to explain that she actually was drunk, but it wasn't alcohol-induced; she was drunk on Rome, and the previous evening, and writing. Hell, just his touch caused her blood to pump at unsteady intervals. She was very aware of the heat radiating from his hand into her waist, and her fingers swelled from the heat off his forearm; maybe she was drunk on him too.

Their eyes locked and Diana stifled a strange giggle, clearing her throat to break the momentary spell brought on by his touch. "Maybe something to eat," she tried to gracefully slip out of his hold, "and another coffee. I think I'd like a cappuccino."

At the bar, Giovanni caught the attention of the barista and after a long-winded order, of which the only word Diana caught was *cappuccino*, the barista turned back to the espresso machine.

"I paid first last time." She fumbled for small talk.

"We'll pay before we leave, but please, I suggested this café and now that you're here, it's my treat."

Diana thought about arguing, but whispers of the women she'd just met overrode her instincts. This was bucket list stuff, and when bucket list stuff presented itself, you lean in.

*Handsome Italian man buys you coffee in a café near the Pantheon in Rome: Check.*

However, even bucket list stuff could be unnerving. Too much time had passed since she'd been this close to Giovanni, so she was grateful for the practiced movements of the barista; his casual speed, the music of saucers and spoons being set together on the bar, the hiss of steaming milk and the final twirl of the cup as he placed it onto the saucer.

Diana nodded her thanks and started back to the table with her drink, but Giovanni lingered. She turned in question and was given a moment to study him. He wore a new shirt, a soft sage green, short sleeve button-down that looked a little large on him, with khaki pants and brown shoes. A slight hint of bicep muscle was visible now, showing off his athletic build. The green accentuated his Italian skin and the angle of his jawline was more pronounced this morning.

The barista placed a plate with three delectable pastries on the counter, all elegant in their sugary glazes that played in the overhead lights. Giovanni retrieved the pastries and his cup. Back at the table, they quietly filled the awkward silence by arranging themselves, their napkins and cappuccinos – neither making eye contact.

It was the awkwardness of the light of day Diana missed. There had been a power in the dim light from the bar and the darkness of the night. *She* had felt powerful in the moonlight. Powerful enough to flirt and hold hands with this man.

Small little facts emerged as the light of day shone on the edges of reality. For instance, she was engaged.

*Engaged isn't married.* Renee's words screamed between her ears.

"You make me nervous." Giovanni rushed the statement, drawing Diana out of her internal thoughts. Perplexed, she scrunched her face as she blew out a snort of a laugh. "I make *you* nervous?"

His blush created uneven red blotchiness that ran up his neck. "Last night, I was just going to meet an old friend, have a glass of wine at the end of a long day of work and catch up. I never expected to be swept up so immediately by someone so captivating."

An excited rumble of butterflies erupted against her chest. She opened her mouth to retort that she wasn't captivating, or that *he* was the fascinating one, but instead admitted, "Well, if it's any consolation, *you* make me nervous." She picked up her cup, but before she took a sip added, "It was much easier in the dark, huh?"

"God, yes." He laughed and the unease slipped away. "I also look better in the dark."

"You look good anywhere." The words were out before she could even try to reel them back in. Diana's eyes widened at the honesty, his became bright. She cleared her throat and gestured out the window behind him. "It's an amazing view. I'm glad you suggested it."

"I thought you'd like it," he said softly before nodding toward her notebook. "I thought the poet in you would like it," he amended.

She lightly ran her fingers over the leather fleur de lis, unwilling to take it off the table. At the moment it was a lifeline to a previous life and to the ghost of something that was tempting her to return to her once upon a time. And she wasn't in the mood to hide it or hide from it.

The symbolism of it warmed her as she tapped the notebook. "You call me a poet and I want to deny it, but this morning ... I actually wrote a short story," she whispered.

"How do you feel about it?"

Diana breathed out a soft laugh. "You know, in less than twenty-four hours I have been asked questions that have me reevaluating my life."

"Is that a good thing or a bad thing?"

"I'm pretty sure it's a good thing, but it's unnerving. It was Michele who told me I was asking the wrong question yesterday while we were talking." *Was that only yesterday?* She'd lived a lifetime since then. "And the whole idea has been like an aspirin that gets caught in your throat, you know? No matter how much water you drink to try and wash it down, you can't dislodge it."

"What was the wrong question?"

"Yesterday, Renee asked me how old I was ..." she took a deep breath, shaky with the morning's honesty, "but before I could answer, Michele said that was the wrong question. The question should have been 'how old do I *feel*?'"

"Yeah, that sounds like Michele."

"How do you know her? I never did ask last night."

"It wasn't a story I had time to tell, I was a bit preoccupied last night ..." He tilted his head and took such a long pause Diana didn't think he'd continue. "The most enchanting woman caught my attention and the more I got to know her, the less aware I was of everyone else."

She picked up her cup, an attempt to put something substantial between them, because this felt like the kind of moment where he'd reach across the table to take her hand in his and caress it. Or place a chaste kiss on her knuckles, or give her a hooded gaze and lick his lips and make her insides get mushy and confused.

While she tried to relish the thrill of being attractive, the woman, whose sister had already planned her wedding, tried to be a screaming voice of reason. So before the internal struggle truly got underway, and since she was being so honest in this daylight, Diana said, "I'm engaged."

Giovanni shrugged. "You can be engaged, it doesn't change the fact that I'm attracted to you."

Maybe she should put a damper on all the honesty.

He continued, "And I think it wouldn't be too much of a stretch of the imagination to think, fiancé or not, *you* are attracted to me."

*Definitely putting a stop to the honesty.*

He continued, "And while you make me nervous, I think that attraction makes you nervous too."

God, was she that transparent, and what was going on with her? She needed to interrupt him, stop all this talk of attraction and–

"But Luna, your engagement and my nervousness doesn't mean I'm not intrigued and excited to see where this goes." He gestured between them.

Diana sat back against her chair, really not wanting to interrupt someone who called her intriguing. But even as the compliment continued to tingle through her veins, she allowed propriety to whisper, "I should probably go."

"Spend the day with me." Giovanni leaned across the table.

"Aren't you tired?" Diana whispered.

"Aren't *you* tired?" he pointed.

She couldn't hold back a grin as she gave another honest answer, "I am exhausted, but I don't think I could sleep if I tried."

"Bella Luna," his voice was a dark temptation, "spend the day with me."

"You can't call me that …" of course, all she really wanted was to listen to him call her 'bella Luna' until she lost her hearing, "and I can't."

"Do you *want* to?" His eyes twinkled. "Isn't that the real question?

Not if you can, but if you want to."

*Damnit.*

"Please," he gestured between them, "whatever it is between us, let's walk it around the city. Let me show you Rome. One day. Spend one day with me and then I'll let you go back to your trip and your fiancé."

The idea had merit.

Good *Lord*, did the idea have merit.

"If I say yes, it's only because I really do want to see Rome. And I'm tired. But I'm too excited to sleep. And it would just be as friends. Because I don't know the language or the city." She tried to write several clauses into his offer.

"If?" He looked so hopeful.

"And just so we're clear, everything you think you're feeling, or I'm feeling ... it's not real." *It couldn't be, could it?* "It's just a haircut." Wasn't that the true crux of this? It all started with a haircut.

No. It all started with accepting to meet a man for a date a year ago.

Softly, David chose that moment to lean into her side and whisper, '*Someone like him. I'd choose someone alive with life and intelligence and passion.*'

She waved a hand next to her ear and wondered if she should have brought David out of the forgotten box she'd placed him in; especially if he was going to surprise her and show up with his opinion.

'*But it was my opinionated ways that made you a better person, baby. You questioned every one of my opinions and fought to change my mind, and when you did that, you figured out your own shit.*' Diana brushed the hair behind her ear, which was more of a gesture to shoo David away.

He laughed. '*Go with this guy, Lu.*'

"So how did you meet Michele?" She rushed the question a bit too loudly; an attempt to stall and stop David.

Giovanni let the question sit between them for a few seconds before he sat back and began his story, "Michele's boyfriend, when she lived here, was friends with Elsbeth's husband. The five of us hung out from time to time. Eventually, Michele and Elsbeth tried to fix me up with very nice women so I wouldn't be a fifth wheel; even though I always told them I didn't mind it. When Michele left, we kept in touch."

"I think Michele is single now," Diana suggested.

"She is, but she's like a younger sister to me."

"She's wise."

"She is," he agreed.

Diana shook her head in wonder. "I mean, those women, all four of them, are wise beyond their years." And Diana was jealous of them.

She was jealous of their age and their friendship and their sense of adventure. She was jealous that they didn't seem to have let life knock them down. And if they had, she was jealous because it was evident, they'd decided to get back up.

"Do you want to know what kind of woman *is* my type?" He drew her out of her reprieve.

*'It's like he's using every line in the book, but they don't sound cheesy. Hell, I'll go with this guy if you don't.'* David laughed aloud.

"I'm older than you—"

"I've heard this argument before."

She was trying to deflate the situation, deflate Giovanni. Maybe deflate David.

*'But why deflate him? Ride this wave, babe. Do you feel that?'* David got closer to her ear. *'That's life pulling you back into her arms.'*

"Why don't you have a girlfriend, or a wife?"

Giovanni sat back. "I had a wife. I got hurt. I made my life my job for a while, then when I decided to start dating again, I couldn't seem to find anyone that caught my attention. Until last night."

"You can't be excited by someone after one night," she pointed.

*'Yes, you can, Lu. You know that better than anyone.'*

She waved the topic away with both hands and a shake of her head. "Maybe this isn't the kind of thing we should be talking about. This conversation is getting all twisted."

"Poetic women," Giovanni replied. "Just in case you were wondering what my type was. Women who know who they are, who are strong, have an opinion and aren't afraid to share it. With dark hair and an infectious smile. That's my type."

*'C'mon Lu,'* David drew out the words and held his hands out in front of him, *'give this guy a chance.'*

"Okay," Diana said a little too forcefully, "I'll go."

Giovanni's grin widened; to stop it, Diana pointed a finger at him.

"But I'm only going because I want to see Rome."

"I don't care what the reason is, I'm just thrilled you're taking me up on my offer."

She rolled her eyes.

"I was in the Boy Scouts, so I give you my word." He held up the three-finger Scout salute.

Diana laughed. "Exactly what are you giving me your word on?"

"That I'll do everything in my power to seduce you." He winked.

*Oh shit*, Diana thought as David's laugh reverberated around her. '*I really* like this guy.'

# Chapter Twenty-Six

"I have an idea where we should go first." That was the only hint Giovanni gave as they climbed into the back of a taxi and drove away from the city.

"Should I be worried?" she asked as the miles from Caffè Vita Nuova grew.

"You don't trust me?" Giovanni mocked his pain.

*'I trust him,'* David said.

Diana gently shook David's comment out of her hair. "I don't *know* you," she replied.

Giovanni aimed a meaningful smirk at her. "Yes you do."

She turned her attention out the window and tried to focus on the buildings to calm the shiver that ran through her body.

Eventually, buildings and shops distanced themselves and the tree-lined street led through the arch of an imposing wall.

"What is that?" Diana asked.

"The walls of Rome," Giovanni informed her. "The Aurelian Walls, built during the reign of the Emperor Aurelian. He walled in the seven hills of Rome to keep barbarian invaders out."

"Do you just have information like that running around in your head at all times?"

"It's my job." He shrugged.

"And you love it," she supplied.

"I really do."

Outside the walls, four lanes became a winding two-lane road with cypress trees on either side.

After a wide turn, the driver pulled through a small open gate, into a parking lot with two tour buses. As Giovanni leaned forward to speak with the driver, Diana climbed out, a defense against listening to his deep voice utter the language she was finding so romantic in her current state.

But she only felt that way because she was running on adrenaline and caffeine. "Exactly." She nodded with her reasoning. All further emotions were going to be blamed on either of those.

As they walked toward an elaborate villa complex rising up behind a wall of tall hedges, the back of Giovanni's hand grazed the back of hers, to perhaps get a reading on how she would take the action. When she didn't pull away, that was all the encouragement he needed to intertwine his fingers with her. And while muted questions of right and wrong floated past, she took the intimacy for what it was, a tangible lifeline to the previous evening and the conversations and feelings she wanted to hold onto.

Besides, she was sure at some point, when this was all over, she'd find that this man was a dream. A harmless flirtation she'd concocted. Hell, maybe she was losing her mind; she'd already unearthed David, so why not a man who was the embodiment of Italy? She was being seduced by Rome as it was, why not go all the way? Let herself be persuaded to drown in the opulent history of Rome and a man who swore to seduce her.

*'How old do you feel now, Lu?'* David hovered on her other side. *'He looks good on you. Though, I'm not sure about the shoes. What is it with European men and their shoes?'*

Diana raised an eyebrow in his direction; was he really going to talk about another man's wardrobe? Wasn't he the one who couldn't paint unless he had on his lucky Converse, and those stupid black jeans that didn't really fit because they were from his high school years, along with the coin his father gave him tucked in his left pocket?

David fished out said coin and flipped it in the air.

"Over there." Giovanni interrupted her phantom conversation, pointing out a souvenir cart where the hedges met an open gate.

An older man, perched on a stool reading a paper, glanced over the top when the crunching of their footsteps in the dirt alerted him of their arrival.

He squinted as they got closer, but when Giovanni called out a greeting, "Ciao, Signore Lazzarotti," recognition dawned. He tossed his paper on the cart that held various trinkets and souvenirs depicting Rome, then crossed the distance between them as he called out, "Signore Donato!"

Signore Lazzarotti was short with a full head of salt and pepper hair peeking out from a worn black beret, and his eyes, surrounded by sagging wrinkled skin, were bright as he pulled Giovanni in for a hug. Giovanni bent to return the action, but stayed in that position after the hug so the old man could study his eyes. Satisfied with whatever he'd been looking for, he patted the side of Giovanni's cheek with an arthritic hand and launched into a one-sided conversation, gesturing wildly as he spoke, laughing and slapping Giovanni's arm every now and then.

The guidebook Diana had been reading said you could get a lot of cues as to what the locals were talking about by the way they gesture. However, she wasn't sure the author had ever met Signore Lazzarotti.

As he spoke, he gestured toward the sky, to his cart, to her, to the parking area ... there was such a confusing madness to his sweeping hands that she didn't have the slightest clue as to what he might be saying. But she couldn't stop smiling, because the enthusiasm and grin painted on his face during the interaction was contagious.

"Diana," Giovanni rushed her name when the man took a breath, "this is Signore Lazzarotti. He is the gatekeeper of my life."

Diana held out her hand in greeting but the man took her by the elbows and planted an enthusiastic kiss that smelled of cigarette smoke, on both cheeks. She tried to pull away after, but the gentleman held her at arm's length, studying her. "La tua sposata?"

Giovanni cleared his throat. "No."

"Not yet," the man said in a gritty accented English, and winked at Diana.

"What?" Diana asked with a smile.

"You, Giovanni," he gestured, "good marriage."

Diana shook her head. "Oh, no. No. I'm engaged." The pang of guilt was momentary as the signore pulled her in for another round of cheek kissing. "See, subito, good marriage."

He released her and turned his attention to a drawer in his stand. Diana glanced at Giovanni with wide eyes, a silent question to translate.

But Signore Lazzarotti was already talking a blue streak again as he searched. "Eccolo!" he called producing a pouch. He opened it and handed Giovanni a small, but powerful looking flashlight and a key.

"Grazie." Giovanni pocketed the items just in time for the old man to take one of his hands and one of Diana's; glancing between the two he nodded and said, "Non dimenticare di invitarmi al matrimonio."

Diana looked to Giovanni for a translation. "He asked that we don't forget to invite him to our wedding." Giovanni nodded to him and answered, "Certo."

"What did you say?" Diana asked.

"I told him, of course."

The old man raised his finger as if he'd forgotten something very important, took a miniature reproduction of the Colosseum and placed the sand colored statue into the palm of her hand. "Now, always you remember Signore Lazzarotti."

"It's wonderful," she whispered, then pulled the scarf she'd purchased in Florence from her purse to wrap the small icon, and smiled when it was safely zipped away.

He took her left hand and Giovanni's right and joined them together. "Avete una buona giornata."

Diana glanced at Giovanni and he translated, "He told us to have a good day."

"Oh, grazie."

The old man patted her cheek then waved them away, settled back on his stool and shook out his paper.

"Ready?" Giovanni asked, still holding her hand.

But the simple question, with a twitch of a smile that flashed in his light brown eyes, seemed to hold more of a grave meaning than intended.

The feeling of being on a precipice and about to take a leap dried out her mouth. She swallowed and took a deep breath; what should she be ready for? What would happen if she said yes? And what did it mean that she *wanted* to say yes to this man?

'*Jesus Lu, just go.*'

Diana felt the physical push, tripped over her feet once, but gathered herself and gave David a snarl over her shoulder, then turned her attention back to Giovanni who'd squeezed her hand in an attempt to steady her. She nodded once, which increased his smile.

"Over there." He pointed to a large double-sided wrought iron gate, with six foot tall hedges on either side that led into someone's yard. At least that's what it resembled. A white sandy path guided them past the outside of a villa and garden, but after they turned a corner there was a brown wooden arrow with the word 'Catacombe.'

"Catacombs?" she asked.

He gave a jerky nod of his head. "I thought …" He cleared his throat. "It's not part of the top ten list of things to see, but I think you'll find it interesting and I did some work down here and still have a key to the site only scholars are allowed so …"

"You thought it would impress me?"

Another corner and they came to a brown door with the word 'Museo' on it.

Inside was indeed a small, bright museum. Quiet for the morning hour. Giovanni pulled out his wallet as he spoke with the museum employee, and after producing some credentials, they were greeted with a pamphlet and a wave in the direction of the entrance.

Diana glanced down a dimly lit steep set of stairs. "So, the catacombs are that way."

"They are."

She glanced at the employee and thought about the buses in the parking lot; there were other people down there. She began the descent. Down one flight, two, a corner turned, then another long flight of stairs to descend.

The different bricks and building material changed color and size the deeper they went. Spotlights illuminated the darkness, but as the distance between the earth above grew, Diana wondered about this tour.

When the stairs ended, they walked several feet through a narrow passageway lined with four or five rectangular compartments carved into the walls on each side, the kind of space perfect for a body. Diana's head almost touched the ceiling when a touch of claustrophobia she wasn't aware she had began to surface. But it was short-lived as a turn brought them out of the narrow space into a very large room.

She took a grateful deep breath. Intricately placed floodlights lit the space, and there were benches set up facing an altar across the room that stood under an arched outcropping with pillars on either side, and the walls were covered with fragments of white marble.

"A church?" Diana asked.

"Yep."

Diana stood a few steps away from Giovanni. "So, do you often take women you just met into secluded underground areas?"

"Just the ones who speak so eloquently about Rome it makes me lose sleep," he responded.

"You know, this is how every movie about women getting themselves in trouble begins."

"The museum curator knows we're down here. Signore Lazzarotti knows we're here. There are a few buses in the parking lot so any second now we'll meet up with those tours." He crossed the space between them. "And Michele can vouch for me. If you'd like, we can go back up and call her."

He didn't reach out and touch her, but his steady gaze continued. "If you want a better character reference, we can call my sister, or actually, my brother. He'd give you the most honest review."

Diana's lips twitched in a grin and he reached for her hand. "If you're really nervous, we can go."

"I don't want to go," she whispered to his fingers.

"I thought," he sighed as she intertwined her fingers with his, "you said the light of day was a problem. So I figured this tour could get us back into the darkness for a while." His voice petered out.

She glanced up, holding back a laugh. "That's pretty macabre."

"I was desperate. And everywhere else we go right now is gonna be so crowded … I wanted you alone."

Just then 'alone' was the last thing they were as a tour group of at least twenty entered the area.

Diana's eyes crinkled around the edges with laughter as Giovanni shook his head at the timely interruption.

"So, okay," the tour guide began in a thick English accent, "we know this catacomb saw the burial of roughly 150,000. And there are many spaces like this one we stand in now; small burial chambers built so the early Christians could celebrate the Eucharist. Today, pilgrims can make arrangements to do so."

Giovanni squeezed Diana's hand and motioned with his head in the direction the group had come from.

This area was wider, with tall outcroppings that left plenty of headroom, and now overhead lights hung every twenty feet.

They walked side by side, still holding hands. Again, that idea of propriety showed up and wondered aloud about the action. Because if she was so willing to hold his hand, allow him to brush a stray strand of hair from her face, linger as he kissed her cheek … what else would she allow?

*'Jeez Lu, maybe you could* allow *yourself to have a good time.'* David gave his frustrated opinion. And while Diana was delighted to have him around once again, she wasn't sure the timing was ideal.

Still, she was able to shake him off because it was taking all her concentration to ignore how large Giovanni's hand was. How comfortable it felt entwined with hers. And how that hand was connected to a body she'd been pressed against so recently.

*Exhaustion and adrenaline.*

"Are there a lot of tour guides in Italy?" She blew out the first question she could find. "I saw so many in Florence in the big piazzas."

"There are, and Italy takes being a tour guide very seriously. To give a tour in Italy you must be licensed. So, if you're standing around with a group of people talking about a monument and you don't have a license, you could be fined."

"Really?"

He nodded.

After a few more silent moments that left Diana with too much room to overthink, she said, "I know a little about the catacombs, but it's been so long. The Christians hid here to escape persecution, right?"

"What did you write this morning?" Giovanni asked instead of answering her question.

"What?"

"When I first came to the table and caught your attention, you said you wrote a story and when I sat down, you kept a close eye on your notebook …" The long hallway became another room where Giovanni led Diana to the right. "I felt like I interrupted you."

"Oh, no. Nothing like that. I'd just finished when you arrived, really.

I kept staring at the notebook because," she shrugged, "I haven't written in a long time. And today, I filled so many pages ..." She swallowed. "Is there a truth serum in the cologne you wear?"

"Maybe?" A snort of laughter followed his answer.

"You said I make you nervous, well you make me want to tell you the truth."

"Ask me anything and I'll do the same," he whispered.

"Maybe it's the comfort of a stranger. It's easier to tell the truth to a stranger." She made the supposition.

"Is it?"

She rolled her eyes. "I kept close tabs on my notebook because I thought I'd lost that part of myself. I was making sure it wasn't a dream."

Giovanni nodded. "So what did you write?"

She laughed. "The oldest story in the book, girl meets boy."

"Would this girl happen to be a captivating writer who called the boy's city extravagant?"

"No, but the boy was tall with broad shoulders and wrinkled clothes from a long day of work."

*'Interesting.'*

Okay, this was too much truth.

*'How long has it been since you've been completely honest with yourself?'* David asked.

"It's Rome's fault." She whispered her blame on the shoulders of the city once more.

*And exhausted adrenaline's fault.*

Giovanni stopped walking and pulled her so she was standing in front of him, showing off those damn broad shoulders and how much space they could take up. Then he had the audacity to touch her chin and tilt her head so she could meet his gaze, study her face for the breath of a lifetime, all the while moving ever so slowly, inching toward her. Temping her to do the same, daring her to be honest about what she yearned for in this moment. And who knows what she would have done if voices hadn't interrupted.

Giovanni gave a low growl of frustration, then with a smirk, stepped toward Diana, backing her against the wall. When the first member of the tour group arrived, Givoanni pressed his body against hers and whispered the excuse, "They need room to pass."

"You're trouble," she whispered back.

He winked at her and was attempting to rekindle the intimacy, leveling his gaze to capture her attention, but was thwarted when his name was jovially called out, "Giovanni?"

He glanced over his shoulder at the man who called his name and smiled in greeting, releasing Diana so he could shake the guide's outstretched hand.

As the two exchanged niceties, Diana tried to shake off the desire Giovanni had unleashed by putting some distance between them. Her assessment had been wrong. The real danger wasn't going with *this* stranger to a secluded, dark place; it was how he treated her *in* the secluded, dark place; holding her hand, listening to her so attentively and looking at her so longingly.

*Yeah, but she'd bet good money that he'd do those things wherever they went.*

"He does volunteer work with us," Giovanni explained, bringing her out of her reprive. The tour guide was following his group and she'd placed enough space between them so she could collect herself.

"What?" she asked.

"Are you okay?" He raised an eyebrow in question.

Diana nodded and changed the subject, "Do you ever give tours? I know you did a pretty good job of it last night ..."

Giovanni, already facing her, began to walk backward. With a wink he started, "A lot of people come into the catacombs and let their imaginations run wild with horror stories because the culture we live in relates evil to darkness. But really, this is a place of peace and sanctuary. The early Christians didn't have the kind of money it took to bury their dead in the elaborate way most of the rich Romans did, so this was simply a means to an end; a cheap way for Christians to bury their dead in these mass underground areas called Necropoli." His voice echoed softly off the intricately excavated earth. "The catacombs were dug under the property of Christians who owned land. There are hundreds of catacombs scattered all around Rome and the tunnels stretch for miles. Several sections are open to tourists, but just up ahead, is a gated tunnel only accessible to archeologists and scholars."

"You're intimidating. You know that, right?" Diana said.

"How?" Giovanni asked, looking suspect at the comment.

Diana stopped. "Are you serious? You speak four languages. You work as an archeologist. In Rome. And you've got a PhD and probably a few more letters to tag onto your name that you haven't mentioned. And you have a key to an area of catacombs only for scholars."

He rubbed the back of his neck and shrugged. "It's only interesting to people who see value in what I'm doing."

"I see value in what you're doing, and I don't even think I have a grasp on its entirety." Diana's voice wavered. "It's intimidating and I'm jealous." More honesty.

"I think I can understand that ..." he started, but if he had something else to say, he let it pass.

To ease the tension she'd created, Diana cleared her throat and asked, "So how far is it to this special scholarly entrance?"

He pointed in the direction they'd been walking. "Two more tunnels, a few twists and turns."

"How do you know we won't get lost?"

"What if we did get lost?"

"My newfound courage might break apart if we get lost."

"Then we won't get lost." He smiled.

"That doesn't exactly inspire confidence."

"Still, the tour continues." He waved, only this time he fell into step next to Diana.

"Where are all the bones?" she asked.

"Some deteriorated, some were lost to grave robbers, and those that were left have been moved."

"Why would someone steal the bones?"

"Well, some of the early Christians who were buried here became martyrs and saints. At that time, it was believed that if you were buried near one of those people, you'd basically have a guaranteed get into heaven free card. So it stands to reason that if being buried next to a martyr was a good thing, having one of their bones in your possession might help too."

"And you said I'm *not* supposed to let myself get creeped out down here?"

He grinned. "I wanted to show you a restoration project of a fresco in the tombs of the city's ancient bakers  that was done two years ago."

"Is there still a lot of work that needs to be done in the catacombs?"

"There's a lot of mileage down here and many areas were forgotten and lost over time. But slowly, with the interest from tourists and the Vatican and the archeological society, work's been ongoing to use new technologies to investigate, repair, and study more areas."

"I always thought that was interesting."

"Which part?" he asked with a soft smile.

"Do you know the guy who took credit for finding the ruins at Machu Picchu?"

"Not personally, he died before my time," Giovanni joked.

"Bingham." Diana smiled, stopping and turning her attention to Giovanni.

"Now who's impressed?"

She waved the comment away. "Do you know how he *found* the 'ruins'?" When Giovanni shook his head that he didn't know, she gave him a suspicious look but continued, "A farmer whose family had lived in the area for hundreds of years and farmed the land took him there. Then Bingham takes all this credit for discovering this lost place when in fact, locals pretty much always knew about it."

"But?" Giovanni encouraged.

"How do you know there's a 'but'?"

"You're a storyteller, and you're telling me a story, so you're setting up the 'but.'"

Her voice was shaky as she whispered the argument, "You don't know me."

"But," he stressed, "I wanna get to know you."

His careful attempts to ignite her attraction were tangible. She drew out the word to continue her story and shake off this man. "But ..."

Giovanni winked.

"Bingham had the resources to expose Machu Picchu to the rest of the world."

"That is true."

"So here we are in the catacombs that were forgotten, but I bet grave robbers or people who needed places to hide never forgot about them."

She glanced around at the place built by death. "Maybe we're supposed to bury things and forget them for a while."

"I couldn't sleep when I got home this morning," Giovanni said softly. "I kept thinking about all the things we talked about last night and how you lit up when you shared your views and theories." His words stirred to life pangs of desire. "When I walked into the café this morning, I felt like I'd summoned you."

"I thought I'd summoned you," she whispered, then tried to focus on the point she was making before the elusiveness of it escaped her. "I think forgetting that the catacombs existed, just like Machu Picchu, caused this area to take on a mysterious life." She pointed to the long arc shape next to her at eye level. "Like you said, this was just a cheap, safe way to bury the dead. But if the existence and the origins are forgotten, the stories that do survive become twisted into something romantic and holy. This place became an escape from persecution. It was given a heroic element." She turned slowly as her own story fogged the landscape before her and her words thickened in the back of her throat. "So when the new stories are unearthed, they take hold with a vengeance. Conscious once more with the new breath of life."

Giovanni's mouth parted as if he were going to say something, but no words came.

"What?" Diana muttered the question, feeling that maybe her point didn't make sense.

"Alive," he whispered. "Last night I was trying to figure out what it was about you. I couldn't seem to put a name to the thing that drew me to you, but it just dawned on me, you're so full of life."

Diana took a step back and felt her face drain of color.

"Did I say something wrong?"

Her throat burned with the first tear. She tried to shake it loose and offered a hoarse "no" in reply as she forced a smile, but there was no way she was going to be able to stop the onslaught of emotion washing over her.

It only seems right she was having these emotions here; because she'd been living her life for the past years as if she had one foot in the grave. A frantic sobbing laugh escaped and she tried to take deep breaths to settle herself down. But so much had happened in the past week, and now, someone declared the most intriguing thing about her was that she exuded life ...

But she did feel alive.

So damn alive she found her words again and through them brought David back. And the words brought waves of lovely memories, and they brought that girl who'd become a woman and this man who *saw* her.

She had indeed buried herself for a time, so she could hibernate until it was time for the cocoon to open and what had been transmuted could rise out – something lovely and alive.

"Kiss me." The words were so soft, she wasn't sure Giovanni heard them. When his own voice whispered "what?" she repeated the demand, "Kiss me."

The request was barely out before his arm slid around her waist, pulling her body against his, twisting a hand into her hair so he could hold her steady as he hungrily brushed his lips against hers.

Her arms circled his neck, clinging to him as she gave herself over to the kiss. She gave herself over to the remainder of the previous evening. She gave herself over to the dimly lit tunnel and Giovanni and Rome.

And then, the part of herself that had worked so tirelessly for security reminded her of the emptiness that came when passion died. That part of her tied the loose hair back up in a tight bun and with disappointed hands on her hips, inserted her firm belief that there was no future a person could build on a house of passion and romance. Not when there was a clear, steadfast path lined with security and stability and 401ks and retirement funds and Medicare.

She ripped herself away from him somehow and keeping her arms extended, distanced herself from him as she blinked against a war of emotions rushing through her.

"What?" Concern and confusion were in his voice.

"I ... I'm sorry. I need to go." She stepped away.

"Why?"

"I can't stay here." Another step between them.

"Yes, you can."

"Giovanni," she begged, her arms still outstretched.

He clasped his hands behind his back and helped her sudden apprehension by putting one more step of space between them as he softly asked, "What happened?"

"I'm engaged."

"I know."

"I shouldn't be kissing a stranger or holding hands or giving you the impression I'm available."

"Okay."

"Don't be so agreeable." She wiped at her face.

"Diana, trust me, the last thing I wanna do right now is be agreeable. I'd like to tear through all these defenses you're putting up and kiss you again."

"I need to go." She turned and began to walk; only after a second, realized she was going the wrong way and turned back. Giovanni's solid form slouched against the wall, taking up a lot of the space she needed to get through in order to leave.

"You said you *need* to leave, but what do you really *want* to do?" he asked.

"Stop it." She was done with everyone changing the question, insisting there were other questions she wasn't asking. "I don't know you." She threw another defense out.

"Then get to know me." He smiled, holding out his hand, daring her to take him up on the offer.

"I can't." She shook her head. "This isn't me. The hair, the clothes, the ... writing ..."

"It *is* you," he insisted.

"Twenty-four hours ago it wasn't." She nodded her head along with her 401k retirement plan-self. "Twenty-four hours ago I was scared ..." She trailed off because while she'd been scared, even without meeting Renee, Michele, Tasha and Sabrina, or getting a damned haircut, she was already changing in spite of all the fear. "I came to Italy to take a little tour. It's over and now I'm gonna go home and get married and move to Houston."

He shot her a skeptical look. "I don't think you really want to do that."

"Don't tell me what I want. I'm not going to stand here and argue with you about this. It's my life and I have a plan and I need to go now."

"You can plan all you want, but at some point, God, the universe, fate – call it whatever you'd like, but it shows up and changes every plan you've ever made."

Diana grunted. "Fate wanted me to get a haircut and make out with a man in a catacomb?"

"Yes." He smiled.

"No."

"Luna—"

"You shouldn't call me that."

"Bella Luna," he disregarded the request, "stay with me. Let's finish here, let's eat lunch at a nice trattoria. We'll talk about history and art and have more coffee to keep up with our exhaustion. I'm not done showing you Rome." He still stood patiently out of reach, but his voice was taking on an octave of desperation. "Give me just the rest of today. Then, I promise, I'll take you back to your hostel and give you back to the life you think you want. Give me today and then I'll leave you alone."

"In the coffee shop you said you were going to seduce me; *now* you're amending that plan?"

He scrubbed his face. "If you agree to just spend the day with me ... I'll take it. God, even if it means I can't hold your hand, or kiss you or try to seduce you, I'll take it." His breathing had become erratic and his voice was a bare sound when he begged, "Please."

She was just going to have to push past him. She'd march out of the catacombs, call a taxi and go back to the hostel. If she spent any more time with this man ...

As she turned her body sideways, intentionally trying to make herself small enough to pass him he said, "It would probably be ungentlemanly of me to remind you that you were the one who demanded I kiss you."

She reached up and covered his mouth with her hand, which turned out to be a mistake because Giovanni clasped her hand in his and pressed a kiss on the palm.

She wrenched her hand away. "Don't."

He let go but brushed a strand of hair behind her ear. She slapped his hand away. "Stop doing things like that."

"You are driving me crazy. Look, I could lie and pretend I don't want you as desperately as I do. But I can't help how attracted I am to you." He held up his hand when she opened her mouth to stop him. "But if all I can get is one day with you and your friendship, then I'll gratefully take it. So, I'll ask you one last time, please, Diana, will you stay with me today?"

She froze. Not sure what to do because she liked how she felt around Giovanni. Because she could still taste him on her lips. Because she wanted to keep talking to him.

'*Lu, tell him about me,*' David suggested.

She shook her head but he insisted, '*Tell him about us.*'

She stared at David for a long time as he gave her the smile of encouragement he'd always given when she had to do difficult things.

With a barely imperceptible nod, she agreed.

"I got married when I was twenty-one." She forced the words out. "David." Saying his name calmed her down. "I want to tell you a story. But I think I need to walk and talk."

Giovanni gestured in the direction they'd been going, then once again clasped his hands behind his back. Diana took several deep breaths to collect herself.

# Chapter Twenty-Seven

"I met David when I turned twenty, my first year of college in New York. I was working toward an MFA, he was an art student. Some friends took me to an art show, which turned out to be his. I was so moved by one of the paintings, I just stood and studied it for the longest time. Of course, he noticed and came to ask what I liked about it. I told him I liked the color, the subject, the way it made me feel, the edges that disappeared into whiteness ..."

'*I told you right then and there I was going to marry you.*'

She smiled relaying the memory. "Then I suggested a date first, to get to know each other. He took my hand and said 'then let's go.' On the way out the door, he called out to his teacher, who'd helped him set up the show, that he needed to go see about a wife."

'*My grade was dependent on that show.*'

"From that day forward we were inseparable. We stayed up late, we argued about the definition of art. He read all my words. We worked side by side; often all night, breaking when dawn reminded us what time it was. We'd eat at our favorite all night diners to celebrate the work we'd accomplished. After three months we moved in together."

'*We were crazy for each other. I couldn't get enough of you. We were drowning in each other and we thrived in every manic moment.*'

She shook her head as every word she spoke brought David back into view. His memory rose like a phoenix, little details emerged in the dim catacombs, like the way he'd shake his head after he rubbed it down with a towel. How he looked as he stared across the room, not seeing anything really but the work of art he was dreaming up.

She felt, for the briefest moment, David's fingers tracing the life line of her left hand. She closed her fist around it and continued, "The work was never stunted because of our need for each other, our work actually seemed to grow out of the need. He proposed on my twenty-first birthday and I laughed and said we were too young to get married. He asked every month after that. The seventh time was the charm. I said yes on Christmas. We were married a week later at the courthouse with witnesses whose names I can't even remember now."

*'We were flourishing. I was selling my work and you were doing freelance and writing and going to school.'*

"I got pregnant just after my twenty-second birthday and miscarried at three weeks." Her voice sounded as far away as the memory, but the telling didn't hurt as much now. "There were complications and I had a hysterectomy. And while the loss was overwhelming, it didn't divide us. We grew closer, we matured with each other because of the hard times. We used our art to heal ourselves."

*'You were my whole world, Lu. My inspiration. But you knew that. I told you that all the time.'*

Diana cleared her throat several times. "I haven't talked about David for a very long time." She was stalling, because this was the hard part of the story. She'd only told it aloud one other time, even though she re-lived it all too often in the beginning. But as soon as she could, she locked the memories away so very tightly in her heart. Then she locked that up too. "I was twenty-six. A month after our five-year wedding anniversary, David had a new show and it was really amazing work. He'd created a niche for himself and was an artist on the rise." Her pace slowed to a stop as she stared down the past, coming back into vivid view. "We had lunch together; it was a Thursday. It was snowing. David was on his way to the gallery but we met for lunch first at one of our favorite diners. He had a grilled cheese, I had an omelet, and we shared fries. He always made his own fry sauce out of mayonnaise and ketchup, the waitresses would bring him a dish of both, knowing he liked to mix it himself. It was just what he did." More memories twirled, resurfacing. "When we finished, I decided to stay and write some more. It was nothing new, that's what we did. Meet up and talk, then he'd go work and I'd stay and write; I loved the rhythm of diners and coffee shops ..." She touched her cheek. "He kissed me on the cheek and said he'd see me soon."

He'd said it so many times, on the way to school, work, galleries; so many times he'd kiss her, she'd kiss him and say see you soon. Be right back. There was nothing different about that Thursday.

Her heart squeezed as if the words she needed to say next were coming from that source rather than a vibration made with her tongue and lips. "I was writing. There was a lot of commotion outside a few minutes later; I didn't know what was going on, but didn't think much of it. It was New York. One of the waitresses went out to see what was going on, but when she came back, I looked up and she was walking toward me, her face so pale …. and time went on forever, it took so long for her to reach the table." But Diana knew, the way you just know something before it's explained. And she didn't want to hear these words. Time stopped, the blood that pumped her heart slowed and each tick of the clock was an agonizing heartbeat. "The waitress said his name; David. She couldn't say any more, just turned and looked out the window." Diana had been in a dream when she stood and headed toward the window. "I remember the waitress was calling me back, screaming my name, as I got closer to the front of the diner."

And from the window all she could see were David's legs, the rest of his body was obstructed by a bus.

"He was hit by a bus," she gave a sad snort, "and the world stopped turning for me at that moment."

*'It shouldn't have, baby.'*

"It did." Diana smiled sadly. "There was no reason to do anything anymore. No reason to eat, no reason to sleep and no reason to write. So I buried David and my writing and myself and stopped living."

*'Oh Lu, you were stronger than that.'*

She shrugged. *"I was strong, but I was nothing without you,"* she answered internally.

"I was twenty-six, I had no husband, no baby, no life, and no money. So I left New York, moved in with my older sister in Atlanta to help her out with my niece and nephew and became a sort of aunt nanny. When I felt a little more human, I went back to school, got a degree as a CPA and just existed until …" The cold, humid catacombs formed back around her again and she finally met Giovanni's eyes. "Until yesterday." She shook her head in disbelief. "Yesterday," she repeated.

Could it have only been a handful of hours?

"Yesterday a group of strange women on a train to Rome turned my world upside down and time started again." She wiped her eyes. "You know what's even stranger than all of this?" She glanced over at David, standing with his shoulder against the wall, his right foot over his left, nodding for her to continue. "This morning, when I started writing, David appeared." She didn't really care what Giovanni would make of that. She was still trying to wrap her head around it herself, and since she'd bared her vulnerable soul, she wasn't about to stop. "It's like the moment I started writing I summoned him ..." her sob turned into a coughing laugh, "summoned him *and* you, but he's been giving me his opinion on everything since."

Giovanni held out his hand, an offering of comfort. She stepped past it into his arms, dropping her head into the crook of his neck; and in the darkness, in the mass tombs of Rome, with a strange man who liked her, she let the final bits of the dam she'd built against David's memory crumble away completely, and basked in the memories of the life they were lucky enough to share.

She cried all the tears she probably should have cried years ago as Giovanni held her, sitting them down at some point against the wall and pulling her against his side. He didn't brush her hair or whisper soothing words. He just held her and let her cry.

# Chapter Twenty-Eight

"Oh, my ..." Diana whispered her first impression, then caught a glimpse of her reflection in the window and reminded herself to close her mouth, as she followed the waiter leading them to a table on the covered rooftop patio. Of course, the closer they got to the table at the edge of the balcony with a perfect view of the Colosseum, the more difficult it was. "Oh ... my ..." she repeated as the landmark sparkled in the midday sun.

The table sat next to a secure hip-height wall topped with glass so as not to obstruct her view, and after the waiter sat them and left, she leaned over the table and said, "I was in there last night."

Giovanni winked in reply and she realized this was the first full-on view she had of him in the bright light of day.

His light brown eyes sparkled, but there were tired, dark rings beginning to form around them. The small scar was whiter. His short dark hair stood slightly on end, but it looked more bedhead than anything. The dark stubble on his chin now defined the slight square angle of his jaw and his lips were full and red. Sensuous. The word floated by and she tried to shrug it off. His clothes were slightly crumpled, and on his right shoulder was a stain; she pointed and cringed. "I think I cried all my mascara off onto your shirt."

He glanced down and shrugged. "I have other shirts."

"It'll wash out," she promised.

He opened his menu, but before he covered his face with it said, "I might not ever want to wash this shirt again. It smells like you."

The comment, tossed casually, sparked a heat to blaze through Diana, and all she could do was focus on the black menu with gold lettering winking at her in the sun, hiding any flirtation that might have followed.

When she'd exhausted herself of tears in the catacombs, she felt lighter. Only then had Giovanni broken the silence. "Thank you, for trusting me with your story."

"I think you just became my confessor." She sat up and pulled away from him.

"It's the perfect place for it."

Diana wasn't sure what to do next, but Giovanni helped. "Does your David have an opinion on me?"

She gave an exhausted laugh. "He likes you."

"Sounds like a man of good taste."

"Um hm ..."

'*I am a man of good taste.*' David grinned from where he stood against the opposite wall. '*And it's time you listen to me, Lu. You're in Rome. With someone who got you into the Colosseum in the middle of the night. Go finish out the day with him and have fun.*'

Diana let a few more long moments pass before she stood and held her hand out to Giovanni's seated form. "I thought you had a city to show me?"

"Do I?"

"Lead the way."

The first order of business had been to see to their rumbling stomachs. Giovani insisted he knew the perfect place, and he hadn't been lying.

Sitting behind the Colosseum that basked in the warm midday sun, was a hilltop dotted with palm trees and cypress and other Italian foliage that had grown together over the centuries. The buzz of traffic busily swerving around the historic Colossus rose up to join the chirping of birds and the clink of dishes and muted conversation of other diners.

Diana was shaking her head in wonder at the whole scene, trying to figure out what to focus on when Giovanni asked, "Do you like it?"

She tried to hide a smile as she annunciated his favorite descriptive word, "Extravagant."

His face lit up with the word and he promised, "Just the beginning."

A shiver ran through her as the waiter approached the table.

Giovanni talked with him for a few moments, translating the specials for Diana. She nodded, watching his easy smile and the exchange, recalling how informative and calming the rest of the tour had been in the catacombs.

He'd continued his explanation as they began to head to the exit that would take them back to street level. "Two thousand years ago Romans were the center of the universe, at least they thought so. They purposely built this city to impress visitors as well as themselves. You were right to call us an extravagant people."

"Of course I was."

They proceeded through the tunnels that were only open to archeologists and scholars as he went on, "Since about 1990, there's been a reawakening in the archeological field in Rome. New digs are talked about in cafés with the same intensity as the rest of the daily news."

"What is it like to love your job this much?" Diana asked in wonder.

"Did you always want to be a writer?" he asked instead of answering.

"In my youth."

"It's not over," he said, and before she could argue asked, "What did it feel like, the writing, when you were in the thick of it, working at it?"

"Like home." The answer, one she'd given a hundred times before David passed away, slipped off her tongue easily.

'*Exactly.*' David agreed.

Giovanni waved to the tunnel they were walking in. "I like the research and the occasional digs I get to participate in, and I even like the papers I write. But my work connects me to people from thousands of years ago, and who knows, maybe some of them were my relatives. So I understand that feeling of home as well. I'd do this job for free. And sometimes it feels like I do."

A clearing of the waiter's throat brought her back. "Signorina?"

She tilted her head as she admitted, "I'm tired and hungry and starstruck by this view. I'd like the perfect pasta. What do you recommend?"

Giovanni translated, and the waiter gave an inclination of his head and said, "Io so esattamente cosa portare."

"He knows just the thing," Giovanni supplied as the waiter left and another arrived with a carafe of red wine, pouring them each a glass before leaving.

Giovanni held his glass toward Diana. "To you, la bella Luna."

"To Rome," Diana corrected.

"A Roma," Giovanni agreed with a thick twirl of accent that made Diana's skin dance with goosebumps as he touched his glass to hers.

She took a sip and sighed, sitting back in her chair. "I don't know what to look at."

"I do." That lowered voice and telling gaze was intent on her.

She shook her head, "What happened to just friends?"

"I threw the idea away when you stood on the Via Appia flirting with me."

"I didn't flirt." She didn't think she was capable of flirting. If anything, she felt awkward and foolish around Giovanni.

*'You said you were grateful all roads lead to Rome.'* Diana glanced over at the empty table next to them where David was sunning himself, sunglasses in place, legs stretched out in front of him, a glass of wine in hand. He toasted the air in her direction.

"I was impressed by the longest, oldest road in Rome," she muttered before taking another drink.

When they'd climbed the stairs and finally exited the catacombs, Diana's red eyes took the brunt of the bright afternoon light. She felt like she was coming out of a hazy, waking dream and walking into an exhausted reality.

Across the street from the church they exited was a waiting taxi.

As they crossed the dark gray cobblestones she looked in both directions before stopping and bending to touch the warm stone beneath her hand. "This road went all the way to the ocean."

"It did."

She glanced up at him. "You said the Via Appia? This is the road, *THE* road."

"It is."

She caressed the worn cobblestone. "I know you've probably thought this before and most every tourist does, but these stones have been worn down by two thousand years of travelers." She stood and gazed down the tree-lined road as far as she could.

"And now you're one of them," Giovanni stated.

She fished out her phone and took a picture of the road with the dappled sunlight falling upon it. "All roads lead to Rome," she said, thinking that she'd post that photo and tagline. Then she turned to see Giovanni, hands in his pockets, gazing in the direction she had, patiently waiting. "Thankfully ..." The bare whisper slipped out before she could stop it.

He didn't react, so she was sure he hadn't heard her. But in the taxi, she felt he sat purposely close, enough for his arm to rest against hers, but not so close that she'd feel the need to move away.

As he gave the driver instructions, Diana found her attention on the lips that were wrapping around the luscious language. She licked her own in reply before turning her attention out the window just in time for David to turn from the front seat and grin. '*I saw that.*'

"We're just friends." Diana brought everyone's attention back to the moment at hand. Giovanni inclined his head as if he were going to bend to her will, but she had a sneaking suspicion it was a ploy.

'*You don't want him to be your friend,*' David antagonized.

She took a deep breath and thought, "*Listen, you overripe figment of my imagination. If I need anything from you, it's to be on team Diana. That team is going to have a nice day, see some sights and go home. Alone. Back to the United States.*"

'*Whatever you need, babe.*'

Diana took a long sip of wine and waited for her bones to become a bit more slack as the Colosseum preened before her, in shades completely different than the previous evening. It would be something to sit here all day and watch the Colossus change colors.

"Do they have paint stores here that sell colors like: early morning Pantheon gray, Roman sunlight, and midday Colosseum?" The comment was meant as a joke, but saying the words aloud made her fingers itch to write down a list of colors she'd attribute to this country.

"That soul of a poet is gorgeous, you know."

"I have the soul of a woman who hasn't slept in thirty-six hours and is now riding a wave of adrenaline and getting a little buzz."

"Good," Giovanni said.

"Good?"

"When exhaustion mixes with adrenaline, that's when you really get to feel the pangs of being alive. And it sounds like you're waking up more and more with the passing of each moment."

She didn't stifle the urge to write the colors down. After she retrieved her notebook, she glanced at Giovanni; his face was passive. He was giving her room to write; not looking overly excited about the prospect or looking as if the action annoyed him.

She scribbled colors: Early evening piazza yellow. Table wine red. Tuscan cypress green. Smoky jazz brick. Waiter jacket white. Maroon awakenings. (The last one was a hair color, of course.)

Their food was delivered, this time not a five-course affair, but a simple bowl of pasta. Steam rose from the fragrant twirl of thick pasta placed before Diana. She lowered her nose and took a deep inhale as the waiter gave the name of the dish, "Bucatini all'Amatriciana."

"Gorgeous."

A brief nod and he was gone.

"What is it?" she asked Giovanni.

"The noodle is a hollow spaghetti called bucatini and the sauce is called Amatriciana. It's tomatoes, a little white wine, a little spicy chili and guanciale; that's the jowl of the pig which is aged, kind of like prosciutto." He glanced at the bowl, "Looks like they cut the meat into strips and fried it, so that'll add a smokiness to the sauce." He nodded. "*That*, is the most traditional Roman dish you'll get."

She dug her fork in and twirled a bite into her mouth, rolling her eyes as the marriage of flavors met her hunger.

"Good?"

"Buona," she answered with her mouth full, but didn't miss the interested tilt of Giovanni's head.

"What did you get?" she asked.

"Cacio e pepe. Basically, it's pasta with cheese and pepper." He picked up his plate and handed it over so she could try some, and she wasn't about to be shy.

She shook her head after she'd chewed the bite. "How can pepper and cheese and pasta taste so magical?"

They fell into easy conversation, Giovanni explaining the specialty dishes of Rome and the history behind some of them.

But when he asked about her job she wanted to wave the questions off. Her job was simple and boring. It brought monetary stability.

"Actually ..." she began, a frown forming.

"What?"

"I work for an accounting firm, there are only five of us. I have my own accounts that I often visit in order to do their payroll and books. And I've never thought about it ... but while I might not have been writing, I think I was observing." She put her fork down, stretched her fingers and shook her hand.

"Are you okay?"

"Yeah ..." She flexed and squeezed her hand once more as a phantom tingling sensation began. "My hand always did know when I wanted to write before I did."

Giovanni waved to the table. "Please. I won't bother you."

"No," she smiled down at her hand, "I haven't *wanted* to write in a very long time. And I thought it was gone." She squeezed her hand again. "I really did."

"I think our true nature never really goes away, we just lose sight of it."

Diana snorted. "This damn country."

"What do you mean?"

"In Pisa, I met an old man who told me the famous tower leans for no other reason than it was her nature to lean. Then he asked me what my own nature was."

"And?"

"I don't think I've figured it out yet." She licked her lips. "I do think I'm drunk again and you are using your honesty superpower on me."

"Am I?"

"Yes," she pointed, "see, honesty." She picked up her glass.

"In that case, can I ask you a question?"

She paused for a moment before nodding. "Fire away." She touched her glass to his.

"Does the difference in age really bother you?"

"Not really." She sighed and couldn't meet his gaze as she answered, "What bothers me is that you're still young. You have time and deserve kids if you want them."

"We could always adopt," Giovanni offered.

*We.* She scoffed at the idea. "I'm too old for babies. And it wouldn't be fair to a child to have to grow up with an old mom."

"We don't have to adopt a baby. But you're also making assumptions that I want children."

She grunted in reply.

"So, are kids the only reason you won't allow yourself to be attracted to me?"

"I didn't say I was attracted to you," she glanced at him through lowered lashes as she admitted, "though I didn't say I *wasn't* attracted to you either."

*'There it is,'* David laughed, *'get it girl.'*

Giovanni regarded her for a long time. Just before Diana was about to break the silence, he asked, "Do you want a coffee?"

Diana nodded. "I think a coffee is probably a better choice at this point."

He gestured to her plate. "Let's finish our lunch. I know a good place for coffee."

She glanced at some diners who had espresso cups in front of them. "Don't they serve coffee here?"

"The place I know is better."

"Well, so far your recommendations have been spot on."

"I hope you'll like it." He finished his glass of wine with a final large swig.

# Chapter Twenty-Nine

B ack with feet on the streets of Rome, Diana glanced up at Giovanni and asked, "Which way?"

He reached for her hand in reply, and when she allowed it to be taken, gave a squeeze and gestured with his head the direction.

"You have sisters?" Giovanni led as they began the slow walk of people with full stomachs and nowhere in particular to be on a warm afternoon where spring was starting to be phased out by the first blushes of summer.

"Two sisters. One older, Lena. She and our parents live in Atlanta. Our younger sister, Harper, lives in New York."

"And this trip was an engagement present from the younger sister," he said, filling in the pieces.

"That's how she conned me into taking the trip," she muttered, "saying it was a gift for my engagement, but then she admitted that she wanted to get me away from my normal life, my comfort zones, so I could … see the forest for the trees." She shrugged. "A place where I'd have space to really think about what I want."

"What do you want, bella Luna?"

"Comfort," she tried to joke, but it wasn't far from the truth. "I want security and dependability."

"What about passion and excitement?"

"You can't build a life around those," she said sadly.

"I think you can. I think you need to be passionate about someone and excited about what they have to say and what they want to do." His case for passion was calm and thoughtful. "I think we all deserve someone who respects us enough to make the effort to understand us.

Dependability and stability can be born out of that."

*'This is why Harper kicked your ass so far out of your comfort zone.'* David smiled. *'So you'd meet new people and be confronted with new ideas.'*

"I don't know." Diana muttered the lame excuse and veered away from the conversation by asking, "Didn't you have to work today?"

"I called in sick." He pointed to the bus stand they were approaching and pulled out his phone. "It's just a few minutes up the road, and we can give our feet a rest."

"I've done so much walking since I've been here, it reminds me of New York."

"Where did you live when you were there?"

"Brooklyn, but Harper tells me it's changed a lot."

He nodded. "We were in Queens."

"Do you still have family there?"

"My brother and sister moved to Maine. My parents are still in Queens, but they spend about three months a year in Italy, staying with all the cousins, aunts and uncles that live here."

"That would be amazing, to be able to spend three months a year in Italy."

Giovanni's voice lowered. "You could always stay with me."

That sultry tone was working wonders when paired with those mesmerizing brown eyes; and those delicious lips that curved up, Cheshire and bold, when he voiced such propositions.

"I might prefer a villa in Tuscany." She shrugged as the bus pulled up.

"So we move to Tuscany, I can work there, too."

Diana gave him an incredulous shake of her head as she entered the bus ahead of him. She stopped by the ticketing machine, but he held up his phone. "There's an app for that."

"Where do you fall in the sibling lineup?" she asked.

"Youngest by one minute," he responded.

"You're a twin?"

"Fraternal. My brother, Amadeo, and I are nothing alike. He's about an inch taller than me and has a natural curl to his hair."

"Those are the highlights of the differences, huh?"

He shrugged. "Isabella, our sister, is fourteen months older."

"Wow."

"Our parents joke that they wanted to raise kids as quickly and close together as possible."

The bus swayed down a four-lane road, honking occasionally at the cars and scooters that swerved too close to its front bumper. On either side of the road were buildings with businesses on the first floor and from the occasional laundry she spied hanging from windows, apartments above.

At another stop, more people climbed on the bus and Giovanni used the crowdedness to his advantage, slipping his hand around Diana's waist and softly pulling her against him. She looked up and became lost in his eyes; just as she had hours before, when he floated into the bar and whispered, 'Buona sera.'

She raised her hand and brushed his cheek with the back of her fingers. That slight touch lifted her heart rate. He lowered his head and touched his forehead to hers. She turned her palm to cup the side of his face and closed her eyes, because the last time she'd been this close, his lips had been on hers – soft, insistent, wanton – and shockwaves of forgotten physical memories erupted from the very depths of her.

All the defenses she halfheartedly attempted to build were wavering, coming undone like a house of cards. God, she *liked* the flutters and shivers. The exhausted honesty and flirting. She enjoyed the intensity with which he studied her, as if he might miss something if he looked away. And she adored the way he talked about wanting to seduce her with the same delight he had when he talked about the history of the Colosseum.

"This is our stop." The whisper disconnected them. She accepted his offered hand as he pulled her behind him, clearing a path through the crowded bus so they could exit.

They crossed the street, and the shade offered from the four- and five-story buildings was lovely as the warm May sunshine had thickened the afternoon.

The buildings varied in Italian shades of coral, champagne, and cream; and on the corners, the first floors offered a variety of shops: gelato, fruit and vegetables, a pharmacy, a small grocery store and at least two cafés.

Both of the cafés looked good to her, but he made no mention of either, so she figured he must have somewhere else in mind. But since they exited the bus, Giovanni seemed preoccupied. He kept a hold of her hand and at random intervals he rubbed his thumb against her skin or squeezed her hand as if reassuring himself she was still there.

Two blocks from where the bus dropped them off, they came to a large cemented, tree-lined piazza with a fountain in the center. He turned the corner and stopped in front of a large double oak door of a residential building.

"Where are we?" she asked.

He glanced over her shoulder and cleared his throat before he finally answered, "My apartment."

Diana let her gaze trace the beige façade of the five-story building with dark brown shutters on every window, a few opened, most of them closed.

She wasn't shocked that he'd brought her here. Or maybe she was. But more than anything, standing at the precipice of where Giovanni lived was such a humanizing moment.

"Do you really think this is a good idea?"

"I don't know," he whispered honestly.

She pulled her hand out of his. "Why did you bring me here? Just for coffee?"

"Yes." He clasped his hands behind his back, tilted his head and shrugged as if he was lost. "No."

She glanced back up at the building.

"Giovanni ..."

"I wasn't lying when I said I wanted to seduce you."

It wasn't going to be just coffee.

The defenses, the excuses, everything they'd talked about, every slight touch, every look; all culminated in this busy Roman neighborhood, in front of this Roman door.

"I want you." He cleared his throat, pulling up courage to continue. "Ever since I saw you last night, I've wanted you and the desperation is an ache that scares me."

She glanced around her, looking for an answer and an escape simultaneously.

"I can't give you what you think you want from me." Her heart had begun wildly thumping and reverberating between her ears.

"I want you. As you are."

Butterflies erupted in throngs, fluttering through her veins.

"From the moment I held you last night I wanted you. And this morning, when I found you, an *apparition* at the coffee shop ..."

"No one talks like that," she whispered.

"Come inside." He held out a trembling hand to her.

Diana stared at his hand, the gesture causing her to realize whatever she chose would be definitive.

She couldn't breathe.

And it wasn't a good idea. If the kisses they shared in the catacombs had knocked a confession of David loose; what would get knocked loose if she went into his apartment?

"Bella."

"What if I say no?"

He dropped his hand and nodded. "I'll take you back to your hostel."

She shook her head.

"You've shared a lot of yourself with me today," he said. "I don't take that lightly. I hope you know that." He waited for her to nod her head in recognition of the statement, then he continued, "I've tried to be honest with you. I'm attracted to you. I want more of you. And I know the chance I was taking coming here. So now the question, Diana ... are you attracted to me?"

She rolled her eyes. "*Of course* I am. You're handsome. And intelligent and thrilling to talk to," she snorted, "and I like your smile and your damn laugh and the color of your eyes and how your hair won't really lay down ..." She waved her words away because his grin seemed to brighten up the whole street. "Okay, since we're riding the honesty wave, here's the thing," she pointed to the door, "this scares me. Because if I go through that door with you, I'll become human."

He frowned.

"Renee might have made the packaging look good," she gestured to her body, "but there are ... squishy parts." Jesus, she was really going to put it all out there, "And things are sagging. And there are sunspots and wrinkles and gray in my hair." She pointed at him. "I've been pressed up against that body quite a lot and I have an idea that without a shirt, you might look pretty ... good." She cleared her throat, staring at his chest. "Real good." A flicker of how good naked flesh would feel pressed against her own flashed, so she shook it away and snapped her fingers as she remembered she'd been confessing. "... and spider veins and my back aches in the morning."

Giovanni frowned and gave an aggravated growl, and before Diana could react, he pulled her against him and sealed his lips over hers. He pushed his way between her lips with his tongue, and she met the frantic kiss. When he pulled away, he turned her and backed her against the door, sliding his hands into hers, silently insisting she look at him. "Bella Luna, I want you because of the color of your eyes, and the depths I saw in them when I first stood in front of you, it weakened my knees. Then ..." he gave a hoarse laugh, "after talking with you, I wanted you for the way you spoke about art so passionately, and when I held you on the dance floor, God ... I wanted you for the way you fit in my arms." He squeezed her hands to punctuate his words.

She couldn't breathe as one emotion after another slammed against her chest.

"Today you've shared even more of yourself with me. The way your eyes take on a dreamy state when something is inspiring you ..." His words had become a caress. "You've never complained about walking or how exhausted I know we both are. There is no pretense or deceptiveness about your views and you have a wry sense of humor." He gently shook her. "*Those* are the parts I want." He gave another laugh and shrugged. "Hell, I'd be lying if I didn't admit that I want the other parts too. The things you think are imperfect, are fucking sexy as hell. Do you know how much I enjoy the view when you're walking in front of me? Now, tell me to kiss you," he fiercely demanded.

Diana moved slowly to her tiptoes, her body moving a few inches upward so that she was as level as her five eight frame could be with his six three. She tilted her head upward, and that was all the invitation he needed to meet her lips once more.

This time the kiss was sweet and gentle. The heat was still there underneath, promising.

Diana pulled away slightly and whispered against his lips, "Take me inside."

Giovanni groaned and deepened the kiss for a brief moment before he separated himself long enough to fumble in his pockets for his keys. As he opened the front door, Diana laughed. It was the build-up of nerves, the excitement, the exhaustion, the questioning if she was doing the right thing; it was a bubbling over that brought the laughter.

Once they were inside the cool, dark foyer of the apartment building, Giovanni pushed the call button for the elevator and Diana admitted, "I still don't know if this is a good idea, and I think I might still be drunk on Rome."

The elevator opened and Giovanni wrapped his arm around her waist then twirled her so she was facing him as they did an awkward walk into the box. As the doors closed he greedily kissed her, building the desire and heat between them. The elevator, unable to hold all the want and need, allowed it to spill out at the edges.

Somehow they arrived at Giovanni's door. His hands shook again as he attempted to open it, the same shake he'd had when he held it out to her moments earlier.

"Are you really nervous?" Diana asked breathlessly.

He glanced sideways at her. "It's not every day you get to bring the woman of your dreams to your home."

Diana almost walked away then. As the door swung wide, she took a step back and found roughly seven hundred reasons she couldn't be anyone's dream.

*What was she doing?*

Giovanni stood just inside, once more holding his hand out to her, a silent question.

*'Jesus, Diana. It's been nineteen years since you did the right thing. Go!'* David pushed her and she tripped into Giovanni's arms, glanced over her shoulder and saw David standing in the middle of the hallway and grinning. *'I really like this guy.'* He gave a wink and a double thumbs up as the door slowly shut on him, making Diana smile.

She turned her face up to Giovanni, her breath catching. "I like him too," she muttered.

He raised an eyebrow at the comment, unceremoniously dropped his keys and pulled her back into his arms, flaming the embers of attraction into a raging bonfire.

# Chapter Thirty

The moonlight woke Diana. Or maybe it was the ravenous hunger that rolled in her stomach.

She blinked her eyes open slowly and grinned at the light spilling in from the window. She stretched her arms above her head and yawned as a large hand slipped across her stomach.

Giovanni.

The name was as dreamy as the rays of moonlight that blinked into her tired vision.

She rested her hand on top of his and let her head fall to the side. His eyes were hooded with sleep as well, but a soft, sexy grin widened in greeting.

The events from the past several hours flashed; a montage of sweaty bodies pressed against each other, moans, soft declarations of wonder as Giovanni's hands and eyes took in Diana's reclining naked form and made her feel more powerful and sexy than she ever thought possible. There were desperate kisses and delightful cries of agony as each touch stoked a fire. And then there were the orgasms.

Good Lord, Diana bit her lip as she recalled the orgasms. "Is there a goddess of really good sex?" She whispered the question out of reverence to the moonlight and the echoing sounds of sex that still lingered in the room like settling dust.

"Roman or Greek?"

"Roman."

"Well, Cupid was the god of love, desire and attraction." His deep voice, crusted with sleep, settled in her chest and made her shiver. "But he was the son of Venus, and *she* was the goddess of sex, beauty, love and victory."

"Victory," Diana repeated.

"Victory," he confirmed.

Diana sighed. "I think I need to light a candle or something, in offering to thank one of them." She widened her eyes. "Unless I have to kill a goat or something, then maybe I don't want to make an offering to a Roman god."

"Don't worry, for Venus you just visit her temple and leave her a garland of flowers, burn some incense and maybe bring some wine."

"So, standard dating offerings."

Giovanni rolled over so half of Diana was under him as he slid a hand up to cup her breast and simultaneously nipped at her chapped lips. "Of course, another way to thank the gods is to just make love." He moved his lips down her neck and Diana turned her head so he could have better access and ran her hands over his back, whispering, "You feel good."

"So do you." He continued his ministrations, zigzagging from her neck down to her collar bone, following a trail of his own making.

"I want you," Diana said and Giovanni groaned in agreement. Then her stomach growled loudly. "But I'm so hungry."

She felt the smile against her throat. Giovanni pushed himself up onto his elbows. "I can fix that."

"You've fixed a lot of things," she muttered.

One more kiss, and he slipped out of bed, retrieved his boxers and yawned as he shuffled across the room, stopping to look back when he reached the door.

In another life, she would have itched to cover herself, but Giovanni had kissed, caressed and washed away any of the misgivings she had about her body. He'd all but worshiped her. Actually, he'd done that too.

"You look the way the Goddess Diana was meant to look, basking in the moonlight. In all her glory."

"Go make me food," Diana whispered, her courage to bask, wavering.

Giovanni gave a slight inclination of his head. "As you wish."

When he left, she pressed her hands to her face, stifling the urge to give a giddy scream at the top of her lungs in exclamation that she was still a sexual being. That she was still attractive. And she *felt* fucking attractive from the tips of her damn toes to the top of her head.

She stretched her whole body and thought maybe the moonlight was actually heating her skin, stroking her, empowering her; or it was just phantom caresses still lingering among her nerve endings.

She heard the radio come on and the clatter of pans. The soft music and an urge to be close to Giovanni was a siren song she easily gave in to.

She found her 'Italy' shirt, slipped it over her head and smoothed it down with her hands. She was never giving this shirt back. She might not ever wash it, now that it smelled like Giovanni and a jazzy night club and the catacombs. At this point, even if she never wore it again, she wanted to preserve a piece of it forever. Proof for later. Proof that such things as magic still existed.

She slipped on her underwear and took her time walking to the kitchen. She was distracted the first time she passed through the apartment. The light from the kitchen was enough to now study her surroundings.

The hallway from the bedroom to the living room had paintings and photos of ancient places. Black and white sketches of Greek temples, watercolor paintings that looked like English castles, and photographs of archeological digs.

In the living room were strategically placed bookcases that held displays of Giovanni's precious finds, mingled with volumes upon volumes of books. "Early Indiana Jones." She whispered her description of the décor to the room as she crossed the tiled floor and touched a worn copy of a book about King Arthur that sat on top of several Greek history books next to the dark blue sofa.

On the opposite wall was another bookcase, she reached out to touch a small clay vase, dark in color with unrecognizable pictures decorating it, but thought better of it. Who knew how irreplaceable it might be.

She did let her fingers brush over a silver-plated framed picture of what could only be Giovanni's family, frozen in the late nineties. Two boys dressed in matching polo shirts, and a girl in a flowery dress stood next to their parents who sat in the center, everyone grinning happily.

The moonlight caught her attention next. One of the living room shutters was open, allowing the light to spill in. She opened the window and the second shutter, looking up at the moon, still a day or two away from being full.

The moon was brighter in Rome, she thought. It looked like it was sparkling too. It had done that when she'd glanced up at it from inside the Colosseum as well.

"When was the last time I stood in the moonlight?" She whispered the question, but had no answer.

She decided she'd go out every night she had left in Italy and soak up the rays of the Roman moon. Steep herself in the moon's energy.

"Diana, goddess of the moon." She gave a dazed laugh. "You have come undone, darling Luna." That she had; and wasn't in any hurry to tighten back up.

She shuffled into the kitchen finally, sucking in a shocked breath and freezing in the doorway.

Giovanni glanced over his shoulder. "What's wrong?"

"Dear God, put on a shirt." Something about seeing him from across the room, in nothing but tight boxer briefs, in the soft light of the cooktop, in the middle of the night while some sexy Italian song played on the radio, was obscene.

Sure, she'd seen him up close, very up close. She'd studied those strong arms and chest and back with her own hands. And what a man, with those strong arms and hands that spent his free time unearthing ancient secrets.

She rolled her eyes at the thought, but her mouth went dry as she recalled just how those fingers had helped find her secrets.

He looked down at himself and frowned, looking worried. "You don't like how I look?"

Diana was surprised to see actual doubt in his eyes.

"You have to know how you look." She crossed the room and leaned against the counter, just out of reach. "Handsome," she insisted.

"You'll be surprised to find out I was a chubby kid."

"Stop it." The little boy in the picture looked chubby, but in the way kids were.

He nodded as he turned the heat off the stove and reached into the cupboard to retrieve plates. "In an Italian family, food is love. And my mom *loved* us, and because of all that love, I became a really big boy. In high school no one was interested in the big, awkward kid. I didn't have any girlfriends, just girls who thought I was a nice guy for a friend. So, I went down the path of eating to soothe myself because no one liked me, and eating to feel the love of my family." He shrugged. "It wasn't until I went away to college that I figured the food out and replaced the urge to eat with exercising. But it was just a replacement. It took a few more years before I found a happy balance."

She thought about how he wore his clothes, not fitted, just a little loose. He was still hiding, wasn't he?

"I never imagined you'd have insecurities about your body."

"I'm not allowed to have them?" he asked with a tilt of his head.

"No," she answered honestly.

He pulled her against him. "Then you aren't allowed to have them either," he countered.

"Yes, I am."

"Why are you allowed, but I'm not?" Giovanni raised an eyebrow in question.

Diana had no arguments for this, so she bided her time by gesturing to all of him and blurting out the only words she could find, "Because you're a wet dream."

A shout of laughter caught them both unaware.

Diana rested her hand against his chest and softly murmured, "Well, you are."

"We've all got our insecurities," he admitted, "but I don't believe in giving mine too much power. Insecurities can become barriers if you let them."

"Who are you?"

"The man of your dreams." He winked.

"The man of my dreams would have fed me by now." She sidestepped the comment.

He brushed a kiss across her lips. "Then stop distracting me."

Diana sat down at the small round wooden table in the corner. She brushed her hands over the wood and thought about a round tablecloth she'd just purchased that would fit perfectly.

She let her gaze wander back to Giovanni and watched his sure movements as he dished up the food. He set a plate in front of Diana announcing, "A little fresh pasta with some pesto." Then, a wedge of cheese from the fridge, a loaf of crusty bread and a knife were placed on a cutting board and added to the table. After grabbing two small glasses and a half drunk bottle of wine, he finally joined her. Taking out the cork he held the bottle over Diana's glass in offering.

She nodded, but he shook his head and pulled the bottle back.

"What?" she asked.

He stood, opened a cupboard and took out a new bottle of wine, returning with it and an opener.

"I don't mind the bottle that's already open," Diana said.

Giovanni opened the new wine and explained, "My parents drank wine with dinner on Friday and Saturday nights. If there was still some of the wine left from the previous week, my dad would drink it but he'd always open a new bottle for my mom. He always said, 'a woman should be celebrated, even if it just means opening a new bottle of wine for her.'"

Diana watched him pour her a glass and once he'd filled his from the first bottle, he touched his glass to hers and softly declared, "Cin cin."

Diana took a drink and then began to eat. It was heavenly. Every element that added to this moment was heavenly. The exhaustion, the lovemaking, the moon, the midnight dinner companion, the insecurities, the honesty, the music, the new bottle of wine – it all made the simple pasta the best thing she'd ever eaten in her entire life.

"Why aren't you married?" Diana asked when her stomach felt satisfied it wasn't going to collapse in on itself and the wine loosened her bones once again. "I'm sorry, you said you'd been married before, I don't mean to bring up any bad memories."

"They aren't bad memories. It happens. I was married for five minutes, it seems like," he said.

Diana felt a pang of jealousy. But who was she to be jealous? Hadn't she just told this man that her first husband (whose ghost had been hanging out with her all day) had been her entire reason for living?

"We were married for two years. But in the end, I think we liked the idea of being married more than we actually liked being married."

Diana raised an eyebrow in question.

"Oldest story in the book, she wanted more than me. We really weren't compatible."

"Is it rude of me to ask if there have been any major contenders since then? I imagine the girls flock to you."

"There have been several first dates and a handful of second, but no one remarkable enough to want to spend more time with." He leaned back in his chair and after a moment said, "I want to ask you more questions about your life in the states, but ..."

When he didn't continue she thought she knew what he meant. "You still want some sort of fantasy?"

He nodded. "I don't think I want to know about a life you need to go back to."

She rolled the base of her small wine glass back and forth on the table. "That's the same reason I didn't want to come up here."

"Why are you here with me?" he whispered but when she met his gaze he was shaking the question off. "I'm sorry."

"You wanted me here," she reminded him.

"I don't think I'll be able to let you go," he said honestly, then took a deep breath and made a noise blowing it out. "These probably aren't the things we should be talking about tonight."

Diana opened her mouth to try and put him at ease but she didn't know what to say. Instead, she pointed to his kitchen walls. "I like this color, this morning, when I watched the sun rise on the Pantheon, the first gleam of yellowed sky was this color."

"Ah, is that why you asked about paint stores in Rome?"

She nodded. "I thought, if I lived in Rome I would have a kitchen painted the color of the sunrise over the Pantheon."

"Luna," he groaned her name, "you can't say things like that." He scrubbed his face. "You said that you think you've been dead all these years. I may have been too. Or maybe I haven't really been living before, because I've never felt as alive as I have the past two days with you. And you say the color of my kitchen is the same as the sunrise over the Pantheon ..."

She scrunched her face in an apology. "I'm ruining your home now too."

"You haven't ruined anything."

"Well, you might like to know, we're even. You've ruined Rome for me." She grinned and he raised an eyebrow in question. "Rome, the memory of Rome, will always smell like Giovanni and have Giovanni standing in the foreground of every major monument, and sound like

Giovanni."

"You know your voice has a low lilting pitch, like a sweetness to it that can only come from living in a southern state. And when you say my name, it's sexy as hell."

"Giovanni ..." She smiled, she liked saying his name.

She shook her head and gathered all her newfound courage, because she was sure they should get off this current path of conversation. It was filled with too many potholes and realities.

To interrupt these thoughts, she asked for the more intimate action she wanted from him that seemed more acceptable than talking. "Giovanni, can you take me back to bed?"

# Chapter Thirty-One

The sun screamed for Diana to get up. If it had a voice it was the opposite of the caressing moon. This was harshness shrieking for her to get her cheating ass out of bed. *Immediately.*

She catapulted into a seated position and wildly glanced around her.

The first thing she caught sight of was her underwear, wrinkled and alone in the middle of the floor, brightly lit by the sun, as if it was trying to double down on her embarassment.

"Oh my God," Diana muttered. Throwing the covers off her body, she leaped out of bed; realized she was naked, then crouched down, hiding her body.

"What?" Giovanni bolted upright, searching for an intruder.

She looked at his uncovered, naked form in the middle of the bed and gave another groan, "Oh my God." She struggled into her t-shirt then stood and tossed the tangled covers closest to her over Giovanni's lower half.

"What's wrong?"

She shook her head as she retrieved her underwear from the floor and slipped them on. "Nothing. I don't know."

"What are you doing?"

She began to search for more elements of her clothing. "Getting dressed."

"Why?"

"I have to go."

"Diana," he scrubbed his face, "what's going on?"

"I just need to think, okay? I was too tired yesterday. I should've stayed with the girls and slept."

"No, you shouldn't have."

She found her bra hanging off the lamp in the corner and tried not to think about what kind of passion had flung it that far. "Rome drugged me," she muttered as she shrugged into her bra under her shirt.

"Rome drugged you," Giovanni repeated.

"Yes, with help from Michele and Renee and the other girls. And you."

"What are you talking about?"

"And the Colosseum and the wine." She found her pants and a sock then knelt, crawling around on the floor, searching under the bed for the other one.

"Yesterday was lovely and last night was … good." She found the other sock and his boxer briefs, tossed them on the bed and sat back on her knees. "But that was just like a tension release. Like, the thing on a teapot that whistles to let out steam."

"The spout?"

"Sure, yeah. That." She sat back on her behind and put on her socks. "We were just two people who were lonely, and it happens," she shrugged, "and we were exhausted. I mean, when you think about it, I hadn't really slept for almost thirty-six hours, so I definitely wasn't thinking clearly and the moon, the … the moon, it did the thing that the moon does and took over, and we gave into our base urges."

"Okay." His eyes were disappearing from the squint of confusion taking over his face.

With pants in hand, she headed to the bathroom; Giovanni was quick off the bed. "What happened?"

She glanced behind her and waved at him, her voice hoarse. "Put some clothes on." But before she could close herself in the bathroom, Giovanni stepped in the way of the door.

"Luna."

She sat on the edge of the clawfoot tub and began wiggling into her pants, only the ledge was smaller than anticipated and she slipped backwards into the tub.

Giovanni lunged for her and held out a hand. "Damnit, what is going on?"

She let herself slip fully into the tub, turned awkwardly, then stood and finished pulling up her pants. "I don't know. I just feel like an awful person."

"Because you slept with me?"

"I'm engaged," she sighed holding up her pinky finger and the ring Anthony placed on it days ago, "and he's a nice guy. He doesn't deserve to be cheated on."

"That's the ring?"

She thrust her hand closer to Giovanni. "He forgot the ring because he was so nervous."

"He forgot–"

"I need to just go and … just go, okay?"

"Luna, you aren't a bad person. You thought you knew what you wanted, but it turns out you don't. This isn't a big deal."

"It is to me." Standing in the center of the tub, she shook her head to clear it. "I just need to think." She held out her hand for him to help her out. Once she was out of the tub, he pulled her against him. "I don't think I can let you go."

She pushed against his chest and scowled. "Well you need to figure out how."

"Diana." Her name sounded like a plea as he dropped his hands.

She took a step away from him and held up her hand to block out the lower part of his body from her vision that was tempting and causing problems. "Listen, I was starved for attention and scared about moving and really, really tired."

"What are you doing?"

"Trying not to get sidetracked."

He looked down at his body and back at her, a grin creeping up the side of his face.

"No," she pointed, "don't do that kind of thing."

"I want you," he whispered.

"Too bad." She turned and went in search of the pink sweater.

"Amore, you aren't making any sense." He followed her and pulled on his boxers and a t-shirt.

"I'm making perfect sense." After searching the bedroom she went to the living room and found the sweater wadded up on the sofa. "Everything made sense before I came here. And just so you know, none of this is real."

"It's real to me."

She shoved her hands into the arms of the sweater. "This is all vacation stuff. And it's a well-known fact, vacation flings don't last. Vacation *ideas* don't last." She did an awkward circle to get her other arm in, but found that the sweater was twisted, so took it off and began again. "Do you know, three years ago my sister went to France and came home with all these big plans to buy a vineyard? A vineyard, in France! But the idea went away after about a week. Do you know why? It was a vacation dream. And that's what's happening here." Sweater finally on properly, she pulled it around her and nodded.

"You don't love him," Giovanni said softly.

"I ..." She shook her head and made a wide berth around him to retrieve her purse that was lying on the floor next to the keys to his apartment.

She opened the door and Giovanni's voice rose, "What are you doing?"

She glanced back at him, hair mussed, wide desperate eyes and t-shirt hugging the muscles that he didn't show off through his slightly too big shirts.

"Bye," she called and quickly headed down the stairs.

"What the hell?"

"Thank you for everything yesterday." She could hear him coming after her as she tried to hurry down the stairs and not fall down.

She was almost to the front door, and just as her feet stepped onto the ground level, the door opened and an older couple, each pulling a collapsible shopping bag behind them, were struggling to get inside.

Giovanni had caught up just then, and he held the door open and forced a smiled greeting, "Signora, signore."

The woman made an obvious study of his attire and frowned, tisking as she walked to the elevator. The old man patted Giovanni on the arm and laughingly commented before he joined his wife.

Once they were clear, with Giovanni still holding the door open, Diana walked through. She was several steps away when she turned and asked, "What did he say to you?"

Giovanni smirked. "He said he's been where I am."

She grunted and turned, but he yelled, "Damnit, Luna, stop."

"No." She turned back toward him and pointed her finger in his chest. "You don't get to call me that."

"I'll call you whatever I want," he sighed, "I'm falling in love with you."

She threw her hands up in the air and did a circle, coming back with another pointed finger. "Well, you're not allowed to."

He frowned. "I'm a grown man, if I want to fall in love with you, I will."

Diana pursed her lips. "Well, I say you can't."

Several whistles and catcalls from across the street caught their attention. Diana glanced at the ruckus and realized that mothers playing with their children near the fountain, patrons at the café across the street, and groups of people walking by were watching them, quite interested.

She glanced at Giovanni then, no shoes, boxer briefs that left little to the imagination and his stupid tight t-shirt. "You're causing a scene," she whispered between her teeth.

"*We're* causing a scene," he corrected.

She shook her head and took a step but he reached out and caught her hand. "Diana."

She tilted her head, insisting, "Let me go."

He let his gaze dart quickly around them and she caught the barest twitch of a smile before he jerked her into his arms, wrapped his arms around her to keep her in place while he seared her lips with a kiss.

She didn't know what she was more appalled by, the action or the round of clapping and whistles it incited.

When she finally freed herself she wiped her mouth with the back of her hand and looked at him incredulously. "What are you doing?"

"Trying to get you to come back upstairs."

"You're making a scene."

He laughed and gestured around them. "Amore, you're the one who ran out here, and this interaction, by the way, is the most Italian thing we could be doing."

She crossed her arms against her chest and snarled at him, bringing another round of reaction from the watching crowd, a collective 'ohhhh' as if they all knew Giovanni was in trouble now.

"Come back upstairs," he tried.

"I need to go. Where can I get a taxi?"

He scrubbed his face. "Please, let's talk about this. Go get some rest and let me take you out tonight, or this afternoon for coffee."

She pointed in the direction they came yesterday. "I can get a bus if I go that way, right?"

"Are you going back to the hostel?" he asked.

"No."

"I'll pick you up tonight and take you to dinner."

She laughed, this man had lost his mind. "No."

"I'll text Michele and let her know what time."

"I'm not going to dinner with you. This was a mistake. Thanks for making the Colosseum happen."

"It'll just be casual dress, we can go as friends." He smiled.

She should just start walking.

"We tried this yesterday when you said you wanted to show me Rome and you ended up baiting me and bringing me to your apartment."

"And you chose to stay because you wanted to," he countered.

"I stayed because I wasn't in my right mind."

"You wanted me as *much* as I wanted you!" he yelled and the crowd, not necessarily knowing what he was saying, seemed to like the passion and desperation in the phrase and clapped.

"Oh my God." She rolled her eyes. "Thank you for everything." She repeated and began to walk away, a few 'boos' accompanied her. Under her breath she seethed, "Really?"

"What's so wrong with me?" he asked, the hurt evident in his voice.

Diana glanced at the crowd which wasn't budging, so she turned back and crossed the distance she'd created, so she didn't have to yell. This elicited an excited, 'ohhh' from the peanut gallery. "Nothing. Nothing is wrong with you. It's me. I'm a mess," she tried to soothe.

Giovanni's whole face lit up, "I get it. If the current, *secure* fiance dies in the future, your world won't end."

"Good, so you see why I can't go with you to dinner. Have a good life."

He shook his head, pulled her into his embrace and brushed a soft kiss on her lips. Another eruption of cheers. He pulled away and looked into her eyes, "I'll text Michele." Another kiss and he let go, then pointed in the opposite direction from where she was originally headed. "I'll call you a cab. It should be there by the time you walk three blocks."

He gave her a slight push and then gave a bow in the direction of the piazza.

Diana gawked as the crowd cheered. Her mouth hung open as she shuffled away from Giovanni and whispered to herself, "What the hell just happened?"

# Chapter Thirty-Two

"**O**hh, here she is." Renee's voice echoed happily around the room as Diana walked in. "Ladies and humans, the woman taking her first ever Roman stride of pride, Miss Diana Barrett!"

Diana pointed an angry finger at Renee. "I am *not* in the mood."

"Oh?" Renee swung her legs over her bed. "Now I'm really intrigued. Tell us everything."

"Renee," Michele warned with a frown, walking over to Diana.

"You want to know everything?" Diana gave an unladylike snort laugh. "I'll tell you everything. I had the best day of my damn life. I wrote again. The Pantheon is pretty spectacular in the morning. I'm seeing the ghost of my dead husband *and* having conversations with him. I just made a fool of myself in the middle of the street. Giovanni seduced me, though he did admit that was what he was trying to do. And the sex was," she nodded her head comically several times as she paced in a small circle before finally snorting, "amazing ... I mean," she threw both her hands in the air, "it was really *good*. Which means I cheated on a good man and if he thinks I'm going anywhere else in Rome with him, he's out of his damn mind because I don't have anything to wear anyway and I figured out what I'm so scared of and Giovanni was a fat kid but now he's ridiculous when his shirt is off and what if I get hurt again? And you," she whirled around and pointed at Renee as her voice continued to climb to hysterical octaves, "you *witch* of a girl! You changed my life with a stupid haircut and you're no better," she turned her accusation on Michele, "asking questions about not asking the right question." Her voice caught on a sob and she dropped her head in her hands mumbling, "Nothing makes sense anymore."

"Yas!" Renee's glee was evident in the way she drew out the word.

"Okay, okay." Sabrina inserted herself in front of Diana and took her hands. "Look at me," she instructed harshly.

Diana blinked through her tears but did as she was told as Sabrina's yoga teaching kicked in. "You're going to breathe the way I do." Diana nodded. "In for two, hold it, and out." Sabrina nodded encouragement as Diana shakily followed the breathing techniques.

Several minutes passed as Diana followed Sabrina's directives, and when she seemed calmed down Sabrina asked, "How are you feeling?"

"Better. Stupid. Tired." She dislodged her hands but nodded at Sabrina. "Better. I feel better." She crossed the room to where her untouched bed was and threw herself down prostrate, moaning into her pillow.

"Oh my God, he really got under your skin." Renee squealed, skipping to Diana's side.

"Renee," Michele warned.

Diana heard a chair being pulled up beside her. "Okay, we're going to talk about all of this and get it figured out." It was Tasha's turn to take charge.

Diana rolled into a sitting position, Tasha and Michele had pulled up chairs next to the bed. Renee sat down on the end of the bed next to Sabrina who grabbed one of Diana's feet, took the shoe and sock off and began to massage it.

"What are you doing?" Diana asked.

"Settling you down," Sabrina said.

Diana thought about pulling her foot away but it really did feel nice.

"Let's start at the beginning," Tasha said.

"You have a dead husband and you're seeing his ghost?" Renee voiced the part where she wanted Diana to start.

Diana rubbed her face with her hands then shook her head and half-heartedly accused Tasha, "You're treating me like one of your second graders."

"Yes," Tasha admitted in the same tone she probably used for her students when they were feeling overwhelmed.

"But if it helps, we're dying to talk through *everything* you just said," Renee interjected.

"I'm sorry I didn't think to let you know where I was all day." Diana sighed and caught the sheepish glance Tasha gave Michele.

"What?" Diana asked.

Michele lifted a shoulder. "Giovanni texted me and told me you were with him and we shouldn't worry. And that you'd probably stay the night."

"Of course he did, because he's also thoughtful." Diana threw her hands up in the air.

"The beginning," Tasha insisted.

"I'm not sure where that is any more." She shivered. "I don't know if the foot rub is helping because my body is still ..." She stopped herself from what she thought was about to be an improper comment; about how her body was still tingling and flushed from the long evening of attention.

Renee sat forward. "Your body is still ..." she prodded with wide eyes.

"You guys kept me up in Orvieto, the night before we came to Rome. It really pissed me off," Diana said instead. "I thought you were drinking and that's why all the hushing and laughter ... I was jealous. I'd just been scared in Florence ..." She rubbed her temple. "Then I met you on the train and you said it was a concert that excited you and then you ruined my life by asking me how old I *feel.*" She snorted a laugh. "I felt like I was way too old to be talking to a group of young, excited women on a train." The tears were building once more. "I felt too old to stay in the same room with you all. Then you convinced me to update my look and took me to dinner with an amazing group of people; Michele, you know some really wonderful people." She nodded, her lower lip quivering with more tears. She wiped them away and continued, "We weren't even halfway through the meal and I didn't feel old anymore. And I really like how I feel now."

Sabrina moved to the other foot and Diana gave her a weak smile of thanks. She looked at each of the women surrounding her, one at a time, and shook her head sadly. "By the time I was your age, I'd been married, had a miscarriage, and lost a husband to a horrible accident." She took a deep breath. "I couldn't go on living after that. I gave up on everything the same day my husband died." If someone had told her last week she would tell her story in two days to complete strangers, when she hadn't voiced *any* of it to the man she was engaged to ... "And I'm so jealous of you all. Of your youth, of your outlook on life, of your friendships, of what you have to look forward to."

"Your life isn't over," Michele insisted.

Tears had formed again and her voice was hoarse as she admitted with everything in her soul, "I thought it was."

No one spoke for a moment, allowing Diana to gather herself.

"You said you were seeing your husband?" Tasha asked.

"David." Diana nodded as he appeared across the room.

*'What's crack-a-lackin, baby?'* He greeted her the way he always had when they'd been apart for a while. He struck his version of a runway model pose and made a quick kissing gesture toward her.

Diana breathed a laugh and rolled her eyes. "David was an artist and I was a writer and we lived in Brooklyn while we went to school. We were crazy in love." He smiled at her, and she shook her head. "When I say crazy in love, I mean it. We had stupid, mad passion." They had a great story, why had she kept it hidden for so long? "We had this fierce yearning for each other that comes with youth and lack of fear and the audacity of having the world at your fingertips."

"Wow," Renee breathed.

Diana nodded at Renee. "You would have loved him." She smiled. "I was barely making money doing freelance writing and was submitting my work to agents. David had several shows and so many pieces in galleries around town. We were starving artists and we were on top of the world."

"And now you're talking to him?"

"He has a lot of feelings about my life choices," she muttered then held up a hand. "And before you say it's my subconscious and all that, I get it. That's what it probably is, but he's very insistent and opinionated."

They nodded, willing to accept the fact for now. Renee took the lull to sit forward and ask, "What happened with Giovanni? How did he find you?" Her voice lowered conspiratorially. "You said the sex was good?"

"I'm engaged," Diana pointed, "at least I was."

"Did you break it off?"

"No, but I'm probably going to," she said hopelessly.

Tasha calmly said, "This sort of thing happens all the time, a lot of people break off their engagements. That's the whole point of an engagement period in the first place, to give yourself time to make sure you're making the right choice."

"She's an adult, you don't need to talk down to her like she's an idiot," Renee muttered.

"Renee, I'm not talking to her like she's an idiot. I'm just trying to help," Tasha growled.

"There's a difference between helping and talking down to people," Renee defended.

Tasha rolled her eyes. "Whatever Renee. I'm not in the mood for your crap right now."

"Tasha," Michele interrupted.

"Don't be the reasonable peace keeper this time Michele." Tasha pointed, the careful teacher gone. "Renee, sometimes you act so immature ..." She shook her head.

Renee scoffed, "Because I root for love and want people to be happy?"

"Yes." Tashsa shook her head. "I don't know, but sometimes romance isn't enough."

Diana pointed at Tasha. "Yes! Passion can fade."

Sabrina patted Diana's leg. "We've been on vacation together in cramped spaces with no 'me time' for a while now," she explained.

"Did the passion with David fade?" Renee asked.

"It died, same thing," Diana said as Giovanni's words whispered: *If the current fiance dies in the future, your world won't end.*

"Not the same thing," Renee argued. "You said you've been talking to him again, is he here?" She glanced around the room as if he'd appear for her at any second.

Diana frowned but after a moment pointed to the small desk in the corner he was sitting on, biting into a candy bar.

"How do you feel when you see him?" Renee asked.

He winked. *'Yeah baby, how you feelin'?'*

Diana snorted. "I miss him and I remember all the good times and the not so good times and how he made me so happy and mad and inspired and challenged."

"So the passion didn't die, *he* did," Renee surmised as Tasha scoffed, "Renee, c'mon. She's baring her soul, she doesn't need you to grind salt in the wound."

"I agree with Tasha." Michele gave the calm alliance.

"I don't," Renee insisted, "I think this is the very moment she's coming to terms with some heavy shit."

Sabrina gave a deep sigh, her passive aggressive comment on the situation was waved off by the other three.

Renee pointed at Tasha. "I'm sorry your relationship didn't work out with Kevin. We all are, but you can't keep dating assholes and then get upset when the same breakup keeps happening time and time again."

"I don't want to talk about it," Tasha said.

"You never want to talk about it," Renee pointed.

"And we're *not* gonna talk about it now," Michele said loudly.

Diana glanced between the girls. "Maybe we *should* talk about it now."

"We're talking about all of it," Renee insisted. "It all runs along the same lines: Life, love and death."

Diana gave a snort. "And lunar cycles."

Renee nodded, largely agreeing. "And passion."

"I don't even know what we're talking about anymore." Diana sighed.

Michele supplied, "You and Giovanni."

"Giovanni." Diana said his name and flopped back onto the bed, hitting her head against the headboard on her way down. Grunting, she turned her head to the side and stayed in that awkward angle, declaring, "He makes me feel things I don't want to feel."

Renee gave a squeal of excitement.

Diana crawled back up to a seated position and glanced around at each woman. "You all need to know how amazing you are. And how important your friendship is. I'm in awe of you, how you all seem to know who you are and who each other is as well."

"You know who you are," Michele said.

"I'm a sensible CPA from Atlanta who helped raise her sister's kids and feels old and is engaged to a man who never, ever touched me the way Giovanni did." She let a hysterical laugh escape, "This person, sitting in front of you?" She wildly fluttered her hands around her face. "I'm not so sure about her."

"Then get to know her," Renee replied.

"Sure, as long as I don't have to see Giovanni again."

Renee glanced at Michele and Diana sighed. "What now?"

"I've had possibly one or thirty-three text messages from him since you left his apartment. He's going to show up tonight to take you to dinner. If you want, I can try to dissuade him or we can all go out and conveniently miss him."

Diana sarcastically said, "But we'll still find him waiting outside when we come home."

"I don't understand the problem then," Sabrina said.

Diana pursed her lips and glanced around the room. When she met David's expectant face, she cleared her throat. "The physical heartache when David died ... there are no words for how horrific it was." She shook her head. "Giovanni said I want to marry Anthony because he's safe. Because I don't love him, and if Anthony died, my life would still go on," she finished softly.

"You're scared to have crazy passion again, huh?" Renee then pointed at her friends. "See, I was right."

Diana nodded. "And Italy doesn't feel like reality."

"Then what happens in Italy, stays in Italy." Renee winked.

"Diana, what do you *want* to do?" Tasha asked.

Diana covered her face.

*'Aw, Lu. I don't think you can shock these girls and we both know you've already made up your mind.'*

From the safety of her hands, Diana mumbled, "I want to keep pretending what happens in Italy stays in Italy."

Renee clapped. "Yes! Let a nice man take you to dinner and then go home and come to terms with life and death. Because you said yourself, you died when David did. Now you don't feel so dead, right?" She waited for Diana to answer.

"I'm feeling pretty alive." Her body shivered with memories of Giovanni's touch to help her corroborate her statement.

"Okay, so the next step is to come to terms with the fact that at some point in your life, someone you love is going to die again."

"Jesus Renee," Tasha blew out.

Renee shrugged. "Death comes for all of us to endure first and then take part in. This isn't news."

Diana felt like she had the air displaced from her lungs. "No, it isn't news."

Renee nodded her head once triumphantly.

Tasha spoke quietly, slowly, as if Renee's words impacted her so much she needed to put them into a different explanation. "If you marry Mr. Houston or date the handsome archeologist or ditch 'em both; you're still going to wake up tomorrow, and the opportunity to get hurt will still be there."

Diana shook her head in wonder. "Whatever you women do in life, please don't ever stop empowering other women. I already told you how great you are, right?"

"What do you want me to tell Giovanni?" Michele asked.

"That I'll go to dinner," she mumbled. "But you're all going with us. Please?"

"Are you sure?" Renee asked.

"Very."

They all nodded in agreement and Diana put her hand on Michele's arm. "Though, maybe don't tell him he's taking five women to dinner."

Michele winked at Diana in reply.

"Okay." Diana was beginning to feel a little more focused, a little better. "Okay, but I think I need something else to wear tonight and I don't think I like my old wardrobe," Diana admitted.

Renee jumped off the bed. "Yes! How much time do we have?"

"I don't know."

"Give me twenty minutes and I'll get this all figured out." Michele stood as well.

"And his side of the story?" Diana said.

"I mean, I was planning on texting him the second you're out of sight anyway." Michele gave a sly shrug.

"What else do you need?" Tasha asked.

"A shower. And I'm hungry."

Sabrina nodded. "We were going to the little bar across the street, Michele said they have a good pasta lunch."

"I should take a nap, but I don't think I'll be able to sleep. So I was thinking I'd write some this afternoon."

Renee nodded. "Okay, Michele works a little in the afternoons." She got up and began to rummage through her bag. "You can go with her.

She finds all the coolest coffee shops to work in."

Diana was feeling properly pieced back together now. "Can I tag along with you, if you go see more of Rome?"

"Of course," Tasha said emphatically, "I'm not sure of the schedule but know the Spanish Steps and Trevi Fountain are on the list, and tomorrow we're going to ride scooters and have lunch with Angelina."

"That sounds so nice, if you really don't mind me tagging along."

Renee slapped Diana's arm. "We adopted you; you're ours now." She handed over a bottle of water, aspirin and a set of disposable under eye pads. "These will take the puffiness down. Use 'em after you get out of the shower."

# Chapter Thirty-Three

"He's here." Michele put her cell phone away and sat down to finish putting on her shoes.

Diana's stomach did an impressive flip as Renee, who was walking by her, reached out and gave her shoulders an excited shake. Diana slapped at her hands.

"What am I doing?" she muttered to herself.

"We," Tasha offered, "are going to dinner."

"We." That helped. "We." She nodded and then with a roll of her eyes, turned to Renee and held her hands out to her side, a silent question, did she look okay?

She was wearing a white, short sleeve faux wrap shirt; a pair of black, wide leg pants, made from such a soft fabric it was like silk and cotton had a baby; a pair of wedge sandals; and large hoop earrings.

"You look gorgeous." Renee wiggled her eyebrows. "How do you feel?"

"I *feel* wonderful," Diana replied.

That afternoon, once Diana had completely calmed down and enjoyed another spectacular bowl of pasta, the group meandered over the geometric patterned cobblestones of Rome to the base of the Spanish Steps, littered with midday crowds soaking up the sun.

Renee's head was on a swivel however, as this was the shopping district and store fronts beckoned the shopper with giant yellow and red signs screaming 'Saldi' and promising '30, 40 or 50 percent off.' But this was part of the plan for the afternoon, to help Diana buy a new outfit or two.

Renee excitedly pulled Diana with her and proved to be tireless in her shopping abilities.

Diana thought maybe they'd go to a department store like the one she'd found in Florence and find a shirt and a pair of pants. Instead, they were on the sixth store with only four items purchased.

Diana finally admitted defeat, "Renee, I'm done. I appreciate everything you're doing," she laughed, "but if you want to keep buying things, you know my sizes. We'll go find an ATM, and you can continue without me."

"Deal," Renee happily agreed, and Diana turned an incredulous look on her friends who shrugged, as if they'd spent years trying and figured that leaving her to her own devices was the best compromise.

Michele pointed out the ATM, took Renee's phone, made sure she had the proper address for the hostel and waved her goodbye.

The women went to a café and sat outside in the shade so Michele could work. Diana was happy for the late afternoon stop, her fingers and brain needed to write. She thought she'd feel strange writing in front of these women, but Tasha pulled out a book and Sabrina sat back in her seat, cradling her tea and perhaps meditating.

When they returned to the hostel, Renee had the colorful wardrobe of seven shirts, two pairs of pants, two kimonos, a dress, and a pair of shoes that would go with everything laid out on the bed. "How much do I owe you?"

Renee grinned and handed over a few coins from the two hundred euro Diana had left her with. "What, really?"

"I'm amazing," she beamed.

And the young woman *was* amazing, Diana felt so good in the clothes.

"Okay," Tasha announced, "I think we're ready to go."

Thankfully, Michele led the way to the common area of the hostel. Diana was a bundle of nerves, she fidgeted several times with the waist of her shirt. She had handed her phone and wallet over to Tasha to carry, and had never missed her purse so much in her life.

"Buona sera, belle ragazze." Giovanni grinned as they came to stand in front of him. Diana watched as he greeted each woman with cheek kisses, and how Michele elbowed him knowingly.

"Bella Luna," She thought his breath caught on the endearment, but she couldn't be sure, her heartbeat so heavily echoing in her eardrums. But nothing was wrong with her vision or sense of smell.

"C'mon," she implored, as he stepped toward her.

Giovanni wore a black short sleeve button-down, the top two buttons undone and tucked into a pair of dark gray slacks. He'd washed his hair and used some product to achieve that attractive bedhead look. But it was the short stubble he hadn't shaved that pulled the remark from her; because she was well aware why he'd kept it; it was all because of a comment she'd made about how good it felt against her skin, so he promised to never shave it.

"What's wrong?" he asked as he leaned toward her. She took a step back and shoved her hand out between them to shake instead of offering her cheek. So the monster took her hand in both of his, brought it to his lips and looking at her through hooded eyes, carefully bushed a kiss on her hand.

"Okay, okay." She pulled her hand away.

He grinned and turned to the women. "Are you all headed out for the evening?"

"They're going to dinner," Diana informed him.

Addressing the others, he asked, "Where are you all going?"

Diana enjoyed this, as she innocently gazed up at him and inquired, "I don't know, where are *we* going?"

He caught on quickly, and gave a slow nod. "So I suppose I should change the reservation."

"Probably." Diana smiled.

"Alright then." He held the front door with a smile. "Ladies."

Michele asked him which way they were going, so he suggested the metro. "It'll be fastest."

When he held out his arm for Diana, she graciously slipped her arm through his. "You needed reinforcements to be with me, huh?" He asked.

"I didn't agree to this dinner."

"Fair's fair." He patted her hand. "You look gorgeous by the way."

"You don't look so bad yourself."

At the restaurant, Elsbeth and her husband, Oliver, were waiting at a table big enough for eight. Diana eyed Michele but she held up her hands. "I didn't say anything, I swear. I just arranged the meeting time."

"I had a feeling." Giovanni said as introductions were made and seats arranged.

The wine flowed and conversation reminiscent of her first evening in Rome began to take shape. When it came time to order, Diana sighed in defeat and leaned over to ask Giovanni, "Can you order for me?"

"What would you like?"

She laughed. "Something to go with a night of good friends and good wine and conversation that revolves around travel and Rome."

He winked at her. "Did I tell you how good you smell?"

She tried to ignore the physical reaction that had become a series of unexpected aftershocks.

Instead she turned her attention to Michele. "Is it always like this? Do Italians eat dinner together in big groups and talk about such interesting things all the time?"

"I wish," Michele shook her head, "but no. This is very much a friendship related standard. I spent a lot of nights eating alone when I lived here."

"Where did you live?" Diana asked. "Not that I'm all that familiar with the city, but I guess I know where the Colosseum is."

"The American University of Rome, it's on the other side of the river, away from all the historical monuments."

Tasha laughed. "*Is* there a part of this city that is away from historical monuments?"

"Kind of." Michele smiled, not minding the ribbing. "When we rent scooters I'll make sure we go past it, it's near an overlook that would be fun to visit. Great views of the city."

"Do you miss it?" Diana asked.

Michele shrugged. "I do. But I was so homesick, I hadn't anticipated that. So I figured out how to work for a company that's located in Rome so I can visit now and again, but live close to my family."

Sabrina asked, "What about the people we met the other night? You weren't all hitting the jazz club every Friday night?"

Michele shook her head. "I didn't meet these wonderful humans until my last year. But we were all so busy, we couldn't always meet like this."

The meal was a whirlwind of various dishes, none of which ended up with their original patron. Appetizers of fried artichokes, cheese stuffed zucchini flowers, more burrata and prosciutto. Then there were pastas; Bolognese, lasagna, something Diana was sure she heard translated as ox tail, along with sausages and broccoli and roasted veal. It felt like she was in a food coma. The full-bodied wine was red and gorgeous, and Giovanni's warm scent was decipherable amid the fresh food smells.

"Oh, I'm stuffed." Renee sat back and stretched. "Can we take a walk?"

Giovanni motioned for the waiter to take his card, but Diana felt bad. "Please, let me split it with you. I made the girls come with me."

"And I made Elsbeth and Oliver come with me."

They regrouped in front of the restaurant and Michele asked Renee, "Do you have three euros?"

"Do you need them now?"

Michele shook her head but gave a wink that said she had something up her sleeve.

"So that's where we're headed?" Elsbeth asked Michele.

"It'd be a shame to miss it, we're so close," Michele responded.

Renee glanced between the two women. "Okay, what are we missing?"

Michele just gave an incline of her head and the group followed.

"I swear this whole city is more ember than it is a harsh fluorescent." Diana offered the observation to Giovanni.

"Can I hold your hand?" he whispered.

She hesitated, and then because she'd been dying to touch him all night, and he'd been a proper gentleman, she did what they'd done as they walked up to the gates of the catacombs. She touched the backside of her hand against his.

He grappled for her, as if he was starving to touch her too and gave her hand a squeeze.

The sound, a loud noise of voices raised greeted them first, and when they turned a corner, like so many details of the city that seemed to be hidden in plain sight, blue and white lights illuminated the stage of the Trevi Fountain.

"Oh, yes!" Renee jumped. "Okay, how many coins do I need?"

"I've got it." Giovanni fished several coins out of his pocket as they made their way to the edge of the fountain. The sound was louder here, water spilling from the sides of the sculpted scene, where a giant Roman god exploded out of the middle, with his two trusty steeds rising from the depths of the water.

He handed the coins out and leaned into the center of the women as they gathered around him so he could give instructions. "With your back to the fountain, take the coin in your right hand, and throw it over your left shoulder. The first coin is to return to Rome. The second is to return to Rome and find love, and the third is to return to Rome, find love and have a good marriage."

Renee found a spot between the crowd and grinned at Michele who had taken her phone out to take pictures. She kissed each coin before she tossed them and then traded places. When it was Diana's turn, she tossed one coin; definitely of the mind that she was going to return here one day. She paused on the second coin, and mistakenly she looked into Giovanni's eyes. He was daring her to toss it and she wasn't one to back down from a dare. However, the third coin, she kissed and pocketed.

"Why'd you do that?" Renee asked loudly.

Diana glanced up. David was leaning against a railing, sketchbook in hand, his forehead pinched with a concentrated gaze. "I had a good marriage," she replied.

"C'mon Giovanni," Michele pushed, "your turn."

Crowding around him, they watched as he tossed his coins, and Diana was glad for his genial quickness. No overt eye contact or innuendo.

"Everyone sit down next to him," Michele called. "Group photo."

Renee turned Diana and sat her directly next to Giovanni; his arm slipped around her waist and his fingers squeezed her hip, releasing another bodily sense memory. Sweaty bodies pressed against each other, his strong hands squeezing her hips to pull her harder against him. She ground her teeth against the recollection and hoped her smile wasn't giving away what she was thinking.

"Luna." Her name was a whisper she could still make out over the loud rush of water and congestion of visitors. Against her better judgment, she turned and was captured in the warm twinkle of his eyes. "Go to Venice with me," he requested softly.

"What?" she scoffed. Diana tried to stand, but he kept her in place. "Please," he urged.

"You're out of your mind."

"I am. I'm out of my mind for you. Let me show you Venice, before you leave Italy for good. Let me spend a few more days with you."

"No."

"Why not? Give me one good reason." She opened her mouth, but he shook his head. "One that has nothing to do with some guy we both know you aren't going to marry, or a made-up insecurity."

"I don't want to." She jutted her chin out.

That slow grin started at the corner of his mouth, pulling at the edges of his eyes, growing until his whole face lit up and the scar at his temple turned white. She could almost make out a dimple in his stubbly cheek. "Michele can help you buy the ticket. I'll give her all the details, but I'm paying of course."

"No."

"Bella, I can't let you pay." He leaned forward and brushed a kiss on her cheek, his lips lingering, his scent stealing her cognitive reasoning abilities.

"No, I'm not going to go."

He pulled back so he could look into her eyes, "Imagine seeing the Grand Canal filled with all sorts of boats and gondolas." He brushed a kiss on the edge of her lips.

"No," she sighed.

"Imagine sipping prosecco at a restaurant with a view of the Rialto Bridge."

"Giovanni."

"Say you'll go. Before you leave Italy, let me have just a little more time with you."

"Tell me this isn't the craziest idea ever," Diana muttered, her vision fluctuating between tunnel vision and a wide spectrum of a floodlit Rome at midnight.

"Girl, this is how every love story ever told starts," Renee insisted.

Diana never gave him a solid answer, as they'd been interrupted by a family whose children chose that moment to lean over the edge of the fountain and start splashing each other and everyone else around them.

Renee had spotted people with gelato and ushered the group into a nearby establishment. Elsbeth and Oliver had to call it an evening, having to work the next day. And as they all said their goodbyes, Diana pulled Giovanni aside and whispered, "When would we leave?"

"Day after tomorrow?" he suggested.

"How long?"

"Two days." He rushed the number like he wasn't asking for enough *and* asking for too much.

She shook her head, worried her bottom lip for a moment before she mumbled, "Kiss me and say good night, then text Michele the details and I suppose I'll see you the day after tomorrow."

A growl accompanied the force with which she was swept against him and her mouth claimed in a kiss.

When he kissed her with all the promise of what was to come and finally let her go, she had to hold onto him for several moments. He'd stolen her equilibrium.

"Buonanotte, bella Luna," he whispered, and then said his goodbyes to the women and walked away with a spring in his step.

"Holy shit." Renee was at her elbow, eyes wide.

"Yeah, holy shit."

# Chapter Thirty-Four

Yawns were exchanged as the five women shuffled into their room. "Family meeting," Michele called out as they entered. "First things first, Diana can I see your passport?"

"Already?"

"Our boy does quick work," Michele bragged as she sat down at the table in the room with her laptop, a map of Rome and a piece of paper, while everyone else changed into comfortable clothes and grabbed water bottles and chocolate bars.

Diana held out her passport, but when Michele went to take it, she pulled it back with an uncertain frown

Sabrina laughed. "That's a good call, you shouldn't trust Michele. Because I suppose it's time we tell you what you've really gotten yourself into with us. We're a secret gang of Tupperware saleswomen, and our initiation is sending you to Venice with handsome men."

Tasha added, "Then please sign me up for the initiation again, I missed this part the first time around."

Diana handed the passport over and Michele motioned to the computer. "You can watch," she offered, "so you'll see I'm not doing anything nefarious." She filled in Diana's name and the passport number, then handed the ID back.

"Do I owe you... or Giovanni ...?"

Michele waved her away. "Take that up with him."

Everyone lounged around the table and when Michele was done, she nodded. "Okay, Diana's flight for Venice leaves the day after tomorrow at ten am."

Diana was sure she paled.

"So we only have one day left with the fair Diana; what do we want to do? Keeping in mind, we have lunch with Angelina."

"I love her," Tasha said. "Do you know she's eighty-three? And she still travels so much, and supports the arts and I think she even has a boyfriend. She's just so interesting and lively."

"I know we talked about renting scooters," Renee said excitedly. "I think Diana should get to ride a scooter in Rome before she leaves."

"Have you seen how people drive around here?" Diana asked.

Renee waved her concerns away. "We'll be fine. Michele wouldn't let us do anything too stupid."

"My big thing was seeing the fountain, and we crossed that off the list," Tasha added.

"I just want to wander and look at the streets and the laundry hanging out the windows." Sabrina laughed then nodded to Diana. "What's on your bucket list?"

"Do you know, I didn't even know I had a bucket list until I met you all."

Renee wiggled her eyebrows. "You've been filling that list out rather nicely the past few days."

Diana stole Renee's chocolate bar in retaliation and after taking a bite said, "I'd like to write a little tomorrow morning at a café and, I was up last night looking at the moon. I thought it would be fun to ... since being in the moonlight at the Colosseum, I just thought it'd be fun to go out every night I have left in Italy and be in the moonlight."

"Oh!" Sabrina nodded enthusiastically. "I know a great moon flow that you'd all love."

Renee groaned but held up a hand and defended, "I know I know, it'll probably make me feel great."

"If we rent scooters tomorrow," Michele began, "we can see some cool sites and if nobody minds, there is a museum I'd love to show you. It's one of my favorites."

Nods of agreement abounded, so Michele sketched out an itinerary and then pushed it to the middle of the table. "Now, I'm exhausted. I'm going to bed, you can all do whatever you'd like."

Sabrina touched Diana on the arm, "I'll go outside with you for a few minutes if you want to see if the moon is high enough in the sky."

"Yeah, thanks."

Out on the gray, rainbow shaped cobblestones, they looked up in search of the moon, but it was difficult to see with the buildings in the way.

"There is a piazza up the road a bit, we might be able to see something from there," Sabrina suggested.

"Thank you for coming out with me, this just felt right, like something I needed to do."

"Those are the whispers we need to give the most attention to, sometimes."

Light fixtures positioned halfway up each of the buildings cast a soft natural glow onto the streets. Most shutters had been closed to the night. A few soft echoes of televisions and muttered conversations rolled past them, but mostly it was their footsteps that were loud in the night air.

"Can I ask you a question?" Sabrina asked and Diana nodded. "How did you know you loved David?"

"Oh, well. I couldn't think about anything else. I couldn't eat or sleep and I couldn't wait to see him. That was at first, of course, and I thought it was just lust." She smiled as David fell into step beside her with a wink.

"It hurt to be away from him and I longed to tell him about my day and ask his opinion and just be near him. I felt whole and complete when I was just sitting near him. Once we got married and the lust settled down, I couldn't wait to see him at the end of the day, I couldn't wait to be near him." She laughed softly. "The wholeness I felt then was a fullness, I felt like I was rounded out and had room for so much." She swallowed a lump forming. "I'm sorry. I don't know if that answers your question."

"But you knew it was love."

"Oh, I knew it was love," Diana reiterated emphatically.

"And it's different with your fiancé?"

Diana frowned. "I don't think I should call him that anymore."

"But it wasn't the same?"

"No, and that's what I like about him. What I liked about him." She rolled her eyes. "But I wasn't looking for extraordinary passion. I just wanted someone nice and caring. Someone I could talk to."

"Someone safe," Sabrina said. "I think we do that as we get older, we look at life realistically. People are attracted to others for as many different reasons as there are people. And safety isn't anything to take lightly."

They rounded a corner and the piazza opened up the sky view, and the moon shone down brightly on them.

"Giovanni is not safe," Sabrina whispered, though whether it was a question or a statement, Diana wasn't sure. And really, it could have been both.

"No," Diana agreed.

"Can I show you a yoga move? Nothing crazy; just something I think we should do right now, to help you gather the power of the moon, for the next phase of your life."

Diana smiled at Sabrina. "Yoga in the moonlight in Rome. Check."

# Chapter Thirty-Five

"**A**re you ready?" Renee yelled over her shoulder.

Diana shook her head and yelled back, "No!"

Renee's laughter rang out and mingled with the passing traffic before she called, "Too bad," then twisted the handle of the pale blue scooter they'd rented and pulled into the midday traffic of Rome. Diana wrapped her arms around Renee's waist, squeezed her eyes shut and tried to keep herself upright as Renee followed the other women, all on their own scooters. Why she ended up with Renee, she'd never understand, other than it just added to her original theory that the woman was a witch.

Renee gave a squeal of delight and Diana opened her eyes. They were moving now, and Michele had led them off the main road so they could travel down less crowded streets. It was a blur of excitement and sites.

Diana developed a phantom brake system, a hint as to what she would like Renee to do: Seated upright, her hands lightly on the woman's waist, meant Diana didn't need Renee to brake. Clutching her fully around the waist, her helmet clad head hitting Renee's meant *slow the hell down.*

It was during an insistence of 'slow down', (that Renee refused to acknowledge), when Diana caught a glimpse of a giant three-tiered building that looked like a re-creation of something from the Roman Forum, with horse-drawn chariots at the top and Italian flags in front whipping in the wind.

The afternoon went on like that, a dazzling blur of history and sites. They drove to the top of one of Rome's seven hills and parked, stood at the edge of an outcropping and gazed at the sea of Rome: terracotta rooftops, beige white buildings, a cloudy blue sky against a hazy mountain range. They posed for selfies and Michele pointed out landmarks.

Michele elbowed Diana and pointed. "Giovanni lives right over there."

"The sight of my infamous public argument," Diana mused.

Michele leaned into Diana's side. "I'll vouch for him with everything in me and more. If you want more proof, I'll get you more proof; he's a really good guy," she said avidly.

Diana leaned back into Michele. "That's great, but I don't really know you either."

"Touché."

"Thanks for the offer though. I know he's a good guy, I honestly wouldn't have agreed to go to Venice with him if I didn't think he was. There's just a lot to rummage through and figure out in my old life first."

Michele nodded. "I get that. But just so you know, living in Rome isn't out of the realm of possibility."

The realms of possibility continued to expand and morph as the minutes and hours passed in this country.

As they walked back to the waiting scooters, Renee asked Diana, "Do you wanna drive?" Diana stared at the scooter as Renee handed over the keys and insisted, "Yeah, you wanna drive."

*'Yeah, she wants to drive,'* David encouraged.

"I'll ride with Michele." Renee headed over to her friend, already having made the decision.

Since Diana had paid attention when they were all getting the ten minute 'how to' instructional from the rental place, she knew what to do. She centered herself, started the bike and edged the kickstand up.

*'Lookin' good, Lu.'*

"Get on." She gestured with her head and as the women started back down the hill, she didn't follow right away; she swore she felt David's phantom arms slip around her waist.

It was the worry that they would get too far ahead of her that prodded her into action.

Once they crossed a bridge over the river that was the lifeblood of Rome, and twisted more through the city streets, they came to the gates of a villa. Michele helped everyone park the scooters next to those already present.

"This is my favorite art gallery," she said as they gathered their things and began to walk down the park-like lane toward the white villa. "It's called the Galleria Borghese, and is the old villa of the Borghese family. But don't ask me for any more information than that. I was just here for the art." She laughed.

Diana overheard Michele drop Angelina's name and like some magic trick, they were able to walk right in. Though any questions she had died on her lips as the cool entrance opened into lavish gold and white filigree covered walls and ceilings that echoed with hushed conversations.

Every inch of the walls and ceilings were covered with frescos or paintings or sculptures, and even the floor was a marble masterpiece.

*'Jesus Christ, Lu! It's a Caravaggio.'* David ran in front of Diana pointing, *'And that's a Raphael!'*

Michele let them wander slowly, but she had a reason for being here and she continued to gently insist on the direction they should go.

"There it is." Michele pointed as they entered a new room. This one was done in glossy tans and golds, the lights dimmed so that all attention was on the Baroque sculpture in the center, a young man reaching for a young woman. "Apollo chasing Daphne," she supplied releasing the deepest sigh, as if she'd finally come home and was seeing a good friend once again.

"Tell us about it," Tasha said as she began to circle the statue.

"It was carved by Bernini who was only twenty-four when he started working on this."

"Jeez ..." Sabrina shook her head in wonder.

"It's beautiful," Renee sighed.

"So Apollo has just been shot by Cupid's arrow," Michele began; the mention of Cupid caused an eruption of emotions to spark through Diana. "He's just reached Daphne, but she doesn't want anything to do with him, so she's saved by being turned into a tree, and this is the exact moment that begins to happen. Her fingers are turning to leaves and her feet are sprouting roots."

"It's your favorite," Diana said and when Michele nodded, asked, "Why?"

Michele smiled. "When I came here for school, after the first six months, I was pretty homesick. I skipped school that day and just started wandering. I came to the park that's out in front, and it started raining, so I came inside. When I saw this sculpture, I just started crying. To me, it felt the way I was feeling, wanting to do so many things, pulled in so many different directions."

Diana glanced back at the pure white marble, and saw a woman who didn't want the reality of love so much that she was willing to allow herself to die and transform into something else. The kinship was a shock. She wiped an unexpected tear away as David caressed the roots spilling from Daphne's foot. *'Nah, babe. You already took root, you're blooming now.'*

She nodded as Renee looped her arm over her shoulder and said, "I hear there is lunch in our near future."

They drove a few minutes up a quiet road and Michele once again instructed them on parking. The restaurant was nearby and when they arrived, they were taken to an outside table where Angelina was waiting.

She stood to greet them. "I saw you drive by. You all look so wonderful on a scooter! Have you had a good day? Were you able to get to the museum?"

"Yes," Michele said, "thank you for setting that up."

She waved the thanks away and gestured for everyone to sit as a waiter showed up with a bottle of sparkling and regular water, then poured out a glass of wine for each woman.

"I ordered already, I hope you don't mind. But I think you will like it," Angelina informed, then held up her glass in a toast: "To young women taking on the world."

They sank into the noon meal. Hors d'oeuvres of bruschetta and fried balls of rice with mozzarella in the middle were served. There was a small bowl of carbonara, and some fresh cheese that Angelina instructed everyone to drizzle honey over.

After the meal was over, Angelina declared, "Oh, I would love una passeggiata, a little walk. There is a café nearby we could walk to."

Everyone readily agreed so Angelina stood and began to leave the restaurant.

"Who do we pay?" Diana asked.

Michele sighed. "She invited us to lunch and when she says I picked out the menu, it also means she already paid. If you can figure out a way to sneak one past Angelina, please let me know."

Back on the quiet street, when Angelina reached out to take Diana's arm to steady herself, Diana was happy to offer the support.

"So, you have a new beau." Angelina started the conversation.

"It's a tricky situation," Diana excused.

"Of course it is, it involves a man." She patted Diana's hand and laughed at her own joke. "I had three of them in my life." She leaned her short curled dark gray head toward Diana and admitted, "But those were just the ones I married."

"Are you a widow?"

"Three times over." Angelina gave a worn smile. "It's an awful word, an awful situation."

Diana admitted, "I am too. I lost my husband David when I was twenty-six."

Angelina made a tisking sound. "So young, life is just beginning at twenty-six."

"Mine ended then."

Angelina nodded her head gravely. "I suppose that happens too. So, now you have a new man who excites you."

"I'm engaged."

"Oh," she squeezed Diana's arm, "I didn't realize. I should have, the way he looked at you all night, especially when you danced."

"No ... not him."

"Ah," she breathed with a smile, "I see. Tricky."

Diana grunted. "Tricky."

"But good, you have options. It's good for a woman to have options."

"You are unlike anyone I've ever met," Diana said with wonder.

"I keep friends, old and young, lots of them. That helps. Always surround yourself with different people who have different interests. And find yourself a good lover, that never hurts."

"Do you have a lover?" Diana squeezed her lips together, embarassed that she'd asked.

"Of course."

Diana glanced at Angelina and tried to hold back a wide smile, "So those are the secrets to life?"

"Some of them."

"I don't think I ever felt like I had any secrets to life, because my life felt like it was over so long ago," Diana confessed.

Angelina grunted. "Ridicola, ridiculous."

"Maybe I waited too long."

Angelina shrugged. "So it took you a few years to shake off the difficulty." She waved the years away. "How old are you?"

"Forty-five."

Angelina laughed. "What's forty-five? Young. You can choose your age and your life."

"You can choose your age?" Diana sounded skeptical.

"Of course. Age is a gift and an illusion. I knew some women when they were twenty, who looked like they were a hundred. I know some at eighty that look like they are sixty ..." She turned her head toward Diana and winked. "I'm one of those women."

"You are," Diana agreed.

"I love this life," Angelina said forcefully, "all the ups and down. It's fun, and no matter how old you get, when you sparkle, you draw life and energy to you that keeps you vibrant and young at heart. You must never forget that."

"Age is relative." Diana summed up the thesis.

"Age is relative," Angelina agreed. "You are only forty-five. Go for walks. Drink wine. Open your eyes and let life in." She gave her cocktail recipe for life, then snapped her fingers, as if she'd forgotten the most important thing. The wise woman stopped Diana, pulling her in close before adding the secret, "And use olive oil as a moisturizer."

# Chapter Thirty-Six

D iana tightly gripped the extended handle of her bag as she tried to gather her warring emotions.

"Okay, follow the signs," Michele pointed, "it should be pretty simple from here on out."

Diana's new friends took the train with her to the airport. She tried to dissuade them and insist she would be fine on her own and didn't want to waste their time. But no one heard her argument, mainly because the last little piece of information Michele delivered as the train pulled up to the airport, was that Giovanni would meet her in Venice; at a water taxi station in the center of the city.

Now, it was time to say goodbye and Diana felt like she was leaving summer camp.

Sabrina hugged and held her hands the way she had when Diana had been so upset, then leveled her gaze and advised, "Listen to your heart, but as the yogis teach, your heart whispers so you have to be quiet." She winked and added, "But when in doubt, breathe."

Next was Tasha. "You can do anything you want. Nothing is ever set in stone, and life is meant to be experienced." She hugged Diana. "And have fun."

Michele brushed a tear away and shook her head. "This is ridiculous. We've only known each other a few days and I feel like you've been a friend for a hundred years."

"I was just thinking the same thing," Diana said.

"Keep in touch, you have a phone, you know how to use it. We want to see pictures of Venice."

"I'll send you pictures and I'll keep in touch." Diana reassured.

Renee stood back and looked Diana up and down, then reached out and touched the soft bob of Diana's dark hair. "Next time you get your haircut, ask for long layers and have them add texture to the ends."

"I'll probably just call you and hand the phone over," Diana admitted.

"You look good." She eyed Diana's outfit; white Capri pants, a white tank top and a black chiffon kimono spotted with white and maroon flowers.

"Thanks to you." Diana laughed. "You know how amazing you are, right?"

"I do."

Diana smiled, "If you are ever in New York, please, look up my sister, the two of you would get along so well."

"Oh, we're already friends."

"What?"

Renee shrugged. "The picture I put on your account, I tagged all of us and your sister reached out."

"Why didn't you tell me?"

"I thought *she* would." Renee said.

Diana shook her head and glanced once more at each woman. "All of you, you're bright shining lights in this world and we need that a lot." She wiped a tear away.

Renee pointed. "*That's* why you always use waterproof mascara. Now," she handed over a tissue from her purse, "send pictures and have fun and don't feel guilty and let that sexy ass man spoil you."

Diana didn't know how to leave, she wanted to say something more but all the heartfelt words swirling around didn't seem like enough, so she simply settled on, "Thank you all. Truly."

"Go," Michele directed with a smile as she hugged a teary Renee close to her side.

With a deep breath and wave of her hand, Diana turned and headed toward the airport entrance to go see about a man in Venice.

After she went through TSA, she had a little time, and she was so nervous, she decided to call Harper.

"Hello!" Harper screamed, answering on the first ring.

"So you and Renee are friends now?"

"As much as you can be friends with someone on social media."

"Listen, I'm going off itinerary and heading to Venice for two days." There was no comment so Diana continued, "I'll still be able to make my flight home from Rome though."

Harper *still* didn't say anything. So Diana sighed. "How much do you know?"

"Not a lot, but Renee posted a picture last night of a group in front of a fountain and the dark haired drink of water you were sitting next to looked like he was rather cozy with you."

Diana groaned. "Fine, that's why I'm going. I just thought you should know."

"Just in case you end up dead in a ditch in Venice this time?" Harper supplied.

"Yes. No. Look, I'm just trying to be responsible about my safety but I don't want to talk about it."

"Luna," the smile in Harper's voice was undeniable, "as far as I'm concerned, from the looks of that man, you don't need to be doing any talking. You need to be—"

"Yes, thank you Harper."

Laugher was followed by a deep sigh. "I love this trip for you."

"Well, it's been interesting, that's for sure."

"Okay, so when does your flight leave? Do you land in Venice on the water? How does that work?"

"I leave here in twenty minutes, arrive on land. But then I'm supposed to follow the signs to the water taxis and get a private one that will take me for a forty-five-minute ride into the heart of Venice."

"Oh my God, then what are you still doing on the phone? Go away, have a great trip. I'll talk to you in a few days."

"Yeah, a few days."

Standing in line to get on the plane, David caught her attention and said, *'Have fun kid.'*

"You're only a month older than me," she muttered, hesitating. He took a step away and she raised an eyebrow, "You're not going?"

*'You don't need a crutch, baby. You just need to let go.'*

She didn't want a crutch, she just wanted some company on the flight.

The woman behind her pointed out that it was her turn to board. She let David wave at her once more, giving her a wink and jutting his chin toward the plane, the indication for her to go.

On the plane, she pulled out her journal and guidebook and attempted to read about Venice or write something, but concentration evaded her. So she settled on fidgeting; adjusted her seat eight times – much to the chagrin of the passenger behind her; flipping through the two provided magazines without looking at them; and ripping her paper coffee cup into shreds.

As the plane came in for a landing at the Marco Polo Airport in Venice she used the breathing technique Sabrina taught her as she tried to differentiate between the elements of excitement, guilt, apprehension and anxiety that were all coursing through her.

And the last thing she did before she deplaned, was to slip the small engagement ring off her pinky, and put it in the coin section of her wallet so it would stay safe until she gave it back to Anthony.

She followed the signs to the water taxis; the walking helped ease her anxiety. When she found a few taxis lined up, she caught the attention of a driver and showed him her phone that had the name of the place she was to go, ferry terminal 'Ca' rezzonico.' The driver gave several nods as he took her bag and said, "Va bene, you sit now."

The boat had an open air seat for the driver with a window to block most of the wind. The middle of the boat was a covered area with wooden benches on either side, and full windows surrounding the space; while the back was also open air, with curved seating.

Diana opted for the less windy option inside as they drove though the choppy waters. It was noon and the sun was hidden by large lazy clouds crawling across the sky, obstructing the heat of the day. Now she had another long wait before she arrived at her final destination.

The boat seemed to head into the ocean until a coastline began to take shape. She opened her camera and took a photo of the buildings she could see, not sure what she was looking at in relation to the city. She did forward it along with a note to Renee that she'd made it to Venice and was on a boat.

Immediately she was answered with a cacophony of exclamation points, kissing face emojis and eggplants, along with a gif of fireworks erupting and the information that Renee was going to create a group text.

She laughed and sent the same photo to Harper: *Somewhere in Venice.*

Harper also immediately texted back: *Get some.*

To which Diana replied: *You and Renee need to meet.*

She put the phone down and stood, stretching from side to side, a bundle of nerves. Soon she would arrive at the terminal and according to Michele, Giovanni would be waiting.

*"What the hell are you doing?"* Diana's opposing side appeared opposite her, hair so tightly wound she could only criticize.

She looked past her, at the reflection of Italian Diana and whispered, "Going to Venice because of a man." The uptight Diana dissolved, arms crossed over her chest, a frown in place. When she was almost gone, she winked and called, *"I'm melting. Melting ..."*

"Jesus ... I might need a shrink," Diana mumbled to her *real* self. "Or an exorcism."

But she'd deal with that later, she'd come this far.

She moved to the back of the boat so she could rest her arms on the top of the covering over the middle section. The city skyline of Venice appeared, rising out of the water. It was all pointed steeples and bell towers that materialized first. Then appeared the terracotta outline of domed churches and buildings of a city built by opulence and kept adrift by merchants and romantic ideals.

The driver slowed and turned toward the crowded city. The buildings parted, opening up their waterways in greeting. Cream and peach colored buildings sat atop the water rocking, as their exposed brick winked and life bloomed around her.

There were more boats now, a few slowly passing, several moored along the side of walkways, bobbing in the wake made by other passing boats.

The first bridge appeared and Diana sat down as the boat passed under it, craning her neck to glimpse the black underbelly as she thought, even the dirt had life in it.

The buildings squeezed the water into thin passages, before releasing the boat into a wide canal.

This, Diana thought, must be the Grand Canal. There was a mass of traffic with no rhyme or reason. Buildings were faded pastel colors, sparkling off the water. So many lacy, arching windows carved into the façade of buildings facing the canal. leaving plenty of room for everyone to have a proper view of the Venetian waters. The water itself lapped against the boat, keeping raucous staccato time with Diana's excited beating heart.

The driver followed the curvy canal and there it was, the Rialto Bridge, one of the few things she'd read about.

Diana couldn't bring to mind why it was important or if it was just popular, but what she did know was that it was an iconic staple of Venice and here she was, slowly floating under it. She stretched her hand and her fingertips, barely brushing the dark gray foundation. She was really here.

Water traffic multiplied around the grand bridge. Gondolas, flat boats hauling stacks of large boxes, water buses loaded with tourists and smaller boats played friendly games of chicken on the water. Her own driver slowed and twisted his way through the throng.

They passed a gondola with a couple snuggled together, smiles plastered on their faces as their gondolier's bold tenor serenaded them.

Another slight turn of the canal and the driver steered closer to the edge and slowed. The visions of Venetian life were lost on Diana as a floating box, a watery terminal wrapped in yellow, clearly read Ca' Rezzonico. Her destination.

The driver pulled aside the opening. Diana's emotions were on overdrive, her breathing shallow as she searched for him. It took too long for recognition to travel from her optic nerves to her brain, though the butterflies were far more adept in perception.

Giovanni stood just inside the windowed box; a tall, handsome figure, hands clasped behind his back, his forehead drawn in worry. He wore khaki pants and a white button-down, a little too big, with sleeves rolled up just below his elbows and the top two buttons undone. It was such an Italian look, it sucked the remaining breath out of Diana's lungs.

The worry melted from his face and his smile grew, a smile just for her.

They locked eyes for a lifetime before the driver's insistent call to her broke through. "Signorina?"

Diana felt off-balance as she made her way to the front of the boat, arriving at the same time as Giovanni. He was reaching for her and she seamlessly climbed from the boat into his arms, then clung to him as his lips settled over hers.

"Ah, scusi. Signore?" The driver, once more, pleaded them back to reality.

"Hi," Giovanni breathed out, pulling back and gazing into her eyes.

"I missed you," she whispered honestly

"Thank God." He pressed his forehead against hers as a visible wave of relief washed over him. "I was worried once you arrived at the airport in Rome you'd just go home."

"What would you have done?" Diana asked.

"I would have waited here for two days then followed you," he admitted.

The driver was impatient now. "Signore."

Giovanni paid him in return for Diana's suitcase. He pulled the handle and held out his hand to her. "You ready?"

He'd asked her that before. The weight of the question thickened the air in the same way it had the first time. Saying yes to him was saying yes to so much more now.

"Yes." This affirmation was about saying yes to an adventure. Saying yes to herself. And saying yes to the way a sexy ass man looked at her as if he were starving and she was a damn buffet.

Giovanni took her hand and led her up the dock into the twisting streets of Venice.

# Chapter Thirty-Seven

The early morning light danced on the ceiling, sparkling and waving, a reflection of the sun flickering off the canal into the room.

As Diana watched the flutter and shake of light, she realized that light was different in Venice. With each passing moment of the day, the light seemed to bend and twinkle, float and alter; a true chameleon. The light would also be dependent on the time of year, the presence of clouds or sun; and throw in the numerous cloud formations and how they affect the light, it was no wonder artists spent lifetimes attempting to capture the everchanging light of the floating city.

"Amore ..." Giovanni's voice was thick with sleep. "Che fai?" *What are you doing?*

"Watching the light," she whispered, so as not to disturb the flickering show.

He opened one eye and glanced at what had her attention. After a moment he said, "fa la vecia," and moved through the tangled morning sheets to pull Diana into his arms. She snuggled into his embrace. "Fa la vecia," she repeated.

"It is a very Venetian phrase, it means to squint, but the real phrase means to do as the old woman does," he explained, leaning his head down so he could brush a kiss across her shoulder. "When the light of the canals reflects in the house it causes one to squint, to fa la vecia."

"I can't figure out if I like the light the most or the sound of the water lapping against the stones." They'd left the window and shutters open all night for the sake of the moon. Just then, nearby church bells began to ring the hour and a soft smile brushed across Diana's lips. "I should probably add bells to the list."

"Want to know my favorite part?" Giovanni propped himself on his elbow and began to trace his fingers along the side of her body. A man couldn't be this romantic, or maybe it was Venice that couldn't be this romantic.

She was at ease, that's what it was.

And they were a far cry from the awkward, stuttered beginning they'd had the day before.

The day apart had built up her apprehensions. What would Lena think? What would Anthony think? Giovanni, for how kind he'd been, really was a stranger.

To which Michele had defended, that was how people got to know each other, as strangers first.

Then Renee insisted that none of this was a big deal because a woman had the right to do what made her feel good. How could Diana explain that it took her six months to let Anthony touch her intimately, and he still hadn't come close to doing a tenth of what Giovanni had already done *to* her and *with* her.

So instead, she laughed and cringed as she explained, "You have to understand, in my day, we were *supposed* to feel bad for jumping into bed with strangers."

But that was the real problem. She felt bad about *not* feeling bad. Because in the middle of the dark nights, wide awake in her lumpy hostel bed, Diana replayed every caress, every kiss, every moment she'd shared with Giovanni while David pointed out how those were the same feelings she had for him after the first few dates.

*'Remember Lu? You couldn't sleep. You tried to write out how you were feeling, and got so upset when you couldn't express how you felt?'* He opened an imaginary book, pretending it was one of her youthful journals quoted: *'... erratic beating heart, the phantom caresses you could feel on your skin, the smell of me stained on your sheets.'*

She waved him away.

And those minutes that took forever to pass in the middle of the night, folded in on themselves, and she was in Venice, on a boat and there was Giovanni on the dock. A vision, a temptation, an excitement.

And Diana went willingly into his arms.

Giovanni led her through the winding streets of Venice. She was dazed by the winding streets, the bridges that rose and fell over the canals, joining one section of the floating city to the other.

"It's just around the corner," Giovanni had said after a few minutes.

Of course, just around the corner in Venice was a deceptive direction. The streets yawned and widened in some areas, and in others, four-story buildings held their breath and sucked in their stomach, creating just enough room to walk single file. In those moments, when Giovanni took the lead, Diana didn't let go of his hand. She wasn't interested in breaking the connection she had with him, she needed to feel the reassurance of his warmth. The link to him gave her courage to be here.

They turned another corner, crossed another bridge and followed a small, lazy canal with boats docked on either side, as crowded as any street in Rome.

It was strange, to want to take in all the sights and sounds yet at the same time, there was an urgency to get where they were going. It had been a long time since Diana felt the pester of anticipation.

An eagerness built up in thick layers with each step they took. The suspense, too much and so delicious, left yearning and needing and wanting rolling around under her skin.

When it grew to be too much, when she was ready to ask Giovanni to stop and kiss her – even if it meant they would melt into a ridiculous public ravaging on a random street in Venice – he turned a corner and stopped, nodding at a thick, dark green door. Faded and worn with the years, it managed to look better than the rough concrete doorframe that held it up.

She craned her neck to get a better look at the building, painted a tired terracotta. Chunks of paint, stripped away by the weather, revealed the gray building material underneath. The windows all had wrought iron planters below them. Dark purple-red geraniums crowded each other in an attempt to show off.

Giovanni opened the door and pushed his way into a foyer. It was a smaller version of his building in Rome. At the back of the foyer was a flight of stairs. He nodded toward them and for the first time, Diana let go of his hand. There wasn't enough space for his shoulders and her bag. Up they went, passing the second and third floor apartments.

Diana asked, "So you have an apartment in Rome and Venice?"

"Just Rome." He smiled as he finished the last flight of stairs and placed her bag down. Two doors faced each other across a hallway, and standing in front of the one on the right, he fished keys out of his pocket, but didn't open the door.

Their labored breathing from climbing the stairs echoed in the small hallway. Giovanni rubbed the back of his neck. "We've been here before."

She nodded.

"This is a colleague's apartment," he explained. "He's doing work in Turkey for the year."

Diana reached out and pressed her hand against Giovanni's chest. His erratic heartbeat under her fingers matched her own. "I had a speech planned about how this should just be a trip as friends and nothing more. About how I agreed to go to Venice with you, but that's it."

"Did you change your mind?" Giovanni asked.

She tilted her head; ever since she saw him on the dock, hands clasped behind his back, five o'clock shadow, hungry eyes searching for her boat, she had the image of a wolf. And now she stood at his feet and wanted to throw herself at him. "You are the wolf from stories that mothers tell their daughters to watch out for." She grinned.

Giovanni put his hand on top of hers and pressed it to his chest. "And you Bella Luna, you tempt the wolf to howl in her light."

She laughed and was glad for the release of tension. "There is still a lot of worry and fear," she admitted.

"You wouldn't be human if there wasn't."

"So what do we do now?"

"Whatever you'd like, I can put your bag in the apartment and we can go explore the city. If you really don't want to stay in the same place, I'll find you a hotel."

"Really? If I said I want to go to a hotel and I'll see you tomorrow, you'd be fine with that?" she tested.

He gave an encouraging smile. "I'm willing to do anything. I asked you to come with me to Venice–"

"Insisted," she corrected.

"But you *came*. You're here. I have everything I could ever ask for," he said passionately. "The memory of kissing you, of holding your hand as we walked along the canals will last me a lifetime if needed," he assured her.

*Holy hell.*

Diana gathered all her courage and straightened her spine. "I want more than just a memory of hand holding."

"What do you want?"

"You," she admitted, and because she wasn't quite ready for what wanting Giovanni entailed, she added, "and maybe a drink."

Giovanni unlocked the door, but before he opened it said, "My colleague is a bachelor, he's very intense and highly intelligent. However, the uhh, little things in life ..." he cleared his throat, "like upkeep on an apartment, are difficult for him." He pushed open the door.

The apartment was as antique as the city itself. Bookshelves lined the walls, and books still overflowed onto the ground, creating concentrated, tall Jenga-like stacks that might crumble if one book was added or taken away.

Two large leather armchairs sat in the middle, between them a shared table with a lamp. Across from the chairs was a dark mustard colored sofa, and against a wall behind the sofa, was a maroon loveseat, coffee table off to its side.

A table with three chairs was pushed up against the wall to the right. The walls that were exposed were red brick. And on one of the open walls hung a tapestry portraying life around the Rialto Bridge several hundred years ago.

Giovanni gestured around the room. "I stay here when I'm working, and I knew it wasn't ... I came early to try and straighten it up." He looked at Diana standing in the middle of the living room. "We can find a hotel."

"No." Diana breathed the word out as she glanced around at the dark exposed beams and the dust layers on the bookcases. "It's perfect."

"The kitchen is through there." He continued the tour.

The kitchen was functional. One wall had an intricately carved wood table pushed up against it, where a maroon and gold table runner had been laid across it, and in the middle was a bouquet of colorful flowers. The wall opposite the table held a stove, oven, fridge, cupboards and sink; all self-contained and put together so the most was made of the slight available space. There was a bottle of wine and a bowl of fruit on the counter.

"The bathroom and bedroom are down the hall. I'll just put your bag in the room," he said.

Diana followed Giovanni down the hallway. She peeked in at the bathroom, it would offer what was needed. It was obvious Giovanni had spent a lot of time scrubbing. Pipes hung from the ceiling, one dark one connected to the toilet, one to the washing machine just beside the toilet. There were steel pipes that ran into the wall and came back out to meet up with the tub and sink; the whole of which was surrounded by a strange tile pattern of browns and tans.

"What is this colleague like?" Diana called.

"Brilliant, socially awkward, oblivious to the current world around him," Giovanni replied.

She followed his voice, arriving at the bedroom. He was standing next to a chair in the corner where he'd placed her bag.

The room had the same exposed brick, and was furnished with an armoire, a dresser, a nightstand and a queen size bed. The headboard was a heavy twisted design of gold flowers and filigree that wrapped itself into a lovely peacock plume. But it wasn't the headboard that caught Diana's attention, it was the candles placed on the dresser and a vase of red roses on the bedside table.

"What's your favorite flower?" Giovanni blurted the question as he watched Diana study the room.

"I like wildflowers," she whispered.

"As I was getting ready, I realized I had so many questions. What's your favorite fruit, your favorite flower? What do you like to drink …? I got excited about having the opportunity to find out the answers." His neck was splotchy with color from a blush. "There's one more thing I'd like to show you." He led her out of the bedroom and back down the hallway.

She was grateful because when she saw the bed and Giovanni standing next to it, the only thought she had was of what he'd done to her the last time they were alone and horizontal.

And as much as she declared to him she wanted this, she was still nervous.

He opened a door next to the kitchen, revealing a set of stairs. Diana glanced at Giovanni and he nodded his head in encouragement.

There wasn't much room in the stairwell and the worn steps were steep. Diana wanted to ask him how many more tight staircases she would have to climb with him, but as soon as the question entered her mind, she brushed it away because a very small whisper of an answer called, *all of them, for as long as she could.*

A few more steps brought her to a door, she pushed it open to reveal a rooftop hideaway. A large patio covered with an intricate pergola that provided ample shade. A hip-height wrought iron fence bordered the patio and in the center of it all, a wooden table with four chairs snuggled among a bevy of planters.

Flowers and greenery created a secret garden. There were deep purple-maroon bougainvillea, and white, red, and pink geraniums. A lemon tree bloomed happily in a large pot in the corner and there were still more blooming bushes and flowers of which Diana didn't know the names.

And from this vantage point, the tops of the terracotta roofs had been set ablaze by the afternoon sun.

Just below them, two small bridges reflected their simple arched beauty in undisturbed water, creating a circular effect. One of the canals they'd walked along stretched a watery arm toward unseen connections. There were church spires pointing exclamations into the thick of the floating scene. Giovanni stepped in the center of it all, and Diana shook her head – in that one move, Venice would forever be flowers, balconies, light and Giovanni.

The table was set with two champagne glasses, an ice bucket attempting to cool a bottle of prosecco, and another bouquet of flowers with colorful peach, white and greens this time.

"It's too much," Diana whispered.

Giovanni matched her tone, admitting, "It's not enough."

"I don't know what to say."

"La mia bella Luna," he said softly, "I just want to be with you. We can sit right here for the next two days or we can go see all of Venice. You don't have to say anything or if you'd like, you can tell me everything you've ever thought. I just want time, and you're giving it to me."

"I can't remember the last time I did something I wanted to do."

"I'm sorry." He looked defeated.

Diana shook her head. "No, it just dawned on me ... the date with Anthony was my coworker's idea. Moving into the guesthouse had been Lena's idea. Even this trip to Italy was Harper's idea."

"Venice was my idea." He muttered.

"But that's not all true ..." She was reasoning with herself. "Writing in a café in Rome, *that* was my idea. Not allowing fear to conquer me in Florence, *my* idea." She raised an eyebrow. "Accepting the proposal, me. Accepting the help, accepting the trip, those were my choices. I could have said no."

He nodded his head in understanding.

"Going with you in Rome, going to bed with you ... those were my choices too." She peeked at Giovanni. "And I came to Venice because I *wanted* to come to Venice." She swept her gaze over him.

"Prosecco," Diana pointed to the sweating bottle as she sat down, "and the sunset. That's what I want. To sit next to you on this wonderful rooftop in Venice and drink a bottle of wine."

He poured them each a glass then pulled his chair so he was seated next to her. But in the same manner he'd done in the taxi, he was close but not so close that she might change her mind; though she could still make out his body heat permeating into her side. She glanced sideways at him; hell, she'd probably be able to feel his body heat radiate into her from across a crowded room.

Diana touched her glass to Giovanni's and was going to say 'cin cin,' the typical Italian toast, but instead her voice cracked, "Thank you, Giovanni."

"The pleasure is all mine," he said fervently.

# Chapter Thirty-Eight

"**W**hen you invited me to Venice, is this what you imagined?" Diana asked, turning her attention from the ceiling and the prior day's memories back to Giovanni.

He rolled onto his back, an arm under his head, the other snaked around Diana's shoulders, pulling her close; she lazily drew circles on his chest.

"I imagined a lot of things and it caused problems."

"It did?"

"I spent all of yesterday trying to figure out where we should stay. I thought about taking you to a small romantic hotel, or a world-famous one. I kept changing my mind about this apartment, it's so jumbled, but the neighborhood is quiet."

"What was the final deciding factor?"

"Privacy," he admitted. "And the terrace. Not too many places I know have a terrace like this one."

"Who keeps the flowers watered when he's gone?"

"The neighbor."

"So your colleague isn't good with people, but it looks like he *is* good with flowers."

Giovanni gave a short laugh. "Yeah, he's a nice guy, but people confuse him, unless they lived in the past. There, he excels; writing about the past, and taking care of plants."

"I love the bouquets you bought me. Did I tell you that?" She smiled. "I don't care if I did, thank you for the flowers."

"You're welcome."

"You said you got here early to get things ready." It was more of a question.

Giovanni smiled. "I didn't give myself enough time."

"Right."

"I just wanted to freshen things up, but when I opened the door, I forgot what this place looked like. When it was just me staying, it was no big deal. But for you, I wanted more."

The idea that someone wanted more for her fluttered against her ribs.

"There were so many books everywhere, dust, dishes still in the sink, and I needed to wash the sheets and some towels. And the bathroom ..." He sighed. "I wanted to find flowers and go to the store so I did what I could, but kind of put most of my attention into this room ..."

"Mmhm." Her grin widened, bringing attention to her chapped lips. She ran her tongue along the rough edges, raw and well kissed; worn out from the night's passions.

The sun had begun to set, and with the bottle of prosecco finished, Diana had melted into the open arms of Venice. And because the canal water could be heard occasionally lapping, or because of the way the early evening light danced, or the way the colors around her changed, she stood and stepped between Giovanni's legs. He had just a moment to give her a questioning gaze before she bent forward, rested her hands on the armrest of his chair and brushed her lips against his.

She would blame everything on Venice. But really, at this point, maybe she should blame Italy. Italy had released her longings. Or maybe it was Anthony asking her to marry him that released her longings.

Anthony's memory put an abrupt wedge in the moment and she righted herself.

"What?"

"Anthony keeps popping up at inopportune moments."

"You're not going to marry him."

"No," she admitted, "but I still feel guilty."

He opened his mouth with an opinion, but whatever he'd been about to say drifted away. He rubbed the back of his neck and stood. "How about dinner?"

She nodded, and in an attempt to put them back on track, tried to joke, "Let me guess, you know a great place?"

"I do."

"Do I need to change?" Diana gestured to her clothes.

"No, you look beautiful." He studied her for a moment and corrected, "You *are* beautiful."

"You're not so bad yourself."

They retraced their steps, or at least she thought they'd retraced their steps, but after the third bridge, Diana was happily lost.

"Is it too early for dinner?" she asked. "I've been told Italians don't eat until eight."

"It's fine," he reassured, "we're tourists, we can do whatever we want."

"If that's true, then I need to go back to the Colosseum; there was a marble column that would look great in my bathroom."

He gave a relaxed laugh. "If you don't mind that I get fired and we'll both end up in jail, I'll help you steal it."

"I suppose." The small street they were walking opened up into a piazza with shops on the ground floor, and three restaurants, denoted by stereotypical umbrella-covered, outdoor seating.

"So when you're Italian, you eat dinner late and stay up 'til five in the morning having philosophical conversations about art and life?"

"Only if you're lucky." He pointed to the restaurant by the canal, where above the door was a small awning with bright gold lettering. "Enoteca ai Artisti," she read.

"Enoteca means wine cellar; ai artisti, of the artists," Giovanni translated as they stood near the sign asking patrons to wait to be seated in English and Italian.

"You have a way of translating that isn't condescending," Diana said.

"Why would someone be condescending when they're translating?"

"I don't know," she shrugged, "I was just thinking that if I knew several different languages, I don't know that I'd have the patience you do."

"If the person you were translating for was truly interested, you'd have the patience," he assured.

"Could you teach me some Italian?" she shakily asked.

"I'd love to."

The restaurant had six tables outside, all set for two with white tablecloths and a rounded candle in the center of each. Inside were several more tables, placed precariously close while still maintaining the illusion of being separate. A maître d' returned from seating another couple and greeted them. After a brief conversation, Giovanni asked Diana, "Would you like to sit outside or inside?"

She glanced at the canal and the way the lights from various windows of surrounding buildings shimmered off the water. "It's so nice outside."

The maître d' sat them with a flourish at one of the tables. He presented them with a menu but continued to talk and gesture. Diana smiled, while she didn't understand, she appreciated the show. When he left, Giovanni filled her in. "He suggested we order the swordfish because it's a full moon."

"No he didn't," she scoffed.

Giovanni widened his eyes. "I swear to you, he did. Tonight's a full moon, and there are all sorts of superstitions that go along with it."

"What does swordfish have to do with a full moon?"

"Well, in this instance it might be a marketing strategy," he guessed.

"What other full moon superstitions are there in Italy?"

"The full moon is the perfect time to get your hair cut."

"*Now* you're making stuff up."

He lowered his menu. "And you should always fall in love during a full moon."

Goosebumps rolled up and down her arms, which she accompanied with a roll of her eyes before turning her attention to the menu. "Other than swordfish, is there a specialty of Venice I should try?"

"Fish," he said, "it comes from the lagoon and today's fresh fish is swordfish and sea bass."

"Sea bass then."

They ordered and wine was brought to the table. Diana glanced around at the half full tables and shook her head. "I can't believe I'm here."

"Neither can I," Giovanni said softly.

"You really thought I wouldn't come?"

"I may have been obsessively texting Michele every hour to make sure you hadn't changed your mind."

"Well, that makes me feel better." She picked up her glass, but before taking a drink, muttered her own confession, "I might have asked Michele incessantly if you really liked me."

Giovanni sat back in his chair with his glass and began an impromptu Italian lesson. "Che cosa *(kay koz ah)* means 'what.' Most people don't use both words together, they drop one of them, so if anyone asks you a question and you don't hear it, you just say 'che?' or 'cosa?'"

"Cosa?" she repeated, and he nodded.

"And che fai *(kay fie)*, means 'what are you doing?'" He nodded toward Diana for her to try.

"Che fai?" she whispered shyly but loved how the foreign words sounded on her lips.

"Amore," he didn't hold back the twinkle in his eye, "means 'love,' but it is also an endearment, like honey, sweetheart," his voice softened, "darling, beautiful, gorgeous, bella ..."

"Wolf." She pointed at him.

"A passionate one."

She gave a humph in reply.

"Posso *(poh soh)* means 'can I or may I?' Posso is a super word in Italian."

"Super, like with powers?"

He chuckled. "No, it's just powerful. You can add 'posso' to any Italian verb and you've got a sentence and you don't have to remember a ton of verb conjugations when you're just starting out. But the best use of it is posso avere *(poh soh ah veh ray)*, which means 'can I have?'"

"Posso avere," she repeated.

"Sì," Giovanni leaned forward and in a whisper said, "puoi avere tutto ciò che il tuo cuore desidera."

*God, that sounded sexy as hell.* "Did you set me up?"

He nodded. "I said you can have anything your heart desires."

She shook her head. "I know 'sì' and 'no' and 'grazie.'" She also knew how empowered she felt just talking about another language.

"You're off to a good start."

"Grazie."

"Prego," he answered and when she raised her eyebrow in question, he mirrored her. She frowned until she recalled another lesson, so searched for the phrase then slowly said, 'Che vuol dire prego?" *What does prego mean?*

"Perfetto." He grinned. "Prego means 'you're welcome.'"

"Ah, so not just a spaghetti sauce in the states."

The appetizer came, four rounds of yellow polenta topped with a creamy white sauce.

"Baccalá mantecato," Giovanni said, "it's creamy salted cod on polenta. Very Venetian."

She took a bite, shocked at the light, creamy texture and the rich flavor, not at all what she'd expected upon hearing creamed fish.

Next came a piece of art. Gorgeous linguine tossed with a light butter and herb sauce, topped with a filet of grilled sea bass.

Diana studied her food for several moments.

"Do you want something different?" Giovanni worried.

She shook her head. "No. I was just thinking. Each meal I've had here has been an art form."

"Food *is* an art form in Italia."

"In the states, we've made food a crutch. It's become something to be ashamed of or to aspire to eating." She looked at the simple plate in front of her and laughed at herself. "Sorry, it just occurred to me."

"No, you're not far off."

"I was just thinking that if we could get back to the beautiful basics of food the way it's been presented to me here ..." she trailed off, because it was such a lovely idea, but not just for food.

Could she get back to the basics of love and respect and living a life for her art and her heart? When she returned to the states and the moonlit dream of Italy was nothing more than a mirage, *was* she capable of rebuilding?

"Are you okay?" Giovanni asked.

"Just admiring." She picked up her fork and sighed when the taste was as good as the presentation.

The last rays of daylight faded, allowing darkness to pull a shade over the city. The lights of various windows spilled out bright now, sparkling their reflection in the canal. In fact, when Diana glanced around, it seemed the whole area had taken on a glittery lens.

"Do you want some dessert?" Giovanni asked when she finished.

She nodded. "I haven't had tiramisu yet ... I thought I saw it on the menu?"

He caught the waiter's attention and ordered the dessert, then looked shy as he asked, "Can I take you somewhere tonight?"

"Will it impress me?" she teased.

"I think you'll like it."

"Is there a dress code?"

"It's a little dressy, but casual. What you are wearing now is perfect, but if you'd like to change, we can go back."

"I think I'd like to change."

He nodded as the tiramisu was delivered. He gestured for her to take a bite, then followed and together they both rolled their eyes in appreciation.

# Chapter Thirty-Nine

Renee had purchased a knee-length, black wrap dress that did impressive things to Diana's decolletage; if she did say so herself. It was simple, elegant and she felt good in the fabric.

She slipped on the black wedge sandals and twisted back and forth in front of the mirror. Harper was going to blow a gasket when she finally saw Diana.

She took out her phone, snapped a picture of her reflection in the mirror and sent it to Renee: *You have super powers I can't comprehend. Thank you again for helping with my wardrobe. I love this dress.*

Renee immediately sent back a page of hand clapping emojis and the reminder: *Take the black wrap.*

Diana double-checked her makeup and walked into the living room. Giovanni was coming out of the kitchen. He'd changed into black slacks but kept his white shirt. When he saw Diana he stopped moving.

She did a slight curtsy, but when she righted and he still hadn't reacted, she lowered her arms in worry. But when Giovanni stepped closer, intently narrowing his gaze and declared "Gorgeous," all her worries dissipated.

She took a deep breath and Giovanni's scent of coffee, aftershave and Italy wafted around her. "You don't look so bad yourself."

She touched the skin that showed from where his top buttons were undone. "Is this an Italian thing?"

"What do you mean?"

"I mean, I've seen several men now in button-down shirts who leave the top ones undone."

He shrugged. "Do you like it?"

Like it? It made her mouth dry. She found herself wanting to press her lips to the exposed skin. She nodded in response, then Giovanni bent and kissed Diana's neck. "You smell as good as you look."

"Renee helped me find my Italian scent." She sighed; the visit to the perfumery had been a whim, and then it had been so daunting and laborious that Diana had turned into a whiny kid having to get new shoes for school. But when they found a scent Diana liked, Renee squeezed her shoulders and promised, "You'll thank me."

God, now she needed to text her another thank you.

"Do we really need to go out?" she whispered.

He brushed a swift kiss across her lips. "Yes."

"Then we should probably go before we don't want to."

He eyed her for a moment, and glanced at the door several times, until he made up his mind. "Yeah, let's go."

They walked back toward the Grand Canal and jumped on a water bus. When Diana climbed aboard she said "hmm" a little too loudly.

Giovanni raised an eyebrow but she waved him off until they sat down. "It looks just like a bus in here. I just thought water bus meant something different."

He leaned close to her ear and softly said, "I remember another bus ride that was very enjoyable."

"Too bad we have to sit down in here," she whispered.

The bus cruised through the Grand Canal to show off the glowing city. Different hues than Rome; Diana would swear there was an undercurrent of pink in the lighting here.

At the stop they exited, there was a church directly in front of them that was lit with spotlights and had people mingling near the open front doors.

Diana glanced up at the church façade and said, "You know, today I keep thinking that a lot of these buildings and streets are sucking it in to stand a bit taller, so that they can make everything fit on this island."

Her attention was drawn by a giant sign next to the entrance of the door that showed a picture of several people holding their violins aloft. Across the bottom was an announcement in Italian and English: 'Concert Tonight,' and the only other word that seemed important – 'Vivaldi.'

"Vivaldi," she whispered. "He composed and performed in Venice." It felt childish to point out the obvious, but when she glanced at Giovanni, he wasn't looking at her as if it were childish. "What?" she asked.

"You asked about the information I have running around in my mind; I think your mind is equally intoxicating."

"People don't talk like that, you know."

"Said the woman who wishes she could paint a kitchen Pantheon sunrise." He pointed to the door. "Should we go in?"

"What?"

He led her into the church, onto the red carpeted entrance, then produced two tickets and handed them over to the greeter.

"This is where you wanted to bring me? For real? We're going to hear Vivaldi? In Venice?"

"Is that okay?"

She nodded emphatically, glancing up at the high ceilings of the church vestibule, and at the heavy red curtains hung across arched doorways, meant to help with the noise, one of which was draped back to allow entrance.

The main body of the church was simple, only one nave with large vaulted ceilings. The sound of the gathered crowd excitedly bounced and twirled, a foreshadowing of how the music would dance through the church.

"Is this *his* church? Where Vivaldi really played?"

"It is. Santa Maria della Pietà. It was built in the seventeenth century," Giovanni softly explained as they walked down the aisle toward their seats. "Now it's used mostly for concerts."

A man holding a violin came out to where the chairs were set up for the ensemble in the front of the church. Giovanni pointed to the seats in the third row that were theirs and they quickly settled as the voices of the crowd died down and the man began to introduce the evening's entertainment. Diana felt a strange pang of disappointment when he began by speaking in English. A far cry from the woman who was worried about being alone in this country, unable to communicate, just a handful of days ago.

When he began the introduction in Italian, she smiled, slipping wholly into the culture. A wave of his hand given and the smiling ensemble took their place.

A single note was drawn across the strings of the violin of the man who'd made the introductions. The rest of the ensemble matched the note and when everyone seemed satisfied they were in tune, they shifted in their seats as a muffled direction was given. Then, as a whole, they inhaled and the first three notes of a single violin rose into the air, and when those notes caressed the ceiling, a few more musicians joined, creating an elegant lilt.

With the excitement of being together in this place, the whole of the ensemble built the notes into a gorgeous frenzy of delightful sound that resonated in a space of Diana's soul she'd abandoned for so very long.

Behind the rising and falling bows stood the statues of saints and angels – gatekeepers of the altar they framed – draped in romantic Roman twists of fabric. But Diana thought perhaps they were also guardians to this moment, to this church, to men's souls. Behind them, the wall was a decorative marble arched with a bold painting of Mary.

"Amore?" Giovanni whispered concern in Diana's ear and brought attention to tears she didn't realize she was shedding. She patted his hand and shook her head as if that would express how moved she was at the majesty of this moment and how she was okay.

If someone asked her what it took to shake off all the layers of self-doubt and age and grime that build up in a person's life, she would declare that visiting a historic church in Venice and listening to Vivaldi, would be a very, very good start. And she thought she should tell Angelina. The woman would appreciate the observation.

As Diana soaked up each note, she gripped Giovanni's hand and shook her head in wonder. When the last note floated to the ground, she leapt out of her seat to join the applause.

After the clapping ended, Giovanni grasped Diana's hand. She glanced at him and was shocked at the raw hunger in his eyes. She was unsure who helped her move her legs to hastily follow him through the crowd, down the steps of the church, and around the first corner they came to; but she was already out of breath when he pressed his back against a wall, pulled her into his arms and began kissing her. Diana held on for dear life as they kissed themselves breathless.

It was a lifetime before they were interrupted. "Excuse us," a group trying to pass them called loudly.

Giovanni smiled into Diana's eyes. "I couldn't help myself."

"We had Vivaldi in our blood," she reasoned.

"Luna, people don't talk that way," he groaned, then framed her face between his palms and brushed his thumbs against her cheeks. "Did you like the concert? I didn't even think to ask if you liked classical music."

"It was amazing. Bucket list stuff."

*See Vivaldi in Venice: Check.*

They walked hand in hand along the well-lit street, with water lapping to their left and Venetian opulence on their right. After a few more twists and turns, and over more small bridges, Giovanni finally stopped, getting in line behind a couple. They'd arrived at a small ticket booth, right near the water, where several gondoliers waited in boats.

"Giovanni," she gasped. The second fact she retained about Venice was that gondola rides were not cheap, and even more expensive at night. But before she could insist he save his money, it was his turn and he was already making arrangements.

She was waved over to the next gondolier in line, and encouraged forward by Giovanni's hand on her lower back.

As she floated from the dock into the boat, the gondolier happily welcomed her, "Buona sera, Signorina." And then Giovanni was next to her, putting his arm around her shoulders as the gondolier was handing them a blanket against the cool night air.

The boat pushed off and drifted through a small channel straight into the middle of the Grand Canal. It was crowded with life, even this late on an evening in May. She'd forgotten what day of the week it was the second she left Pisa.

"It feels like I was in Pisa months ago," she said. "And in Rome for weeks, and in the catacombs for several days at least." She chuckled. "Angelina said time was relative. I think people feel time differently in Italy."

"It's you," Giovanni offered. "*You* make people feel time differently."

"Hmmm."

Once they were in the center of the waters, surrounded by the yellow and pink glow of light spilling out from street lamps and windows, the moon beginning her rise, a gondolier across the canal from them began to sing. They heard a deep baritone holding out the notes of an impassioned Italian song. Their own boat changed course and when they were close enough, their gondolier began to join in the song. Diana and Giovanni smiled at each other, happily shocked by the unexpected event.

Giovanni threaded his hand into her hair and kissed her. The affection infused in that kiss and the romantic vapor settling on her skin was delicious; she eagerly returned the kiss as the opulent city that worshiped love sang to her.

The gondola dropped them off closer to the apartment, which Diana realized just meant the other side of the Grand Canal. They walked slowly, Diana in a dream state.

"Can we get a Bellini?" she asked. "Michele said we need to have Bellinis in Venice."

"I think there's a bar still open near the apartment."

"Why Bellinis in Venice?" she asked.

"This is where it was invented. We could actually go to the bar where it was first created." He slowed.

"How far away?"

"A ways."

She shook her head. "I'd rather be closer to the apartment. Besides, if it's a Venice drink, I'm sure other bars know how to make it."

"They do."

They found a bar still open, crowded with patrons inside so they opted to sit outside near a propane heater. Diana draped the wide wrap around her shoulders as Giovanni ordered.

Two stemless champagne flutes, holding deep pink hued drinks with a sliced peach wedged onto the rim, were delivered. Diana held her glass up and said, "I've never toasted this much in my life."

"Good." Giovanni touched his glass to hers and took a sip.

They lingered and flirted, Diana filling the night with soft sighs of contentment. At one point she gazed up at Giovanni and observed, "You look tired."

"It doesn't matter."

She reached out and gently touched his cheek; his eyes were slightly sunken with his exhaustion.

"We've kept some strange hours lately," he said.

"Let me run to the restroom and we can head back." There was a lot of innuendo in the sentence, because they had played all day, trying to ignore what they most wanted to do.

She excused herself. The restroom was small,  an all in one space, and after she locked the door, she turned and caught a glimpse of herself in the mirror. She still hadn't gotten used to it, but she was beginning to feel more and more like that reflection every day.

When she went to wash her hands, there were no faucet handles, just a spigot. She turned in a circle and when she glanced at the floor and spotted a red lever to step on, she shrugged and tried it. "Well that's clever."

After drying her hands she took out her phone to take a picture and saw several messages had come in from Anthony.

Her heart sank, and bile rose in her throat, as if she'd been caught red-handed, as if Anthony knew what was happening. The flames of excitement that had been building all day, fell to the ground around her feet, in ashes.

The messages were simple.

*Sorry I missed you.*

*Hope you're having fun.*

*I can't wait until June.*

*Talk to you soon.*

She felt awful. It was as simple as that.

Embarrassed and confused, she made her way back to the table, didn't sit back down, just picked up her drink and emptied it.

"Luna?"

"I'm fine." She picked up his glass and finished the little bit he had left as well.

"I paid the check, we can go anytime," he said, on guard.

She gave a half smile of thanks, still not making eye contact, and began walking.

But the thought of what lay at the end of the road, a single queen bed covered with rose petals, froze her in place.

When Giovanni caught up to her, she asked, "Which way is the apartment?" He pointed and she began walking in the opposite direction.

Giovanni kept pace with her and after she'd turned two corners, crossed a bridge and became properly lost, she faced him. "Where are we?"

"Where would you like to go?" he asked softly.

Diana shook her head and took off once again, gazing around her perhaps trying to find some inspiration. However, when she turned a corner and came face to face with a large embedded shrine that held a statue of Mary, the mother of God, with faded blue robes and a forgiving smile, it wasn't the inspiration she needed.

Diana pointed. "What is this? I've seen several now in Florence and Rome." She didn't wait for an answer, just added, "I can't do this."

Giovanni clasped his hands behind his back and inclined his head toward the shrine. "It's called a Madonnelle. The ones in Rome are placed high up on the corners of buildings at intersections. But the tradition of a godly image being put on a corner, is actually an ancient Roman tradition. They believed that demons could come out of the underworld at night and hang around at the crossroads. Since gods were meant to be protectors, images of them were put on corners all over the empire. When Christianity took over, it was an easy tradition to continue."

Diana crossed her arms over her chest. "I can't figure out if you're the demon at the crossroads or the one trying to ..." She shook off the sentiment.

"I'm not a god, and I'm not trying to protect you." He finished her thought, his voice harsh. "I'm just trying not to lose you."

"I missed texts from Anthony," she admitted, glancing back at the

Mary, looking for another sign. "It made me feel like shit."

"I can understand that."

"Do you think this is a sign?" she whispered, nodding to the statue.

He took a deep breath. "If you want it to be, it can be. It can be a sign you're doing the wrong thing, coming here with me. Or, it can be a blessing that you've chosen wisely," he tried to joke, but his steady voice wore the undercurrent of thunder filled with fear and building desperation.

"I don't know why I'm so scared of you," she said.

He rubbed the back of his neck and sighed. "God, I tried to give you space to come to terms with everything that's going on for you, but you have to understand, all *I want*, is to throw you over my damn shoulder, take you back to that apartment and never let you go."

Her hands were shaking. "I want you too," she whispered. "Then I think about being fifty-five when you're in your forties. What then?"

"Really?" He let his frustration slip into anger. "Is there an age difference between us, yes. Do I give a shit? Absolutely not. Is this the wall you're trying to hide behind now?"

"I'm not hiding, I'm being practical."

"You're grasping at excuses because you're scared," he pointed.

Diana gave a laugh of disbelief. "I already said I was."

"Luna, you and I are going back to that apartment and I'm going to tear off your clothes and show you everything I've wanted to do to you since you left my bed. You aren't going to get married and Anthony will be fine."

"Will I be fine?!" she shouted.

"Of course you will!" He tossed his hands in the air, "Damn but if you aren't the most stubborn, strong-willed woman I've ever met ..." He shook his head in disbelief.

"What?"

"Do you know what kind of willpower a person needs to lock herself away from her life and then keep herself in that cage for almost twenty years?"

"I didn't—"

"You did, and you know it. Just because one thing went wrong."

She opened her mouth to refute Giovanni, but turned and walked away. He was on her heels instantly, and  stepped in front of her to stop her progress. "Not one little thing, I didn't mean it that way."

"Please move."

"No." His voice became more gentle. "You had every right to close yourself off after experiencing such a loss—"

"I don't need your permission—"

He held up a hand to stop her. "But thinking of going back and staying there behind those walls can't be the answer."

"I didn't say I was going to close myself off again."

"But if you leave, you might."

"Because of you?"

"Yes, because I'm here." He emphatically pointed to the ground beneath his feet. "I'm here, *now*. I reignited a passion in you that you thought was dead and you are a fucking passionate woman. You need to move forward, not backward."

"Why can't I move forward *and* walk away from you?" She put her hands on her hips and raised her chin in defiance.

"Because you'd be selling yourself short."

She pursed her lips and moved around him. "This is the most ridiculous argument I've ever had."

"Why, because I'm making sense?"

She whipped back around and crossed the space she'd put between them and jammed a finger into his chest. "None of this is real, you know." She waved all around her. "The moon, the tides, the crossroads, the attraction ... *none of it*, is real," she insisted. "It's all a lie."

"No," his voice was soft as he argued, "the *lie* is the life you've been living; hiding from everything as well as your true self. That's the lie."

His words stung the back of her throat.

"This life," he took her hand and held it against his chest, "it's going to be difficult and have heartaches. But there will be laughter too, and dancing and tears. That's the point. You know better than I do the number of poets and writers who have spent their lives dedicated to defining what a perfectly lived life is." He wiped a tear that slipped down her cheek. "Life is light and darkness, crossroads and demons, success and failure. It's the wolf and the moon. And you, amore, are made up of all of it. Hell, every story you've told me of your life so far has an element of you fighting to live again."

"Stop."

"I'm not going to stop until you see that you're finally the woman you're meant to be and I'm the man you're meant to be with."

"No."

"Stop looking for excuses, stop overthinking." He looked up into the sky and gave a desperate laugh. "I think I fell in love with you the moment I held you in my arms, and since that evening, the mundane suddenly looks extraordinary. Everything seems possible. There's magic everywhere. And I know you feel it too." He pointed at her. "I *know* you feel it."

"I want to ..." she said, then thought better of her admission. "I want to go home."

"You are home, amore," he whispered fiercely.

"I'm in Italy."

"You're with me," he growled.

"Giovanni ... I just met you."

"And you still know me, just like I know you."

A lifetime passed as they stared each other down. Each breath that passed between them seemed to carry the years they'd been apart. Giovanni was daring Diana to make a decision, more long term than a few days. And Diana was doing the same.

Her eyes began to take on the sparkle of their surroundings, to widen in delight at the way Giovanni challenged her. And that sparkle and delight turned to yearning. She let herself drown in it. She wanted to be thick with want and need.

She never took her eyes off Giovanni, and he waited for her to move. He was a patient carnivorous plant, waiting for her to land just within his grasp so he could swallow her whole. And she wanted to be consumed. Oh, did she want to be wholly, madly, and fervently consumed. And there it was again, all was madness. And it was delectable and delicious and she wanted more and more of this feeling until she drowned completely.

All she had to do was make one move, one slight movement in surrender toward Giovanni, and he'd catch her. She waited for a moment, but Italian Diana gave a tisk and snarled – she'd been waiting for far too many years already.

Diana gave him a slight upturn of a smile, and he enveloped her, the argument and building intensity winding them into a blur.

It was deep kisses and searching caresses. She pulled at Giovanni's shirt, desperate to feel the warmth of his skin beneath her hands. He moaned when her fingers slipped up his torso. His large hands gripped her hips, pulling her to him.

Against his lips, she muttered, "Apartment." And somehow, they tore away from each other. Giovanni took her hand and pulled her, running and laughing behind him.

Their breathing and the lapping of the water against the canal kept a strange time. Her heart didn't know which beat to match and decided to match both rhythms.

Giovanni struggled with the front door of the apartment building while Diana hugged him around the waist from behind, and slipped her hands up his shirt. He pressed her hands to his chest with his free hand as he opened the door, then maneuvered her so that she was through quickly and against the wall in the small foyer.

When the need was more than she could handle, she pushed at his chest and turned her attention to the stairs, jogging in front of him, taking them two at a time. She knew he would follow with the same speed.

He was at the door of the apartment moments after she arrived. They were both laughing, a result of their pent-up emotions and beating hearts and the adrenaline of anticipation.

Once inside, Diana moved just out of his reach as she rid herself of her shoes and shrugged out of the wrap dress. Giovanni, following Diana's lead, unbuttoned his shirt and dropped it on the ground. She backed down the hallway, slowly unclasping her bra.

He followed, not stopping until she had rid herself of all her clothing and was scooting back onto the bed, laying back on her elbows as she watched him in the soft lights shining through the window. As he crawled over her body, out of the corner of her eye, slipping against the wall, she thought she saw the shadow of a wolf.

# Chapter Forty

The light across the ceiling, the *fa la vecia,* faded as the morning became afternoon and well spaced, fluffy white clouds created a game of dimming and increasing the sunlight.

When the complaints of their ravenous stomachs outweighed their passions, Diana and Giovanni put on enough clothing to be decent and tripped up to the covered terrace with juice, espresso, fruit, cheese and pastries.

"This still feels like a dream," she sighed as she bit into a sticky croissant.

"Then let it be a dream," Giovanni said.

"You know," she licked her lips and glanced over at him through hooded eyelids, "you can't just fall in love with someone after a few days."

"I thought you fell in love with David after just one date."

She shrugged. "He was the one who fell in one day. It took me almost two weeks."

"Are you still seeing ...?" He pursed his lips and shook off the rest of what he was going to say.

Diana smiled. "Seeing and talking to my dead husband?"

"God, there's no good way to ask that, is there?"

"He waved bon voyage and left me at the airport in Rome." She swallowed, she hadn't really thought about it much. She'd been so concerned with creating Swiss Alps sized issues out of grains of sand. "I don't know if he's gone for good."

Giovanni was silent, giving her space to think about the consequences of that.

"But he's not really gone, is he? I'm finally talking about him and remembering him and telling his stories."

Giovanni nodded. "I'd love to see some of his art one day."

"His art … that's another thing I haven't thought about in years. Do you know, until the Borghese Galleria Michele took us to, I haven't been to a gallery or art museum, on purpose, since he died?" It seemed so right then, that she'd gone to the Galleria with David in tow.

"Would you like to go to an art museum?"

"What did you have planned today?"

He sat back and studied her, his eyes catching a glint of the sun as it peeked out of the clouds for a brief moment, drawing the lighter browns out. "I didn't plan anything. And I planned everything." He sighed. "I have a few ideas if you want to leave the apartment; hell, I have a few ideas if you don't want to leave."

She had strong opinions on each option.

"Giovanni," she whispered, but when he glanced at her expectantly, all she could think to say was "how did I get here?"

She dipped her nose into the collar of his white shirt she'd pulled on and buttoned loosely to come upstairs. It smelled of Venice now, and a secret rooftop, wine, the canal water, Vivaldi and coffee. Her bones were still liquid and her skin still craved more wandering caresses.

It all stuck in her chest and coiled about, a knot of unending possibilities.

"Giovanni." She smiled and he answered, "Bella Luna?"

"Show me Venice."

They weren't in a rush, and they slowly walked, unaware of the existence of a world outside their bubble. The sun was more obscured by the clouds now, shading the floating city in gray shadows; yet another light aspect for an artist to attempt to capture.

"Some Japanese art movement only used the color gray to express the sense of an entire nature scene," she said as they strolled the errant streets. "The singular color was meant to express the values of the people. A reverence for the natural world, the order of nature." She let out a snort of laughter.

"What?"

"Everything keeps going back to the old man in Pisa. Here I am trying to say that Venice covered in gray, void of color, lets us glimpse more of her true nature." She paused for a moment, then declared, "I'm moving to Pisa. I'm going to spend my mornings on that bench and ask weary travelers what their nature is."

"Have you figured out your nature yet?" Giovanni asked.

"Not yet. You know, I never asked, what's your nature?"

"To dig." He responded so quickly Diana chuckled.

"To connect," she corrected him. "You connect the past to the present."

He squeezed her hand. "I like that."

"So," she gestured to the quiet street in front of her, "if the Tower of Pisa's nature is to lean, Rome's nature is to seduce—"

"Is it?" There was a smile in Giovanni's voice.

"It feels true."

He nodded his agreement as she finished, "Then what is the nature of Venice?"

Giovanni considered the question for a while before answering, "Well, Venice was built as an escape from the world. A group of people wanted to escape their land so much, they figured out how to build a city on the water. Then, Venice became known for her opulence and for her love; and now she is stuck in the past."

"Which means?" Diana asked.

"I think people forget the purpose of this city was momentary. Yet they built churches and monuments, forgetting that wasn't the nature of Venice. And now she's sinking and they have this arbitrary date when the whole city will finally be under water, and while that is an appalling verdict, it is her nature. I think Venice was meant for the momentary glory of opulence."

"So the nature of Venice is fleeting beauty?" Diana parroted.

Giovanni brought her hand he was holding to his lips and kissed her fingers. "Coffee?" he asked.

"Certo," *Of course,* she answered in Italian.

"I know a place." He eyed her with a grin as she muttered, "Of course you do."

They emerged into the Piazza San Marco. Across from them stood the church the piazza was named for, St. Mark's Basilica.

Giovanni led her across the piazza with birds and artists taking up space to view the ornate church. Surrounding the piazza, chairs and tables, extensions of the restaurants, were set.

When they were close enough to take in the whole church, Giovanni stopped and allowed Diana time to contemplate the golden painted archways with paintings of saints yawning into pointed spires.

"Is this city really sinking?"

He nodded.

"What can be done?"

"I like to believe the Italians will figure it out."

"You can't hinge the fate of an entire city of such beauty, just on hope." Diana frowned.

Giovanni raised an eyebrow. "But it's her nature to sink."

She gestured to the church. "But it's so beautiful."

Giovanni squeezed her hand. "You saw the Duomo in Florence, right?"

She nodded.

"Did you know, they started building that cathedral before they had the engineering capabilities to actually finish it? No one knew how to construct that kind of dome when they started."

"Really?"

"They just had faith that someone would show up and figure it out."

"You know, one could argue that Italians aren't very good planners." She smiled.

"Italians are very good at taking a leap and knowing that somehow, the net will appear." The comment was soft and directed. And just in case she wasn't sure of his meaning he whispered, "If you take the leap bella Luna, I promise, your net will appear."

Diana swallowed and couldn't bring herself to nod her head in agreement, but she also didn't dismiss him. Thankfully, he smoothed over the moment by looking back at the basilica and agreeing, "It is stunning though. C'mon, I wanna show you something I think you'll appreciate."

They walked toward the nearby water, where island met lagoon. On their left Giovanni pointed out the Doge's Palace connected to the Basilica. Intricate arches met atop windows creating a lace-like parapet. In his best tour guide voice he said, "The Doge's Palace is the best example of Venetian Gothic style."

"And what does that mean?"

"The Venetians were obsessed with lightness and light. Land is scarce on these islands, so every inch was covered with thought to the weight it was putting on the ground. Venetian Gothic architecture was a style where the very arches of the windows actually supported the structure."

"I'll tell you this much, you are handy in a tour situation."

"You're welcome."

They arrived at the water where a walkway along the lagoon's edge met a watery parking lot of unused gondolas bobbing up and down to a rhythm only they could hear. Lamp posts topped with three branches of lanterns lined the edge of the walkway. "Weren't we here last night?"

"Just up the way," he nodded, "but we took a different route to get to the gondolas."

Giovanni led her to a bridge, and when they stopped in the center, he pointed down the canal to an overhead bridge that connected two buildings above the canal and was covered on all sides. "That's called the Bridge of Sighs," he began. "It connected the prison to the place where a prisoner would meet his demise. This bridge was the last point where condemned men would be able to view their beautiful city of Venice one last time before their death."

"A sigh-worthy view," Diana murmured as she studied the bridge floating in the air, connecting the third floor of two buildings.

"The poets and writers of Byron's day loved the idea of this Bridge of Sighs."

Diana wondered if you came early enough, or late enough, and stood in this spot keeping your ears open, could you hear the lingering sighs of condemned men who were long gone?

"The bridge lore took a turn over the years; now it's said if you're lucky enough to be in a gondola under it at sunset, and kiss the one you're with while the bells of the Basilica chime, you'll find eternal love and happiness."

"So I bet there's a gondola back up at sunset right there." She smirked. "I never knew Italians had this much folklore involving a person's love life."

"You can blame the gods for that." Giovanni urged Diana back the way they came.

"Really? The gods told Italians to throw coins in fountains, get haircuts during full moons, and kiss at sunset in gondolas?"

"The gods taught us how to be superstitious," he corrected, then slipped his arm around her waist and brushed a kiss against her neck.

A vision of a young couple in Pisa, bound for Venice flashed. The daydream created, as she watched the young man kiss the woman's neck, sparked memories. But the idea of having that passion again seemed so unattainable

But here she was.

Bridge of Sighs indeed.

They continued their tour though the city on their way to the promised café. Giovanni would stop and point out the importance of certain buildings. History came alive as he painted scenes for her to imagine and her fingers itched to write the stories down.

He bought a newspaper then pulled her into a small café for a snack. "You have your notebook?" he asked as they settled themselves. Diana gave him a sideways glance. "I do."

"Good, I won't feel bad if I read the paper and ignore you."

"If I didn't know any better, I'd think you somehow knew I wanted to write."

He gave an exaggerated shake of the paper and began to read in reply.

She opened her notebook and wrote at the top of a new page: "Blame the gods."

It seemed apropos.

# Chapter Forty-One

After their feet were rested and bellies sated, the tour continued. Diana was content to admire storefront windows and lavish displays of goods, but it was a store that sold notecards and paper that finally tempted her inside.

"Oh, look … paper. The writer's drug of choice." She laughed.

The small space had a wall covered with dowels that held newspaper size prints; another was lined with greeting cards; and the last was bookshelves filled with bound notebooks and a sign explaining that they were handmade on the premises.

Giovanni struck up a conversation with the man behind the register as Diana explored. After she'd done her first round, she joined him at the register, placing three bookmarks with Venetian scenes, a canvas bag that said 'Venice,' and a small journal with a watercolor gondola for Harper on the counter while he explained, "This is the owner. His family has owned this business for six generations; they still make paper the way their ancestors did."

"That's amazing. I can't think of what business my relatives were even in six generations ago." She shook her head as Giovanni translated. "Wait, that's not true. Six generations ago would have had something to do with sheep and farming in Ireland."

The old man laughed and gestured to the store. Giovanni translated his reply, "This is a better way to make a living."

Diana agreed when her attention was captured by a basket of what looked like hand stamps with letters – that belonged at the beginning of illuminated manuscripts. She found one with a woman and a unicorn and all the scroll work along the sides. She didn't need this souvenir, she *wanted* this one. She placed the stamp on the counter and nodded that she was done shopping.

Giovanni picked up the stamp and turned it over, studying it.

The owner began an explanation and Diana thought she heard the word 'luna' in there, but wasn't sure. Giovanni didn't interpret right away, but asked the owner a question. The man nodded and went into the back of the store.

"What?" Diana asked.

"You'll see."

He returned with an ink roller, took a nearby sheet of paper, rolled the ink on the stamp, then stamped it and handed it over to Diana saying, "La luna splende sulla signora incantata."

She glanced at the scene, so delicate, complex and lovely. A woman sitting near a window, with robes and scrolls strewn about, a unicorn by her feet with his head on her lap. Outside the window the moon shone brightly.

Giovanni finally translated, "The stamp is called: The moon shines on the enchanted lady."

Diana opened her mouth to wave away the moment and say something along the lines of 'all this talk of moonlight ...' and love and gods and superstitions. But she didn't want to. That was the other part of her, the cold closed off part that had been protecting her from believing in such foolish things as love found in moonlight.

"It's perfect," she said instead.

Giovanni wouldn't let her pay, so she watched in rapt attention as her treasures were wrapped together in a piece of gold paper, a ribbon and finally a sticker seal that had the shop's name on it.

Italy even made tourist shopping extravagant. She looked out of the corner of her eye at Giovanni; he was watching her, so she signaled to the package and said, "Extravagant."

"Where else can I take you?"

"Masks." So many stores sold carnival masks, and she wasn't sure if there was a difference between homemade and possibly mass-produced masks.

"I know a store you may like."

It turned out, he didn't just know of a store, he knew the owners of the shop; a husband and wife whose families had been making carnival masks since the seventeenth century.

After exclaimed niceties, the couple took Diana and Giovanni to the back room where they worked and explained the history of the shop and the art of making masks.

There were so many to choose from. Gorgeous full face masks, masks that only covered the eyes and nose, and masks that covered the entire head as well; as far as the designs went, those were countless.

In the end, she chose a half mask, small enough to fit in her luggage, done in golds and blues with lacy patterns in pink flowing across the nose. "It reminds me of the water of Venice," Diana said as she touched the mask.

"Sì, yes. This is what it was inspired by." The wife was delighted with Diana's assessment.

When Diana tried to pay, the store owners wouldn't allow it. "L'amore di Giovanni will not pay. You see the water in our creation, is enough you understand our art."

Another carefully wrapped package was handed over. As they left, she shook her head. "I miss talking to artists," then added, "I miss talking about art. In the world we lived in, David and I were always surrounded by other writers, photographers, poets, sculptors..."

"No wonder the dinner the other night made you feel so at ease."

Giovanni led them through more tight alleyways. "How do you know Venice so well?" she asked.

"I've done a few lectures here for some archaeological exhibitions. I stayed with my colleague, whose apartment we're borrowing, and he showed me around."

If it was possible, they arrived at an even smaller alleyway, off of which was a dark green door that was open. "I think you'll like this next shop," Giovanni said as they turned into a short courtyard, lined with weather-worn books leading to a main entrance, above which was a sign that read: Aqua Alta.

She repeated the phrase and Giovanni supplied, "High Water."

She stepped inside and grinned. "A bookstore."

Stacks of books were on raised tables, but so many others were in containers: a bathtub, a gondola, several table size planters. It was a bright shop with no obvious rhyme or reason to the way the books stacked, other than the owner must have taken decorating advice from a hoarder. For Diana it was love at first sight.

Giovanni explained that the containers kept the books off the ground during the months the water rose, so the books wouldn't get wet. Although, several of them still suffered the effects of the humidity.

In the center of the store was a gondola; though it was difficult to make out at first, the inside of the boat being stacked with teetering piles of books. Above the gondola hung two very large, gaudy crystal chandeliers, but all of the store's elements came together to create a wonderland.

Together they began to sift through the books. As the reasoning for the collections began to make sense, she ran her hands along the spines and breathed in deeply the moldy paper smell.

"See anything you like?"

"I don't know, I don't want a book in English, I feel like it should be in Italian, and I can't decide. I think I just like being here."

He nodded and disappeared, finally returning with a bag of books.

As they continued their walk, she took the bag and pulled out his purchases. The first two books were on Rome.

"I thought you were an expert on Rome," she said.

"I never said I was an expert."

"I thought you knew a lot about Rome," she corrected.

"I had these two books before and gave them away, thought I'd replace them."

She pulled out the next book, an Italian language book.

Giovanni tapped the cover. "It's a good book, a good place to start."

This was exactly the kind of book she needed to have acquired from a gondola in the middle of a bookstore in Venice.

"Thank you."

"You'll be fluent in no time." He winked.

An unexpected pain pushed at her ribs. She didn't want to pack up her paltry things at her sister's guesthouse and move to Houston. She wanted a decadent change of life. She wanted to pack up her things and become fluent in a second language and find a small apartment with a kitchen the color of Venice at sunset.

She handed him the bag, but opened the book and began to ruffle through it as they walked. After silently attempting a phrase, then feeling more assured, she said aloud, "Ti piace qui?" *Do you like it here?*

A smile pulled at the corner of Giovanni's mouth as he stopped and faced her. "Mi piace così tanto qui, voglio rimanere per sempre." That deep baritone of Italian was powerful, reverberating in her bones the way a thunderstorm in the middle of the hot Atlanta summer could.

She kissed him and the electricity sparked.

"How close are we to the apartment?" she asked.

"Can you run?"

"God, yes." She laughed.

# Chapter Forty-Two

With half-laden eyes, Diana stared out the open shutters while Giovanni mindlessly rubbed her arm. She lay on his right side, her head in the crook of his neck as she attempted to soak in the moment, to somehow etch every bit of it on her skin. The sun had set some time ago, so only light spilled in from lamps and neighboring homes, giving the sky a luminescence.

"What are you thinking?" Giovanni asked.

When she didn't answer right away he brushed a kiss on the top of her head.

"I think the Bellini is pale pink to match the light in Venice," she finally said.

She heard the grumble reverberate in his chest. "But that's not what you were really thinking."

"I need to go home." The words were out finally. They both knew this would be how things ended.

He didn't say anything and Diana knew, from all the declarations of how he cared about her, how he would do anything to keep her with him, that the words singed him.

"You gave me what I asked for," he whispered, but she could hear the hurt in his voice.

"I need to go home and tell Anthony I'm not going to marry him." Saying the words felt powerful, and a little frightening.

"And then?" Giovanni asked.

"I don't know," she answered honestly. "I need to weigh all the new against my old life. I need to see how I am on my own two feet."

She heard his attempt to say something, changing his mind several times until finally, he whispered, "When do you want to go?"

"My ticket is for tomorrow morning. That was the plan all along. So I'll stick to that." She sat up on her elbow and studied him; his face, as shadowed as it was, couldn't hide the resigned look.

"But Giovanni ..."

He cupped the side of her face, his fingers splayed wide into her hair in reply.

She whispered her last request, "I don't want to sleep tonight." He gave an animalistic growl of agreement.

# Chapter Forty-Three

E leven hours and two planes later the pilot announced, "Ladies and Gentlemen, we are now beginning our descent into Atlanta. We'll be on the ground in about twenty-two minutes. The local time is 9:18 p.m. and the weather is about sixty-seven degrees with clear skies."

Diana stared out the window as the night-lit coastline of Georgia came into view, and chewed on her lip, not sure which world had been the dream.

Giovanni insisted on taking her to the airport. "The least you can do is let me have an epic goodbye kiss at the airport," he joked.

But as the distance from the apartment grew, Diana wished she had found enough courage to say goodbye to him there.

They held hands and quietly watched as the water taxi ate up the miles. Once shuffled into the ticketing area of the airport, like mutineers being forced to walk the plank, they stood to the side of the security checkpoint and turned into each other's arms. Still no words came. Diana pulled away, looked up into Giovanni's darkening eyes and traced her fingers down the side of his face.

"A più tardi," he whispered.

She repeated the phrase, "A più tardi *(ah pew tardy)*."

Giovanni gave a sad smile. "It means 'see you later.'"

They wouldn't say goodbye. She snaked her hand around the back of his head and pulled him down to her, brushed a kiss on his lips and then stepped away.

He clasped his hands behind his back, and she nodded. After she and her bag arrived on the other side of the x-ray machines, she glanced back and smiled.

Giovanni winked but his smile looked forced.

With a final wave, she turned then continued to move forward in a fog until she boarded the plane.

Every nerve ending in her body was short circuiting from the memory of Giovanni's touch. She was lost in a daze of fully exhausted, entirely awake and wholly back to life.

It was a short ride from Venice to Rome, and then Rome to Zurich where she switched planes. And as the doors of the plane to Atlanta were shutting, David rushed in, a grin on his face. He waved his ticket at her and as he got closer said, *'Right on time.'* As he dropped into the empty seat next to her. Diana suppose she should be grateful for the space to have a nervous breakdown and allow David a place to sit.

*'Miss me?'* She teared up, and David sighed. *'Aren't you happy to see me?'*

She nodded emphatically.

*'What's wrong then, is it the new guy?'*

Another sob escaped.

*'Then where are you going, babe?'*

"Home." She wiped the tears away.

*'I like him, Lu.'*

She liked him too.

Diana stared out the window and tried to stop her tears as they took off, and once the giant metal bird hummed its way over the big blue ocean, they moved to a fully telepathic conversation. Which was really easy to do, since David wasn't really there.

*'Lena would have packed up all your stuff and shipped it to you,'* David said.

*"I just need to see what it's like. I ran away the second you died."*

*'And you hid.'*

*"I need to see who I am again,"* she reasoned.

*'Sure. You need to see if you're back.'* David stretched his legs out in

front of him. *'If you want my two cents' worth kid, I think you already know, and this is a futile trip.'*

"I hated when you acted like you were so much older and wiser than me."

*'Because I am.'*

She grunted.

*'I liked who you were in Italy.'*

"Exactly, and that's what I'm doing. Going to see if I'm the same at home."

*'What if you aren't.'*

"That's what I'm scared of."

*'Then change it.'*

"Is it that easy?"

*'Lu, it's always been easy. You made it hard.'*

*"It was easy because of you,"* she insisted.

He scoffed and scrubbed his head, making his hair stand on end, then he smoothed it down. *'You aren't remembering any of it correctly, you know that, right? It was you.* You *were the reason we stayed up late working.* You *were the reason I did the best work of my life. I was trying to keep up with you, we all were. You brought out the best in everyone around you.'*

She shook her head as the memories fractured and swirled. Writing groups at the apartment; potluck dinners with paper plates on laps as everyone sat around the living room talking about art; her scouring the internet and papers and local magazine for submission calls for artists and writers and passing them on to everyone; letters of interest from magazines about her short stories; friends showing up for weeks after David died; letters and calls and emails and hands that were all a blur, trying to reach out and keep her afloat.

"I could have stayed in New York," she whispered. "I could have figured out how to pay for it all. I could have kept writing. I'd already figured it out when I was going to school. But without you ... there were too many memories." She glanced at the ghost of her past. *"Every damn street had a memory of us. Of you. You made your mark on that town. All those reminders, they broke me."*

*'I know, baby.'*

*"Would you have stayed if the tables were turned? If something had happened to me?"* she asked.

Though she didn't really need David's ghost to answer that question. She knew he would have been heartbroken, but eventually would have gone on with his life because he would think he owed that much to Diana. To continue to live his best life in her name.

"*Do you think less of me?*" she asked.

'*Never.*'

"*Really? I wasted so many years. So much time. I flushed it all away.*"

'*You were the love of my life too. I understand why you did what you did. I just wish you could have found a way to move through the pain.*'

"*I did find a way.*" By closing the door on everything and everyone.

'*But here we are, and you're through the darkness, Lu. You found the light.*'

Colored lights flashed at the mention of light: iridescent orange, moonlight white and Bellini pink. "I did find the light." She grinned fondly.

'*But those are all Italian lights.*' He elbowed her. '*I'm serious. I like him.*'

"*Of course you like him, what's not to like? He's personable, funny, so damn smart and passionate in a very reserved way that when it comes out, it's like a volcano that tries to burn you ...*" She waved her hand. "*I don't want to talk about him.*"

'*So what's the problem?*'

"*For starters, I brought my dead husband back to life so he could annoy me with his opinions.*"

'*You're welcome.*' He tilted an invisible hat to her.

Diana laughed. "I miss you," she said aloud.

'*Do you miss Giovanni?*'

She pursed her lips and snidely snorted. "*Of course I miss him. I can still smell him and feel his touch on my skin, is that what you want to hear? Cuz it feels weird to tell you about a guy who has me all hot and bothered.*"

'*But babe, you said it yourself, I may be your husband, but I'm your* dead *husband.*'

"*David,*" she warned.

'*Okay, okay,*' he held up his hands, '*it's a bit weird. I get it. So then let's talk more about your overthinking.*'

"*You're relentless.*"

*'Always have been, always will be.'* He blew her a kiss. *'I just think this is also a good time to talk about how stupid I think it is that you think your life is over.'*

"Yes, thank you. A very nice Italian woman named Angelina gave me the same advice."

*'You finally going to listen? How many more strangers do I need to put in front of you, telling you the same thing before you get it?'*

"You *put in front of me?*"

*'The world works in mysterious ways, Lu. That's the universe's nature.'* He winked.

She rolled her eyes; not really wanting to discredit the idea.

*'What was your favorite thing about Rome? I saw so much art,'* he supplied.

*"Did you?"*

*'While you were otherwise engaged,'* he wiggled his eyebrows with the innuendo, *'I saw as many works of art as I could.'*

*"I love that."*

*'What was your favorite part?'* he repeated.

"That stupid moon," she blurted aloud, trying to sound angry. But the sigh and grin that followed her words were a giveaway. *"Italians have a lot of superstitions, and many are about the moon."*

*'The full moon brings out the animalistic side of people.'*

*"Is that what it was?"* Diana shook her head. *"He'll be okay. It'll be good to be home and regroup and Giovanni will get over me. He's handsome and smart and Rome is crowded, he'll find someone that'll be good for him. He'll have a good life."* She nodded as if that would give her the courage she needed to go on.

*'God damnit, Lu. Don't hide again from feelings that are too hard.'*

*"I'm not hiding."*

*'Your first move; the second you feel alive again is to run away. I hate to break it to you, but you're getting ready to go underground again. You're about to hide from someone who saw you. Don't belittle the guy,'* David warned.

She glanced out at the tarmac as the runway lights blinked and waved, welcoming her back.

*"Help me?"* she asked.

He nodded. '*Why do you think I'm still here?*'

She choked on another sob then. "Because I'm having a psychotic break," she announced to the empty seat.

# Chapter Forty-Four

Diana shuffled through the long line at customs, punchy from lack of sleep, the imagined conversations with David, and the onslaught of memories of her time spent with Giovanni.

The scene before her – excited travelers, exhausted toddlers, loud business calls – disappeared, replaced by a mirage; a montage of nuanced memories. How he rubbed the back of his neck when he was pondering how to answer a question; the blush that was a splotchy red mass creeping up his skin; how his smile filled up his face, lightened his eyes; how his skin felt beneath her hands ...

"Miss." There was a tap on Diana's shoulder, and the mirage cleared. A frowning woman at the customs desk in front of her took its place.

The woman took Diana's passport and scanned it asking, "What was the purpose of your visit?"

She cleared her throat. "Travel."

"Business or pleasure?"

Her voice was hoarse as she answered, "Pleasure."

"Do you have anything to declare? Did you bring anything back from Italy with you?"

Diana's gaze grew as she whispered, "Myself."

The security officer frowned. "Ma'am, I don't appreciate the flippancy."

"No," Diana shook her head, "I'm sorry..." A tear slipped down her cheek and she smilingly wiped it away. "It was just the trip of a lifetime."

The disgruntled woman nodded through pursed lips as she stamped the proper paperwork and slid it back to Diana. "Welcome back, Miss Barrett."

Diana whispered to herself as another tear slipped, "Welcome back, Luna."

Through a fog of happy exhaustion, she navigated the crowds, and headed for the sliding doors where she would find waiting taxis.

"Luna!" The yell stopped her and scanning the area, a movement caught her attention. It was Harper happily running toward her.

"Harper?"

"Oh my God!" her sister screamed as she hopped, skipped and clapped her hands in Diana's direction.

"Harper?" Diana asked again, confused.

"You are gorgeous! You look so good! You look like *you* again!" She screamed every phrase as she excused herself through the crowd until she was finally close enough to slam into Diana's shocked body, hugging her close.

Diana released the hold on her bag and slid her arms around her sister, and what should have been a quick hello of a hug, turned into the hug of long-lost spirits reuniting after years and years apart. Harper was sobbing, and Diana tightened her grip as her own tears fell.

"I'm sorry," Diana whispered over and over as they stood suspended in time, mourning for what had been lost, and reuniting with the joy of what had been unearthed.

Harper shook her long auburn hair and wiped the smeared mascara from under her eyes but even when they finally separated, she never looked away from Diana. "Lu, jeez, you look better in person."

"I'm sorry," Diana repeated, and the tears she thought had stopped, started up once again.

"For what?" Harper stepped forward and rubbed Diana's arms.

"For so much."

Harper shook her head with a soft smile, as if everything had been forgotten and forgiven in that moment. When she pulled aside the collar of Diana's shirt, her eyes widened and her smile became a laugh, and in her best southern acccent said, "Why miss Luna, I do declare, you have got a hickey."

That stopped the tears. Diana slapped away her sister's hand and pulled the collar upward, the touch on her skin immediately bringing back the feel of heated worship that put the mark there in the first place.

"Oh my God!" Harper exploded into bouncing again. "I'm so happy!"

"What are you doing here?" Diana tried to change the subject.

"I'm here to pick you up. I booked the flight, remember? I knew when you were getting in." she said as if it was enough explanation.

"No, what are you doing *here*? In Atlanta? How do you have ticket money after sending me to Italy?" It came out sounding accusatory, but it was more curiosity; she'd forgiven Harper the ruse.

"Mom paid for my ticket so I could come help with the thing."

"The thing ... the fundraiser?" Diana rubbed her temple, Harper's explanation was confusing her.

"Yeah, I volunteered so that I could be here when you got home. Mainly because of that man you went to Venice to see *and* I figured I needed to either face you and apologize or face you and let the rain of 'thanks' wash over me." She took Diana's bag and centered it between them. "Which one will it be?"

"Well, I think I'd like an apology first."

Harper took a deep breath. "Luna. I know it wasn't right for me to trick you into going to a foreign country alone, where you don't speak the language."

Diana nodded. "A little too practiced and lame, but I'll take it. Now," she pointed at Harper, "I am going to thank you, but from this day forward, if you are going to go around sticking your nose in other people's business, promise me you'll just talk first. No outlandish plans."

"Deal."

"Thank you," Diana said with all the sincerity she had. "It was the trip of a lifetime. Bucket list stuff."

Harper gave a hoot of joy and jumped in a circle.

She linked her arm with Diana's and dragged the bag behind her as she led her out of the airport. "Now, start from the beginning and tell me *EVERYTHING*! Oh my God, I'm so glad I guilted Mom into buying me a ticket. I'm so glad I came to pick you up! This is going to be one hell of a weekend."

"What, the fundraiser?" Diana asked as they started to cross the street.

"No, Anthony showed up this afternoon at Lena's." Harper excitedly exploded with the information.

"What?!" Diana stopped in the middle of the crosswalk, but Harper laughed and tugged on her to keep them moving.

"He came by to talk to you."

She stopped again and shook her head as the light turned green and cars started honking at her. "He's in Houston on business." Diana reached up and touched the hickey on her neck, as Harper grasped her other hand and pulled her out of the street toward the parking garage.

"He's not there now. He's back in Atlanta."

"He's in Texas ..." Diana trailed off, allowing Harper to drag her toward the car. "He never said anything to me about coming back."

She thought about his last few text messages; bland, with nothing of importance mentioned. She knew she hadn't missed a phone call and there'd been no request for her to call him.

"Harper, are you sure it was him?"

"No, Lena's suddenly taken to lying about really weird stuff," she said sarcastically. "Lena told me Anthony said he'd come back tomorrow morning."

"Where did you say I was?"

Harper shrugged. "Italy. He knew you were in Italy. Lena said he'd just forgotten about the time change or whatever."

She nodded her head. "That's right." He knew where she'd gone.

They were almost at the end of the first row of cars when Diana caught sight of Lena's Cadillac Escalade. "Did he say what he wanted?" Diana asked.

"I don't know, he's not my fiancé."

"He's not my—" Diana bit, stopping the words.

Harper whirled around, her eyes bright, and Diana thought her sister was preparing herself for another round of jumping. "Does this have to do with Mr. Hickey?"

"Harper."

"If he isn't a fiancé, what is he?" Harper whispered the question.

He *was* a security blanket.

"You'll be happy to hear that it isn't about what he *is* to me, but what he's about to be." Diana no longer wanted security. She wanted to be passionate about life again.

"Which is?"

Diana sighed. "An ex."

Here came the jump twirl. Harper squealed then stopped abruptly and gave a properly solemn look at Diana. "I'm really sorry."

"No you're not."

The solemnity shattered. "No, I'm not."

Harper held the button for the trunk to open and helped Diana put the suitcase in. "Start from the beginning ..." She waited until they were both in the car and continued, "Don't leave out one detail. Tell me eh-ver-ree-thing." She elongated the word.

Diana pressed her lips together and glanced in the rearview mirror. She was greeted by the old Diana pulling her hair up into a bun, saying something ridiculous about propriety and age, but Diana shut her up with a shake of her head. *We're done here*, she chided, running her fingers through her short hair and turning her body toward Harper. She took a deep breath and began, "I started writing again."

"Oh." A shocked inhale and shaky exhale accompanied more tears. Harper wiped them with the back of her hand. "If you came home with nothing else but that, then it was all worth it."

Diana waited for Harper to pay for the parking and when they were finally on the road, started, "His name is Giovanni."

Harper honked the car horn, making Diana jump in her seat. "Oh my God! Start with the buildup, Pisa, Florence. Renee. She did your hair, right? Did she help you with your look too? She seems like a kick. I love your clothes, by the way."

Diana took a deep breath, it would be good to tell someone the whole story. To hear it aloud, to reason it out. To hold onto it even tighter. "I was pissed when I got to Pisa and you weren't there," she began. "Scared shitless too."

# Chapter Forty-Five

Harper was attentive, interrupting occasionally with the same exclamatory statement: "Holy Shit!"

She cried often, so Diana dug out Lena's endless supply of tissues and kept handing them over.

When Diana yawned and insisted on a quick drive-thru stop so she could get something to eat and drink, Harper admitted, "It's been so damn long since you told me stories."

"I used to tell you about my day like it was a soap opera."

"I missed it so much." Harper cleared the buildup of tears from her throat. "Do you know the reason I know so much about New York is because of you?"

"I knew that, even if I never talked about it." Diana nodded.

In the last few miles to the house, they shared fries and Diana told her about all the food she'd eaten in Italy. The sweet sugary pastries in the morning and midnight glasses of wine.

"That sounds so decadent," Harper said as she pulled into Lena's driveway then continued to the front of the guesthouse. "I'm staying with you tonight."

"I figured." Diana yawned and Harper shook her head. "Oh no you don't. You can't sleep until you've finished this entire story."

Diana opened the guesthouse and stopped in the doorway, unable to breathe. It was stifling, not from heat and humidity, but from blandness. There was no color on the walls, they were all beige. The same beige as the furniture. There were no stacks of books. No trinkets laid about from travels. No artwork on the walls. She realized, as she glanced around at the appropriately decorated, bland room meant for company, that she was comparing it to one-bedroom apartments in Rome and Venice. Hell, she was comparing it to a dorm room in Pisa.

"You okay?" Harper asked.

She had to press her hand to her chest to force her breath once again before she whispered, "Has it been this way the whole time?" It was a modern-day mausoleum.

"You were unreachable. Inconsolable at first and then you disappeared." Harper didn't pull any punches.

Diana nodded in sad agreement as she glanced around the place she'd called home for the past nineteen years. "I'm moving."

"I think you should."

"I'm not sure where I'll go," she admitted, but thought, wherever it was, she was going to paint the walls Pantheon sunrise, Venetian blue, and cypress green.

"Take a shower, then you can finish telling me about your trip." Harper coaxed Diana back into the bland land.

"Giovanni Donato," Harper sighed. They were both sitting on the sofa, a bottle of wine on the coffee table almost gone, the pizza Harper ordered at midnight completely gone. "God, I want one!" she exclaimed. "Do you have a picture?"

Diana tilted her head at the question, shocked. "No. I ... it didn't dawn on me to take a picture."

"It didn't dawn on you?!"

"Harper, you have to stop yelling everything you say." Diana laughed, and she felt that lightness again. "But no, it didn't dawn on me because I was so busy when we were together. The only picture I have is the one Renee posted of the whole group."

"Does he have any brothers?"

"A twin."

"Really?!" Harper sat up straight.

"They aren't identical." Diana shrugged.

"Well, still …"

Diana stretched her arms above her head, the yawn loud and long.

"We're not done." Harper leaned forward and gave a playful slap on Diana's face.

"Ow."

"I'm serious. Keep going."

"I'm sorry," she whispered to her little sister, who'd been her friend, her cheerleader, and never given up on her, even as she watched Diana deteriorate and close herself off.

"Jeez," Harper said, "if we keep apologizing to each other, I'm never going to get to the end of this story."

"You know, I think I really started changing about a year ago when I agreed to go out on a date with Anthony." She moaned after saying his name. "I guess it's good he's in town. I was actually thinking about going to Houston to break things off. It doesn't feel right to do something so important over the phone."

"Look, I feel bad for the guy, okay? I'm a good person at heart. Now, get back to Giovanni." Harper rubbed her hands together.

"The distance helped, you were right about that. It helped to have to struggle through some fear and just be in an entirely new setting."

"I'm sure the handsome archeologist didn't hurt, either."

"Nah," she tried to shrug off his obvious importance, "he was a footnote. It was really the nature of Italy that did the trick, and the jazz and artists of Venice." She grinned.

"What artists in Venice? I don't think you're going in chronological order any more."

"I'm not," Diana said, exasperated, "I'm exhausted and punchy and a little drunk now."

"Fine, finish telling about the artists and then we'll get back on track."

*When was that?* Diana wondered. *Two days ago, two years?* "We were walking back to the apartment, and the Venetian streets are like a web. As we turned a corner to go over a bridge, we heard music. A boat was slowly drifting on an unseen current, they had a wireless speaker with some romantic music and it was just a group of people chatting. But there was a woman sitting in the front of the boat with a sketchbook in her hand. She was frantically drawing, and when they passed under the bridge, I could see her sketches; they were just studies of the windows they were passing. But the whole thing felt like a blessing. Because we went to a cafe after that and I wrote about it all. I had the power to reach out and take a moment and capture it."

They fell silent as Harper and Diana both lost themselves in the phantom music that played through the small guesthouse. Harper continued to study her sister and with another incredulous shake of her head said, "I wish I could have done this years ago and pulled you out. I'm so sorry it took so long."

"Jesus, why are you sorry? Harper, you told me I deserved to stand in the middle of Rome and be inspired and I was." Lord, if that wasn't the truth. "Harp," she licked her lips and leaned toward her sister, "I cried in front of Bernini's statue of Apollo and Daphne. I ordered my own espresso in a café in Floence. I drove a scooter in Rome. I listened to Vivaldi played live in the church where *he* used to perform. And in the darkness of the catacombs in Rome, I came to terms with David's death and my life. It was a lifetime of bucket list stuff that came to fruition. And *you* made that happen."

Harper had tears in her eyes as she asked, "And David came back in Rome? I miss talking about him. You know, he became my brother. When he died, I was hurting too."

"I know."

"What have you two been talking about?"

"You don't think it's weird I started having visions and conversations with my dead husband?"

"Nope."

"Lena's gonna want me to talk to a professional if she finds out."

"Yup. But I say don't tell her. What did you and David talk about?"

"Everything." Diana shook her head. "We talked about us, about art, about Italy. Why I hid, how things are going now." Diana smiled and buried her gaze in her wine glass as she admitted, "He likes Giovanni."

"So what happens now?"

"Nothing." Diana shrugged. "Something ... I don't know. Giovanni kissed me and we didn't say goodbye –" *a più tardi*, "I don't think either of us could." Diana smiled at her sister. "Or did you mean what happens to my mental health now that I'm admitting to seeing my dead husband?

Like, do I go to the doctor and get a brain scan?"

Harper smiled. "I don't think it's a problem. I'm just glad you're talking to him and about him, Lu."

"Giovanni calls me Luna," Diana whispered, "Bella Luna."

Another yawn and Diana closed her eyes for a second, just to rest.

"Luna!"

Diana blinked her eyes, they were scratching and burning, and her body ached from exhaustion. "I don't think I've slept for ten days ..." Her head bobbed down on her chest as her eyes slid closed.

Harper's laughter woke her. "Okay, go to bed. Can you make it by yourself?"

"Cake of piece."

Harper sighed, "I missed you, but just so you know, we're not done. Tomorrow you finish this story."

Diana shuffled to bed and mumbled through a yawn, "Don't worry Harp, I'm not going anywhere this time."

# Chapter Forty-Six

"Diana." Someone was harshly calling her name, "Luna, come on, you gotta get up!"

It was Harper yelling so that must mean it was Harper shaking her as well.

Diana slapped at the hand on her shoulder as she tried to force her tired, crusted eyes open. "What?" she muttered angrily.

Harper shook Diana again. "Anthony just called, I answered your cell. He's on his way."

Yup, that was the bombshell that would help her wake up. She bolted upright and looked around wildly.

Harper was at her dresser pulling out clothes; she tossed a sports bra, t-shirt and sweats at Diana's head. "Time to face the music, Lu."

"Couldn't you just break up with him for me?" Diana groaned in her hoarse voice as she dropped her throbbing head into her hands. "I need an Aspirin or Advil or headache pill ..." she muttered to her palms.

"I'll find something and this is all you baby, he's not my fiancé."

If only Diana's head would stop spinning, she could focus. "What time is it?"

"Nine-thirty." Harper left the room, hopefully to retrieve something for her hangover.

Diana grabbed at the clothes, and with one eye open she tried to pull on the sweats. After getting one leg in she figured that was enough productivity for the day.

Harper returned with a glass of water and one Advil. Thrusting the glass at Diana, the water sloshed over the edge and down her tank top.

"Hey," Diana slurred.

"Oh my God, we do not have time for this Luna." She handed the pill over and bent to help her sister finish putting on her pants.

"One Advil?"

"That's all I found. I'll call Lena and make her bring more over."

Diana took the pill and let Harper help her into a standing position. "I'm tired."

"You're gonna have to be tired later," Harper said, followed by a knock at the door.

They looked at each other, eyes wide. Diana let a snicker of ridiculous fear escape. How had she gotten herself in this mess? She was exhausted, probably still drunk from the wine, and her throat was molten lava from all the talking and lack of water. She took another drink, then put the cup down and picked up the bra when another knock came. With bra in hand, she pointed toward the door and raised an eyebrow toward Harper, who in turn, shook her head and whispered, "*I'm* not gonna get it."

"Harper, please," Diana begged, then began to struggle into the bra as Harper conceded with a snarl.

Bra on, she smoothed the front of the wet tank top and went to glimpse herself in the mirror in her room; her hair was standing on end and her eyes were bloodshot.

She dipped her fingers in the water cup, tried to smooth some of the wildness out of her hair and nodded. This was as good as it was gonna get this morning.

She wasn't sure what kind of outfit was protocol for breaking off an engagement with someone, but this was probably at the bottom of the list.

"It's not Anthony!" Harper yelled just as her older sister called, "It's Lena." Their screaming was causing tinnitus in her ears, but she took the relief that came with a bit more time. She pulled on a cardigan and went into the living room.

Lena was smiling with her arms across her chest, and when Diana stepped into the room, she shook her head. "You're a mess."

"Harper's fault."

"You did a poor job of keeping in touch when you were gone," she scolded.

Diana frowned, trying to focus her eyes to see if Lena really was disappointed. "I was trying something new," she defended, and the soft smile on Lena's face calmed her.

Lena shook her head and Diana caught a glimpse of her glassy eyes before she was pulled in for a hug. "The hair looks better in person."

"I look insane," she muttered into Lena's shoulder.

"Harper's fault, I'm sure."

Harper ignored the comment and instructed Lena, "Look in her eyes." Lena did and Harper was next to them both as she whispered, "She's back, baby."

*'Yeah she is.'* David walked out of the kitchen with a bag of chips under his arms. *'They look good. I can't believe Lena has kids. I can believe Harper is still a whirlwind.'*

"Wanna know how Luna got her groove back? She found an Italian stallion who seduced her under a full moon." Harper laughed as Diana groaned.

"Oh really?" Lena said.

Harper nodded. "Tell her about the art and the romantic dinners and the orgasms."

"Jesus, Harper," Diana groaned.

Lena snorted. "Yeah Diana, tell me about the orgasms."

With a full mouth, David laughed.

"No," Diana said and squinted her eyes as she admitted, "I think the wedding is off."

"Oh crap! That's why I came over. Anthony is on his way."

"We know," Harper said. "How do you know?"

"He called me." Lena narrowed her gaze and asked her sister, "Is this what you want?"

"For the first time in a very long time; I am one hundred percent positive about this decision," Diana responded.

Lena tilted her head. "It must have been quite some trip."

"Life-changing," Diana affirmed.

"Just wait, Lena. The story is amazing," Harper promised.

Lena opened her mouth to say something when there was a knock at the door. Whatever she was about to say was replaced with a whispered, "That's Anthony."

*'Oh,'* David sat down on the sofa, making himself comfortable for the coming show, *'I finally get to see this guy.'*

Diana's strength wobbled, she nodded her head at Lena but she didn't move.

Another knock.

"Are you gonna get it?" Lena asked.

Diana gripped Lena's hands a bit harder and shook her head.

"Do you want me to get it?" Lena asked.

Diana nodded, this was big sister stuff; and that's what she needed.

Harper reached for the edge of Diana's sweater and pulled it up to cover the hickey. That helped prompt Diana to finally release Lena's hands and with a groan she pulled the sweater around her neck. Lena bit back a laugh and patted Diana's shoulder before she turned to answer the door. Harper hopped behind Lena, and Diana, thankful for the obstructed view, held her breath as the door swung open. She wasn't ready for this yet.

"Well, hello." Harper moved from behind Lena to stand next to her, her voice having turned sultry. Lena looked over her shoulder and shrugged. "Not Anthony."

"Is Diana here?" a deep voice asked.

Harper and Lena parted, giving Diana a perfect view of the owner of the voice.

*'My man!'* David announced with a whoop.

"Giovanni?" Diana whispered the name.

"Giovanni!" Harper's voice radiated excitement.

Lena glanced at Harper. "Who's Giovanni?"

Harper didn't even try to hold back the giggle. "He's the Italian stallion."

He glanced then at the women on either side of him and gave a terse smile. "Your brother-in-law said you were back here."

"What are you doing here?" Diana was having a difficult time trying to find her voice.

Harper closed the door and held out her hand. "Hi, I'm Harper, the younger sister." She shook Giovanni's hand then pointed to Lena. "This is the older sister."

"Lena," Lena offered, shaking Giovanni's hand in wonder.

"Nice to meet you." He glanced between them and then across the room. As if he'd made up his mind, he dropped the leather messenger bag he'd been holding, crossed the room and pulled Diana into his arms and seared her lips with his.

"Oh. My. God!" Harper exploded.

Diana pushed Giovanni away, but he continued to hold her gently around the waist as her arms rested atop his forearms.

She heard Lena ask again, "Who is he?"

Harper was happy to explain, "The girls Luna met in Rome took her to dinner with a group of people. She met Giovanni there and he showed her how to get her groove back. Italian style."

"Harper," Diana groaned, but Giovanni winked and agreed, "That's a fair explanation."

Lena cleared her throat. "This is really intriguing and I would love to hear every last detail, but Diana, we've got *company* coming." She raised an eyebrow at the innuendo.

"Giovanni, this isn't a good time," Diana insisted, but before she could explain any more, there was another knock. She leaned her head against his chest and moaned, "Oh no."

Lena said, "Look, why don't you all go into the bedroom. I'll tell him to come to the house, say that you're getting ready, and give you more time."

Giovanni frowned in question, and Diana sighed, dislodging herself from his arms. "No. This is my mess. I need to clean it up." But she didn't move.

"I owe you one," Harper said as she opened the door.

"What's going on?" Giovanni asked, but no one answered. All attention was on the door.

"Is Diana here?" She heard Anthony's voice and stepped away from Giovanni, then took a deep breath.

"I'm right here," she called.

*'This is amazing.'* David wiggled into the sofa. Diana snarled over her shoulder at him.

Harper moved out of the way and Anthony shuffled into the gathering in the living room. He blinked at the crowd before him, from Harper to Lena, then Giovanni and finally Diana. He looked startled when he saw her.

"Diana?"

"Hey Anthony." She pulled the sweater she wore around her.

"Anthony," Giovannni whispered to Harper who'd moved to stand next to him, "the fiancé?"

Harper nodded in answer.

Anthony touched his own hair as he spoke to Diana. "It looked different in the picture."

"I ..." she cleared her voice, "I'm really tired and I was up late last night talking with Harper. I need to wash it."

He had a frown of confusion on his face and Diana felt the way she had when she first opened the door to the guesthouse; stifled and disappointed.

Anthony was a nice man, but he too, was so very beige. He was so safe he was ... '*Death*,' David whispered as he walked around Anthony, looking at him up and down. '*Oh babe, you almost married this guy?*'

Anthony nervously wrung his hands together and cleared his throat as he focused on Diana. "Diana, can we talk?"

She nodded.

He glanced around at the group and again cleared his throat. "Can we go somewhere ...?"

"No," she said a bit desperately, then smoothed herself out. "I need to tell you something and I think it would be better if I just got it out now."

He cleared his throat a third time. "But Diana, I've been thinking," he took a deep breath and exhaled, "and I think ..." He gave another nervous glance around the room before leaning close to her, his eyes wide as he apologetically whispered, "I don't think we should get married."

A snort of laughter escaped from Harper followed by a soft slap and hiss from Lena. Anthony glanced between them all but continued, "I'm so sorry, Diana."

"What happened?" Diana asked.

Harper muttered, "Do you care?" and this time Lena's hiss was louder.

He continued, "In Houston, it was like I was seeing my life for the first time. And I'm so sorry. It's just, I like being single." He shrugged.

"You like being single?" Diana repeated.

"Yeah, he likes being single. This is a win-win for everybody," Harper said enthusiastically.

Anthony frowned at Harper so she explained, "Diana was about to reject you too."

"Harper!" Lena and Diana both yelled at her. She shrugged. "We're all adults, no need to beat around the bush."

*'Lu, are you angry?'* David asked, more out of curiosity than anything.

She nodded and answered aloud, "I think I am."

"You think you are what?" Harper asked.

"You don't want to marry me either?" Anthony seemed relieved.

"Do you know how much time I could have saved … how much worry …" she began frustratedly.

"What are you talking about?" Harper asked.

*'Even if you knew he didn't really want to get married either, you were still gonna come up with a million reasons to try and run away from Giovanni.'* David offered.

"Yeah, because of you," she insisted.

"Luna," Harper frowned, "this is getting hard to follow. What are you talking about?"

"I'm not talking to you, I'm arguing with David," she seethed.

"David?" Anthony asked at the same time Lena's face paled. "David?" she said with apprehension.

Harper rubbed Lena's arm. "She's been having conversations with David's ghosts since Italy."

"Just since Rome," Giovanni offered.

Lena looked aghast between them both.

Anthony finally seemed to become cognizant of Giovanni. "Hi, I'm Anthony."

"Hi," Giovanni held out his hand, "Giovanni."

They shook hands before Anthony frowned and asked, "Who are you?"

"A friend of Luna's."

"Luna?"

*'Time to stop being a victim, stop blaming others, pick the pieces back up and let the magic put you back together.'*

"A victim?" she bit.

Harper whispered, "If David just called her a victim, they're about to get into it."

"They fought all the time," Lena supplied.

"No we didn't," Diana argued.

"They were full of passion; about everything. Especially Lu," Harper added.

*'Lu...'* he sighed, *'victim, martyr... I don't care what you want to call it, but you have to accept that you fell in love and the consequences of that are vulnerability. But instead, your identity became wrapped up in my death.'*

Lena told Giovanni, "They were so young, and had so many ideals they were working through, they fought all the time."

"It wasn't fighting, it was misunderstanding that I was always right!" Diana yelled, but the ridiculous words made her laugh.

*'We fell in love so fast, and everything seemed heightened. We were in a hurry to experience the whole wide world as it opened up before us.'* David sighed.

"I felt like I could do anything then. I thought it was being young that made me feel that way. I thought you only get to feel that alive once in your life."

"But you don't," Giovanni supplied.

She turned her gaze to Giovanni, "I'm scared to be vulnerable again." He nodded.

"So is someone else here?" Anthony asked, confused.

"Don't worry about it," Lena soothed.

"Are you mad at me?" Anthony directed the question at Diana.

She shook her head. "No. I'm not. I wish you the very best and will always look back on this last year fondly."

"We had a nice time," he agreed, "but I always thought you might have wanted more."

*'So much more,'* David said pointedly. *'What do you want, Lu?'*

"I want friends and laughter. I want to talk about art and philosophy until five in the morning." She licked her lips as she met Giovanni's eyes. "I want to see operas, sit in cafés with decadent pastries, watch the sun come up over ancient ruins, and I want to write about all of it."

*'There she is,'* David said as Harper cheered.

"Ah, well," Anthony shrugged, "then this is for the best."

"What else do you want?" Giovanni asked.

"Romantic dinners in the moonlight?"

"I know a place." His voice was a caress.

"Of course you do." Diana smiled.

Anthony had been looking between them as if he were a spectator at a tennis match, his frown growing, he asked once more, "I'm sorry, who are you?"

"Diana met Giovanni in Italy," Harper explained.

"Oh." His forehead wrinkled.

Giovanni gave him a shrug and admitted, "I'm in love with her."

"Oh," he glanced around the room, "then maybe I should ... go?"

"Wait, Anthony," Diana called.

Between her teeth Harper said, "This is going really well for you, Lu, what are you doing?"

She ignored her sister and stood in front of Anthony. "I need to apologize to you."

"For him?" Anthony nodded toward Giovanni.

"No ..." how did she explain this, "well, yes. I'm sorry I cheated on you." She pushed the words out.

Anthony's eyes widened as if he hadn't thought of it that way.

"I need to apologize because I was using you, Anthony. I felt old before my time. I buried myself the day David died. In a way, I've been waiting to die since then too."

Anthony nodded as he tried to follow the explanation.

"I duct taped the loneliness and heartache up and I was using you for security." She narrowed her gaze, a quiet question if he understood. His nod became a shake, he didn't understand.

She touched the lapel of the brown suit he wore. "I thought you were someone who would be safe, because I liked you, but I didn't have any real passion for you. And I'm sorry for using you that way. You deserve better."

He gave her a sad smile. "I knew you didn't love me the way you loved your first husband."

"I'm sorry."

Anthony nodded once, twice, then extended his hand and announced, "Apology accepted." She smiled as they shook hands and after a moment, he tilted his head. "You look like you're ready to take on the world now."

"Thank you, Anthony."

"If you'd like, I can return the ring to Rita."

Diana went to retrieve the ring from the zippered coin compartment of her wallet.

*'I'm glad you don't want to sit around and wait to die anymore,'* Daivd said.

"Me too. And you were right," she said as they both walked back into the living room, Anthony still looking confused.

*'Of course I was.'*

She handed the ring over to Anthony. "Good luck, Anthony. With everything."

He closed his hand around the ring. "You too." He took a few awkward steps backwards then turned and saw himself out of the guesthouse.

"And then there were four," Harper whispered. "Or are we still five?"

"Okay," Lena grabbed Harper by the upper arm, "we're going to give you two some privacy."

"No!" Harper cried dramatically as she followed Lena out, but before she closed the front door, she peeked around the corner and said, "You still haven't finished telling me everything about the trip and now this is happening, so take good notes."

With her sisters gone, Diana took a deep breath before she turned to face Giovanni. "I can't believe you're here."

"I went back to the apartment. Did the dishes and laundry and called Michele and got upset and the next thing I knew, I was at the airport in Munich with Elsbeth helping me fix my entire schedule ... because I am not about to let you go without a fight."

She nodded several times as David rolled his eyes and threw his hands up. *'What the hell are you waiting for?'*

Diana turned her full focus to Giovanni. "Everything about you scares me," she began. "How much I want you. How much I like you. Even the damned apartment with the right color walls that I can see myself writing in, scares the hell out of me." She swallowed. "What if something happens to you?"

"What if something happens to *you*?" he volleyed, then held out his hands. "But the reason I got on a plane and rushed over here, not knowing how you'd take the gesture, is because I'd rather have five minutes with you, than a lifetime without you."

"I've been thinking about the nature of things again," she whispered. "I turned my back on my nature long ago, but maybe it wasn't really gone."

"Did you figure out what your nature is, la mia bella Luna?"

"Yeah," she wrinkled her nose and smiled, "I think it might be perseverance."

*'Do you know what the antidote for death is?'* David grinned. *'Love.'* He moved over to put a phantom arm around Giovanni's shoulder. *'Damn, I didn't realize how tall he was. Ah, I still like him. He's good for you, kid.'*

She smiled in agreement but knew what was about to happen. She was about to lose David again. She stood still for as long as she could, memorizing his face and his smile, that cocky youthful exuberance that he walked around with.

*I missed you*, she thought. But the pain wasn't searing. It wasn't unbearable.

*'Ah Lu, you won't forget me. But stop using me as an excuse, okay?'* Always the reasonable one, he gave Diana a wink and slapped Giovanni on the back; to which Giovanni glanced over his shoulder with a frown. He turned in a circle, obstructing her view of David, and she knew when he moved out of the way, David would be gone.

"That was weird," Giovanni said, "it felt like someone …"

"I want you," Diana announced.

His attention darted to her face.

She finally crossed the space that separated them and breathed in the scent she hadn't been sure she'd ever smell again. "With all the pent-up crazy, mad, passionate kind of want a woman can feel, I want you."

The side of his mouth raised in a smile.

"We might fight," she reasoned.

"Probably."

"I'm strong-willed."

"So I've noticed." He tilted his head. "We're going to have to work at this."

"We are," she agreed.

"Are you up for this?"

Diana slipped her arms up around his neck and met his lips in answer. She was more than ready.

She held him tightly and thought she was the kind of woman who deserved ridiculous amounts of love, and since she'd found it again, she was planning on holding it close for as long as she could.

When they were finally able to separate themselves from each other, she rested her hands on his chest and looked up at him. "I'd like to introduce you to everyone, properly."

"I'd love that."

"We should take a selfie and send it to the girls, Renee will lose her mind."

He nodded in agreement. "Michele is probably waiting by the phone too, anxious to find out what happened."

Diana traced the side of his face with her fingertips. "What else do you need?" he asked gently.

"Well," she wiggled her eyebrows, "I *need* to make sure to add olive oil to my grocery list."

# Bucket list
### Diana's ~~Italian sightseeing checklist~~

- ~~the Leaning Tower of Pisa.~~
- ~~Micheangelo's David~~
- ~~Duomo of Florence~~
- ~~Uffizi Museum~~
- ~~See a medieval Italian town~~


* Daydream on a train while riding through the Tuscan countryside.
* Stand in the Roman Colosseum in the moonlight.
* Let an Italian man buy you coffee from a café near the Pantheon.
* See Vivaldi in Venice
* Watch the sunrise over the Pantheon
* Drive a scooter in Rome
* Be swept away in Venice
* Come undone
* Let a piece of art bring you to tears
* Find a story
* Be intrigued

# Note to the reader

I hope you enjoyed the time you spent with Diana and Giovanni. I know I did.

1 – Wouldn't it be so damn cool to be in the Colosseum in the middle of the night under a full moon? Well, guess what? I found out it's not completely unreasonable! It turns out you can actually take nighttime tours during specific months, without the crowds or the heat. A quick search online and you'll find the companies that offer this. And you *know*, I'm adding that to my own bucket list.

2 – If you are in Venice, go to Harry's Bar to have a Bellini; that's where they were invented. And at the time of writing this, you can get tickets to see orchestras performing Vivaldi in the church where he composed and performed. The church of S. Maria della Pietà or della Visitazione is also known as the "Church of Vivaldi."

3 – So does olive oil really work as a moisturizer? Well, my mom has been using it my whole life and she claimed it was because of an interview she read about Sophia Loren. (But the interview my mom heard was before this one that I found so I could quote Ms. Loren.) "In 2005, she told the *Sunday Times* that her trick to defying the aging process was "a love of life, spaghetti and the odd bath in virgin olive oil."

Now my mom doesn't use a ton, just a pea size amount and rubs it on her neck and face a while before bedtime, because it needs to soak in. And according to sources, if you want to bathe in the stuff, add about three capfuls to one full tub of water and soak up all those good antioxidants.

As for the spaghetti being age defying, well ... I'll get back to you on that one.

4 – Of course, the guidebook I refer to is Rick Steves' books. I have

several of his books covering all of Italy. I love how accessible he's made the country to me. And the man knows travel.

5 – They are doing a lot of cool work on the catacombs in Rome. I'm not sure if the catacombs where Giovanni took Diana have an area closed off to the public, only open to scholars and archeologists on a whim; but it's a fun plotline. The idea came from my Roman History professor who was invited to Rome several times to study some areas of the catacombs that only scholars are allowed to enter. I've always loved that idea. It's very Indiana Jones. There are several virtual tours online of the Domitilla Catacombs in Rome if you are curious.

6 – I'd forgotten about Stendhal's syndrome until the kind British gentleman showed up and helped Diana. It's real. And I myself have suffered from it once. (Or twice.) I was standing in front of the statue of David at the Academia, and all of a sudden I didn't feel well. I had to sit down because I thought I was going to faint. At the time I thought I was just hungry, tired and dehydrated. But in doing research for another book on Italy I'm writing (who knew?) I found the mention of this syndrome. "The staff at Florence's Santa Maria Nuova hospital are accustomed to tourists suffering from dizzy spells or disorientation after viewing the statue of David, the art works of the Uffizi Gallery, and other historic treasures of the Tuscan city." -*Nick Squires (28 July 2010). "Scientists investigate Stendhal syndrome – fainting caused by great art". The Daily Telegraph. London. Retrieved 1 October 2019.*

# Thank you!

Oh, to write about Italy again has been wonderful.

It takes a lot of support and behind the scenes work to bring my books to life. And there are so many people to thank.

First I'd like to thank Ariane Kimlinger, my grammatical guru, my friend and the best support a writer could ever have. Seriously, y'all have no idea how many times this amazing human has to reassure my artistic nerves. If you are a writer, or are just starting out, find yourself an editor who has your back. It makes all the difference in the world. And Ariane, I hope you know how amazing you are!

Thank you Michele Tomlinson, my alpha reader with amazing 'eagle eyes,' I so appreciate your friendship, continued support and help.

Have you SEEN the cover of this book? Magic, that's what A. M. Rasmussen does for me, creates magic to make my dreams come true. She also moves mountains for me, literally. Thank you for sharing your wonderful talent, your friendship and hard work

Some of the first folks to view this story were my old writing group; thank you Sharli, Jess, and Emery for all your feedback and support.

To my ARC readers, you are wonderful! Thank you for gifting me your time and for being part of my hype team. A big shout out to Kimberly who's been part of every book ARC to date!

Thank you to my mom and dad, my sister and brother, I miss you and love you. Thanks to my extended family and my cousins and aunts and uncles for all your support and love.

Amy, Ashelee, Gina, Jewell, Shannon and Sophie – Thank you always, for the continued support and cheerleading.

Thank you for your friendship: Crystal, Barbara B., Amy B., Elaine,

Jeremy, Alison, Vanessa, Josh, Gabe, Biggs, and Bryan and Tammy. And those I'm forgetting because I might be a little tired. You know who you are and I love you.

My fellow writers who continue to support me, thank you!!

To my husband and my precious "A," I love you with all my heart, it's as simple as that.

And lastly, thank you my dear reader for your time. I know how truly valuable it is in this day and age; and I appreciate that you spent it on my words and story.

# Want to read more
# by Nicole Sharp?

Try another
Italian holiday

**or**

get started on

Legend has it that Nicole Sharp was born to hippies during an ice storm in Stone Mountain, Georgia. While confirmation of said events cannot be agreed upon, one fact is for certain, it was a Tuesday.

By age twelve, Nicole was sure of two things: 1) She wanted to be a writer and 2) She wanted to travel. She begged her parents to allow her to voyage alone to exotic lands. They permitted her to go from California to Boise, Idaho to visit a great-grandmother.

After muddling through her college years, Nicole graduated with a Bachelors in History (think Greeks and Romans). Why not study English if she wanted to be a writer? There were better stories in history class.

Nicole is Italian. According to Ancestry.com it's a rather low percentage, but she feels she is at least 51% Italian. She's visited the homeland a handful of times, studied the language and loves the Italian cappuccino.

Nicole's first concert was to see the bluegrass group The Seldom Scene when she was a fifteen-year-old, thanks to her parent's bluegrass phase. However, she never admits it, and instead tells everyone that They Might Be Giants, whom she saw in college, was her first real concert.

Her first car was a yellow Chevy Celebrity and her favorite job was working as a docent at a museum in an old Colorado mining town. She has written extensively about both.

Visit NicoleSharpWrites.com for more entertainment.